URBAN NARRATIVES

KEN CHAMPION

For
Steve, Tim, Toby
and Les

ART HOUSE

'A beautifully written and poignant story.'

Ronna Wineberg, Bellevue Literary Review ('06)

RELIGIOUS AFFAIRS

'In this story Ken Champion provides highly developed characters that contemplate their relationship to Christ, to culture and to each other. His character, Steve, develops a relationship with a younger African student, Thandi Mnede. Even when these characters are together, they are worlds apart, Steve's sense of isolation deriving from his intellectualized disbelief in faith.'

Monica K. Mankin, The Literary Magazine Review, University of Wisconsin ('06)

THE BEAT YEARS

'I found some beautiful writing here.'

Susie Reynolds, Chimera ('06)

FRACTURE

'I really do like this story. He deals with a potentially melodramatic ending with real elegance and lightness of touch. The last two lines are heartbreaking.'

Jonathan Ware, Silkworms Ink ('10)

VERSTEHEN

'I think his work is amazing.'

Sarah Kayss, Post Poetry Magazine ('12)

CONTENTS

ART HOUSE

I'd seen him around the college, he worked in Business Studies; big man, late fifties, intense, almost marched along, tweed jacket, unpressed worsted trousers, the sort of face you wouldn't want peering through the playground railings of your child's school.

He had read my parody of Edu-biz buzzwords and phrases in the house magazine, '...*proactive encouragement of student-centred assimilation of conceptual bridges to facilitate non-arbitrary criteria of recourse-based parameters for...* etc.' and, literally bumping into me in the foyer, had told me how much he'd enjoyed it. I was mildly pleased; he may well have been the only reader not to take it seriously.

Though I had never spoken to him, he obviously knew of me and perhaps knowing I taught an art course to mature students at the same college, and had done so for the last ten years, told me he bought paintings, mainly Victorian, mostly at auctions and would I like to see them. He owned a large detached house in a Victorian estate in East London and lived on his own, as did I, in a small, rather minimalist flat near my workplace.

The next afternoon I went to see him. He lived on a street with an abundance of established trees in front gardens hanging over walls of London brick - the same as the houses, though some of these had been rendered and painted.

His house was large and unprepossessing; scruffy, uncared for, shallow pediments above pseudo Georgian windows - I again wondered why Victorian architects, with the embellishments of colonial masturbation, had enjoyed destroying the perfect proportions of a twelve-paned box sash - and a roll of barbed wire across the top of the castellated garage. It was a sunny day, though the porch was dark, unlit and the maroon door had paint over the original glass from badly cut-in glazing bars. The bell didn't work. There was no knocker. I tapped lightly on a muntin and the door opened immediately as if he had been standing behind it. He smiled me in with a weary gesture.

It was the kitchen I noticed first; handle less cups on a dark wooden table, ketchup spotted floor, oil bound distemper peeling off walls, the smell of gas and a butler's sink that was so full of pots and pans and bacon rind that I felt even he wouldn't piss in. I followed him up the stairs; railings missing from banisters, Napoleonic grotesque glimpsed through a dusty bead curtain, sofa, the back of a headboard, a mahogany mirrored wardrobe perhaps tired of his naked reflections, walls of stripes and roses, a patterned pub carpet, the tinkling crystals of a chandelier.

The paintings were in crude wooden racks in the loft, possibly fifty or more, their frames dust covered. He began pulling them out, looking at each one with a sort of apprehensive wistfulness before replacing it. There were cottages, fields, sheep, town hall faces, smug eyes, snug waistcoats, mayoral chains, nearly all covered in heavy varnish. A canvas fell to the floor, he stared at the back of it, then looking above my head - he had rarely looked at my face since I'd been in his home - muttered nervously that he wasn't well. He started to stutter.

'Th-there's a lot here, they'll take them. They'll take them.'

'Who will?'

'People. They'll get in, they'll take all of them.'

He looked straight at me. 'B-Belmayes, I have to go to Belmayes.'

I wanted to press my knuckles into my ears, pretend he hadn't said those words.

Again he said them, exactly as before, but whispering. Then, louder, 'Take me there, please, I'm ill.' He said this last very quickly.

He scuttled down the stairs, through the kitchen and into the long back garden. I followed. The door slammed behind me. He asked if I liked his 'little plot' and apologised for it being overgrown. He strode towards the back door of the kitchen, tried to open it and announced it had locked

'I think the f-front door's open.' he said. 'There's a ladder here.'

He pointed to a few rungs showing through the long grass. I pulled the ladder up and leant it against the back of the garage; climbed up, and realising I couldn't drop down from the front because of the wire, dragged it across the roof and slid it down the front of the garage. Awkwardly stepping over the coiled wire I came down and went to the front door again. It was open. I went into the kitchen, unlatched the back door and, following him again, went through the hall, out and around the side of the house where there was an old Citroen, the grass partly hiding its hubcaps. Opening the passenger door he slumped into the seat and beckoned me with a flippant wave to sit behind a mould-splotched steering wheel and drive.

The smell inside was foul, but surprisingly the car started first time. I bumped and stalled along for a while before I could control the vehicle adequately enough to trust myself on the main road. He sat there like a silent scream. I passed my own street ten minutes later; it looked darkly unreal. Two miles or so further on was the familiar chimney in the grounds of Belmayes Hospital. It wasn't just the chimney that was familiar - that was a local landmark.

I had been in Belmayes as a young man and didn't expect, nor wish, to return for whatever reason. It was the local Bedlam. I'd stayed months; needle-pierced in early dawns, drifting into insulin-deep sleeps because they didn't drop you into cold baths any more and playing football by order with a sugar water bottle in my fist, defying instant comas and watching a crazed goalkeeper stopping shots with his face. I dug the hospital allotment without knowing why, watched someone from Ward 4 scrape a pick across a long-stay's scalp, blood covering his smiling teeth, and the stiff dances in F Ward with glazed-eyed girls were no incentive to leave my glass-walled mind.

Fifty yards inside the gate now I stopped in a small, asphalted space outside an incongruous glass door at the bottom of what could have been a medieval keep and looked across at him. He was frowning and nodding rhythmically. This went on silently for minutes. Quietly I asked him what he wanted to do. He glanced at me, clambered out the car and walked hastily towards turreted psychiatry.

Following him in I saw a stocky Jamaican behind a counter asking if he could help.

'I want to see a doctor. Could I see him now, please?'

There was no desperation, he had asked his question almost apologetically. He seemed to have stopped stuttering.

He was told to wait. I think he was crying, his hands rigidly flat on the top of his legs. Quietly he told me to go. He'd be alright, he said.

The man put a phone down and said someone would be with him soon. I didn't know what to do or say. Tentatively I put my arm around his shoulders, not really wanting to touch him. Then a young doctor appeared, gently took the elbow of his potential patient and both turned into a narrow corridor and were out of sight.

Driving back I wondered why he hadn't packed a bag with some washing stuff, toothbrush, pyjamas, for surely he wore those. I put the car in his garden, churning the grass. For a while I sat, noticed there was still a small patch of mould on the wheel, then looked down between my legs and saw a smear of blood on my sock. The barbed wire must have cut me. Sunset suddenly silhouetted the house. I got out of the car and walked quickly away, as if fleeing childhood.

The next day he rang me in the staff room. He was speaking from home. He wanted to sell his paintings and wished me to be executor. There were forms to sign.

I looked around the room, usually a chattering chorus of pedagogy, a communion of roles across coffee spilt desks. At this moment there were only three of us; Colin, lording it over his empire of three desks, grin legitimating his loveable crassness, Durham accent ruling okay as he gleefully repeated how lucky we were that evolution had got it right by giving us thumbnails so we could scratch our arses, and Alan, head of our department, provincial man, established victim, cold wife, colder kids, a Co-op ceilidh the highlight of his month. It was ordinary, familiar, almost incestuously so. Now, here was this strangely authoritative voice telling me that I must take official responsibility for the sale of an art collection

I told him that I had no classes and could get to him about two. I'd mentioned yesterday to no one.

Stepping off a bus and turning into the long street I could see a cream coloured pantechnicon parked some two hundred yards away. I slowed, almost stopped, and then thought of him a few hours ago inside that square half mile of Neo-Gothic dismay.

Moving more purposefully along the street and getting nearer to the vehicle outside his house I saw two men in brown smocks leaning paintings against the rear nearside wheel, then returning to the house again to get more. On the side of the van was written *'John Baines, Art Auctioneers, Cotteshall, Essex.'* The front door was wide open and a dustsheet thrown over the porch step and part of the hall. I went inside the house a little way and waited hesitantly. One of the men came down carrying a large painting of several sheep in the lea of a hill, the burnished gold on the tops of their heads and backs shouting second-rate Pre-Raphaelite. I asked if the owner was in the attic and receiving an affirmative nod went up the stairs, the second man passing me on his way down.

He was looking at me through the open loft door, his eyes wide, greying hair sticking up as if it was gelled.

'Do you think they'll take them to Baines's? They could take them somewhere else, couldn't they? They could take them to another auctioneers and do some sort of fiddle.' He seemed frightened.

I asked him if he had spoken to the firm's office, he said he had, and I tried to reassure him that his paintings would get there. I didn't inquire about the previous night.

I gestured to him that I'd help take some of the paintings down. He pointed to a few of the smaller ones. I took them outside and leant them against the others. After bringing a few more down and realising how hungry I was - lecturing, or rather the way I proselytised, burnt up a lot of energy - I asked him if he'd mind if I went to a café somewhere for a quick bite. I didn't want to eat where I was. Nodding, he said,

'Don't be long.'

I hurried to the other end of the street to the main road, but didn't see any cafes. I wandered around asking people. Someone told me of a place near the Flats where I used to play as a child. I found it, ordered something. It took a long while to get to me. I ate it quickly, had a coffee.

I walked back along his road, looking at privet hedges, scrolled gates, the black and white diamond tiles of front paths, and then looked up. There was no van. I stopped, feeling self-conscious. I wanted to run to the house, but couldn't. I stood outside; doors and windows shut, the long grass, the car at the side where I'd parked it and the ladder still against the front of the garage where it had been all night. Neither of us had noticed it. I laid it alongside the car, went to the front door, knocked tentatively on one of the coloured glass panes, then harder. There was no sound from inside. I waited ten minutes or so, not knowing what to do. Remembering I had a class that evening I walked slowly back to the bus stop. Looking back along the street the air seemed dense and hard. I didn't phone him. I think I was frightened to.

13

I wondered about him for a week or so. Had he gone with the men in the van? Had he decided to trust them and, maybe, gone back to the hospital again? Was he strong enough to get well in that place? Where were the forms for me to sign, did they exist?

My interest in answering these questions gradually waned and after a while the episode faded away.

Six days ago in a café opposite Liverpool Street Station I saw him. He was munching a meal and staring steadily at a far point just above my head. I had been there, eating and reading, for at least twenty minutes and hadn't noticed him. I also hadn't realised just how big he was. He looked well, was wearing a raincoat, tie and was well groomed. I was tempted to speak to him, give him a casual grin and ask coyly if he remembered me. Instead, I got quietly up, walked past him and crossed the road to the station.

Leaving the train before my usual stop I went to his street and stood outside the house. I wasn't quite sure at first if it was his - it had been four years - until I saw the rusting barbed wire.

I sat on his front wall, my back to the road. I started swinging my heels rhythmically into the bricks, felt bits of pointing crumble away, kicked harder, wanted to smash the wall down, to pull the gate off its hinges, rip the grass from the garden, kick the side of his car in - though it wasn't there anymore - wanted to put my foot through the front door, rip the wire away until my hands and arms bled. I don't know why. I walked quickly along the road, started running, fists clenched, till I felt my fingertips would push through the palms of my hands. I was weeping.

VERSTEHEN

'Have you noticed,' he asked, all skinny jeans and stubble, 'that the parents who complain loudest about paedophiles are those who have kids no one would *want* to shag? I lie. *I'd* shag anything.'

His metier was obviously sick humour, and in this context it was a competent beginning, earning satisfyingly outraged and knowing laughter.

The comic was Freddie Weels, the venue *The Paltry Plate* pub just east of the square mile on a Thursday comedy night. During the five minute spots the hyper-active MC hovering nearby would, after four minutes, put one foot on the side of the six inch high 'stage,' stand on it thirty seconds later, and then threaten to kick the arse and grab the mike of a performer if he ran over time.

James Kent was there also; for two reasons. One, being an invite from an acquaintance whose stage name seemed to be Johnny Glasgow - with his 'I go to a draper's warehouse; get my best material there' puns for beginners - the other was Weels. James had a particular interest in him.

He'd been a therapist for almost five years, using the study of his East London home to see clients - at one time thinking of moving to a house in nearby Nutters Lane, but hadn't - and had noticed amongst some of his patients, near maniacal moments of shrill hyperbole, building, often from bland, everyday comments, a whole pyramid of ludicrous and sometimes hilariously funny narratives and bizarre incidents; and then, when they'd stopped, sometimes suddenly, the emptiness behind their eyes.

He wondered whether comics, established and otherwise, shared these characteristics and why. He disliked the often self-fulfilling nature of socio-psychological labels, especially the master statuses they became, but something must be called something. We search for order to understand our past and present conduct and to predict future actions. Constructs, especially meta ones like 'society' - behaviour removed from the randomness of chance - and 'God,' provide it.

Weels was a successful comedian and well known at venues in both east and north London and had done gigs at the Edinburgh Fringe.

He'd been recommended by a colleague, Thomas. 'This one's more up your street, James, if you can spare the time.'

He could. There'd been a recent drop in his client numbers, and other than filling his time with poetry, films and watching a local lower league football team, there were professional time gaps that needed filling. Weels had gone to Thomas's deep purple, valmier-rugged, Art Nouveau Marylebone office just once and had walked out, distressed. James wasn't told why. Perhaps it was the colour scheme.

The rule governing much therapeutic practice is to attempt 'detachment.' He invariably struggled with this, had to fight off an immediate urge when meeting new patients to intuitively, empathetically understand them; *verstehen,* to 'become the other.' The argument against this is similar to the situation of the anthropologist who, not being content to remain 'outside' of a tribe he's studying in the Amazonian rain forest, turns native, thus moving from being a non-participant observer to a non-observing participant. He'd been in therapy himself, mainly to learn to separate his own feelings and attitudes from clients so as not to project them. Not always successfully.

Freddy Weels - who Johnny Glasgow had mentioned was on the bill - continued blasting the sensibilities of the few older people in the audience while making the rest love him. He was wearing make up: rouge on his cheeks, eyebrows s accentuated, and had an almost clown-like persona. James was standing at the end of the bar, the room was dark, the stage barely illuminated. Weels didn't see him. He didn't want him to. James was due to meet him in a month for the first time. He'd briefly encouraged him to come sooner, but he wouldn't

After lots of clapping and whooping from the audience, Weels sat down at the back and left soon afterwards. Feeling rather surprised that the man would play a venue like this - there was little talent on show, mostly first-timers and others a little more experienced trying to hone their spiel - James made a few observational notes and left.

He forgot about him for a while, partly because he was excited about one of his early patients who he'd seen monthly for over four years and who had, during this time, just sat perfectly still, looking down between his knees and only looking at James for a second just before he left at the end of his Tuesday session. During the final minute of his last one, he'd suddenly looked up and smiled. James had never seen his teeth before. He wanted him to smile next time and maybe one day, to speak.

Quite accidentally he discovered that in a few days Weels was appearing on a Friday evening at a small theatre in suburban North West London. He went.

The place was small, most of the seats taken. Not wanting to watch the second half acts - retro music hall jugglers, ventriloquists, a couple of impressionists - he went in just before Weels' last-on slot.

He was barely recognisable: well groomed, hair shorter, smart jacket, open necked shirt and shiny shoes He stood motionless, saying nothing, eyes slowly scanning the audience, who, after a long hiatus, began to get restless.

'*All* wine is served at room temperature.' he began, deadpan and slow.

It took a while, then a few people began chuckling.

'I took the dog for a walk round the block. It fell off.' Again, an expressionless delivery.

'My friend's a radio DJ. When we walk under a bridge I can't understand a word he says.' More chuckles..

'I divorced my wife. We split the house fifty-fifty. She got the inside.'

The audience began a spell of almost continuous, modulated, often head-shaking laughter, his act becoming increasingly surreal.

'When I woke this morning all the furniture in my apartment had been stolen and replaced with exact replicas.'

The slight frown, the relaxed sharpness were all of a piece, a whole.

This was a different crowd than at the pub: a rather older, well-heeled demography, one that appreciated his crafted, urbane performance.

Again he left the building soon after vacating the stage. James watched him from the shadow of a side door. He felt like a private detective, but that's largely what psychiatry was: helping someone trace their behavioural genesis, finding the trauma, facing it, feeling it.

Weels walked to a soft top Audi, his posture different from the first time James had seen him; more erect, casual, in control. He opened the door and sat behind the wheel almost elegantly; not the loose-limbed, often crouching prankster of the other evening. He was beginning to intrigue James.

He was unusually busy for the next few days; As a registered practitioner for the borough in which he lived, he was on-call for certain times of the year, and this time it was a little frantic: a hospital patient who had, apparently, molested two nurses, an ex-client who pitifully and then aggressively demanded to see him, and a curt reminder that he was to appear soon in a law court to give expert testimony in an assault case and which took hours to prepare.

Unlike last time, it was intentionally that he found out where and when Weels was next appearing. It was a club in Dalston.

He recognised that he was trailing this man - stalking being too strong a word - around London. A flash of film noir came to him,

Hey, this comic, Marlowe, waddya want with him? You wanna find out what he really is? What does that mean? What sort o' guy are you?

He smiled. He did want to know him, wanted to …be ready, wanted to know some things before they met professionally.

It was a small venue; dim lighting, a pale spot on the stageless space at the back and a mike. He started off similarly to his pub act; crude, gross, lots of emphasis, shouting, but not as funny. Then he stopped, looked around him for a while, again the slight crowd restlessness, then, slowly, deadpan,

'I do very abstract paintings, no paint, brushes or canvas, but I did buy some second hand paint in the shape of a house.' A long pause. 'My friend has sideburns behind his ears and wears braces on his false teeth.'

People didn't really respond, they looked a little confused. They'd been given a genre, offered a mindset they'd taken willingly. Now, here was another, a very different one. Only towards the end did they, rather warily, respond. The clapping was muted. He went out of the room quickly, carelessly, annoyed.

As James was leaving the building he walked through the foyer. It had obviously been a thirties cinema and although its original function had, presumably, long gone there was enough of it left - the lamps, some walnut marquetry, curved handrail, chevrons engraved on a broken mirror - to prompt a flash of teenage excitement, anticipation, magic. He looked for Weels at the front, with its two chipped lotus leaf columns and curved café windows, but he wasn't there. He went to the car park at the back. He couldn't see him. Then as he got into his car he saw Weels' Audi move away. He'd been parked close by.

He began following him. He was thinking of his disparate acts: the zany, exaggerated crudeness, occasional wild-eyed look, the stooping, pacing restlessness, and the calm, unhurried, perfectly pitched delivery of the other. Were these projections of a classic schizophrenia - roses are red, violets are blue, I'm a schizophrenic and so am I - or was he trying to find the comedic presentation that most suited him, worked the best? Perhaps they were both a rather desperate effort to find himself, find *a* self. He wondered what Thomas would say from the depths of his forty years psychoanalytic experience. He'd told James nothing about him, except that he was a comic.

It was quite easy trailing him eastwards, there was relatively little traffic. He had no idea where Weels lived. After half an hour the car turned into a tree-lined avenue north of Woodford Station and stopped outside a large, double bayed, red brick Edwardian house with wide mullioned windows, black and white chequer pattern path leading to steps, a porch and the original front door, painted jade green - the marker of affluent, liberal middle class conventionality. He went in. A light in the upstairs front room came on. James could see bookshelves and a fifties table lamp before the curtains were drawn.

He looked away, stared through the windscreen, felt like a cunning child doing something rather dirty, something he shouldn't be doing. He was annoyed at himself. He didn't want to be a detective following someone in his car, a man he was going to meet formally in a few weeks.

How long you gonna keep this up Marlowe? Why can't yer be content just sittin' around listenin' to Joes all day?

He drove home, feeling flat.

There was a message on his phone from Lorna, Thomas's daughter, who he'd been friends with since soon after he'd met her father at the beginning of his intended career. She wanted him to go with her to a local drama group that was rehearsing a play to be put on in a few months time. Her father had taken her to a local TheatreCoach as a child, which she'd attended into her teens, but, apart from appearing in plays at her university, with the occasional leading part, she'd done nothing since. She wanted him to 'join in' with her. He had an aversion to being one of the crowd, especially starting cold, knowing no-one. But it was Lorna, so he said yes. It would, he rationalised, have some interest for him: seeing how a show was built, a script changed and tightened, the lighting, sound, props, and, perhaps, the precise moments when cast members emotionally recognised that the roles were theirs.

A few days later they were at the studio, previously a school hall that now had black walls and ceilings with matching curtains and floors. The rehearsals were on a weekday evening and had begun three weeks previously. They stood quietly inside the black entrance door.

They were obviously late. Twenty or so people were standing in a half circle facing them while a man in the centre paced repeatedly towards and away from them.

'Think of a number from one to ten, trace it with your fingers on each others backs, those with the same number stand together.'

He seemed immediately familiar. They separated into small groups, scrawling, being scrawled upon.

'Look at someone's eyes, same colour, same group.'

Some women had two or three men looking closely into their faces.

'No, you're dark brown, she's hazel, different groups. Walk about, just walk, don't act. You're walking anti-clockwise like all the groups do, walk straight. You're trying not to act. It shows. Relax till I give you a quality. Right, anger…excitement…vengeance.'

The light was dim, James could see only his back; the others, if they'd seen them, took no notice. These seemed to be warming up exercises.

'Okay, so you're traffic wardens, and you love it, the uniform, the peak cap, all of it, you're full of hubris, move like it, look in a wing mirror to comb your hair before you book 'em. Now I'm holding a beach ball, see it? I'm going to throw it to someone, then they throw it to someone else, let's have five balls and shout out the name of the person you're throwing it to. Stop. How many have we got now? Where's the missing one? You've got dirt phobias, clean something, get manic, more manic.'

They started throwing invisible balls to each other, many then scrubbing floors in ever widening circles, using imaginary brushes while some polished tables or scratched away tiny bits of non-existent dirt from invisible furniture, others vigorously dry-washing their hands.

The back of the Director's head seemed increasingly familiar to James, as was his energy and enthusiasm, and that quick crouching when he wished to emphasise, and of course the voice, though occasionally sounding rather posh, drawling, luvvy. A second before glimpsing his profile, he embarrassingly knew who it was. The unexpected had blunted recognition, though a part of him had known from the beginning. He didn't want it to be him, didn't want them to meet before they should. As Thomas often said, denial's underrated.

He wanted to leave. Lorna, with her large, sensitive eyes, was almost quivering with excitement in anticipation of being part of it. She looked up at him, grinning. He decided that when they eventually had to give names, not to give his surname. And he felt only a little guilt this time; this was an accidental voyeurism.

Weels carried on with his quickfire instructions:

'Speed dating, anyone done that? There's more men than women, put the chairs in facing pairs, women sit opposite the blokes, the ones left can stand at a bar, put some chairs there. When I blow the whistle all the boys choose another partner and so on, then we'll have the girls doing the same. Go on then.'

They quickly moved the chairs.

'Can we be ourselves?' someone asked.

'Up to you.'

Off they went.

'You nervous?' 'Yeh.' 'First time?' 'No, I've been nervous before'... 'Hi, you don't know me, but I'm Mister Right' 'Yeh, my wife was so fat that wherever I sat she was always next to me'...'Your legs'll start aching tomorrer, they'll be runnin' through my dreams all night.

Lorna's fascination was palpable.

They continued, not always sure whether the people they were facing were being themselves or acting created personalities. He watched a diffident teenager walk across to a young Eurasian girl.

'Do you, er, live round here often?' he asked. James wasn't sure whether it was intentional or not.

They waited till the coffee break before going over to Weels, Lorna leading. He greeted her warmly, James perfunctorily as he mumbled his name, then left the room.

Lorna went across to a small group and talked to them while James slowly sipped coffee. After a few minutes Weels came back and gave sheets of A4 to everyone, including Lorna, who he talked to for a while, pointing at what James assumed was the script and then wheeled away to stand towards one end of the hall. They began again, more or less still roughly in a half circle, while James leant against a wall and watched.

A large skinhead with a cockney accent, adopted or otherwise, began with,

'Don't forget, some day you're the pigeon, uvvers, the statue'

One by one the others joined in, Lorna too, speaking with a surprisingly realistic contemporary East London accent. The setting of the play was obviously local; the physical and cultural characteristics were all there, summed up by one of the cast's,

'The posh bits, the dirty bits, the swanky and the wanky bits, big house with dog shit on the pavement, wisteria up the walls, piss in the gutter..' the fatalism, Len and Hazel getting ready to win the night's bingo, overlaid with a sound track of Roy Orbison singing 'All I Have To Do is Dream,' the humour, 'I started out wiv nuffink, I got most of it left'...'Whatever look you're tryin' for you've missed'...' I told him I wanted to practice safe sex, he said he'd put more paddin' on the 'eadboard...' and an Asian rhetorically asking, as if he was a comic stand-up, 'What's the favourite name for Asian lesbians? Minjeeta.'

There was a whole *pot-pourri* of seemingly tenuously connected scenes: a character, Girly, with a blow up male doll, Orbison singing 'Only The Lonely' in the background., 'Thug', with fantasies of using his controlled savagery to destroy the figure that was always looking at him from across a road, a park, a room, and which turns out to be himself,

This was interesting James now, and it was obvious who'd written the show. The author was quite still, not looking at the script in his hands, just silently mouthing the lines, occasionally nodding or suggesting someone read something in a different way, to make it quicker, slower, lesser or more emphatic.

James became more interested in Weels' creation than in him. Perhaps he was just a good professional, neurotic maybe, but not really disturbed by anything traumatic from his past, not really having to come to terms with any ontological lesions festering since infancy; perhaps just wanted to express his creativity in the field he'd chosen, or had maybe chosen him.

This reading went on for an hour or so, then, as a caretaker came in pointedly swinging his keys, Weels called a halt and they all, gradually, left, but not before he asked James whether he wanted a part in his play. He thanked him, but refused, saying he was merely an interested spectator. He just nodded and then, with a smile that made James aware that, when dwelling in this apparently more relaxed persona, he was, with his thick, dark hair, wide smile and patrician nose, a handsome man. He could see that Lorna agreed.

He thought about him during the following week, but felt less intrigued, less interested, and had little desire to drive around London after him. He decided not to go to the next rehearsal after Lorna told him that she wasn't going. This was a little surprising after her obvious enjoyment at, as she clichéically put it, 'treading the boards again.'

A week before James was due to see him as a new client, his interest in Freddie was reinvigorated. Lorna rang to tell him that she hadn't gone back to the group again because 'the Director' had invited her to have a drink with him and she'd accepted. This seemed to be a contradiction - unless she didn't want to mix pleasure with business.

She hadn't done anything like this before, not that he was aware, and he intuitively knew that it hadn't, or soon wouldn't be, just a drink. He felt suddenly shaken, as if a complacency which had cloaked him for years had been torn away. He became aware that she meant more to him than the interests they shared and the affection they'd built for each other. Now, he emotionally recognised, admitted, how

23

attractive he found her, how much he'd been thinking of her sexually; and something he'd done nothing about.

This made it more painful. He tried to work out why he hadn't. Perhaps it was because Thomas had, in helping him through his initial psychoanalytic doubts, of wondering whether he was temperamentally suited, was emotionally strong enough, resilient enough to be what he wanted to be, had become, in his psyche, a father-like figure; was symbolically his father. And he began to see how he'd looked at the situation through the morality of his respectable working class parents and which, unthinkingly, he'd skewed into an almost quasi incestual barrier, a warped parameter that, somehow, he was forbidden to tread past.

He wanted to tell her all this, wanted her not to go out with Weels, wanted to… begin again. The only way he could do this, he felt, was by blurting it all out to her; He could almost see himself physically shaking her, hear himself shouting, 'Do you under*stand*? *Do* you? That biblical, almost cruelly analogous advice of 'Physician, heal thyself,' whirled around him deafeningly.

She was, he realised, loudly repeating his name, almost screeching it. He put the phone down, detached, in slow motion, wondering if an intelligent child with a knack for understanding psychological and clinical theory, and with discretely placed, but see-able framed diplomas on his walls and a deep, spacious couch and muted lighting, could help *any* one.

But, *verstehen*. He wanted to see Weels now, though whether he'd understand him or not, would he, he wondered, be able to give him anything? Help *him* understand? Would he want to now? And then, another realisation: empathetic interpretation could be an excuse to fill himself *with* the person he was trying to understand. Then, of course, he wouldn't have to face himself, or his early distress within the dynamics of his own family. He could theorise this, articulate it.

Now he was excited. He wanted to work on it, it was an insight deserving of research. He could get a paper out of it, maybe in the British Psychological Review and, a further insight, this intellectualisation *itself* could be an escape from…

He remembers kicking the desk that held his computer, smashing a fist against the solid pine door of the study and, an ultimate irony, throwing himself onto the couch, sobbing.

Freddie Weels didn't keep his appointment. Lorna didn't contact James again, nor he her. A little of the, 'but we've shared so much, how can you...?' came and went without warning, but with decreasing frequency. They hadn't, in retrospect, really shared much, but enough for her absence to hurt. It was painful, also, that her father hadn't rung him, something he would often do to offer advice or, though rarely, when he himself had a particularly problematic patient.

He wasn't really sure how it had happened, something as ordinary, mundane, even edging the arbitrary, as meeting someone to share a drink, to... He stopped his retrospective rationalising. He'd recently seen the outcome in a waiting room celebrity magazine: Weels stepping out of his car with a laughing, groomed Lorna, her hand touching her designer windswept hair, alongside an article, which he tried not to read, about a new TV show, *Freddie's Ready*. The professional part of him wanted to watch it, to look for behavioural clues, for bits of behaviour that didn't fit with other bits, to see how much he could delineate what was and wasn't an act, to search for... he didn't know.

He was getting even less clients now. He'd begun ringing other practitioners he knew to see if they had people they didn't really want to treat and thought that, maybe, he could help them. They hadn't.

How's business, Marlowe? Like show business - no business? Dames, uh? Maybe you learnt things about yerself, Maybe you ain't so clever. Better luck next time.

There would be a next time. But he didn't know how many of them. Somebody once told him economic historians were failed economists. He wondered what, if anything, would or could be said of unsuccessful psychotherapists, except, maybe, failed comedians...

RELIGIOUS AFFAIRS

He was leaning against the back wall of the classroom, hands in pockets, body arched forward a little, right leg bent, heel resting on top of the skirting and head cocked slightly to one side like his childhood photos; hiding a sulk, a shyness. A 'little camp' was the description offered by one student. She herself, so debilitated by her family that she had succeeded at nothing, was getting through the course because he was writing virtually half of her work for her.

Her brother, who had abused her as a child, had burnt himself to death in his car by throwing petrol over the inside and igniting it. She, too, had attempted suicide, driving her car at speed into a lamppost. The vehicle had split almost in two, she stepping out with a grazed face. Her sibling she'd seen as selfish, there being nothing left for her to remember him by.

Mature students, generally, had many problems, especially women. The majority on this course were females and half of them were starting the long road to economic independence and, for some, hoped-for single parenthood. Their male partners were largely unsupportive, insecure and suspicious of those who were helping their women stretch to new vistas; a colleague had recently seen one of them standing in the car park looking grimly up at the staff room windows. Fresh bruises seemed a weekly occurrence. The younger girls, minimum age twenty, were not exceptions.

For six months he had been lecturing this group in both the sociology of deviance and of medicine. Most would go on to a nursing or social work degree. Two hundred students were split into groups called 'cohorts' by management. He'd told the latter that as a cohort referred to a tenth of a Roman Legion and he hadn't seen a toga or a sandal since he'd been there, the term was inappropriate.

He disliked management and their sycophants; their eager grabbing of Edu-biz buzz words and throwing them into the air like linguistic status symbols at staff meetings, at the end of which, having remained silent throughout, he would quietly place a scribbled list of code words in front of the frowning Chair.

The students he saw as 'his,' as he did the subject he taught, and was aware that this proprietary urge was a vestige of a working class background; his father, a caretaker, owning nothing, would claim psychological ownership of 'his' building, his mother, a cleaner, 'her' bank.

He was doing role-plays with them and had suggested a scenario or two; the Jehovah's Witness parents of a young, injured child who were refusing to allow a life-saving blood transfusion - what would, could, the medical team do? A similar question was posed by an extremely sick menstruating woman being treated by Orthodox Jewish doctors. It was a delight to watch two Yoruba Nigerian women and a Kenyan man play the doctors.

With encouragement they'd create their own situations and act out one or two a lesson. They particularly liked making up stories that enabled them to dress up - tongue in cheek he'd suggest nurses' uniforms with fishnet stockings and stiletto heels would be appreciated - and, if they justified it in the context of a genuine ethical dilemma, to use music. The head of school would look through the door and frown perplexedly at them. Once, she had marched into the classroom and demanded they changed rooms, this one having been overbooked. He'd told the class not to leave.

'You can't treat them like this.' he'd said to her.

'And I hate the way you behave towards me in front of students,' she'd hissed angrily, and using her authority had had her way. He wondered if she'd have acted thus if most of the students had been white.

Thandi Mnede was delivering a baby - a large black doll - from a fair-haired Spanish student, slightly shorter than the doll, lying on a desk surrounded by other 'medical staff' who were laughing and screaming with delight. He liked the innocence, the ingenuous nature of African women, except when it came to religion.

He told them of European oppression and control through Christianity, that God was a construct, all predictably met with surprise, anger and, sometimes, pity. God was involved with the things that they wrote, their essays and research projects - particularly the latter where, in their acknowledgements, they would thank various organisations and individuals who had helped them, often including God. He'd suggest they put him higher on the list than God. Some took him seriously.

Pulling a chair across he sat down, watching them. Maria was holding her new-born tightly and miming breast-feeding while Charity, the youngest in the class and wearing a stars and stripes headscarf, was jumping up and down with glee. It was she who, after he'd told them that sepia photos of ringed female necks a foot long and 'savages' with bones through their noses had been part of his early upbringing, had insisted to the group that the bones were fashion statements. On her mobile he knew that it permanently said, 'I love Jesus and Jesus loves me.'

Thandi was enjoying herself, grinning at him. She was tall, slim, with short frizzy hair, almond-shaped eyes and that slightly jutting curve at the top of her buttocks. He was seeing her that evening.

Recently she'd been passing the staff room when he'd beckoned her in and asked what work she did. Most of the women had caring jobs outside college; she was looking after adolescent boys. He offered to help her with her project questionnaire and handed her a sheet of paper which asked if she fancied a drink one evening, under which he'd drawn a large square with a 'yes' under it and a small one with a tiny 'no. 'Please tick appropriate box.' it said.

She'd folded it in quarters slowly and perfectly and in her slightly brittle Zulu accent had said, 'Why didn't you ask me before? I knew you wanted me as soon as you walked into the classroom.'

'It would have been too early then, I may have frightened you off.' he'd explained.

Disdainfully she'd lifted her head and walked away.

It had been rather different in the early days when she'd been with other students chattering eagerly around his table in the staffroom waiting for their marks and calling him, 'Mister Steve.'

They met in a pub near where she lived, he arriving before her as intended. It was a dismal place; flock wallpaper, match boarded dado, fifties lampshades and a tattered, miss spelt notice stating that there were rooms to let. When Thandi came in he gestured at it and said that the landlady would probably have told any potential guests that she couldn't shake their hands, she'd just finished putting lard on the cat's boil. She looked bemused.

Sitting down opposite him and with her Nefertiti head inquiringly angled she said,

'Well, are you bisexual?'

He asked if it was the earring - he wore a small gold one. Pints were pulled and a darts matched ended before she told him it was because he wore tight jeans. He jokingly sneered at her African stereotypes, until she reminded him that he'd told them that sociology was a generalising enterprise and not to apologise for it.

She couldn't stay long; she had a shift to do, and briefly told him about herself. Brought up outside Johannesburg in a large, extended family - he envied aspects of African culture; babies huddled in slings between their mother's breasts, having lots of 'mothers', what could create more security? - she'd managed a restaurant before coming to London and its gold-paved streets. She was single, had a son Nono - pronounced with clicks after the consonants - and was thinking of adopting Tshepiso, her absent brother's teenage daughter who he had ill-treated from an early age.

'I want to show her and teach her love.' she said.

Two evenings later he was quickly shaking hands with other household members: an aunt, uncle, two cousins, a half-sister, and a sister who she shared a room and a bed with. She gave him a glimpse of the room; a few African carvings, bright traditional dresses inside an opened wardrobe door, a photo of herself in a Diana Ross wig taken on the sea front at Clacton when she'd first come to Britain four years before.

In the train on their way to see 'Umoja' she wore a black velvet hat and, picking up a newspaper from a seat, started reading. He asked her if her not talking to him was an African thing.

'We don't show love or hold hands.' she said, and enquired if his son was well. He was divorced, as he told his classes in response to their questioning, and his young son stayed with him some weekends. Later he was to find that she revelled in disinterest; not asking who he'd seen a film with, but where, not who had accompanied him to a gallery, but merely a polite raising of an eyebrow.

He asked her why she had worn her hat in the theatre and hadn't clapped and sung as many in the audience had.

'We wear our hats inside. And I didn't want to make a noise because I could see the way you looked at people when they were unwrapping sweets. But I told the people behind you are my teacher and to take no notice.'

There was a smile in her eyes, but he felt frustrated that she hadn't expressed herself, had misunderstood.

In class she acted as if they hadn't been out together. Occasionally he rang her at her work place; she always seemed to be working and could rarely talk for long. She called him 'darling' on the phone and he noticed she greeted her student friends in the same manner. Childishly, he felt annoyed.

One Sunday she rang to ask him to help her with a communications essay, the title of which she'd been allowed to choose herself. Despite precise instructions she got hopelessly lost. He drove to where she was parked and led her back to his flat.

Standing by his side while he looked at her work and wearing salwar kameez trousers around her head, braided extensions pluming above them, she looked utterly African.

Without looking up he asked her quietly when she was going to sleep with him. She pushed him playfully to the floor and stood astride him, eyes black and still. But it was church day and she had to leave and, holding her folder, walked to the gate while he returned to the screen where her essay title still read, '"Thou shalt lie only with whom thou love.' Discuss.' He wondered if she recognised the irony.

They went to the Passion play, 'The Mysteries.' Knowing his views on organised religion she was surprised at his choice. How many times had he told them of social inequality being legitimised by hymnal lines such as, 'The rich man at his castle, the poor man at his gate, all creatures high and lowly, God ordered their estate.'

The director had encouraged members of the South African cast to act in their own languages. She casually said she could speak five of them. On the way back he mentioned that the lead black singer, the best voice on stage, should have played Eve. She made no comment, just shrugged. He tried to get her interested in the songs, the humour, the scant, but effective scenery; like the stockade made of Peter Stuyvesant cartons in which a near naked group had sung, 'You Are My Sunshine.' and received a standing ovation. She shrugged again, then said,

'I will stay with you tonight, then.'

He drove her home. In his bedroom she began undressing quickly, a sudden dark shape slipping under the duvet. After telling him that it was too early for them to make love, she added disinterestedly that she would still satisfy him. He delivered a short lecture on the myth of joyless servicing, but gave in to her plea that she never slept naked by letting her wear him for most of the night.

In the morning she made herself breakfast with food she'd brought with her, picking up pieces of cornmeal to soak up her thin stew, lips making soft smacking sounds and occasionally smiling. Unravelling her cornrows into a tightly curled wedge and rubbing in sulphur cream, 'Because this is what they do back home.' she transformed his kitchen by putting dishes away as if she had lived there forever instead of staying a night. Looking briefly around his minimalist home she announced she'd be late for college and that when he took her class he mustn't anger the women again by jeering that infibulation was about male control and that they didn't have to lie back and think of Africa.

As she started the engine of her car, barefoot on the pavement he anguished his frustration through the car window.

'But I made you cum.' She frowned and drove away.

During the summer he saw her only once. She had passed the course and was beginning a nursing degree at university and was working nearly all of the time, mostly with the boys. On most days he rang her and if there was more than a three-day gap between calls she would ring to remind him of 'the contract,' referring to a promise he'd made to phone her regularly.

One evening she asked him to meet her at the street where he'd picked her up when she'd got lost. When he crossed the road to her, she wound down the side window and gently took his hands and pulled them inside the car and pressed them to her breasts. He felt awkward, like a teenager, and wanted to take her home. Grinning at him she said she had to go back, and drove off. Always she seemed to be driving away.

She'd been at university a month before he saw her again; for the first and only time she'd arranged for someone to stand in for her at work. She walked in with a parcel of fish heads and yams and began washing up while they warmed and noisily sucked one of the eyes while he opened the wine, though she rarely touched alcohol. He found it pleasurable to watch her eat with her fingers.

She hadn't spoken since coming in, then, with eyes darker than her lashes and blacker than her fountained braids, looked up at him and said, in long, continuous sentences and barely pausing for breath,

'When you mimic me your accent is too strong, I am Zulu not Afrikaans, and when you come home with me at Christmas it will be very hot, but you must wear a suit to show respect for my mother and you cannot sleep with me.' She carried on eating for a while. 'I am beautiful inside as well as out, and if I were a virgin you would pay a thousand pounds for me, and when I go back I even give them my panties because we are poor and when I was a child my uncle said I was spoilt because I didn't sweep the yard and cook tomatoes in the big pot like the other children and I walked like an old woman, but I hold my shoulders back for you because I am glad you took me out, though I don't think you will come home with me at Christmas.'

She looked down at her plate again. He didn't know what to say.

She stood up and began swaying with the music he'd put on, a languorous wisdom inhabiting every glance, then, moving nothing except her wrists, bending them rhythmically downwards, she was nonchalantly clutching all the sex in the world.

There was a familiarity about the bedroom struggle to remove her clothes, until she clamped his wrist and he noticed the rag tied around her waist, which she'd said she wore for fasting. This meant that nothing was to enter her body except sips of water.

She laid down with her back to him, braided hair now in a loose knot on her shoulder before flowing down almost to her hip.

'I am a wounded soldier making love on the battlefield.' she whispered, and went to sleep.

When he woke she was parading naked around his bedroom, buttocks clenching Zulu style and intently mirror-gazing. She murmured repetitive 'mmms?' to his thick-throated questions about when he would see her again, and her bumping into a stool, hair extensions loosening, did not interrupt her delighted solipsism. After she had gone he could still hear her sharp vowels telling him she was leaving, and lay still on the bed as he scrawled on the calendar an imaginary cross for some day next month.

She started work-placement at a local hospital, after which she came to tell him that as her family had moved to Nottingham, and she had flown back to her childhood home to bring Nono back with her as well as adopting Tshepiso, she now had nowhere to live.

'I have now been seeing a man for some while.' she added, with that slight irregularity of English use he usually found endearing, 'He is not African, but he will provide a home for us.' Her eyes were sad, and also asking him to offer her his home.

This news hurt and confused him. The flat was not large enough, his son still stayed with him, though less often, and he wasn't sure he could cope with her two children. He felt weakened, told her he couldn't have her, was sorry

Then, at the end of her first year at university, instead of the dutiful relationship she had with God being little more than a socialized response, she really did find Him.

She asked him to come to church with her and listen to her testimony. He hadn't been to a church since a child. It was a Victorian building whose builders would never have envisaged the nature of this congregation. There were many people present, mostly ethnics, the majority Africans. The pastor, white, tanned, grey hair, tailored sports jacket, briefly shook his hand.

'Hi, I'm David.' he drawled in an American accent, and moved into the hall.

'Hi, I'm a sceptic.' Steve said under his breath as he climbed to the back of the balcony. He stood watching the keyboard player hitting the chords with a gospel band and, pointing to the hymn-filled screen above the stage and telling them that this was their God for the morning, he led the congregation into their devotional karaoke. Matrons sang, clapped and swayed and towards the far side of the balcony he saw two students he'd taught the previous year looking across at him, eyes wide in surprise. He exaggeratedly raised his shoulders and gestured with open hands to them.

Thandi arrived late, African time, shook his hand - he fondled hers - and introduced him to her lover, a protestant chill momentarily freezing the music. He was a pleasant looking Afro-Caribbean who welcomed him warmly and asked him to sit with them. He stayed where he was. After a sermon and further hymns it was time for her testimony. Standing in front of the audience she told them how she had come to God.

She recited it very quickly and emotionally and he could understand little. After she had finished, with more clapping and singing from the now packed church, she came up to the balcony and gently squeezed his arm and asked him to take her back to the flat so she could tell him what had really happened. Her partner would take the children home.

Sitting at his table with him, she held his hands tightly together as if he were praying and, with her eyes closed, told him that when she was seventeen her ancestors had occupied her spirit and told her to remain chaste - a command manifested in the white rag appearing around her waist - and when it was time for her to work for them she would be told. She assumed that, like chosen others in her country, she would 'go away' for two years then return as a healer.

Two weeks ago the ancestral spirits had demanded that she walk into the sea and there would be a crocodile waiting for her with open mouth into which she would climb. There would be snakes, a festive party and great happiness inside the creature. There she was to stay until ready to heal the sick.

As she told him this she spoke rapidly, became excited; several times he gently slowed her down. She became more agitated, almost frantic, when she announced that she had, wearing the rag, white knickers and white dressing gown, set out to obey these wishes two weeks ago at Southend-on-Sea while her younger sister and her boy friend had watched from the beach.

Resisting explaining the phallic symbolism of the snakes, he imagined her, oblivious to the sounds of boy racers, the pier train, the fun fair, go-karts, the smell of vinegar and chips, moving deeper and deeper into the sea.

Part of him wanted to laugh, almost hysterically, at the sheer incongruity of the town she'd chosen, but he believed her; believed her when she told him that as her head was going under water, God had exploded inside of her and told her to renounce what she was doing and to do His work, and only His.

She had waded back to her sister and pleaded with her to find a priest. They'd driven back and found the church - the one she had been speaking in an hour before - and she'd told David what had happened. This had been her first visit since then.

She began to cry. Releasing his hands he gripped hers. She opened her eyes; they shone with excitement. This was a different reality for him, a spiritual universe he couldn't enter, and didn't wish to. He wanted to tell her that many frigid women who gave themselves to Jesus could do so in the knowledge that they didn't have to make love to him. She would, her humour and patience jettisoned, have cried out that it was profane, an insult. She wasn't in the classroom; he wasn't teaching her. He held her tightly for a long while before she left.

He went to church with her once more. It was the last time he saw her.

She picked him up at his home and drove northwards. In the car Tshepiso ate greens with her fingers while Thandi threw them around back streets telling him that the preachers used private jets, while he proselytised about ruling classes and God until they arrived.

In a hangar on Hackney wasteland gantry cameras arced over them like crows, people waved at screens, puzzled they were in profile, and envelopes for Jesus magically appeared. Outside, he'd noticed how permanent the fast-track buildings were, how organised it was. As well as hot food and drinks there were all the cogs of capitalism; stalls housing loan firms, insurance companies, mortgage and investment brokers, banks, estate agents, a funeral director, even an adoption agency. And inside, a bass voiced pastor was telling the congregation that all that they looked upon is all they may have.

Knowing those who had nothing, he stood up, squeezed past Thandi with a tight smile and walked towards an exit, remembering irrelevantly the gifts she'd brought him every time she came to see him; the lemons he never ate, the popcorn he never made, the t-shirt he never wore.

At the door he turned; saw her head with its short tufts of hair, Tshepiso and Nono grinning back at him, and under the starry night ceiling of the stage, standing in a lake of lilies, the wild hair of a singer hitting Whitney Houston notes. Turning sixties pop into gospel, Jackson Five look-alikes strutted to the front and a thousand believers raised their hands.

MRS. GAINES

It was a book launch - his working class roots writhing at that last word, filling him with images of Home Counties public school complacency, pseudo-intellectualism, and the taken-for-granted expectational norms of childhoods so different from his own. It was on the second floor of a pub in the West End. He was purposely late. In a long, narrow room with coloured, leaded glass windows and a bar were fifty people: a malice of poets, a swirl of grey haired men, asexual Germaine Greer and Anne Bancroft look-alikes - Oxbridge and casually slumming - and all rather expensively dressed.

James Kent had come to see Jilly Bates, an old friend who he hadn't seen since they'd both read their poetry at an extra-mural event at the L.S.E two years previously. With her bulging blob of black hair and fringe she reminded him of a page boy at the court of one of the Henrys. She had wide hips and was standing, jeaned legs apart, at right angles to the bar with an almost beatific smile from her large teeth. She was a lawyer and as she saw him they both said, as if orchestrated,

'Scientists use lawyers instead of rats now; 'cos you can get too close to rats and there's some things even rats won't do.'

She laughed, gave his cheek a kiss and then turned to someone who shouted 'Jilly!' and who gave her a crushing hug. The recipient raised an eyebrow at James, signalling, he assumed, that she wouldn't be spending much time with him this evening, further confirmed when a long-haired man with a Welsh lilt said hello to her and to whom she turned with that grin.

Someone, one of the support poets he guessed, started reading. He heard 'fecund land,' a line later, 'soul,' then an adjectival glut and some neo-surrealist poetry dwelling in its own arse. Jilly had disappeared inside a huddle of pearls and Chanel; but he could email her tomorrow.

Half way down the stairs was a toilet: a mixture of urine stench, turbo jet drier and, from a speaker embedded in the ceiling over a cubicle, the quiet, slow, insistent:

'Say, English, *Ingles,* Say, do you understand? *Entiendes?* Say, you do not understand. *No intiendo.* Say, do you speak Spanish? *Hable*

Espaniol?'

It was mesmeric, its seeming randomness fascinating him, soothing the bludgeoning, self conscious erudition of the poetry a few moments before.

He went back to his office, relieved to return to it and finish off the discreet san serif lettering on the door. Not many therapists can signwrite, but he'd earned a living doing this and painting murals - and other things - before a psychology degree, training and, now, five years in practice.

As he wiped the smudged 't' in 'Kent' there was a foot on the stairs. He looked down, noticed her cloche hat, retro fox fur, wedge heel shoes and, as she looked up, the auburn hair and dark lipstick. He was reminded of what his mother's posh sister wore when he was a child, and which went perfectly with her front garden rockery, chevron'd door and curved crittall windows.

She was tall, slim and without a trace of estuary as she asked whether he was in.

'I am,' he said, pointing to the letters. 'That's me. And you're...?

'Beth Gaines'

With her black, pencil skirt he imagined her taking shorthand before translating it onto a Remington. She looked slightly Jewish.

'Am I a little early?'

He'd forgotten about her, something he hadn't done with a potential client before. Deciding to leave the wondering why till he was on his own, he beckoned her to come in and then excused himself to go to the toiled to wash his hands, they smelt of paint. There was no speaker, no Spanish - if he was to learn a language he would prefer Italian, with its deep, rolling aesthetic, both simultaneously beautiful and aggressive.

He returned to see her sitting on an arm of the chair in the corner of the room facing his desk. The office was large, bigger than the adjoining room where he saw his patients and which he'd painted a pale green, the most psychologically restful of colours. Recently he'd decided to live downstairs in his picket fenced, terraced home and use the upstairs as a working area. He'd only just finished decorating it.

She gave a tight smile as he sat down on the edge of the desk facing her.

'It's about my husband.' Another cliché born of truth.

She looked down at her hands resting symmetrically perfect on her stocking'd knees. Her dark eyes looked up. He gave her an encouraging smile.

'He just sits there, so…distant. He doesn't care, doesn't let me do anything for him; cooking, ironing. It sounds old fashioned I know, but, that's me.'

'I'm assuming there's no…he doesn't touch you? I'm sorry, but I want to establish basics.' She briefly shook her head.

'You can cry if you need to, it's allowed,' he offered gently.

She took a deep breath, held herself upright, emotionally shook herself

'I don't know why.'

He asked her how long they'd been married.

'Five years.'

'And how long has -'

'Nearly two. I don't think there's another woman.'

She gave a mock laugh. 'How many times have you heard something like *that ?*'

'Often.'

She looked straight at him. 'I'm sorry I insisted you see me now, but I had to do something.'

'I'm guessing there are no children.'

'No.'

She looked away, out of the window. She was seeing rear gardens with long established trees, the back of the corner off-licence, Victorian brickwork, chimney pots, and the ever-present hovering cranes, emblematic of the area's 'regeneration.'. As somebody born and bred less than three miles away he couldn't take 'Yuppie Rebirth' or 'Stratford Village' seriously. But he was looking at her: the strong but vulnerable profile, the slight, smooth wave in her hair, the small mole on her cheek.

He asked if it had happened before, and if there was, maybe, an age gap - he was visualising an older partner. She answered no to both questions. He asked her if she had told him, hinted, that he needed help.

'Yes. He just puts on this face, just flippantly shrugs or walks away. Will you see him?'

He told her he would, asked her to get him to ring him.

'He won't, and I don't think he'll come here.'

He informed her that he didn't see clients in their own home and, presupposing the questioning response, added that there was a comforting familiarity there, that her husband would use it as a haven to protect himself from him, from what he would symbolise. Here, he could try to establish some neutrality, difficult of course, as it was his own home.

'He won't come. I know he won't.'

'Mrs. Gaines, ask him to see me, tell him I'm a nice man, user-friendly.' He reminded her of what he charged.

'Yes, I know, I'll pay for this. But he won't come.'

She stood up, puckered her lips, looking disappointed. She pushed her palms firmly down her thighs, turned and walked towards the door, saying,

'I'll try, Mister Kent, but don't hope.'

She turned towards him and held her hand to be shaken. He was mildly surprised, and a little sorry, that it wasn't gloved.

She rang him at lunchtime the next day.

'He won't come, he's adamant. I'll try again, but I can't keep trying.'

He asked her if he was there, his name and what his job was - questions he should have asked before. He suggested she get him to speak to him. It was at least two minutes before he heard a hardly audible,

'Hello.'

'Alan, it's Mister Kent. James. I'd like you to come to see me. You don't have to say much if you don't want to, just come. I can see you tomorrow at four. That okay? Another long silence. He tried to bribe him, as he would a child.

'You're a graphic designer, aren't you? I've got some sketches and a couple of water colours I've recently done, I'd like your opinion. Would you ?'

It seemed as if he'd said, 'Alright,' then silence again. James was about to put the phone down when he heard her voice.

'I think he may come to you. I hope so. Thank you. Goodnight.' She sounded relieved, but tense.

He was on time. He was average height, wiry, neatly buttoned up, crisp collar and tie. He went straight to the couch, sat on the edge and stayed there for almost ten minutes, looking down.

I feel...so terrified. I'm so... I always have. I'm not real ...it's not real.'

He looked up, not at James' face, a little lower.

'Your jacket, it's the wrong colour for you, and your left shoe's scuffed on the outside of the toes, and you've got a slight cockney accent and I *hate* cockneys.'

'So have you. We need to know why you hate yourself.'

'But I ...their 'fuck awfs,' their...Bill Nash, a bloke at work when I was sixteen, used to say, when we were talking about women, 'lick it aht, lick 'em aht.''

'Tell me about sex, Alan.'

He had his head in his hands, then thumped a knee. 'I feel awful. I get an image of her and...when I'm out, if I see something in, say, a shop window, an... electric fire or...a big book, I feel it's going to hurt her, hurt her vagina. Oh God, I'm so frightened.'

James knew that for the man in front of him, it would take years, and, possibly, he would never return to full reality, if indeed he'd ever had it.

He was gripping the hair above his ears. James let him calm himself. It was too early for free association, and certainly for a Rorschach test - too easy for the patient and merely an indulgence for the psychologist - but not too soon to tell him what he intuitively thought; talking of his latent homosexuality could come later.

'I think you felt your mother was trying to destroy you at birth, that's where your terror lies. You've pushed this away all your life, and you've struggled all of this time; but eventually the pain of unreality becomes greater than what you've blotted out. The little I know of you, it seems quite amazing what you've actually achieved. You've had, I assume, relationships with women, held down jobs, you married... I think that you're too frightened to leave the womb, and too frightened to stay in it. You're trapped.'

It reminded him of an early patient who, recently, had suddenly told him that he was being born, and then seemed to try to burrow his way into the couch, to get inside of it, and then screaming for a full half minute before he sat, trembling, for the next half an hour. It was horrible. James was surprised that it had taken only the few years that it had., though he guessed that the man would, the next day, carry on as before, having little or no emotional recollection of the incident.

This dragged up memories of his training, and of visiting a psychiatric ward at a hospital in Essex where he'd seen a man writhing on his bed, and the doctor he was shadowing referring to the two nurses walking behind them, saying, 'Noticed the tits on the tall one, James?' He could look only at the patient systematically putting his pillow over his face, then turning over and placing his face in the pillow, repeatedly, till James left the ward, looking backwards, nearly walking into its door.

Alan looked up at him, a second's eye contact, then away. James knew he would have given almost anything to have cried, to release it all; fear, pain, horror, but knew he wouldn't, couldn't - this only happened in movies. He would need an intellectual recognition initially, then years to become emotionally aware.

His patient looked at the drawings above the couch, dismissing them with hardly a glance, seemingly more interested in the water colours, but these too he dismissed as mere technique. He talked about art, fine art, animatedly articulating it, but not looking him directly in the eyes. James let him continue, flowing - the staccato had gone - knowledgeable and insightful, until the fifty minutes were up, knowing that he was intellectualising, escaping from telling him more about himself, his parents, his childhood.

Alan's wife called him late that evening to ask how it went. He suggested she view him as an atheistic, confessional priest guided by a code of confidentiality.

'Please tell me something,'

How could he tell her that her husband was not psychologically born yet?

'He's very ill. He copes. It will take a long, long while. He has to do the work, not me. There are no magic wands. I'm tempted to say, just…continue loving him, but you have to be yourself, it has to be real, authentic.'

He felt he was guiding her more than he should. He said goodbye to her.

'Call me Beth,' she said.

He wished her goodnight, asking himself from long habit what his old friend Thomas would say, but since breaking up with his daughter he hadn't contacted him, and missed his long-practised professional advice.

Two days afterwards he was shopping, watching objects of necessity or mild avarice being plucked off shelves and wondering if it was possible that others disliked the activity as much as himself, when he saw Mrs. Gaines - Beth - behind him at the checkout. She smiled a little tensely, being unexposed to behavioural guidelines appropriate to meeting her husband's therapist in a supermarket. He paid and waited for her, struggling a little with her bags, and offered to take one. They walked into the car park and after the occasional polite grins at each other, he said,

'Do you, er, shop here often?' She smiled, genuinely.

'Okay, you think of something then,' he suggested.

'Well, just behind my car over there in the corner there's a road with a little café.' She raised her eyebrows.

They put the bags in her car, walked to the cafe and sat down.

'I should think,' she said, 'that walk took about eight minutes and we didn't say a thing.'

He laughed, felt both relaxed and suddenly stimulated. She wore a beret, dark lipstick again, tailored jacket, tight skirt. She looked younger, lighter, than at their previous meeting.

'Let's get this done with,' she said. 'I feel relieved that he's come to you, that he's beginning the process that - '

'Let's talk about, I dunno, literature? movies? I bet you loved Brief Encounter.'

'Of course I did, that surprisingly real script.'

'The hubby was a convenient stereotype though, wasn't he? And with that beret you could have been sitting at a table in the station café.'

She smiled as if he'd satisfactorily confirmed the success of her style. They talked a little more about films, her telling him that she occasionally went to the NFT on her own, her husband being more interested in the theatre.

'I'm hungry,' she said, 'let's have lunch here, unless it's too greasy spoon for you.'

He told her it wasn't, but thought it may be for her.

'Oh, *contraire,* I love stodge and fry-ups.'

He perversely liked her for this; he, having partly re-constructed himself years ago and, at least symbolically, moving away from that culinary environment, and her defying conditioned taste buds and shifting towards it.

It was an enjoyable two hours; largely extending their conversation on films. They seemed to laugh a lot, she was easy to be with. Then he realised he'd be late for a client unless he moved quickly.

'Let's see a film,' she said as, apologising, he paid and left the café quickly.

He rang her the next day, telling her he'd book for 'An American in Paris' a few days hence, if she could make it. She sounded pleased, she hadn't seen it for years. Half way through this conversation he felt a dull, dispiriting warning that he shouldn't be having it, especially when realising that her husband had an appointment with him in less than a week.

He met her at the NFT entrance, the restaurant, now under a new franchise and without the film posters and LCD's showing clips of Fellini or Tarkovsky films, appearing a little less welcoming to cinephiles. She briefly squeezed his elbow and, inside, listening to the intro by an elderly man who had been something like second assistant chief grip gaffer on the film, interminably intent on detail and which the boy in him didn't want to hear, wishing to believe that Leslie Caron was still 22, leant her shoulder against his. He got used to it quickly. It felt warm, flirting, pleasant.

He slyly watched her enjoying the film, noticed how small and well shaped her ears were, one side of her hair pulled back, how smooth her skin. It was an effort to turn back to the screen.

Halfway across Hungerford Bridge - a committee's seduction by Nordic technology - she put her arm inside his, affectionately, without proprietary. It was increasingly relaxing to be with her. They found a bar, and between the laughing - her humour alternating between the droll and sharp and interrupted by a lilting laugh - he saw how dark her eyes were, how full her lips; and that this was a woman who was holding so much in, so much distress, so much giving and who, by long practice, was hiding it. He wanted to release it, wished her, selfishly, to give it all to him. For a while she didn't have a husband, or he a patient.

It was getting late and as they entered an underground station one of the annoying side effects of his job, and of his own character, came back: the analytic training, his inclination to let it surface, to *know* why he was feeling something, experiencing it. This was the child wanting a mother-Madonna, a glistening, fantasised object - men wanting to have, women needing to be.

On the train back he sat a little stiffly next to her. They didn't speak much, though the silences weren't unpleasant, but he felt there shared realisation of who and what she was going back to.

They got off at the same stop, reminding him how near they lived to each other.

'That was so nice, a lovely evening.' Her voice was noticeably smoother, her accent less clipped than when he'd first heard her speak. She squeezed his hand tightly. He stepped back from her.

'I'll...see you.' he said, grinning a little too much

He watched her walk down the steps opposite the station: the poise, which hadn't registered before, her hand bent out, fingertips sporadically touching the handrail, her high heels on each step at the same angle of descent, shoulders moving smoothly down, her bag swinging like a pendulum.

He walked home thinking about her, trying to push away his obvious attraction to her. By the time he was in his study, sitting staring at the effortful, but clumsy watercolours, he saw her differently; felt that at some level she was walking around in a forties railway station, playing the faithful, but unfulfilled, unhappy wife: that slight tilt of the head, the occasional brave smile, exaggeratedly cheerful grin were all of a piece, a complete, but inevitably flawed performance. But it was doing no harm, neither to herself nor her husband - if he ever noticed it, was conscious of it. It was a coping strategy, the need probably engendered as a young girl, created later by people she knew, aspired to and, a little, by movies, theatre; reinforced certainly by the man she married. She was vulnerable, therefore attracting him more. He wanted her. Wanted to go to her.

Of course he didn't - inevitably society wins in the end; in this context, by his social role of 'the professional' and its attendant behavioural norms with their notions of diligence and responsibility. Like 'society' a role is an abstract noun, a concept that is reified, like duty or loyalty, so that it *seems* real and tangible, and he was beginning to bear its inescapable weight of guilt; for he was about to treat and attempt to help make better someone this woman loved, or at least, had.. Social roles become a large part of our identity, they dominate us to a greater or lesser degree, so that we betray ourselves in order not to betray their demands. He was denying a desire to, potentially, fall in love, *to* love, surrendering to his role's imperatives.

He rang to tell her, gently, but clearly, why he wouldn't be seeing her again. He felt her disappointment. It matched his.

He needed to escape for a while. The day after her husband's second appointment with him he would be in Spain for a few days, albeit in East End gangster territory - from laundered money Essex farmhouse to Majorcan villa - but there were cheap drinks and sun, and he could afford the former and needed the latter. He also wanted time on his own, to think things through, if he could.

And maybe he would learn a little Spanish, anyway. '*No intiendo. No intiendo…*'

THE BEAT YEARS

The same battleground. Smells of cooking fat, polish, disinfectant, oven heat and new coconut matting filled the cramped scullery, pushing their way around the living room and beyond. The sounds of slippered feet, a moist hand agitatedly wiping a brow, then the same hand using an apron as a towel, the squeal of a fork inside a saucepan, the knocking of crockery, all became a whole, unutterably familiar.

His mother, tall, angular and in her mid-forties, with a thin face, worried eyes, and clothes which in spite of their obvious age still retained a neat, well pressed appearance, scuffled from the kitchen with two laden plates and placed them hurriedly on the tablecloth, almost dropping them. She drew her breath sharply and putting a hand to her mouth urgently sucked her fingers.

Shaking her hands quickly she wiped them heavily down the front of her apron, went back to the kitchen again, reached up and pulled the window sash down. Returning, she seated herself and with quick nervous gestures patted her black, greying hair.

Sitting opposite her was his father. His eyes were small but rather bulbous, his nose creased, causing his upper lip to bare an expanse of gum and a ragged line of nicotine-stained teeth. He looked like an angry rabbit eating cabbage.

'Len, must you make so much noise?'

She tried to ask the question pleasantly, only a glimmer of disapproval showing. She waited for a response and when none came she leaned forward with her wrists resting on the edge of the table and her knife and fork raised at the same angle as her body leaning toward him.

'Must you make so much noise?'

A disinterested mumble came from under his nose at this carefully enounced repetition and the munching noise increased. She leaned back with a sigh of fatalistic acceptance and began eating.

It did not then occur to Chris that she was an unwilling captive. It was 1950. He was sixteen years old.

His father was a security guard-cum-fireman at St. James's Palace, his mother a shop worker who was rather proud of her husband's uniformed job.

He had one of the previous Sunday's papers spread out on the table to the side of him and in between scooping large mouthfuls of food into himself he inclined his head to one side and read the cartoon page slowly and carefully, his cheeks bulging and lips silently forming the captions. Occasionally he stopped chewing and frowned, his mouth hanging open. Understanding would come and with an infantile, sucking laugh he shook his head, tutting with pleasure as he looked down at his plate, flicking small particles of food from his bottom lip and, sticking a fork through a new potato and a cube of meat, would guide the heaped piece of cutlery into his mouth as he turned his attention to the paper again.

After a few minutes his head jerked up and he frowned once more, looking across the space between him and his son.

'What's the matter with *him*, then?' he asked, jerking a thumb towards him.

Observing this nightly enacted scene from an armchair, Chris continued staring at the earthenware butler sink six yards away while their meal was finished in silence. He leant forward and pushed a hand under the cushion he was sitting on and pulled out the book both Tony and he had bought copies of the day before. It was Jack Kerouac's *'On The Road.'* He slumped back and with aggressive interest began to read.

His mother cleared the table, opened the door on the side of the scullery and through the net curtains he saw her open the outside lavatory door. Out of the corner of his eye he saw his father lean across to the television. He tensed. The quick look at him before flicking the switch told Chris the mood he was already in or which he had unknowingly put him.

He gripped the underneath of his chair and half-sitting turned it and himself around to face the set no more than three feet away and stared blankly at it. The room lightened as the blue-grey glow appeared. Despite himself Chris looked across and saw a detailed close-up of a small, fat, hand with tiny tapering fingers. A smooth voice explained that it was a detail from, '...one of his greatest works, 'Madonna And Child.'' He didn't know who 'his' was, but certainly wanted to find out. The hand disappeared into the bottom of the set and the finely executed folds of a garment with minute cracks interlacing the whole area slowly followed. The curved, unblemished chin and the small thin lips of a woman slid into view and then the buttons underneath were suddenly pushed in and snapped out again and there was the noise of cheering and applause as a bulky woman announced in a proud and jovial voice that she came from Manchester, at which the tall, lean-faced man hovering restlessly above her laughed wildly and shouted,

'Has anyone got an umbrella?

The unseen audience cackled uproariously. The man held his hands in front of him and waved them up and down and when the noise trailed away pulled grinning, giggly faces at the camera, repeatedly crossing one knee over the other and asking her what prize she had in mind. It seemed she was going to win something simply by living in Manchester.

Straining to speak as gently and as pleasantly as he could, Chris asked him why he had switched channels, why he had 'turned it over.'

'Wha'? Oh, it was only talkin',' he answered quickly and grinned with delight as the fat woman complained jokingly that if she didn't win her husband would divorce her.

Chris looked at him; his thin, uncombed mousy hair hanging loosely from a barely discernible parting, the weak, stubbly chin, the watery eyes and that complacent grin. He turned back to his book and the meaningless words. He stared at 'Moriarty' and kept repeating it quietly, over and over - like 'ever' which he said endlessly as he tried to sleep at night and to grasp the concept with a final 'ever' - the same word, until it was just an absurd sound, and felt the loneliness, the anger again.

Turning his face to him, voice quivering, he stammered, 'Do you know, you put that thing on regardless of...of what's on, what time it's on, you watch...inane, trivial...anything that makes you think, challenges you...you...'

Chris was clenching his fists on his knees.

'Look.' his father bellowed, standing up, hands tightened on either side of his thighs, 'What about you and your bloody books? Read, read, bloody *read!*'

He grabbed the paperback from Chris's hands and threw it at the wall behind him. It seemed to float before it hit and in a moment of schizoid irrelevance Chris wondered what pages it would lay open at as it landed

He saw his surroundings with frightening clarity; his mother, returned from the lavatory, bending over the sink, her blotchy arms, the speckled grey gas cooker, the tiny living room, the grey fireplace with its stepped sides, the worn floral mat raggedly spread thin on the linoleum, the dingy passage seen through the distorting frosted glass panels in the door. And like a final perception, the claustrophobic inevitability of it all. It wasn't the only time it had happened. He was eleven when he first did it, but now the shock wasn't quite as great.

At least he could tell Tony about it.

He'd known Tony since they'd started at the local Tech. in the East End four years before where they'd learnt the rudiments of the building trades and had both opted for painting and decorating. ('Get a trade in yer 'ands, son' was the stereotypical advice from his father). They'd seen each other virtually every day since. He had come across to Chris, all blonde hair and blue eyes, while the latter was nervously waiting outside the main entrance on the first day with scores of other boys. He told Chris a joke.

'This bloke goes to the Council for a job. The interviewer asks him if he's done military service. 'Yes.' he says. The man says, 'That gets you five points. Do you have any disabilities?' 'Yeh, I had my genitals blown off by a mine.' 'That gets you another five pints, enough to get you the job. The hours are eight till five Mondays to Fridays. Right, we'll see you at ten on Monday then.' 'But, you said you start at eight. Why d'you wanna see me at ten?' 'Well,' the man says, 'we usually stand about scratching our bollocks for a couple of hours and that's no good to you, is it.' Chris liked him immediately

Tony took to him, he once said, because although he played football he looked as if he wrote poetry as well.

Tony had a younger sister with dark hair and eyes who looked rather Latin and who he occasionally and affectionately called 'kid', much to her fifteen year old annoyance.

It was she who opened the door to Chris. Tony was behind her in the passage, but she obviously hadn't seen him. Then she turned, jumped up and put her arms around him, her legs for a second kicking back behind his waist and nearly pulling him over.

'Tone-eee', you're back, you're already home.' she shrilled as if he'd been away for a month instead of returning from a building site, then playfully biting his ear, said a quick hello to Chris and ran, giggling, through to the kitchen before coming back again.

'Just a minute, hold on.' said Tony, 'Is that lipstick you're wearing?'

'Yes, it *is* lipstick, I'm wearing it because I *want* to, I'm going out in it and I intend to *continue* to wear it.' She puckered her face.

'Quite satisfied?' She looked very pretty.

'Thank you,' she said sarcastically, taking silence as assent. The front door opened and shut quickly, the sound of her hurrying heels could just about be heard.

'She's gorgeous,' said Tony warmly, taking a tobacco tin from his pocket and rolling a cigarette. He didn't roll it very successfully. He never did.

Chris liked the feel of this house, solid, but light, and envied him his relationships, especially with his mother, who he could hear moving around upstairs. His father had left soon after his sister had been born. He never spoke about it.

It was raining. The colours of streets and buildings were washed away and a steady drizzle dropped flimsy layers of cool wind and a fine blurred greyness around people hurrying along. They walked quickly, sometimes with one leg in the gutter, playing a game with themselves, trying to maintain a steady speed without leaving the pavement completely and having to admit failure as they gave wide berths to groups of teenage girls leaving the local cosmetic factory, mincing along in their tight skirts, their umbrellas held in a raggedly line above their bouncing, giggling heads.

Tony liked the rain, it sent peace down to him, he said, and he could wander about and look at people in their self-sufficient little worlds and stand on corners and gaze at the cars as they waited for the spots of colour to give them the right of way. He thought that in the rain things in cities became themselves and were nearer to their own particular truth. They were alone then, virtually ignored by people whose dominant perceptions of them were as shelters of some kind, not as aesthetic objects, part of our designed material world, rising, sometimes awkwardly but firmly in the rain.

They marched down the street, the rain heavier, blowing into their faces, Tony's jacket flapping behind him, the front of his shirt turning into a clinging brown. Chris didn't know where they were going, it somehow didn't matter with Tony, but he guessed it was Lou's. Tony stopped and took his jacket off, putting it over his head and clenching the bottom of the lapels around his neck, looking suddenly feminine, like a factory worker with a thick headscarf tied under her chin.

There was a bus shelter further down the road, the rain splattering from its roof in the red neon glow from the fascia of a late-opening pie and eel shop. Chris ran towards it. Leaning over a tubular bar, getting his breath back, he saw Tony standing in the middle of the road, cars splashing past him, putting a foot tentatively forward each time tail lights went by. It was fascinating to watch. It was like a slow motion film sequence of a dancer stranded from the chorus and uncertain of her routine. But whatever he did, and he did sometimes look a little unsure, unknowing, it was, somehow, impressive.

Seeming to guess the picture in Chris's mind Tony flung his arms rhythmically in the air and as a gap in the line of cars appeared he made swimming motions, pawing his arms through the wet air to the shelter. He leant against the inside, took deep breaths, patting his chest. Then he sniffed.

'Is that vinegar?'

He looked across to the pie and eel shop and screwed up his face in pain, his full, blue eyes blinking. Some people have an allergy to pollen, some to cats, Tony's was vinegar. He suddenly looked pathetic, didn't appreciate Chris's laughter.

'Do you know what that brown stuff is?' He pointed to the shop. 'It's evil, intellect shattering, it's… I can't breath, can't think. I'd like to write an advert.' He moved his hand across in front of him, thumb and forefinger curled, shaping the words, ''Do you want to be a moron? Have plans to be a cretin? Then buy our vinegar!' Let's go to Lou's.'

'Intellect' was a word Tony used and alluded to a lot. They would debate, argue, discuss, were opinionated and often uninformed. Chris would cross the park to Tony's house, his mother usually letting him in, and he would be pacing around the living room agitatedly.

'Don't you see? its a con,' he would say, 'we're tied to our behaviour by a piece of metaphysical string, always being pulled back to actions, intentions, attitudes.'

'Are we talking 'conscience' here?' Chris would ask.

He'd spin round. 'Yes, yes, but where does that come from? Is it innate? Internalised from the world around us? And it's all about control, isn't it.' he'd say excitedly. 'You could perm all of our values and behaviour with programmed and learnt behaviour - there's so many options - but whatever's doing the asking, 'conscience' as you call it, it's socially controlling us and...'

And so he'd go on and Chris would go on; at his house, at Chris's house - their respective mothers hesitantly bringing them cups of tea in the front rooms - walking around the local streets, the parks, sitting in cafes, especially these, talking, babbling, gesticulating into the night, feeling that there should be people flocking around them with gold pens glinting in the street lights, writing down everything they were saying.

Of course, nothing they were saying was new. There were bits of Marx, Freud, existentialism, psychology, sociology, philosophy, and a lot of what they said was probably sheer nonsense. They weren't aware.

Lou was leaning across his counter, elbows on a newspaper spread between milk and sugar-filled cups and, for once, was not telling anyone who would listen that he could have been a 'coifurer' because in Italy his father had been a hairdresser and he was to follow in his footsteps, never explaining why he hadn't. The café's steamy, sour warmth, tobacco smoke, and damp clothes hanging from the brass hooks of the clothes stand was a familiar, welcoming cavern.

They hung up their soaking jackets, Tony wiped his face vigorously with a handkerchief, his shirt dark and saturated. He sucked his tea noisily and put it down again on the chipped marble topped table.

'I want to get away.' he said, looking down.

He glanced up at Chris, waiting for it to sink in. Chris couldn't quite understand what he meant.

'Get away? Where?' Get away and do what?'

He tutted impatiently. 'Just get away, somewhere, anywhere.'

'What about your job? Your apprenticeship? You can't just pack it in.'

''course I can, I can always go back there if I want, and there's less reasons stopping you than there are me. You're not exactly in a state of bliss at home, are you.'

Chris incongruously giggled, stopping himself instantly, unsure of what was underneath it, what sounds and turmoil it would turn into.

Tony stretched back in his chair, smugly, as if he'd proved a point. He was so sure of himself. Chris felt annoyed. He didn't know why.

Tony leant forward eagerly.

'Don't you see, it's simple, really it is.'

'I know it seems like it, but…'

He didn't know what he wanted to say. Tony rubbed his hands over his face, like a child might; pushing its nose up and pulling its eyes down to look like an ogre.

'Well, are you coming with me?'

Chris felt more annoyed. He criss-crossed a pool of spilt tea with a finger and flicked little splashes of it away from him.

'I'm still going.' Tony said quietly.

He could see Lou amongst his crockery reading his paper and wondered how he could stick inside this place all day with its stained ceiling and walls and the, 'two airships on a cloud, mate.' and 'babies on a raft, Lou.' for sausages and mash and beans on toast, and while mechanistically producing them, thinking, perhaps, of pleasant banter as he trimmed people's hair back home in the sun.

'I'm going tomorrow.'

'Tomorrow?' Chris asked incredulously.

Tony leant closer to him, 'I'm going to get the tube, and the nearest main line station it takes me to, I'm…' he shrugged.

'There are only two lines you can get from our station.'

'Don't tell me; don't tell me, I'm just going to go. Anywhere. I don't want to plan anything, just go. I'm taking fifty quid with me, that'll do, should be enough. I'll take my chances with digs and things.'

'That sounds all right sitting here, but...'

He held his hands up in front of him, 'I'll be okay.'

Chris stared down at the table, the spilt tea about to drip between his knees.

'You're not sure, are you,' he asked.

'I can't.' Chris almost shouted.' I just can't.'

Tony said nothing. He sipped his tea, eyes looking at Chris over the cup.

'I'll send some money home to help them out, of course.'

'I don't suppose I'll be coming, Tony.'

He slowly got up. 'Okay.' he said softly.

'Ta-ta boys,' said Lou as they went out, not looking up, still smiling.

Chris sat in the bus absently counting the fag ends and matches in the channels of the wooden floor, with Tony bending his head back and looking into the night through a condensation-free patch on the window that he'd wiped with the side of his fist.

'What's your mum going to say?'

Tony looked blankly in front of him and shrugged, as if he hadn't grasped the question.

'I don't know where I'm going to go. I'm fed up with streets, though,' He waved his arms expansively. 'Still, if I land up in streets, well...' He shrugged again.

'I want to do things I'll remember. Do you understand?'

There was no answer. Neither of them said anything until they got off the bus and walked the short distance to Tony's home. He asked Chris in, he declined.

'Come with me.'

'Drop me a line,' Chris said, forcing a grin and playfully punching his arm. He walked away, not looking back As he turned the corner he kicked a stone viciously along the road, it ricocheted and clinked into the base of a lamppost. Behind it, a dog, resenting the interruption to its ablutions, barked at the dingy world around it and trotted away.

Chris tried to finish the last few pages of Kerouac's book that night lying in bed, and realised he hadn't talked about it with Tony. There hadn't been time. He'd imagined them sitting in Lou's bursting with it; its energy, rawness, poetry, the adventure, the colours, all of it, talking about it until Lou started putting the chairs on the tables and still continuing outside long after hearing him bolt his door.

He didn't sleep, he wondered where Tony was going; would he actually *go*? He imagined him wandering around somewhere on his own, stopping someone and saying,

'Tell me about things.'

This could have meant anything, but they were really feelings; feelings from bits of wood, a doorknocker, clouds, from an old woman, the silhouette of a child playing around a lamppost, an articulated lorry, the smell of paint, of hotdogs at half-time at Upton Park. Tony had an almost psychotic obsession at times to become other people, not just those that were obviously different, anyone; it was a rampant empathy. He wanted, when the mood took him, to become even programmed creatures. Chris had seen him sit on his haunches for half an hour staring at his sister's kitten, hardly moving, saying nothing, like a method actor performing in abstract for his introvert audience of one. He would talk to, or merely observe, a stranger and barely out of earshot, say,

'I know that person, I *know* him.'

And his intellectualising. They would, perhaps, be walking silently in a park, and he would jump on a bench, an imaginary lectern in front of him, frown down at someone in an imaginary front row and say gravely,

'There must be no 'your' truth, but a whole truth, there can be only one; an unfeeling intellect devoid of everything *except* that intellect. Even the most unemotional intelligence distorts the object of knowledge. We need an...untouched 'isness' - I like that, sounds like a virgin Greek goddess - an intellectual god, some sort of mythological machine, and if the work gets too much for it - and don't forget, there is one whole complex truth in every square millimetre of everything - it should have a whole group of these machine-like gods to help it, an authoritative intellectual body, an AIB, without emotions...human character. Nothing must distort clarity.'

He'd scythe his hand as if he were decapitating his audience, which would consist of Chris and possibly a pigeon strutting disinterestedly in front of him. He'd look down at Chris, shrug his shoulders dejectedly and ask him what truth was, as if his friend had known the answer all the time and had purposely withheld it from him to make him miserable.

Chris couldn't picture him away from England, he couldn't see him in scenes of rural wilderness, endless deserts, the hot, orange-groved landscapes of California, wearing a T-shirt and not his tie - the mark of the skilled artisan however paint spotted it might be - putting beer before food, he was too young to legally drink alcohol anyway, and instead of coffee and benzedrine it would be weak tea and Tizer, and it wouldn't be jazz, sex and aimless driving sitting next to Sal Paradise gazing out of a car window at the continuous road - perhaps it was *him* who wanted to be sitting there - nor LSD, mescalin and free love, rather Wills Woodbines, and sketching from the black and white photos of happy, healthy looking women with their brushed out private parts from Health and Efficiency magazines, rubbing a pencil line on cartridge paper with his finger to emphasise the curve of a breast till the paper wore through.

There would be no New York jazz joint or Mexican whore house, his would be no tale of chill dawns and madness, He couldn't see him being a 'western kinsman of the sun' couldn't imagine him seeing San Francisco, 'stretched out ahead the fabulous white city on her eleven mystic hills.' Perhaps didn't *want* to.

Chris cried that night

When his father died some years later he didn't cry, though he tried to, but was reminded of both him and Tony when, clearing out his life shortly afterwards before moving from the East End, he found Kerouac's story, dog-eared and torn, at the back of a bookshelf. A week later, in the early morning mist by his father's grave, he laid it carefully on the wet grass like a book of remembrance.

Twelve years after this he heard that Tony had been living in Liverpool and was now back in London. He'd never communicated with him. He wondered if a city in the north west of England had been his 'search for the edge.' He was given his address, it wasn't far from where Chris was living.

He never went to see him - sixteen years was a long time, at least it felt like it then. What had happened to him? How long had he stayed in Liverpool? Had a nasal twang replaced his posh cockney? Had he married? Obvious questions he let lie unanswered. He did, though, see him once more.

A few months ago Chris was coming out of a shop in Carnaby Street - he was working nearby, still decorating - when a tall, very slim, rather exotic looking woman brushed by him, giving him a quick smile, drawling, in what sounded like an American accent, 'Hey, excuse me,' and ran across the road to a smartly dressed man half turning away from her as she put her arm in his. Twenty yards further on he opened the nearside door of a blue sports car and she slipped casually in. It moved away, the man driving. It was Tony.

ACHOLI

Walking through the crowded concourse of Liverpool Street Station James Kent suddenly found himself sprawled on the ground. Covering his outstretched arm was a grey jacket, next to it a small pink and black travel bag with wheels and a five foot long extended handle, at the end of which a short, podgy woman was frowning down at him.

He placed the jacket on top of the bag, picked up his sunglasses and stood. The woman mumbled a reluctant 'sorry' and continued walking. A few seconds later at the top of an escalator he told her politely that her bag could have been carried.

'Why should I?'

'Because people can fall over it at.'

'It was your fault.'

'Then why apologise?'

She lifted her head in the air and strode away off the bottom step on her pneumatic legs. The first thing he noticed as he got in the tube train was the smell of fried chicken and a greasy food wrapper being thrown on the floor. James picked it up and dropped it gently into an open bag on the diner's lap.

'I believe this is yours.' The woman looked confused.

Strolling along Union Street twenty minutes afterwards, a motor bike swung off the car-jammed road and came slowly along the pavement towards him. James stopped, stood legs apart and spread his arms. The rider came close up to him and then swerved away with a vehement, 'Fuck off'.

He wasn't really sure why he felt angry. He went to the Island Café, had tea and lemon cake and as his mood was sweetened away thought of his psychiatric patients and the reasons for what he'd been feeling. Some were living within inert, leaded minds, a few hardly able to speak to him, and others so agitated they never sat down during any of their fifty minute sessions. He felt depressed that, other than one whose schizophrenic sparks were gradually dimming as a real self began to emerge, they were not, it appeared, getting any better. He thought he'd got used to them taking such a long time to show improvement. He obviously hadn't; their impoverishment fed upon itself; a morbid, repetitive arc of cause and effect.

He felt sour again, and needed to banish it He went to Putney for a walk past his favourite Georgian Thameside cottages, where he was reminded of his publisher who, tongue in cheek, had suggested 'Through a Georgian Window' as a working title of James' recent poetry collection.

When he got home there was a voice message from a 'Lucy' waiting for him. He didn't know a Lucy. After listening for a few seconds he remembered her; Lucy Kenyo. She was one of the students he'd taught twelve or so years before when a social worker friend had asked him to take some lectures and seminars for a term at his university annexe. He rang her back.

After a few mundane pleasantries she asked him whether he knew where she could get hold of her Psychosocial Studies Diploma. Telling her he knew little of the Faculty's administration he suggested she contact the college. She told him she'd recently been back to Uganda because she was converting a building in Kampala into a guest house and holiday home.

She continued with, 'I was woken one night by what I thought were the rats. I got up to chase them away and there was a man in the doorway. He hit me with an axe on my shoulders and arms and then he suddenly stopped and ran away. I think he wanted to steal my things. I think he thought I was rich. There is so much poverty there.'

Her voice, more modulated than the African accent he remembered, was rather quiet, precise. He suggested that if she wanted to talk more perhaps it would be better for them to meet. He did so without wondering why he had.

They met at a café next day near to where she lived in Hainault. He didn't recognise her from the back. She was the only black female - the only customer. He sat down opposite her.

'Your hair's longer, 'he said.

'Yes, I let it grow.' What he did recognize was the slow, gentle smile.

'I wondered if you would look different, but you don't. There's a man living in my street who always reminds me of someone, and, of course, it's you. He's Jewish.'

It had happened before. Recently he'd been walking through Broadway Market when a man selling curtain material from a stall asked him what shul he belonged to. James told him he wasn't Jewish. 'Of course you are, what shul?' But then, he'd been mistaken for Italian, Spanish and even Mexican.

She placed her elbows neatly on the table and began.

'I will tell you what happened after this man attacked me. I went to a clinic and they helped me. The next day I went to my mother's house and she told me that I couldn't stay there, and my brother also said that I was not wanted there. I went to my older brother's house and he came back with me and started fighting with his brother. My mother was laying there and had blood on her head so I got between them and stopped them. I went back with my brother and when he left for work next day two policemen came and told me I must come with them. They drove me through the town. When I asked where they were taking me they wouldn't tell me. They took me to a place where other women were. It had faeces on the floor. I knew it was the mental hospital. Some of the women told me that their families had put them there. I was lucky because some people who I had grown up with had spotted me in a supermarket some days before and wanted to find me. They traced me. So I then went back to the guest house, and came back here again.'

She related this in a flat, almost matter-of-fact manner as if it was about quite ordinary, everyday happenings Picking up her cup she said she was expecting a call from an agency about a job.

'I. need to go. Ring me.' She carried her cup to the counter and left.

He sat there and tried to remember her from years ago. All he could picture was her smile, her quiet way of expressing herself and the way she'd moved. As she'd walked out the café he'd noticed again the easy, casual manner in which she held herself. He rang her the next day and they met the one after.

It was her local pub, one that looked a certain candidate to be on the list of rapidly disappearing suburban drinking houses. Other than bar staff they were the only ones there; he wondered whether they were doomed to meet in places where there were no customers nor, perhaps, ever had been - if there *was* a next time

She seemed a little more animated. He thought she looked rather like an American Indian with her elliptical eyes, and her black hair curling inwards at the nape of her neck Childhood words and images popped in his mind: Hiawatha, Minnie Ha Ha, and a Hanna and Barbera animated cartoon of Big Chief Rain on Face with a grey rain cloud constantly floating above his head. She asked him what he was smiling about. He told her. She laughed; it was a deep, almost husky sound.

He realised she attracted him. He then wondered what the connection was between character and face shape; a receding chin suggesting 'weakness,' a jutting one, 'strength.' How could there possibly be a connection between the shapes of bone growth and ... he was aware that this anaemic splodge of irrelevance was a way of blanketing what he'd begun to feel.

'Are you with me? You seem far away.'

'Of course. Why did your mother and brother say - '

'Oh, money reasons I suppose,' she said, dismissively flicking her long fingers.

'Look, just before I left to come here I had another call; I need to alter my CV. You know how it is. Afraid I'll have to go again. Sorry. Ring me.'

A measured walk towards the exit on her long, almost thin legs, a quick look back at him and the door swung shut behind her. She'd hardly touched her coffee. He stayed, thinking of the fading bruise on her upper arm, a memento, he assumed of the attack. He rang her that evening and suggested a pub in Epping Forest during the coming weekend.

At her request he went to her flat. She came to the door in a dressing gown holding her wet hair high above her head.

'Sorry,' she smiled, 'I won't be long, make yourself at home.'

She gestured towards the front room. He sat on a sofa looking at a painting of palm trees ringing a white beach, a large African rug and two wire Giacometti-like African sculptures, and on a teak coffee table amongst some papers he recognised a research project he'd helped her with towards the end of her course:. 'That Africans in the UK feel that sexual abuse within the family in their home country may be becoming the norm.' It could have been better phrased he thought, and it wasn't the only one concerning that subject he'd assisted the other African women with. Perhaps she'd got it out to mention on her CV

He didn't hear her enter the room. She wore a white dress and red, high heeled shoes. He was about to point out that they were only going to a pub, there was no need to wear... when he thought of his late mother dressing up for one of her rare journeys outside the house: the powder puff, lipstick, the brief tissue between her lips and the quick pulling down of her dress in front of the wardrobe mirror. The image held a comforting pleasure. He asked her if the painting was of somewhere in Uganda.

'No, Uganda's a land-locked country.' She grinned

They were quiet on the walk to the station and on the short train journey, but easily so. On the way to their meal he occasionally glanced at her, prominent cheek bones and the long, slender neck; reminding him of old sepia photos of tribal women with metal rings round their necks to elongate them.

'We're here now. This is it.'

It looked a typical London gastro-pub: cleaned-up Victorian bricks, the fascia and windows painted dark grey, potted plants by the entrance and inside, a deep red dining area. They sat and ordered. Her dress was a shining contrast to her dark, almost glistening skin.

He heard himself say, 'The head of UKIP said recently that he'd spent twenty years building the 'brand.' How's that for an example of the dominion of corporate-speak, of politics being just another part of globalised capitalism?' Again, the inappropriate quasi-intellectualising to steer himself away from her.

'Why are you looking at me like that?'

'Like what?'

'Well, as if - '

'I probably looked at you like that when you taught us. We used to talk about you, you were mesmerising. I don't know what it was; your body language, voice, the little gestures you made with your hands... something. You disturbed me.'

'Did you know that 'mesmerise' comes from Franz Mesmer, the first man to practice hypno... You don't want to know, do you.'

'Not really. *Do* you remember me?

'Yes, you were the quiet one.'

She looked at him steadily then said, 'I will tell you about my father.'

He recalled now that towards the end of his lecturing stint she'd told him that her father had been a Vice President of American Tobacco, that she used to be taken to school in a limousine and that she'd worked for a while as a presenter on Ugandan TV.

'I was raised on a 3,000 acre estate north of Kampala near the Sudanese border where, as well as tobacco, my father grew maize, tomatoes and red peppers which he would send to the local market or export to Kenya. He also had cows and a business which imported tyres. My mother ran an agency that sold the tobacco to other agents. He was assassinated.' There was no change in her tone.

'He had just picked up a new Land Rover when he was stopped by three men. They wore no uniforms, but had pistols. They were from the Secret Service. He was a big man so there was a struggle to get him out of his car into theirs. My mother was with him. She was beaten around the head with a pistol. The night before, his brother, who ran Central African Airlines and was a minister in Amin's government and a personal adviser to him, came to the house and talked with my father all night. I heard them. They kept waking me. He left the country for Kenya next day. The rumour was that Amin was going crazy and was charging around with a hand grenade. He'd gone to my uncle's house who'd called some men to help get the grenade away. Another rumour was that Amin went to the barracks where my father had been taken and interviewed him, and when he found out who his brother was, shot him himself.'

James was about to use the line beloved of screenwriters, 'Why are you telling me all this?' but quelled the impulse. He was strangely glad she was, but she was relating it with a resigned sense of inevitability, as if this was just what happened in Uganda, in perhaps, all of Africa. Their meals came. They ate mostly in silence.

'There are other things to tell you, but not at the moment.' she said as they finished their dessert. Wiping her lips with a napkin she asked him what he knew of Africa.

'Perhaps the first thing that comes to mind is infibulation. Does a woman really have to lie back and think of the washing up?'

She smiled. 'It's not just about genital mutilation. The Loh tribe, who have a clan in Kampala, practice the opposite; they try to enhance a woman's pleasure. They start when a girl is twelve. They stretch her over a stool and spread the petals of her vagina between finger and thumb.' She rolled hers together in demonstration. 'And they also can make it long; it looks like a cow's teats. Mine's not long,' she said as a smiling afterthought. 'The muscles are somehow strengthened so a man cannot penetrate if he tries to rape her.'

She rose from her seat. 'I am tired, I need to go.'

'Again?'

'Yes. But there's an Alumni event at the college on Friday. I haven't really kept in touch with the others, but it would be nice to go. They'll remember you. Will you come with me?'

James nodded. He paid and they went out into the evening and back to her station. At the entrance she told him there was no need to walk back with her. She squeezed his hand and had gone. That evening he received an email from her.

'Thanks for seeing me today, it means a great deal to me. Thanks.'

The next day, a clientless one, he went to Turnham Green and walked around the Edwardian estate near the station. He thought of his recently deceased brother naming period houses, 'Georgie,' 'Vicky,' 'Eddie,' and his occasional touching of James' hand to draw attention to something; an architectural detail perhaps; an ogee arch, a pilaster, a Roman capital. He missed that touch. He missed him.

When he got home there was a voice message for him. Lucy was saying in her level, rather self-absorbed manner, 'I wanted to tell you. I have been left the 3,000 acres and I was thinking of maybe starting a school there because nothing's growing there now. I think that would be good. Maybe you could come with me and reconnoitre. I think that's the word. You could tell me what you think. It would be fun. Thanks. I will see you tomorrow. Goodnight.'

He listened to it twice more. Laying on the couch, one that had felt the weight of many clients, he thought of the continent she had come from. He saw Africa, unknowingly, through the words of Ali Mazuri. 'You are not a country, Africa. You are a concept... a glimpse of the infinite.'

His first image of Africa wasn't really of female circumcision, an act born of the insecurity of the African male and the fear of his woman enjoying sexual pleasure with other men - paralleled in the imposition of burkas and hijabs in Islamic countries - but almost mystical names that came crowding into him: Mogadishu, Burkina Faso, Djibouti, Cape Verde, Mauritania, though he knew little about them nor where they actually were. And the events of unquestioned colonial grandeur, glory and adventure: the Boer War, Rourke's Drift, the discovery of Victoria Falls - which he'd once mentioned in class and had been told by a Zimbabwean that Africans had been there for centuries before it was 'discovered' by a white man - a salutary reminder that definitions and many social constructs are created by power - Timbuktu, Togo, gold mines, large rings through women's lips.

Should he, could he, actually go? A neighbour could look into his house occasionally, his clients could be treated by a colleague who shared James psychiatric perspectives and… He picked up the phone and rang her. There was no answer.

They met in a café-bar next to the main university building. .She walked in wearing a long, tight, pale blue and turquoise dress. He got their drinks. Their were covert glances towards her from several men and, to give himself a little time to adjust to what he was feeling, he raced into another stream of deflective disinterest.

'Did you know that Nigerians are genetically nearer to Norwegians than they are to Kenyans? People outside of Africa think that the whole place is a kind of state inhabited by a homogenous whole; which is understandable at a superficial level because of skin colour and.. '

He stopped. She was looking at him with a smile like an African Mona Lisa.

'I remember you saying in class that we were programmed to react to people and things that are obviously different from ourselves. You mentioned responses like fear, hostility, suspicion. But do you think opposites might attract?'

This time there was a slightly teasing shape to her lips. He looked at her dress, the top low enough to show the hint of small breasts which, for James, had a subtle sexuality that was infinitely preferable to those that made their owners look like galleons in full sail.

'Perhaps we should dance,' she said, still smiling. She hadn't mentioned the request she'd made in her phone call. They went into the hall. There were sixty or so people either standing or sitting around the sides and a six-piece band that was coming to the end of warming up. She looked around her, shook her head slightly. There was no one there yet that she knew. She looked levelly at him for a while and pointed to a door at the far end of the hall.

'Come with me.' She grasped his hand .to lead him across the floor. The door opened into a changing room. She pointed to a bench. She seemed different, almost authoritative. Sitting next to him, but rarely looking at him, she began.

'Five years ago I brought a man back from Uganda who I lived with for two years. At least he came through the door and not the window,' she said with a smile. 'My parents knew his. We are bound by family, that's what it's like in Africa; family, family. But they are useful sometimes; aunties teach you how to roll around in bed with a man.' She smiled again 'He left, but we kept - keep - in touch by phone. He is now in England again. He wants to come back to me, to live with me. My mother keeps calling, telling me to have him back.' She turned her head towards him. 'Please come with me to Uganda. We can... I'll show you my old school, the guest house and the house I grew up in, you could meet my brothers. Just see the land, get the feel of it. It would be fun.' She stopped. James could see an excited glint in her eyes.

'You know, you said on your last day of lecturing us that you weren't really interested in teaching, but you enjoyed it with us. You're good at it. Wouldn't you like to teach children? They wouldn't get your jokes, like we did, but you'd be... I don't even know if you're still a psychologist. I assume you are. Isn't there anyone who could look after your patients? '

There was a lull in the music and then a female voice not far from the door was saying, 'Lucy. Where's Lucy? Someone said she was here.'

She turned her head. 'I know that voice.'

She went to the door, opened it, looked quickly around. A large African woman with a huge, astonished grin suddenly embraced her. Lucy turned to James.

66

'I won't be long. I'll come back. Wait for me.'

She pushed the door shut with her foot as if to keep him there till she chose to release him. He sat there feeling used; a man she'd known for one academic term being utilised to escape from another she'd lived with for two years and had known for at least five. Then a sudden, hard conviction: that she knew if this man came back to her she would forgive him - as, James suspected, she already had at a level of consciousness she was hardly aware of.

Turning his head he could smell her faint, sweet, earthy odour; a strange scent, but having a kind of primitive familiarity. If he went to Uganda with her he would be the 'evidence' for her family to believe she'd found someone else, and ease the pressure from them to return to her lover. He wanted to be with this woman, but not if she was split between the desire to escape from something and the need, however unconscious, to run towards it.

He felt restless, stood up, paced around. There were two football shirts hanging on wall hooks, a pair of muddy boots under a bench - another mnemonic of dubbing, cinder pitches, of tabernacles, Brasso, the flicks. But this was now, and he wasn't about to run on to the field behind the college, cut inside a defender, nutmeg another and then charged down, the ball gone.

How apt it was, he thought, for her to lead him to a changing room: she having to change her life; to stay or to go, he to push himself away from his picket-fenced little house and into what could be an adventure, perhaps helping to create something; both tangible and, in the context of affecting future lives, intangible.

He opened the door. Music, voices, laughter sliced into him. He could see her at the far side of the hall laughing with a woman of similar age, someone she was obviously pleased to see. A man tapped her on the shoulder, she turned and, wide-eyed, hugged him. As he held her he guided her into the dancers and started dancing with her She seemed to be taller than any woman in the hall. She moved away from him and started swaying, slowly, relaxed, occasionally looking at the man, grinning, widening her eyes; almost fluttering her lashess, bending her body subtly, sensuously.

He went back inside, feeling ridiculously alone. He could smell grass, see himself kicking a ball, hear his father shouting at him to, 'Get rid of it. For Chris'sake cross it!' He went out again, started walking around the edges of the hall in her direction. She saw him, said something to her dancing partner and moved towards him, weaving through the dancing couples. He stopped by the double entrance doors. She stood in front of him. Angrily baring her teeth, she said,

'Were you going to leave, then? Just walk away?'

'No. I... '

She pushed through the doors. He followed her outside. She walked quickly into the coiffured garden, stood by a trimmed evergreen bush

'I will tell you something. When we all left your class we went to that club place, it was our last day there. Do you remember?

'I remember you giving me a video of Acholi tribal dances in - '

'And you and I were sitting on our own and you weren't really listening to me, you were looking at one of the student's legs. If you had *really* been with me I would have asked you home with me. I would have pounced on you. I would have given you my body.'

Her eyes were narrowed. She flicked her long fingers dismissively away from her again.

He tried to joke. 'So I blew it then?'

He did remember; she'd asked him to stay, but even then he continued thinking, as he had done for most of that day, of a potentially suicidal patient he was particularly concerned about; and he probably did, absently minded, watch a woman's legs, walking, sitting, whatever.

'Were you going to leave because I was dancing with someone? Couldn't you have waited a few minutes for me, or is it that you don't want to come to Uganda with me. Are you frightened?'

James took a deep breath, stretched a little so he was taller than she.

'This man; are you sure you're not using me to - '

'Using you? Using you?' She was shouting. 'What for? I asked you, suggested, you come back with me to look, and what *about* him? I lived with him, and even when he left I was faithful for three years.'

She made an effort to calm herself. 'I've had men friends since, but... '

That flippant shake of her hand again.

'*Is* he coming back to you?'

She glared at him, bent forwards, beat her fists on her thighs.

'I... Oh, why do you ask?'

She looked anguished, looked away from him, She was motionless for a while then turned to face him. She seemed lost, smaller, as if she'd shrivelled inside her dress.

'I only asked you to... '

There were tears in her eyes. He could read a silent, 'I don't know,' see the tears now streaming down her face, running into the down of her lip. Suddenly spinning around, she ran falteringly back to the hall. He could see a couple sitting by the door look up at her as she moved stutteringly across the floor

He wasn't sure what to do, wasn't even sure of what he felt. A little heeded grown up voice told him to go to her, offer comfort, treat her as he would a client, give her confidence in him as someone worth giving trust to.

He looked at the doors, could faintly hear the music. It seemed to have happened so quickly: from a voice message on his landline ten days before to an emotional confusion, a sense of some sort of loss - though he had never owned her, and had done so little with her except sit in a café, a pub, a changing room.

Turning his back on the building he walked to the station. He went home, but couldn't lie on his couch this time, he was too agitated, restless. He made himself a drink, sat momentarily on a chair and looked at a patch of soft evening sunlight falling on the front room wall; the shadow of the window's centre bar and his hanging spider plant looking like a giant splash on a thick, dark horizon. He tried to imagine African light. Saw it blazing across vast spaces of cracked, red earth, across a splintered, inimical terrain.

He went out again, strode quickly to his station, wondering about her, trying to grasp her personality. To him, now, it seemed elusive, contradictory, like a slowly moving quicksilver. There was a depth to her, she was shallow, attractive, ordinary, self sufficient, dependent... and were the phone calls from an agency, or her ex-lover? His brother, again, came into his head and he wondered what use to human evolution was the knowledge that we are going to die.

And the quick realisation that the question itself was a deflection from an attempt at self-analysis.

He could feel himself getting angrier. He crossed a road hardly aware he was doing so. A car stopped a few feet short of him with a shrill of brakes. He was tempted to put a finger up to the driver, but couldn't bring himself to - his expressions of anger were learnt in the days of the V sign, his early conditioning loyal to that.

What he really wanted was to prowl pavements looking for cyclists with long-handled wheelie bags trailing behind them, discarding chicken bones and greasy food wrappers so he that could stand in their way like a colossus and destroy them as they came within firing range.

GEORGE

There is, of course, no beginning; attempts to find one being merely arbitrary. The aetiology would involve too many variables; the infinite regresses of their permutations neither known nor knowable.

Just after an amicable divorce and several years after finishing a degree in sociology, Mark Talbot began lecturing at various colleges in and around East London.

Immediately after graduating he'd been invited to take seminars in an annexe of a local poly-soon-to-be-university. This had been his old junior school. Sitting in the main hall and looking up at the oriole window of the headmaster's office was a disquieting experience, as had been the voices of schoolboy friends and foes he thought he could hear swirling around the staircases when, as an ineffectual monitor and telling the noise makers to be quiet, he'd be answered with, 'You ain't nuffin' Talbot.' ''ere, 'e's tryin' to tell us wot to do.' 'Teacher's pet, an' 'e,' and looking out of a first floor window thinking he could see the girls doing handstands against the carpentry shop wall, skirts falling over their faces and knowingly showing their knickers.

One of the colleges was in Havering, Essex, where he had a one year full time contract which included a Friday evening class for mature students. Most of the people sitting in the classroom - he saw it proprietarily as his - were indigenous working class pupils and recently arrived Africans, all wanting to get to Higher Education.

Yolande, as usual, came in late, swinging her hips in a yellow and green Cameroonian football shirt - this being a world cup year - and yet again, Prudence, one of the older women, was frowning at him while his eyes unavoidably followed her sister African to her seat. Matronly Prudence had transferred from a day class because, as she'd whispered tearfully to him in an empty staffroom, one of the female students had called her, unjustifiably, a 'prostitute'; an unintentional irony and the ultimate African slur.

At the end of the first month he was finishing theory with a quick round up of post modern meta-narrative - implying, self stultifyingly, that there is no such thing as a meta-narrative - when he noticed Elaine raising her hand at the back. She self consciously put it down as he looked at her.

'Why is post modernism such a small part of the syllabus?'

'I've just given you one reason. Why d'you ask?'

'Well, I wondered if you favoured Marxism, because post modernism would invalidate that and - '

'Thus if I were, you thought I might be getting my own back?'

'Yes, I suppose so.'

'Well, any proponent of an established, overarching sociological theory, including right wing ones, would dislike a scattered string of opinion and conjecture that emphasises an individualistic subjectivity and denies social class and... do you know any Marxists then, Elaine?'

It was only the second time he had spoken to her in class, the first being to call the register on starting day. She was rather mournful looking, sad, tall, with a model's shoulders and something quietly deliberate about her.

'Well, my ...guardian is.' She looked briefly awkward and shy. There was a little pause in the class and he carried on in his proselytising manner. When they'd finished he briefly answered someone's question about an essay he had set then left the room. Elaine was just in front of him, awkwardly putting on her coat. On impulse he pulled the collar up at the back for her. She smiled a little shyly and thanked him. He guessed she was about thirty four, the same age as him.

'It's going pretty well isn't it.' she said

'The evening class?'

'Yes.'

'Do you come far?'

'About eight miles or so. I live just down the road really, but I'm staying with a friend tonight.'

They walked in silence through the main doors.

'I tell him what you're teaching. He's...suspicious.'

'What of?'

'Well, being a Marxist, he - '

'Your guardian?' He smiled at her.

'Yes. He'll be happy about your demolition job on post modernism, though.'

It was her slight, friendly awkwardness - and her wide smile with those slightly protruding front teeth - that tipped the words out; 'Maybe I could meet him sometime.' He was walking through the car park with her.

'Maybe,' she said with a dull pragmatism, and as she got into her car added, 'Oh, did you know that Annie, the dark haired lady who sits next to me, is a niece of Gramsci?' She smiled and drove out the college grounds. He'd mentioned the uncle in class, but nothing more than the name, aware of how little historical knowledge he had of Italian political activists.

She didn't turn up the next week, but the week after as they reached her car at the far end of the car park he asked her if she fancied a drink one evening. 'Yes,' she said simply, as if she'd been expecting him to ask.

He met her in a pub near the college a few nights afterwards. She was little different from her student role he thought, as if her ability to express, the glints in her eyes were dulled by a reluctantly enforced stoicism. She told him she had a ten year old son whose father had left them both years ago. They then talked generally, her saying that the class had gelled well, had a good camaraderie, that she was enjoying the subject, but wouldn't tell him why she had become someone's ward. She did tell him that it had occurred when she was sixteen and that George, her guardian, was now eighty. Mark calculated that he was about sixty when he entered her life He was a 'well known communist' she said with a seeming indifference, but quiet pride.

He'd left Oxford, she said, half way through his degree to join a merchant ship that was gun-running for the Republicans in the Spanish civil war. He was eventually torpedoed. All this delivered, again, with a matter of fact casualness as if, somehow, everything that she'd experienced had happened *to* her, unavoidable, outside of her own volition, and that she looked out at a world she expected would treat her dispassionately and a little unkindly.

A month after this they slept together at her flat on the top floor of a converted ex-council house. For a while they saw some films, went to alternative comedy venues - small rooms above pubs, working men's clubs - the occasional restaurant, a play, and then, after the last evening class of term, she suggested they pay a quick visit to the farmhouse. 'Just to meet George,' she said, 'we won't stay.'

Elaine drove. He sat silently next to her, a little unsure of how he should feel, as if he was about to meet the father of his 'intended,' about to ask George's permission for her hand, to seek his approval of him, of his abilities as a teacher, his knowledge of and, perhaps even commitment to, Marx or Marxism and to test his knowledge of political history, political ideas; a sort of box-ticking exercise. Would he, Mark wondered, want to know what he knew of the Second Spanish Republic, whether he favoured anarchism or Trotsky, what knowledge he had of the Basques, Colonel Beorlegui, of the siege of Madrid. The generic answer would have been, very little.

He wasn't in love with George's 'daughter.' There was a quiet practicality about her that he liked, she was pale, leggy, with a gauche artlessness; she had an honesty, a consistency and was, he felt, beginning to fall in love with him. He didn't want to hurt her, but sensed she knew this.

They walked towards the house through a small, lit, apple orchard, the lights under the symmetrically planted trees making them look like enchanted fans, the dark bulk of the building looming in the background. There was a porch lamp above a narrow door at the side of the black painted, barn-like house. She put her key in the lock, reminding him of the neighbours in his childhood terrace street who would 'let themselves in,' nearly all, it seemed, having keys to each others houses.

He felt George was some sort of absolute certainty in Elaine's life; there was a shut off implacability, a fatalistic acceptance when Mark thought of her in relation to George - as if he was a symbol of some authoritative, atheistic deity.

As they entered, George was looking down at them from a balcony. He was tall with long grey hair, leaning slightly forward, fingers casually curled on the wooden handrail in front of him. He looked from Mark to Elaine, nodded, turned and walked towards the top of the narrow staircase. Mark looked quickly around: grey-blue walls, high pitched cream ceiling with oak joists, the doors of the rooms off the balcony in the same dark, polished wood as the handrail all the way around the four sided gallery, beneath which weren't turned spindles or metal rods, but wooden carvings from the Karma Sutra of women being penetrated by men in a variety of acquiescent positions. One of these was a female with puffed cheeks kneeling behind a priapic male figure and holding one end of a straw to her lips, the other just behind his testicles. He wondered detachedly if this was the origin of 'blow job.'

George came down the last step and walked towards him, deep set eyes, hair swept back from a lined, tanned face, a full, trimmed moustache and dressed in dark grey almost completely. An ideologue, and a seemingly rich one, thought Mark.

They shook hands, a tiny smile in George's eyes, a casual, but almost formal grip. 'Come through,' he said. Mark followed him into a large kitchen, noted the eclectic mix of the new and old: two small windows with leaded panes, a slatted blind, a long kitchen range, oak table, modern blender and coffee grinder, copper kettle and an incongruous thirties cloud-back chair.

'Do you want a drink?' He had a rather curt, deep, voice. There was the sound of a flushing cistern, quick, light feet, and a boy of about ten with blue eyes and wide, thin-lipped mouth was looking up at him. Elaine, who was filling the kettle, said, without looking round, 'Richard, this is Mark, my friend.' Richard nodded at him then threw his arms around George's thigh and squeezed. George lightly touched the child's hair.

'Elaine tells me she's enjoying her subject and the class are too, it would seem.'

'They do seem keen, though it's a little difficult to get one or two away from God and to politicise them. I shouldn't be doing that, of course, but detachment's difficult.'

George grinned, 'It wouldn't matter much if you rammed Marx down their throats would it? The system can take it, can it not? Bourgeois accommodationism I believe it's called.'

Mark was feeling challenged, though knew what had been said was correct. He told George that though he'd once been called an auto-didactic secular preacher, he was more interested in the analysis of class society than revolutionary Marxism. George frowned slightly, forced a grin and asked again if he wanted a drink. Mark told him he was driving and George then, with surprising nimbleness, picked

Richard up, dropped him over a shoulder and said, 'Well, I'm gonna put this little toe rag to bed and then I have things to do. Hope to see you again.' He said this without looking at anyone and went out of the room. Mark expected Elaine to follow him so she could say good night to her son, but she handed him a coffee and after a few silent minutes beckoned him to follow her as she started walking back through the apple trees as if, somehow, she wasn't allowed to tuck Richard in when George was putting him to bed. She drove them back in silence to the college car park.

'That was...interesting,' Mark said, 'You going back there now?'

'No, the flat.' She drove away.

They went back a few weeks later - again in the evening - for Elaine to pick something up. George was away at a council meeting. Mark hadn't known he was a councillor. While she was upstairs he wandered around, looked in the large through-lounge with its oriental rugs, sixties three piece suite, Art Deco cocktail cabinet and coffee table - a half drunk cup of coffee on a hardback copy of Debord's *Society as Spectacle* on the latter - and a book-lined end wall. But he was taken by the paintings. There were vividly coloured scenes of street markets, fountains on a Madrid boulevard and a stark black and white photo of a vertical half of a *pension,* the other half just chunks of rubble. There was also a crayon sketch hung in the centre of the wall of a girl in her late teens with large, dark eyes, impish grin and an energy in her that made the rest of the room seem almost lifeless.

He walked up the stairs, along the balcony, stopped at an open door. Elaine was putting what looked like a skirt into a bag. She gave a hesitant smile as she came out the room and closed the door, but not before he'd seen a four poster bed complete with canopy and a nightshirt hanging from the dark headboard. As they went out he asked her if it was a painting that he could see at the back of the open garage.

'I think it's a Braque. I don't know much about art.'

He went in and turned it round. He knew little of the artist's work, but recognised the style immediately.

'It's an original,' she said, 'can we go, I'm getting cold.'

It was this almost dismissive casualness, a gentle flippancy that both simultaneously intrigued him and pushed him away.

One night at her flat he asked who the face in the sketch belonged to. She became immediately animated. 'Oh, that was Maria. She was lovely. George met her when he was in Spain, she was about twenty then. It was the *paseos* he called them, executions, both sides were doing it. Her husband was a Republican and they shot him. They came after Maria too, and George hid her. He and a group of others lived in the hills and she stayed with them. She used to come over and stay at the farm, every other year really, and George would sometimes go to her in Spain. She died last year. He was very upset and so was I. She had a little boy, but he died when he was two. She loved Richard. She used to get so excited around him. She would grip his hands and swing him around, and shout, *Ricardo, 'eres un chico encantador y tu papa es magnifico!'* She was lovely.' He asked what it meant. 'Doesn't matter,' she said, 'I miss her.'

Towards the end of the academic year - they'd seen much less of each other, though he wasn't sure why, but she was an ever-present in class - a full time job came up at the college. The evening Access class was the only sociology teaching he had, the rest of his timetable consisting of Communications. This job entailed mostly his subject. The opening had arisen because a lecturer had been sacked. He, David, was a little younger than Mark, short, stocky, ginger haired and quietly intense. He didn't know him that well, he was relatively new there, but liked him. He always seemed to be surrounded by young females both in class and the staff room. They were obviously fond of him and Mark felt there was a political - and politicising - element in their relationship.

The word was that he was an 'anarchist,' a 'trouble maker,' and that management had got rid of him by sending a lackey to keep tabs on him, He was seen going into his class ten minutes late. That, apparently, was all that was needed. Whilst feeling sorry for him and disliking management - in particular and in general - Mark needed the job and applied for it. Three of his fellow Communications lecturers said they would see the Vice Principal and suggest strongly that they wanted him on the staff.

He was surprised and disappointed when told he wouldn't be short-listed. He had a meeting with the Vice Principal and asked him why. 'I do not,' he was answered patronisingly, 'want a communist cell in the college.' Mark felt he was the sort of man who thought a communist meant someone who shopped at the Co-op. He was rendered inarticulate, all he could think of saying was an almost choked, 'But, that's ridiculous,' before the Principal entered the room on 'urgent business' and he left.

He told Elaine. She seemed surprised. The next day she showed him a letter she had written to the Head of the college in which she talked of the difficulty of the subject, the teacher making it such a pleasure for the class and her amazement that a competent teacher of such an important discipline would not be at the college next year. 'I do not look forward,' she wrote, 'to having a teacher perhaps unqualified in sociological understanding and am thus thinking twice about continuing my studies.' It was gratifying, but Mark wanted her to continue. She'd been working as a temp at an IT recruitment firm for the last year and had an ambition to do a social work degree.

A few days afterwards she showed him a copy of the letter George had sent to the Chief Education Officer of the borough in his role as shadow chairman on Further Education for the County Council. 'Whilst I must stress that your selection standards are nothing of my business, apart from their bearing on my daughter's education, I must state that I am disagreeably surprised a to find her progress threatened.' It was signed George Mills, and had the Great Mitchams, West Ockden address.

He didn't see her over the two week Whitsun period - 'I have things to do at George's' - but was in the library preparing a letter to circulate around colleges and to see what teaching jobs, if any, were being offered, when he thought of the charcoal drawing. He wasn't far from the language section and took a book of Spanish-English back to his table. For someone whose knowledge of Spanish began and ended with *dos decaffeinado con leche por favor,* it took him a while to find and interpret what Maria supposedly and ritualistically had said to Richard whenever she'd seen him. He could imagine her, then about seventy he supposed, but still vivacious and strong, swirling around the boy, dancing with him. It seemed obvious suddenly that she had been George's lover for many years .Mark didn't know why he had remembered her words, but he had. Apparently in English it was, 'You are a lovely boy and your daddy is magnificent!'

And this was something else so obvious he'd missed. It reminded him of when he'd stood on the observation floor of the Empire State at night a few years before and, looking at the Chrysler, the Woolworth building and Times Square, had wondered for a second why he couldn't see the Empire State. Richard's father was George.

He sat there thinking of him; someone who had risked his life for something he believed, had saved lives, been, perhaps, responsible for taking them. The nearest Mark had got to any sort of cause was walking half a mile around a university town with a CND banner and once, as an apprentice joiner, had been part of a building site go-slow. He felt admiration, respect, but then remembered what Elaine had said to him one evening a few weeks before; something else he had pushed away, deflected, sidelined. Lying on the bed she'd said casually, as he got dressed to go home, 'George wants us to do it in front of him because he can't any more.' He hadn't replied.

And there was a memory of a glimpse of a crumpled nightshirt dropped in the corner of her bedroom when she'd first invited him into it. Was George, he thought, still sleeping with her, here and at the farm? There was another question: had Maria's child been George's too?

He'd grown fond of Elaine, but realised he'd felt somewhat dispirited when with her, experiences were somehow blunted, any sharing - of humour, situations, of giving emotionally - diluted, impoverished. He tried to categorize it as an interesting, but disappointing episode for he knew he wouldn't be seeing her again and intuitively felt she knew this, too. The only stimulus, other than in her bed, had been the teaching. He could give something to her then; she was intelligent, though carefully, methodically so, as if her intellect was in abeyance and her identity, the sixteen year old self, had no real expression except through or with George.

He wanted to teach, encourage, preach - he had a picture of George nodding in approval as he thought this. Mark had met him just once, but could feel how Elaine had been influenced, invaded, taken over by him.

He had applied for more sociology lecturing, wanting to deal with the empirical, *a posteriori* synthetic truths, people as Durkheimian *things,* to escape into a more intellectualised, understandable world.

He didn't see Elaine again, but did hear her voice. He'd just got home from a class at a college where he had a full time job, when the

phone rang. It was Elaine telling him that George had died in Spain .
For a moment he felt trapped in a ghost story in which he couldn't
actually have met someone because they had died many years before.
He remembered what she said almost verbatim.

'...he hadn't been back there for a few years and wanted to meet up
with Maria's younger brother who he'd helped to get to Catalonia.
Apparently he was away on holiday, so George went on his own to
the hills in Miranda de Ebro, near a monastery by the river, Our Lady
of the Wheel it's called - I remember these places because he often
told stories about them, Richard used to be fascinated. It was where
he'd hid Maria....' She stopped speaking.

'Elaine?'

'It's okay. It seems he was walking around the bottom of a hill - a
couple from the village were picnicking there and saw him. He kept
stopping to look up, probably trying to find the caves they'd stayed
in.' In answer to his unspoken question she said, 'I was his next of
kin, so a policeman rang me from Madrid and told me all this.
George was wearing his black cap, he wore it nearly every time he
went out. He called it his 'comrades cap.' They found it near his
body. He was climbing up a slope. Perhaps he didn't know the caves
had been filled in. He slipped and slid down. Not far, but both his
legs were broken.' A silence again. 'He was eighty two you know.'

He heard a whimper and could feel the effort it took for her to stop it.

'When's the funeral, Elaine?'

'Oh, it's gone. I didn't know what to do. I thought he might want to
be buried there, near Maria. I know where's she's buried, he told me.
He's buried in the next grave to hers. I went over there, and Manuel
and his wife were there. They were very kind'

'Why didn't you...' He was about to ask, in a moment of childlike
arrogance, why she hadn't told him before and perhaps asked him to
go with her, but he didn't. He wondered if she felt that she had no
right to bring George back and bury him; maybe in the churchyard
near the farm.

He told her he was sorry about George and, as he said it, felt regret at
only seeing him the once, at not making efforts to get to know him,
to see if he could have pierced that teak-like exterior, that hard,
selfish toughness he seemed to carry with him. He asked her what

she was going to do.

'I'm going to sell the farm.' At least, she had that, he thought. 'I shall move somewhere I suppose.'

He wanted to say, 'Find something for yourself, Elaine, find what *you* want, convince yourself you can, you're *allowed* to.' Instead, he asked about Richard.

'He's okay. He's sad, but he's alright.'

She asked what he was doing, was he teaching. He mumbled something. She said,

'Well, all the best then, Mark.' and hung up.

Driving on the A13 he took a detour to drive past the farm house, which he hadn't seen for a year. The orchard was no longer there, it was now a paved area with barbecue equipment scattered about, and where all the latticed windows had been were pvc mock Georgian glazing bars. The subtle carriage lamp on the side door had turned into a crass mock-up of an early Victorian lamp, and though the outside was still in East Anglian black, it had now been glossed. It looked rather cheap. The chimney stack, in its crumbling authenticity, was still there.

He didn't stop. He had to get to work - finish off Marx's theory of economic determinism. He felt that George, in a narrow eyed, cautious way, would be quite happy with that, even if conditionally.

As he drove back to his new college he felt empty, specious. He missed George. He couldn't understand this. He knew *of* him rather than knew him. Perhaps he had become, unknowingly, a talisman, perhaps a figure to be emulated, someone mature, solid, complete. But Mark instantly knew he couldn't do this. He had to become whoever he was, was going to be. He drove a little faster, wanting to get back to the students. To the beginning.

PEWS

'Did you understand any of that? I didn't.'

The questioner was sitting next to James Kent in a crowded train slowing into a City station. The unintelligible noise was another corruption of sound that passed for a public announcement - James picking out two 'wivs' and a 'frew' as estuary and Jamaican pidgin skewed the linguistic geometry into shapes previously the habitué of the London working class and Detroit African-Americans.

As he stepped onto the platform he thought about the films he'd watched as a young man that involved railway stations and the significant roles they'd played. He slowed his step, wandered dreamily back to brown carriages, pistons, steam, refreshment room tea urns, trilbies and fox furs, and thought of usherettes leaning against the curtained wall at the back watching 'Brief Encounter,' and perhaps recognising the stifling duty of their own Saturday night giving, bearing the weight, smelling the Woodbines and ale, and willing the heroine to turn and run back to her would-be lover, leap through the smoke, rise above sooted columns, shatter the roof, soar...

Over a coffee in Paulo's he wondered more about the role of the usherette, remembering as a lad his aunts Flo and Daisy standing attractively uniformed under the palms at the top of the stairs in the now demolished Art Deco cinema at Stratford Broadway. With their torch beams gliding over soft carpets and velour seats he saw them as ciphers guiding the audience into jungles, deserts, cities, bedrooms and bars.

He stopped his meandering and thought of his patients and a little rule he'd learnt from Thomas; telling them all at one time or another that they could shout, cry, become hysterical, swear obscenities, but never try to hit him.

He missed Thomas. He hadn't seen his older colleague and mentor for years. He'd been friends with his daughter. She'd fallen for a stand-up comic and he'd seen neither of them since. It was the absence of Thomas that held the deeper emptiness.

An age of Thomas swelled in his mind. He'd been lecturing where James did his degree; mostly the founding fathers, particularly Freud.

He was an excellent speaker; fellow lecturers and students from other disciplines would come to the hall to listen to him - he'd given a lecture at Columbia University in New York to a packed hall that, James was told, had ended with a standing ovation.

James had first seen him at an introductory session in the Lecture Theatre where he'd strolled about the stage pointing up at and singing the names of members of the faculty staff to the tune of 'Welcome to Cabaret,' replacing the last word of the title with 'UEA.' He'd felt an immediate sense of belonging.

During the three year course he saw him occasionally at lectures and seminars; though rarely speaking other than about the work that was required of him. Halfway through Finals Thomas had told him, with mild but genuine concern, that he was doing badly. It woke him up. He eventually did well.

He saw him next at a conference soon after starting his therapy practice. Thomas recognised him and seemed interested in how he was faring. At the next conference he gave him an invite to his office. Rather bizarrely, his father had owned a farm where he'd grown a large acreage of carrots. Thomas inherited, sold it and moved to London where he'd begun a psychoanalytic practice in Marylebone. It wasn't a large place, but had a considered opulence.

As well as introducing James to his daughter he encouraged, advised and occasionally bullied him into working harder to establish himself and move his endeavour in the right directions. In the early days James had sent him some difficult clients, especially those who, at the time, he hadn't the patience to oversee for the long term. Thomas would, in return - James suspected he felt a little sorry for him - send him a patient or two to make up his meagre numbers and help him earn a living wage. When James got home he took a deep breath and rang him.

The voice was just as gruff and seemingly disinterested as ever. James asked him how he was. There was a short, huffing sound.

'I'm glad you rang. I suppose I should have rung you, really. You're better at social norms than me. But, sod those, I'm glad you rang, let's meet.'

They met at a restaurant near Thomas's office. It was rather out of

James' culinary and financial league. Thomas had more clients and, commensurate with his fees, appreciably richer ones. He seemed to James to have changed little: burly, broad shouldered, thick bush of grey hair and voice as tough and rumbling as always. He seemed, in his sometimes rather off-hand way, to be as pleased to see James as the latter was him. They ordered, Thomas insisting that this was on him.

'I want to get this out of the way, James. I thought, guessed, that you were falling in love with Lorna without realising it and I knew she wasn't, she'd never been in love. She is now. I know you were her close friend - our close friend - but... she seems very happy.' He sounded almost apologetic, or as near as he could get to it.

This didn't hurt James as much as he thought it would, unless the bruise came later.

'And of course, it makes me happy,' he continued, raising his eyebrows.

'Yes, I can see. I understand, it's - '

'But I do feel guilty, as if somehow It was me that -'

'Transference,' said James a second before his friend did. They both laughed.

'Of a rather incestuous sort I suppose, but perhaps worth looking into. Let's have our meal first, text books later.'

James hadn't eaten grilled salmon for a while; he let the taste gradually stimulate him. They talked shop as they both knew they would; James telling of his practice, the irregularity of it, disappointments, satisfaction, rewards, Thomas of his full client list and the idea that however rich many of his patients seemed to be, pain was pain, trauma was trauma. James felt somewhat irritated, he disliked privilege, having experienced little himself.

'So, someone who is homeless and in emotional pain is not worse off than a rich guy with similar pain - assuming it could be quantified and compared of course.'

They both knew where this exchange would go ideologically, it had happened before.

Partly in order to get on safer ground - for James had no wish to argue, it was just good to be with his old mentor again - he told him of a thought he'd recently had, but hadn't pursued.

'I was thinking about what sort of society would fit an unsocialized human nature in order to optimise that nature, to fulfil itself, but of course, given the power of the id, the force of the instincts, there couldn't *be* a superego, a hyper-moral parent, there could be no social values countering the id's expression; in short; and dismissing the idea of man as a blank slate, infinitely malleable and educable, there could be only a Hobbesian war of all against all.'

'If that's the case how did we form society in the first place? What made us switch to some form of deferred gratification?'

James couldn't get further; another chicken and egg dilemma, but he did bring up the sociological counter against the 'too generalizing' label psychologists laid on it by pointing out that, for psychology, each individual is a particular case of general law. Thomas grinned wryly.

'Yes, it is so, the oedipal, paranoia, we do generalize, but not as much as... '

He stopped. They both laughed again. This was typical of their old conversations; there were few people James knew now who he could have them with. He felt somehow replete; the meal and... Thomas. It was good.

The latter then casually told James, a little too lightly perhaps, of a client of his.

'I'm overflowing, take him, he'll interest you. He's got a little project. I know you like churches, though for the wrong reasons it could be argued,'

He smiled, knowing James' interest was purely, so he said, for aesthetic reasons.

'He is, I think, being a bit of his usual dilettante on this one. He has problems of course, though difficult to get to, but there may be a real reason for him in this, though he doesn't have to have a reason for anything, he's rich. I think it maybe good if he did have. I see little real pain there; maybe he has more than he presents, but... Forget it. If you want him he's yours.'

After a quasi argument about Freud - James convinced that he'd underestimated the effect of the mother, his friend disagreeing - Thomas reached in his pocket and handed over a scribbled name and telephone number, saying that he would be rung anyway. Knowing Thomas had intended mixing business with pleasure, James was a little hurt, though a pragmatic part of him was glad to have the chance of a new client. His friend looked at his watch, signalled the waiter and raised himself from his chair.

'I know a little of your morality, James, but I think you should force yourself to charge him more than your usual fee.'

He put his arm around James' shoulder as they walked out. And there was Lorna, a little breathless, standing in front of them.

'I wanted to see you, but couldn't get through and the new housekeeper said that...'

And then she noticed him. Her eyes widened.

'Hello James.'

She smiled and held out her hand. James shook it. It was instantly strange and, for a few seconds, the action felt remarkably stilted. She looked exactly as he'd last seen her, an hour or so after indirectly introducing her to the man she was very soon smitten by; excited, eyes gleaming. There seemed to be a maturity to her now, and as James looked at her he still couldn't understand why he'd never told her what he felt for her. He could never do so now. He took a deep breath, squared his shoulders as if he, too, had acquired ... maturity. He felt the odd one out, a reminder that when the three of them had been together he often had. He told Thomas he was going back, thanked him for the meal and that he'd keep in touch. He turned to Lorna, said goodbye, feeling stiff, formal, strangled. She gave a rather over-executed grin, put her arm quickly in her father's and they turned away.

James was in a grey, morose mood on the way home. It lasted till he went to sleep.

His potential client called him three days later wanting to know immediately whether his listener thought he'd 'get on' with him; James assuming Thomas hadn't and, perhaps, had sent him someone perceived as incorrigible. However, it could have been that Thomas had neither the time nor, for some reason, the desire to help him, though James couldn't imagine his friend ever doubting his own ability to help virtually anyone. He told the caller that he would be paying him to help him help himself.

'They all say that.' the voice said, 'We'll see.'

He was as James imagined from his Hollywood construct of a name, Kurt Christian, but more so: long, fair hair, tall, good shoulders, lightly tanned face, confident, estimating blue eyes, clothes that were bought to convey an academic personae; soft, un-ironed shirt, creased linen jacket, faded jeans, suede sneakers. There was a foppish, contrived air about him.

'Hi,' he said easily, hand outstretched, then almost dangling it as if offered for the respondent to lightly stroke. 'How are you?' There was a covertly patronising feel to him which, James guessed, was feigned.

He was asked to sit. He raised his arms a little as if to ask, 'What else?'

James began. 'Firstly, I'd like to -'

'Hey,' his new client said, looking around him, 'rather nice water colours. Do 'em yourself?'

James felt childishly pleased to say he had; compliments on his creativity were rare. He let him talk, saying little himself. Often this was the best way: allowing clients to express themselves in whatever interested them in the moment, however seemingly facile. Sometimes, there were clues, pointers to underlying tensions, discords. But James felt almost immediately that this one needed directing, channelling into areas of unrecalled experiences, feelings, with himself noting what forms his deflections, escapes took - occasionally the latter were softened, fantasised versions of what his patients were so fearful of.

But James was being lazy and it was covertly encouraged by his client talking of the paintings, going into unnecessary detail about them, then subtly asking questions about James which, with his professional guard dropping, he, at first reluctantly then less so, answered. In a short while the patient possibly knew more about his therapist then the latter, him.

James shook himself. 'This is a classic deflection, Mister Christian - and I'm sure not many people of my age, even yours, call you that without wanting to use a Charles Laughton accent.'

'Quite,' he smiled.

His mood changed. 'Aren't you going to ask me why I didn't get on with Mister Fitzroy?'

'No, but I'm sure you'll tell me.'

'He was... hard, almost rough, cold.'

'And you wanted sympathy, a best friend; a father?'

'That's predictable. Are all analysts like you and your friend? Do you always want to win? If I agree with you I'm okay, if I don't I'm in denial?'

'Can you articulate your problem or rather what you feel is the problem?'

'I know a problem's only a problem if it's defined as such, but I'm not happy, I get annoyed, frustrated, so easily. I'm angry most of the time.'

He looked at James for a second, seemingly sincere, without affectation.

'I don't know why.'

Anticipating James' question he said,

'Yes, I always have been. Oh, I've looked at the usual things: boarding school, and yes I did have a homosexual relationship there, my parents splitting up soon after I left. Lived with dad mostly, often in the south of France, occasionally with my mother in Wiltshire.'

'You say 'my mother', yet for your father it's 'dad.' Any significance there?'

Ignoring the question he continued. 'It's text book stuff for the rich kid isn't it. I was also taken in hand, literally, by an older woman when young, the maid, actually. It's all so corny isn't it.' He looked at James defensively. 'Money does bring its own problems you know, or don't you like the 'poor rich' line?

He leant back. 'Anyway, I've just trod the boards for a little theatre company,' he said, flicking his forehead as if he had a forelock to tidy back. 'People seemed to like my little performance.'

He gave a mock modest smile then looked satisfyingly around him again. Finding nothing else he wished to comment on he looked at his watch.

'I don't want to go, but... ' He'd been with James over an hour.

'You should be the one to call time, should you not?'

James couldn't remember this happening before; a client telling him the session was over. After he'd gone it felt as if the last sixty minutes or so had been an airy, affected whirl of his client's effete, fair haired charm.

When he came the next week he wanted James to help him save his local church. It was an Edwardian redbrick in West London which James had noticed a few years before on his London walks. It had an unusual spire and despite the vividly coloured leaded windows it had a rather stately sparseness. The look of it had stayed with him. This was obviously the 'project' Thomas had mentioned.

'They may demolish it. I don't know why. There's a meeting next Monday. I'm an atheist, never been inside the place and perhaps its double standards, though I prefer 'strategic hypocrisy,' but I'd hate to see that building go. Its ... Englishness, its tradition, the archi - . Do come. Come with me. I'm sure your protocol won't let you see me outside of these walls, but every little helps. I don't know your views on religion, but - '

'Similar to yours.'

He gave that smile again, told James the time of the meeting and that he was going to appear soon in another play. He talked about it enthusiastically, insightfully, so much so that his listener increasingly stopped thinking of what was behind the words and the unnecessarily acted charm. But, in a rare moment of detachment with him James saw in his rather self-conscious elegance, in a fleeting expression, heard in a particular arrangement of words that he knew his effect on others and that this, also, was part of the seduction.

This time it was James who told him his time was up. He raised an eyebrow, seemed surprised that he had to leave, that there may be other patients and that he'd have to find another listener for the day.

The meeting was at eight in the evening a few days afterwards. James was twenty minutes late, partly because a client had telephoned him in some desperation needing to talk, and because he wasn't sure about going, anyway. Then an image of the spire and the tall plane trees it thrust itself from won.

There were 150 people sitting on long, curved lines of pews like a flat, mini-amphitheatre. James sat at the end of the first row. He didn't see Kurt. A minister was addressing them. He talked of the cost of the building's upkeep in some detail, that he was the steward of God's money, how small the congregation usually was and that the proposal for forty flats and a café could become an 'iconic building' He used 'needs of the modern age' twice, three 'move forward's' and there was a concerned annoyance when someone mentioned that the proposal for demolition had been with the local council for four years without local residents being informed. The vicar of a nearby parish then stepped forward and in a soft, would-be persuasive voice rhetorically asked,

'How many of you still have your first car? Of course you haven't, it got old didn't it, and you got a newer one didn't you. It's the same with the church, we have – '

That's when James saw Kurt. He strode out from somewhere behind him, grabbed the mike from the speaker, who seemed to disappear into the fabric of the building, looked around him angrily and said,

'This is such a vapid presentation. I'm an atheist. There's only the one thing I'm interested in and that's the building.'

James felt a recognition, an instant's aesthetic sharing.

'Look around you, look at the windows, their colours are falling on you, on your heads, shoulders; look up, look at the vaulted ceiling, the symmetry, the proportions, the oak dado, the rich mahogany organ, the elegant size of it. Just look.'

He swept his arm expansively and dramatically around him as if he'd built the place himself and was offering it to the people.

'This is a developer's wet dream. These unimaginative apologies for faith leaders who conceive of barrack social housing as an acceptable trade-off are deluding themselves that their well-meaning intent justifies their vandalism.'

While he was talking, rarely hesitating, flowing, his face seemed to take on a gloss of enamel, his eyes were brilliant, darting, but he seemed to James as brittle as a dragonfly.

'And it's as if churches weren't built for rich men's social standing; 'I've got a bigger penis than you.' And what sort of analogy is the car one? Are we to destroy St Paul's because it's old? London's a predominantly Victorian city, do we raze it because it's ancient? This man has the brain of an amoeba.'

His effeteness suddenly wasn't so obvious, his gestures were more precise, stronger, he seemed larger, more solid. There was a suited man sitting directly in front of him who said quietly while looking up at him,

'Who's going to pay for it then?'

Kurt stopped, bent forward a little and frowned down, saying courteously,

'Please be quiet, I haven't finished.'

'Well, the fact is, the money's got to come from somewhere.'

The man looked around and behind him, appealing to the obviousness of it all.

'Please don't *continue.*' Kurt hissed.

It appeared so incongruous; anger in a house of worship. The face of the man in the front row went through so many expressions it blurred.

'Ask *God* for it,' Kurt shouted, then began hitting his thighs with his fists. He turned behind him to the corner of the nave. James could see only the back of his head. There was a life-size statue of Mary, her face looking modestly down. She was holding in one hand what could have been a star. Kurt took three steps towards her, clasped his hands behind the neck and pulled it towards him, instantly stepping away. It broke from its plinth, falling forward, face down, cracking open with a clattering explosion on the parquet floor.

It seemed to have happened with an uncanny, violent speed. The silence after it was alien, there wasn't a murmur. Kurt turned around, stood rigidly and began to tremble. Nobody moved for, seemingly, minutes, then just as James was going to stand, not quite knowing what to do, someone from the audience walked firmly towards the shaking Kurt, put an arm around his shoulder, led him towards the rear pews and sat him down. Kurt had his head bowed, hands over his ears. James couldn't see his face. A few people walked out, others gathered around the two men; both ministers were still sitting.

James looked at the segmented statue, the cracked head, face untouched, part of a finger, a wrist, still rolling to and fro against a skirting board. The object in the other hand now looked like a torch, as if the Madonna was a destroyed, useless usherette, the lips like his aunt Daisy's, the dark hair actually similar to his aunt Flo's, and the high-coloured cheeks could have been Lorna's; the cracked, gold-hemmed gown similar to the one she once wore when she and James went to pay homage to her father receiving an award from the British Psychotherapy Association.

For one wild moment it seemed to him that Kurt had destroyed members of his family, part of his childhood, and the memories of an unrecognised love. It was as if an age had ended, not just a significant phase of his life, but a reality that had just… gone.

Most people had left. Two or three of those remaining passed by him with barely perceptible nods. The fuss had died. Two police constables and a paramedic had entered quietly, the latter taking over the caring duty and shepherding James' client out followed by the uniformed men. The clerics had gone, the sun also; no coloured light anymore, just the brown-grey of a forlorn, dead space.

He shouldn't have come, shouldn't have seen it happen. The question now was what to do with it. He had to get to the real causes of the anger; it was from a long way back; his patient, despite the humour, the sardonic wit, was deeply depressed. And the cliche that depression was merely anger without enthusiasm wasn't good enough.

On the train home listening to the resident glottal stoppages, the 'bruvvah's,' 'whatevah's' and the 'So I was like's' drilling loudly through his head, he went to go through to the next carriage, but then stopped. He stood there looking out of windows at gasometers, overhead cables, the edge of the Olympic Stadium silhouetted against a lowering sun and wondered why Thomas really had sent this client to him.

Perhaps Kurt's flamboyance, money, background, had put a slight barrier between himself and his analyst, thus he'd been pushed onto James as a challenge, knowing that this man who seemed initially to have the emotional capacity of a teaspoon would be a reminder to James of the privilege he'd never had and thus envied and also, perhaps, that he could be seduced by it. He felt for the briefest moment that Thomas could be using this man as an experiment, a bet with himself about the way James would deal with him knowing that he would fail, that somehow he'd wanted revenge and that neither he nor James knew what it was for. Maybe Thomas had guessed that his patient had been on the verge of doing something like this and hadn't really known how to handle it.

James had looked up to his faultless mentor and advisor for years; he'd had so much experience of so many patients, problems, conditions. It could be that he was tiring, didn't have the strength now to deal with the pathological world and its wife. If this was so and he'd trusted James with Kurt Christian then this act of respect from him was vastly outweighed by a feeling of loss, a loss of something rock-like James seemed to have been clinging to in the troubled waters of his professional life. Something more had floated away from him, sinking...

As he turned his head to look out the windows on the other side of the carriage it occurred to him that intolerance, indecisiveness, an immature, emotional dependency and an inability to recognise how weak professionalism could be against the massive confrontation of face-to-face reality were not really useful qualities in a psychoanalyst.

They slowed, a goods train thudded by; Maersk, Sealand, P & O, Lorna... He played a little game where he stepped off the train and looked quickly along the platform to see whether his was the first foot that touched. He often did it, knew it was utterly childlike, but didn't care. If he wished he could run up the station stairs three at a time, tango with an imaginary partner on the forecourt, skip along the pavement or play hopscotch as a patient of his had felt compelled to do outside James' home before coming in for his session. It didn't matter. Little mattered He didn't want to be a therapist, didn't care about people enough, was fed up with theory, intellectualism, buildings, roads, vehicles... He was aware he was being perverse. It was part of a huge sulk.

At a bus stop he looked up as two buses, one behind the other, stopped. The number on the first was Thomas' office address, the second said 'Kensington and Chelsea.' .He looked at the initial letters and metaphorically put his hands over his eyes.

He started walking, looking around him reluctantly, unable to turn it into the habitual, almost spiritual experience: noting a dark doorway at the end of an alley, the sun reflecting from a slowly turning chimney cowl, the squeak of a park swing as a laughing child left it for the next excitement. But he couldn't help himself from wondering what Kurt had seen in the plaster-cast Madonna. He saw it again; the innocent female, the gentle, wise, compassionate face, the mother, the quintessential, complete, perfect mother. Did Kurt see this? Did he instantly hate her; the mother he never had, should have had? 'My mother' he'd called her, not the always there, taken-for-granted 'mum' nor, with the social background and education he'd obviously had, the expected 'mummy,' just the formal nomenclature of 'mother.' Perhaps, thought James, he wasn't destroying his mother, but the *absence* of her that the figure had reminded him of, of the mother he'd wanted, needed so much No woman, no earthly one, could be an adequate substitute. Not now. And perhaps this had been Thomas's blind spot, as it had, arguably, been Freud's; the power of the mother He'd glossed over it, and there'd been a flawed understanding between him and his patient; and he'd given him to James.

He knew it could all be guesswork. But this time, despite past errors and flawed analysis, he felt he was right, though again he wasn't sure what to do. He didn't really want to treat Kurt Christian nor, at the moment, anyone, but he knew he would eventually contact him and, if he'd let him, try to help him. Try as hard as he could.

BUNTAH

Six months before I first saw him I was in a shed on Wanstead Flats sitting a test determining whether I went into the Army or Air Force for my National Service. It was 1958, I was eighteen, and had just broken the terms of a four year bricklaying apprenticeship. Though I'd liked the solid, tactile pleasure of laying bricks, after two years of working in and around London, mostly on new-builds with their bland, yellow and grey slabs, often on scaffolding and too regularly scraping ice from spirit levels and trowels, and knowing I had to do National Service anyway, decided to do it at the age most lads did. In the shed I and twenty other youths had to answer questions such as: to start a car do you, a) press the accelerator, b) turn the ignition, or c) depress the clutch. I had no idea about this one; driving cars was for the big boys. The price of failure was the Army. A few weeks later I found myself at an RAF Reception Camp in Cardington, Bedfordshire.

Here we were given haircuts that exposed parts of our heads we never knew existed and were kitted out and given service numbers in a futile attempt to make us look part of an efficient fighting machine. I was dismayed at how ridiculous I looked in a new beret until I learnt to razor-edge it down the side of my face like the three-year regulars, most of whom rarely acknowledged conscripts, thinking they were a nuisance and the latter considering them 'thick' for the obvious reason that they had voluntarily signed on for that period of time.

After a week we were sent to a square-bashing camp outside Liverpool where we were despatched from wagons, herded into a vast echoing hangar and were screamed at. We were screamed at most of the time by little corporals who all seemed to originate from the Gorbals.

We were yelled at in frightening, almost indecipherable terms, to stand to attention, at ease, about turn, fire rifles - not 'guns' - and given orders for every, often pointless, activity that could be thought of for six long weeks

There was, of course, method in their madness; to dehumanise us, objectify us. The thinking serviceman is as useful to the military as throwing a drowning man both ends of a rope.

Orwell's *1984* had recently been dramatised on television and at our passing out parade two months later, marching dead in line and performing tricks with rifles, we saw, painted on the side of the hangar in ten foot letters, BIG BROTHER IS WATCHING YOU! I felt an unusual feeling of belonging and, despite my cynicism, a small moment of something approaching happiness.

The next move was to a radio training school in Wiltshire where we were given a choice of learning either radio operating or working a teleprinter. Having heard stories of the relentless di-di-di-dah, di-di-di-dah of Morse code sending operators mad, I chose the latter. I was taught to touch-type, to read Murray code - a series of perforated holes in paper tape, each combination representing letters and figures - and to understand the general procedures for sending and receiving signals.

The final parade here was a less serious affair than the previous one, especially so when marching ranks of us, turning our heads for 'eyes right,' saw that the famous white horse carving on the side of the nearby chalk downs had had a reproductive appendage added - the result of another overnight sortie - its tip coloured RAF blue.

During our last week we were suddenly transported to a thousand foot 'hill' in Snowdonia where we camped out on six inches of solid ice for two nights. Some of the men were crying. This was an 'acclimatisation' exercise for our permanent camp. Six days later, in the ninety degrees humidity of Singapore, I was trying to breathe.

Flying in a BOAC turboprop Argonaut, it took us four days to reach RAF Changi during which we had overnight stops at Karachi and Calcutta, being entertained during the former in a nightclub by a cabaret singer who asked the audience to give a big welcome to 'the boys in blue.' I wasn't sure how he knew who we were. We were in civilian clothes and had been since leaving England.

The first few nights were spent in a windowless transit block holding eighty men laying on pillows with brown sweat stains from the hundreds of heads that had rested on them before our own and staring at chitchat lizards criss-crossing the ceiling. There were tanned Adonises everywhere, grinning at us and calling us 'moon men.' A few weeks later, turning brown after hours spent lying on our backs on the buoyant, salty water of the Straits in a fenced-off area to protect bathers from sharks, the new boys, too, were calling fresh arrivals, 'moon men.'

Moving into our permanent billet, I noticed inside the entrance a tall, dark-skinned man standing very still, looking silently down. He had a sweep of black hair, small moustache and was wearing what looked like a grey sari, plus the inevitable flip flops. It was the nearest I had ever been to a 'native'. Subliminal Raj words arose instantly: 'swarthy', 'cunning', even 'shifty'. He was our *dohbi wallah* who would take our washing to be done, sweep the three concrete floors of our billet and generally tidy up. He was an Indian Malay we called Buntah. I don't know how long he'd been there. He was just there. I didn't really talk to him, didn't think of it. The first time he took my washing I was standing on the balcony. He looked at me shyly and said,

'You Johnny big bollock.'

I was wearing, above woollen socks and polished boots, a rather short pair of khaki shorts. A sliver of scrotum was showing beneath one leg. I smiled back at him.

The first night on duty in the signals section, in the clacking of teleprinters spewing out tape and paper, and a temperature and lack of air I had never experienced before, I quietly panicked and tore ten operational immediate signals from a receiver, threw them in a bin and then started, with growing efficiency, to log the rest. I was found out, but was lucky, the duty sergeant merely reminding me that we were fighting the 'Forgotten War' and in mainland Malaya - as it was then called - people were getting killed. I was reminded again of this from time to time when receiving signals reading typically, *'Found in jungle clearing: packet of unopened corn flakes, one knife, one fork, 202 rifle, no ammunition, one decapitated head...'*

There were other memory aids. We were told to 'defend' the local military telephone exchange from a Scottish army battalion that was going to cross the Straits to 'occupy' it. We stood or sat around, blanks in rifles, bored and impatient, when we were surrounded suddenly by soldiers in jungle green uniforms. Taffy, who I'd known since Cardington, immediately shot at an officer from six feet away. He could have blinded him. He mumbled apologies and after a little fuss it was forgotten, though he did gain some notoriety.

I did too, in a much lesser way. Falling asleep in the rest room at

4am.on duty in the section I was shaken awake by the sergeant and called a bastard; two signals had come in on my machine. One of the many barrack room lawyers told me that I could get the sergeant into trouble for using that sort of language to a National Serviceman. I didn't really believe him, and my accuser wouldn't do anything about the situation anyway, having been stationed in the Far East for too many years, being perpetually half-pissed in the section and knowing that we knew.

There were further incidents that contained elements of farce, as when the section personnel were split into opposing Red and Blue groups, their members told secretly what groups they were in. As I was about to start the evening shift on this day, an airman who I had worked with for some months suddenly announced that he was a member of Red group, knew that I was in Blue and that the section, and now myself, had been 'captured.'

And on the way to the NAAFI one lunch time, the most memorable constituents of the meal being rubber eggs and salt tablets - we sweated all the time - I passed a female officer, pretending I hadn't noticed her.

'Airman.'

I ignored her.

'What do you do when you see an officer?'

I slowly and reluctantly turned towards her before answering.

'Salute.'

''Salute' *what?*'

'Salute, *ma'am.*'

'Do so, then.'

I hated to be told what to do by a woman. This wasn't just a result of my class culture - my mother's punishing hands had planted the seeds of an unaware misogyny long ago.

I about-turned in my crisp, starched, khaki shirt and shorts, woollen socks around my ankles, exaggeratedly stamping a foot down and, forgetting that I was holding a knife, fork and enamel mug, clipped a hand smartly against the side of my head. I felt blood start to trickle down my temple. She was tall, attractive, groomed and looked like a forties' recruitment poster. She gazed at me for a full minute without expression and marched away. Suddenly Buntah was there, grinning, his usual suspicious, mildly defensive look gone, as had the young boy he sometimes had with him and who I assumed was his son. I had rarely seen him outside of the billet before. He offered me a handkerchief to wipe my face.

I saw him again outside of the billet when I was on 24 hour duty guarding the 'secret' ammo dump, sitting on the grass sweating in secondary jungle as smiling kids came by and said hello. Buntah passed too, smiling again, his tiny moustache and large teeth making him look like an Asian Chaplin as he picked up my rifle, pretended to shoot me, gave it back and left.

Travelling up-country for a fortnight's annual leave to Penang Island, the presence of terrorist activity was again made, almost, clear to us. We were in a train, standing by the windows with loaded rifles. I asked an officer why we had to carry them when there was, apparently, little threat.

'To prevent armaments from being stolen.'

'What armaments?'

'The rifles and ammunition we are carrying.'

'So, we are carrying arms in order to guard the arms we are carrying.'

'Yes,' said the officer and unaware of the tautology continued along the carriage.

This seemed to confirm to me the consensus that 'military intelligence' was indeed an oxymoron.

There were some good things I did that helped nurture my sanity. Occasionally, a few of us would spend our leisure time around a cove on the Straits acting out the scenes we could remember from current films: 'On the Waterfront,' 'Bad Day at Black Rock,' 'Duel in the Sun,' and which we shot black and white stills of with a newly acquired bellows camera. Buntah used to watch us. He seemed to be there every time. Taffy asked him if he'd like to play a role, but he shook his head and continued frowning, concentrating hard on what we were doing. I never questioned why he'd walk a mile from the billet to do so. Perhaps he lived nearby.

There were other things, too: the solid feel of cylindrical packets of Pall Mall cigarettes, the delicious aesthetic of drops of ice-cold water running down the sides of bottles of still orange, the sitting in an air-conditioned bar every pay day simply because it was air-conditioned, and cold Tiger beer.

Some time after Bill Haley's 'Rock Around the Clock', a film that apparently required the Singapore police forming a cordon around the cinema to prevent teenagers 'rioting', real riots took place along with the increasing clamour for *merdeka* - freedom. In the early hours one morning an irate sergeant shook each of us awake and told us to get into waiting lorries which would take us to the city centre to quell the 'gangs of vicious thugs' breaking a recently imposed curfew and damaging property. We were to be given truncheons.

The word quickly spread through the darkened billet that conscripts couldn't be forced into this extra-curricular activity, and one by one most of us turned over and went to sleep again. Why would we want to hit over the head with sticks, polite, well-mannered and generally well-behaved citizens who wanted independence from imperialist rule?

Two days later, Taffy told me that a few of the airmen had gone, not with the intention of using their truncheons, but to see what was happening. One of them told him he thought he'd seen Buntah with a crowd of younger Malays, that he'd been shouting and yelling along with the others, holding a stick, and that the police had charged at them, digging their batons into them and hitting those they could get to across their heads. The observer had been ordered back on the truck and returned to camp, and had seen no more. I realised then that I hadn't seem Buntah for a while. I found a copy of the Straits Times soon after which mentioned that several rioters had been killed. The police were hardly mentioned.

For a few days the most significant thing about his absence seemed to be that we had to clean the place ourselves - someone tried to get a rota system in place, but it didn't work - and that we had to walk a hundred yards to take our washing to be done. Then an elderly Chinese woman came and silently took over Buntah's work

I was on duty when the signal came through for my demob. It was an operational immediate and my name was the last one on the passenger list. On the truck into Changi Airport I was sitting behind the tailboard staring at palms, the ubiquitous banana trees, roadside bars, one with a giant fake bottle of Tiger beer in its front garden, and crossing the road behind us was Buntah's boy turning to look at us. I'd forgotten about him. I stood up and waved He looked sad. He gave a little smile and a gesture of a wave back.

We arrived in England - returning in a civilian aircraft and although taking a different route, also taking four days - and found the hut we were given had no coal. It was November. We started breaking up the furniture for the fire. We weren't yobs, we were cold.

When those from London and points south were dropped off at Waterloo Station we said hurried goodbyes and then I was on an Underground train. Despite the strangeness, the feeling of not belonging - or perhaps because of it - I thought of Buntah; his silent, unexpected appearances, his walking past the foot of my bed swivelling his skinny legs, pumping his elbows, singing 'gonna rocking around clock...' his strangely patronising giggle when he thought I'd done something silly and the day before he disappeared, shouting at him when I found that while tidying my bed space for an inspection he'd thrown away a sketch of a sniper in a tree I'd taken nine hours to draw. He'd looked so hurt.

I wondered what was going to happen when I got home, what I would do for a living, Then, for the last time for a long while, I thought of Buntah again; mostly about his smiling testicular reference, 'You Johnny big bollock.'

ANTHROPOLOGY

He was a new client. James Kent didn't want to see a new client A few moments before he'd knocked on his front door, James, looking for a spare ignition key to leave in the tail pipe of his car for his mechanic to take for an MOT and save him calling and perhaps interrupting a patient's session, had found his mother's old watch. It had triggered a memory he'd buried for years; the moment he had been told she'd died.

He'd been in a local pie and mash shop he hadn't visited for some time, about to enjoy the thick liquor-splashed mash potatoes and the charred, but soft pastry of the minced meat pies, when his mobile rang and his bully boy cousin's voice was demanding he get his arse over there because his mother was dead.

When he'd arrived she was in the living room jammed awkwardly between skirting board and table, her eyes still and staring, with a smear of jam on her chin and a small plate neatly covering her dressing gowned breast. He'd asked to be left alone and knelt beside her, thumb and index finger gently closing her eyes.

His client was tall, thick-set upper body, pale blue eyes, dark hair and beard. He had a slight stoop and was, James thought, in his mid forties.

James smiled. 'Well, tell me things.'

'I don't... don't want to talk about myself. I know I'm here for that, of course, but... that little picture of Catherine Deneuve on your hall table; I'd sooner talk about movies or something, really. '

'So would I, perhaps we will sometime, but for now it's about you. I'm on your side.'

He thought how repetitive this phrase was when he met new clients; letting them know he wasn't a bogey man.

'You look,' said his client thoughtfully, 'although the sun's on the side of your face and it's a soft light, you look a bit... hard, too solid.'

'Too solid for whom?'

Perhaps, James thought, he saw authority when he looked at him, some form of hostile officialdom. His client squirmed on his chair. James offered him the couch. He refused.

'There's nothing that can hurt you... fall on you,' James said quietly, raising his eyebrows as he looked across at him.

'At breakfast this morning,' said his patient, 'I was looking at my piece of toast close up; there was a low light coming through the French window and the butter was like tiny, glistening hills.'

He was lost in the image for a second. A touch of nascent schizophrenia, mused James, then wondered whether he was acting this brief, dream-like intensity and, if so, why.

'I hope you're not a Freudian.'

'Why's that?'

'Well, he thought that sons who desired their mothers killed their fathers and ate them and, in redemption, forced themselves not to want there mothers, therefore not having to kill their fathers. From this, I read, came the idea of marrying out.'

'Yes, the first cultural event leading to civilisation, you might say, though he could have added that the sons were also frightened of being killed by each other. But why does it annoy you?'

James was wondering whether his new patient was implicitly pooh-poohing this view because there wasn't much evidence for early cannibalism and, like many, had delegated it to mere myth or, perhaps, there was something else. His client didn't answer.

'What I want to know is what you *feel,* what you're feeling now, and why you're here, anyway.'

There was a silence, a heavy one. It grew longer. James let it continue, trying not to guess what his client was thinking.

'I think I'll go now. I'll try again next time.'

James said nothing as he left; the running away might just crystallize his client's thoughts over the next week to help him face the reasons why he had come to a therapist.

Other than seeing patients, James spent the next week walking around Ealing and the Common, surrounded by its Edwardian and pastiche houses, and watching two films at the NFT with a friend. He even wrote a publishable poem, which he hadn't done for a while.

When his new patient came again James greeted him pleasantly.

'Do try to relax, Matthew, unless you want to begin by telling me why you've come again. We can talk of other things and leave that a while, but I would like to know before the next fifty minutes is over. That a deal?'

His client nodded. He said nothing for minutes then, with a look of annoyance, broke his silence.

'Coming here, there was a bag of rubbish in a passageway and on the pavement a sofa with clothes dumped on it. I saw a road sweeper walking by, told him about it and he held his phone out and took a picture of it. Why? Was he going to enter it for the Turner Prize? It was Asian stuff; but you can't say it because - '

'If it was, it was, liberalism can't homogenize us. There are whole movements of denial of things outside of current hegemonies; anything outside the moral universe of science, for example, was and still is seen as 'mistaken;' it's a way of dealing with unwanted - I'm sorry, you're here for some sort of help and I'm... Anyway, why does this 'rubbish' stuff, this rule breaking annoy you? Is it that somebody's getting away with something, and you never could as a child?'

His listener took a deep breath and was quiet, looking uncomfortably down. He looked up again, saying,

'Like you say, society tells you what's right and wrong, though there's nothing inherently wrong or even moral in anything, is there? We stick to rules even if breaking them isn't against the law.'

'Legal and illegal deviancy, Matthew.' James looked at his watch. 'Time's ticking by. We had a deal.'

Matthew nodded, looking down again. James thought back over the conversation: behavioural codes, society as a moral community, rules.

'Is there a rule you're frightened to break or,' he leant towards his patient like a chess player across a board, *'are* breaking?'

His client looked quickly at James, stood and said, 'I need to go.'

'You can stay, there's time left.'

'No.' He moved towards the door. 'I'll see you next week.'

As he opened the front door James reminded him that he hadn't kept to their bargain.

'Next time.' Matthew mumbled, hurrying away.

Before James closed the door he noticed a car waiting outside with a fair haired woman in the driver's seat staring straight ahead of her. His client got in. Without turning her head she drove away.

The next seven days were similar to the previous ones: the same friend, a film or two, patients: the only difference was that he went to a poetry reading. A friend, Jilly, had a dozen of her poems in an anthology and, under duress, he went to a Camden church and reluctantly tried to listen to her and other readers. There was a lectern but no mike, and little competence except for Jilly.

At the interval, sipping the inevitable white wine, watching mock smiles and fake handshakes and a well known wordsmith who hadn't read yet lassoed by a fawning ring of elderly women, he heard a voice he knew saying quietly somewhere behind him, 'Celebrity, the pursuit of the talentless by the mindless.'

As James turned, Matthew's eyes widened in recognition. He looked confused and a little apprehensive.

'Hello Mister Kent, I didn't know you were interested in poetry.'

'Why should you?' James asked disinterestedly, hiding his own surprise and not looking at his client. He was looking at the young woman with him; wraith-like, with slightly exopthalmic grey-green eyes which, despite their intensity, managed at the same time to look surprised. Her cheekbones were prominent in a pale, pinched face, the skin having a slight sheen as if perspiring. With her loosely permed fair hair and dark schoolgirl jumper she reminded James of a figure in a forties war poster. It was the woman in the car that Matthew had got into.

He knew from his training and own experience that he should excuse himself and move away from them - this was outside the secular confessional of the green walls and leather couch of his office. - but continued looking at her, and even while he smilingly acknowledged her his thoughts were arcing back to blonde Iris's skinny legs hopscotching on the pavement outside his East End childhood home and, spinning round, showing a glimpse of knickers. He remembered their colour.

'This is Sheila.' his client said tensely.

She slowly held out her hand. James briefly felt that if she'd offered it more enthusiastically it would have been too forthright, too aggressive for her. He gently touched it. He wanted to again. He nodded to Matthew, smiled at his companion and left.

For the next two days, in between listening to clients, James kept thinking of the girl; so much so that it began to annoy him. He knew he had a proneness to seductive images that were, often, meaningless pictures; filmic, theatrical, transient, but this time he kept seeing her face in the car; slightly in shadow, the still profile, unblinking eyes.

On the third day, almost as soon as he'd entered the office, his client went towards the window, looked out and remarked on James' kerbside car.

'It's red. Why did you pick that colour?' There were sly eyes and a subtle smirk.

'Are you going to say its phallic?'

He nodded.

'I think you'll find that a car, of whatever colour, represents the womb. Why do you think there's road rage? Because something, somebody, a sudden braking, a tail-back, has interrupted our warm, pleasantly suspended state.'

He vaguely thought that vehicle congestion perhaps left us waiting in the birth canal while we wanted to get out, get on, and wondered if his dislike of long, straight, terraced streets represented a bad birth canal experience. He stopped himself. This was indulgent; he was also, perhaps, sailing close to the historical residue argument that a brief case represents a cave man's club and a back pack a placenta.

'Just for the sake of it, is there any significance in the car you use being grey? In fact, you seem to wear grey a lot.'

'No, but I hate red.'

'Is it because it's, somehow, visceral?

He looked away, but not before showing a fleeting, apprehensive expression as if he'd realised how valid the question was.

'Incidentally, who's Sheila?'

His client looked around the room as if he was trapped. He stood. 'Could I have some water?'

James pointed to the kitchen and watched him through the louvred serving hatch fill a glass and drink it greedily.

'That's a nice kitchen.' he said, returning to the room, 'all green and white.'

James raised his eyebrows in a silent request for an answer.

'My sister.'

Matthew turned away, walked to the office door and said, 'I have to go now. I'll pay for the whole session'

James shrugged with mock indifference and as he saw him out, said, 'If you want me to help you, you really must tell me why you came to me.'

His back to him, his client nodded in agreement and left. James, however, wasn't overly concerned at the moment about this man; he'd had patients who'd left sessions much earlier and some who'd said far less.

When Matthew came again four days afterwards after ringing to see if he could bring his appointment forward he seemed more animated. He began by talking of his loathing of double standards - James quickly guessing that it was because he was full of them himself, or maybe a single deep, troubling one - and talked quite bitterly of those he'd encountered in his life. This was his theme for virtually the whole of the session with James remaining mostly silent, trying to pick up clues, signs of his troubles, but there were few.

Towards the end, James said, 'This is meeting number four, Matthew, it's about time you told me why you're here.'

He leant back, crossing a leg over a knee. 'I'm in a rather comfortable position; I'm in the warm, occasionally, as you've noticed, looking out on a cold, but sunny day, listening to your reasonably entertaining deflections, and I'm getting paid. But it's unsatisfying. Forgive my selfishness, but what would please me would be for you to keep your part in our little pact. What *is* it, Matthew?'

'I still can't... I will though. I have to leave it now.'

He pulled on a thick black overcoat and placed a grey scarf around his neck. There was a quietly stated, but deliberate retrospective in his choice of clothes.

'Maybe next time, Mister Kent.'

He left. Looking at his notes after he'd gone, James noted how much younger he was than he looked.

A few days later James was at 'The Basement,' a poetry venue in Covent Garden where his collection had been launched two years previously. He'd been asked to read by his publisher whose last event it was before selling the business which he'd started and kept flourishing for ten years. James had the last guest spot. There were almost fifty people there, leaving just a few empty chairs. As he settled on a sofa at the side of the mini stage, Matthew walked through the curtains at the bottom of the stairs. Huddled and tip-toeing he went towards the back of the room. As the curtains closed they were instantly opened again by his sister who stood for a second, turned her head towards the reading poet - a grey haired man with a black homburg hat and matching cape whose self-indulgent attempts to match sound effects to the narratives of his poems were increasingly annoying an impatient audience - then moved to join her brother. A nano-second before the surprise at seeing her James felt a frisson of excitement. He wondered if they were regulars here - he couldn't imagine a client coming especially to hear his analyst read.

Those who had put their names down for the open mike spots began to read; younger ones either full of bright eyed enthusiasm or an almost shaking shyness, and a couple of older hands who read as well as they crafted their work. At the interval James went upstairs for a glass of wine and to chat with a poet he knew from other venues he'd been. Whilst talking he occasionally glanced at the top of the stairs to see whether Sheila would appear. She didn't, neither did her brother.

Downstairs again and just before the compere ushered on more readers, he could see Matthew earnestly turning to his sister and gesturing towards the stage. Before James was scheduled to take the floor the MC asked if anyone else would like to read. Sheila reluctantly stood, brushed her hands down the sides of her thighs, walked quickly past the rows of seats, stood behind the mike and, holding a few sheets of paper close to her breast, began.

She looked taller under the lights and her voice was stronger than James had expected it to be, clear and, in certain passages from her work, lyrical. She didn't look at her poems much, just the occasional glance.

Speaking of metaphor moons, of cliffs, clouds and cormorants, she spiritualized salmon, eulogised larks, yet as her foot tapped to the meter, her groin subtly pushing forward, gyrating, she turned her sentimentalised, neo-Victorianism into the body, into skin and breath and touch, into the visceral just by her bodily movements. There was a contained waywardness about her, an almost disingenuous sexuality; the difference between the contents of her poems and her effect almost dichotomous.

The audience didn't clap between her poems as, sometimes reluctantly and politely, they had done with the other poets. They were quiet. She stepped from the stage and was halfway to her seat before the clapping began, louder and longer than for the previous readers. James looked again to where she was sitting, looking down and as if she'd shrunk inside of herself - though, for him, the way she sat, her knees resting against each other, hands in her lap, still holding her poems, her sensuality hadn't diminished.

It was his turn. His head was full of her, but he couldn't just stand behind the mike and mumble or, as he wanted to, run upstairs and have a lone coffee. He took a deep breath, vowed, as usual, to lose the glottal stoppage, and began.

He knew the poems that worked, where he'd get a laugh, a frown of interest, appreciative nods. He read his favourites: the boyhood ones, the New York, the Prague ones and his well-read surreal piss-take on over-figurative poets. He could just see her at the back of the room; she was still looking at her lap. When he finished he smiled his thanks and sat down, feeling disappointed, like an adolescent who'd tried to impress, had shown off to an attractive girl and who hadn't noticed. He forgot to make his intended short speech of thanks to Larry, his now ex-publisher, who was inviting everyone to join him upstairs for free drinks.

Trying not to look for Sheila, James followed the audience and, as he turned from the counter, wine in hand for Larry, he saw her through the glass entrance door with her brother. She was kissing him. They then walked off in opposite directions. James immediately felt jealous. And then he was being introduced to the new owner of 'Brittle Light,' a man with a pork pie hat who politely expressed a liking for James' work then watched its creator force himself to chat to Larry's artist wife and, soon afterwards, leave.

On the train home James scribbled a poem about her, or rather the images of her, although when he'd finished and remembered some of the lines from her work; the doves, blossom, sunsets, the lambs, he smiled at the ludicrous difference between what she'd actually read and the almost lustful, sensibility he'd picked up from her.

He was between Leytonstone and Wanstead stations when, like a zoom-in close-up, that last image of Matthew and his sister shone from a screen in his head and stayed there. For a brief second he saw his own mouth where Michael's was and as he did so knew why his client had come to him - or had made the gesture of doing so. His training to be aware of any projections of his own feelings, attitudes, desires on to his patients sobered him momentarily. But he knew he wasn't, and that their kiss was much more than sibling affection.

He managed to emotionally corset himself till he arrived home and let his feeling of abhorrence surface. He was aware that it was triggered by cultural experience, the breaking of a behavioural norm; though the strength of the emotion itself was innate. He wondered if it was because she was his patient's sister that so intrigued him, excited him; and knew that his repellence was driven further, deeper, because he wanted this woman, wanted to surround himself with her, with her mouth, hair, clothes, breasts, her carnality.

Opening his study window he took some deep breaths and thought about the incest taboo, something he hadn't needed to be interested in since university days. Although seemingly universal he knew it wasn't an absolute; there wasn't one. There had, he knew, been approved sexual relations between aunts and nephews, nieces and uncles in various clans, and, in some historical elites,' marriages between brother and sister, but... His habitual, almost obsessive desire for analysing himself and the world suddenly tired; he was too emotionally involved to intellectualise, to make it all so theoretical and dispiriting. Not for the first time did he wonder at the discordant gap between his intellect and his emotions.

Was he, as a patient once suggested, playing God? In the arbitrary mess of the human situation who was *he* to meddle in the compromise between an encultured self and an instinctual one in the egoistic battle between superego and id? And anyway, how could we understand the world except in the way we have, in its repressive obeyance, internalized it, the way it has impinged upon us, and then, in turn, that we see it through that process; another tautology. He thought of the simplicity of Shakespeare's 'There is nothing neither good nor bad, but thinking makes it so.'

He had an image of Sheila in the car, and thought he'd glimpsed a tiny six inch figure that looked like her dangling behind the windscreen which, to James, seemed to turn into a painted totem; a clan's symbol not only of belonging, but of the injunction against sexual relations with family members within it. It was as if Matthew was using the very object of denial to smash that denial and to shout, 'Fuck the totem.' But, of course, it wasn't a likeness of Sheila; it was probably just a swinging Barbie doll or air freshener or even a pair of woolly dice.

It was getting late. He made a supper then went to bed and lay thinking of her at the mike; her hair, the bright lipstick, which he'd hardly noticed before, the long dress, her confidence, the *isness* of her.

He got up after a few minutes and climbed into his loft. After some searching he found a framed print of a Victorian nude, at the edge of which was part of a boy's face gazing at her from behind a curtain. He brought it downstairs and put it on the wall under his watercolours, ready for Matthew in two days time.

James didn't really expect him to come. This was to be his fifth visit and so far he'd said nothing directly of what had prompted him to see an analyst. James was wrong. Seeming more huddled than usual his client smiled wanly as he entered and made his rather cumbersome way to the chair next to the sofa. It was a bright day, the sun lighting most of the opposite wall where James' watercolours were hung. Matthew noticed the print immediately and pointed out its incongruity. James was casual.

'Do you think he's a brother?'

Matthew looked at it for longer than was needed for an answer.

'Er, don't know.' He rubbed his hands forcefully together as if preparing to face inclement weather at the beginning of a journey.

'Look, I only really came here to say... it's okay. You've been patient, but I think it's better, really, if I get by on my own. I have to live in my own skin, don't I' He forced an embarrassingly fake grin.

James appeared to take no notice.

'Nothing to do with the painting then?' he enquired lazily. 'I mean, if it's his sister, well... pretty exciting, eh?'

His client reached a hand into a pocket and held out a folded cheque.

'This is for this session. And thanks, really.'

He seemed suddenly likeable. James didn't want to like him.

'So, you're going to tell me at last why you're with me. Yes?'

Matthew frowned. 'I just told you, I need to go.'

'You're not going. Not yet. You're going to listen to me and talk to me.'

His client stood still, face wooden.

'It's your sister, isn't it It's what you and she are doing. I wonder how long it's been happening. Is this the hypocrisy you don't like? Perhaps you wanted her as a boy, but couldn't, it wasn't right, was it. And all around you your mates were getting away with all sorts of things; stealing, bunking in the pictures' - the ever detached part of him hearing the language of his background - 'or whatever they were doing. But you couldn't have what *you* wanted, your sister, couldn't get away with it. You've made up for it now though, haven't you. Interesting that you talking of Freud in the context you did was one of the first things you spoke to me about.'

He realised his voice was getting louder, but as long as he could control it, and himself, he didn't mind He stopped for a few seconds.

'I know I should help you Matthew, but - '

'Then why don't you?' he asked quietly.

'Because... you should have told me before, and then - '

'You fancy her, don't you?' The voice was so quiet now James could hardly hear him.

'You want her for yourself.'

James immediately pushed the words away, he felt a panic. He knew he couldn't answer. It made him angrier.

His patient turned his head towards the window and looked out.

'The car again, Matthew? Don't like red do you? It's vagina, isn't it

112

It's blood, it's your sisters, it's Sheila's blood and you share it.' He could hear his voice filling the room. 'What have you been *doing?*'

James was almost snarling; he was no longer an analyst, he was a man whose professional training and experience may as well not have existed - at that moment it didn't. What did exist was ripping at him; his rage, and even while in it he felt a quick grip of envy for Matthew because he'd had the courage to do it, to break the normative bonds that tied him. But it was an awful courage, a warped, destructive one. He felt paralyzed; couldn't move his body, head, eyes which were staring at his patient's loose, wet lips. He shut them, turned himself away, swung around again. Matthew had moved back from him a little.

'How did it start then?' Smelling her knickers when she was a little girl?'

The knower in James knew instantly why he'd asked the question; to satisfy a pubescent child's curiosity. He'd never had a sister, hadn't known any little girls - or big ones till in his twenties. He stopped himself, searched his anger and knew it wasn't there just because she was Matthew's sister and that they both, like virtually everybody else in the developed world, had ingested the social imperative against incest, but who she was; Sheila; that strange, uneasy amalgam of modesty, confidence, diffidence, self-possession, sensuality…

Matthew sat down, looking at his hands clasped between his knees. James knew that he was, for Matthew, a shocked Dickensian Headmaster telling him off for being a dirty, nasty little boy, and to go and wash his mouth out. But, he didn't really want to know how long it had been happening, didn't wasn't to help his client work out the genesis of his behaviour. Without saying a word he forced himself to go to the bathroom, threw cold water over his face, his neck, half of his shirt - symbolically washing his own mouth out. He dried himself and returned to his office. It was empty.

He couldn't bear to sit in the room again. He went upstairs to his study and sat at the desk. He tried to calm himself. His patient had come to him for help, for guidance from someone who would understand why he was doing what he was, help him manage his corrosive guilt, gently ease him away from her with as little psychic damage as possible and, through the process, to help her, too. It was the first time he'd wondered about her role in this. Perhaps, in some secret way, she had a sort of happiness with him. Now, James was a damming society incarnate, ready to punish. And he felt embarrassed at how pathetic it had been to put the print up as a way of getting Matthew to talk about the relationship with his sister, as if it was a clever, cunning trick.

He got up, went to a bookshelf and brought back a copy of *Incest: A Textbook*. He forced himself not to laugh hysterically at the title, and felt his oppressive, inculcated professionalism diluting everything: his joys, interests, his life, diluting everything; his joys, interests, his life... He craved, in a storm of emotion, to look to the sky and shout, 'I *want* her!'

An image of twelve year old Gwen came back; her smiling shyly at him from across his childhood street, anaemic, fair skinned, pale. Was Sheila a grown-up version of Gwen? Then a short visual travel to his mother, and other textbook words he remembered theorising on the ultimate incest, the Oedipal, and at what stage of psychosexual development it began: *For Freud, it was the third stage - the phallic, ages 3 – 6....*

He had no recollection at all of desiring his mother. As a child he thought he'd noticed her slim legs and how nicely shaped her shoulders were, but those deep-set eyes and long nose made her look like... He wanted to pound his temples for thinking it, to be able to formulate the words. He tried to imagine a patient who would say to him, 'I never fancied mum, she wasn't attractive enough.' and what his reply would be. He couldn't think of one.

What he did remember was that he'd recently booked a short holiday in the Mediterranean, starting in three weeks. He was travelling on his own and staying for the first few days in Crete, then on to Athens, near where, he'd just realised, was Colonus, the supposed birthplace of Oedipus. Another Greek tragedy, he thought, was just what he needed.

The initial barrier against incest, with its emphasis on exogamy, may well have kick-started culture, civilisation. If so, then James Kent felt as if he was swimming in a primordial quagmire that long predated that event.

ARTISAN

He was making good a crack in the main bedroom ceiling. He'd prepared the rest of the apartment and after finishing the paintwork he would be hanging paper-backed silk to the walls. James Kent was back 'on the brush.'

It had been a few years since he and Trev, who he'd met soon after finishing an apprenticeship, had done sub-contract work together and even longer since working directly for a building firm - the last time had involved James lying on top of the furnace in a North London crematorium rolling the ceiling while the man sifting through still hot ashes found a melted gold tooth and ring which he'd casually pocketed. James had done the odd re-dec for friends as a favour, but most of his time, until very recently, had been filled with the business of being a psychotherapist.

It was part of his background he never mentioned to patients, thinking their perceptions of his competency would be compromised or that they wouldn't believe him. He'd found it relatively easy to deconstruct himself before university as a mature student, feeling there hadn't been much constructed anyway; never having been comfortable in childhood with his parent or his milieu. Perhaps this was the underlying drive for his late-chosen profession.

He hadn't wanted to return to decorating, but though his business had grown in the last few years until its present paucity of clients, he had never earned enough to save. He tried to give himself some rational reasons for going back. The money, obviously; he would earn more in this ten day job than in a month as a practitioner, and it would be good to be with Trev again and have some laughs - he remembered when they were on a site once adolescently rolling up putty into small balls and blowing them at each other through lengths of electrical conduit to alleviate the boredom of painting or spraying large areas of wall. He also recalled Trev saying to him, 'You don't see me much anymore 'cos I can't read.' His pal was illiterate and thus sharing the things that interested James was limited, though they had been close at one time. Working together again would, maybe, alleviate his guilt at hardly ever seeing his friend in recent years.

But though these reasons were relevant, none were more so than James having lately failed a client because he couldn't handle the knowledge of the man's incestuous relationship with his sister and, even more saliently, his own desire for this woman, he'd felt a need to absent himself from involvement with new patients. His three long term ones who he knew were never going to get well - had never *been* well - he would continue to see. Working as a tradesman again would be less emotionally draining; there'd be less … responsibility.

It was Trev who had got this small sub-contracting job in some luxury flats near the Ritz Hotel. The old skills returned immediately; this was 'West End' work, he was enjoying it, as he was the six-a-side kick-around in Green Park at lunch times with some builders working in the hotel. He wasn't as fast as he used to be - though considering himself just as tricky - but felt re-energised when he got back to the job and they top-coated three rooms with time to spare in their self-set targets.

Returning to the flats after the game a few days later he noticed, through the grimy window of the area basement, a figure with a woolly hat pulled low over his forehead staring out of the window. There was something rather grim and lost about him He could have been the caretaker. James disinterestedly guessed he wasn't.

He'd been home an hour when his phone rang. It was a call from an ex-patient whose voice he didn't at first recognise. When he did he remembered a self-doubting man whose intelligence and creativity James had worked hard to get him to recognise. He was now, apparently, a director of a large charity which, along with its other work, was currently looking into reasons for homelessness. He appeared to be one of James' few successes.

'What we were thinking of doing, Mister Kent, and we're obviously looking into economic determinants, was a kind of psychosocial study of homeless people, and I thought of you. You probably haven't time, but if you have we'll fund you and it's up to you, of course, how you carry it out.'

He remembered also that this particular patient would never call him by his first name. James thought it might be interesting He'd done a small, investigation into male victims of domestic abuse in his last year of psychiatric training and found it intriguing, other than the number crunching, but he wasn't sure about the idea just presented. An image of the man behind the window then clipped into his mind.

The request seemed to James to concretise his intuition about the man in the basement, it gave him a status: homeless, though he wasn't sure why he felt he fitted it. It wasn't just his appearance; crumpled jacket, old sweater, and unshaven, James, too had stubble, though a little more designed, but, if he was right, here was somebody on his doorstep, so to speak; he could talk to him, find out a few things. He told the caller he would consider doing a small pilot study.

'Fine. Thanks, Mister Kent. Confirm what you intend to do when you know.'

He felt unsure; the man may live in the block somewhere, could actually own the apartment they were just finishing, but if he was homeless how best to approach him? As James was a decorator working a few floors above him he may as well play that role, get friendly with him, show some sympathy. He had a fancy to see himself as a participant observer in an ethnographic study pretending to be without a home himself. He quickly deleted the whim.

The question seemed to be answered next day. James didn't have his kick around, he and Trev needing to finish hanging the silk in the hall to complete the flat so that they could clear their stuff for the furniture to be moved in. At lunchtime he made a quick trip to peer through the basement window, but there was no one inside, though he could see what looked like a pile of rags and clothes against a wall which could have been used as a bed.

Trev had invited James to have a meal with him and his wife at their home in Brentwood so he travelled back with him. At Stratford Station an untidy, unkempt man stepped into the carriage. James felt only a little surprise that it was, as he internally referred to him, the basement man.

He walked straight to the end of the carriage, turned and, holding out a cupped hand and looking straight into passengers eyes, began what seemed to be a well used patter,

'Spare twenty pence, guv? only twenty pence. Need a bit to get by. Just twenty pence, gotta 'ave a cuppa, an' I.'

He continued from the end to the front of the carriage repeating the same spiel, letting his offered hand stay open for about five seconds in front of each traveller and collecting, James reckoned, as well as his own quickly given 50p, about a pound. This could mean eight pounds per train for roughly thirty minutes work. It seemed to be a living of sorts, but what interested James was where he'd learnt his ritual; the steady gaze and the proffered, almost demanding hand, enacted perhaps daily, must have seemed like a long, bitter stretching of time. He said nothing to Trev.

They began the second flat next day and had finished half the paintwork by the evening. Though it was good to be with his old mate again, James had never told him what he'd actually done over the last few years; as far as Trev was concerned his friend was some sort of social worker. James made an excuse tor staying on and, when on his own, went down to the basement door and knocked. He waited a while then went outside and looked down into the window. There was a light on. James pushed some earth with his foot which fell and lightly brushed a pane. The man appeared and looked up. James smiled and gestured to him to pull the sash up. The man did so, frowning.

'Sorry to bother you, but we're working upstairs' - James had kept his paperhanging apron on - 'and I wondered if you had a pair of steps we could borrow. I assume you're the janitor?'

'No. No I'm not and I have no steps, I'm sorry.'

He closed the window abruptly and turned away. James hardly recognised the voice; gone were the 'guvs' and 'lady's,' the glottal stoppage, lack of 'h's' the 'London 'f's.' In their place was an accent of almost lazy elegance, allied to a very different personality. For a moment James imagined he had acted both personas, as if he were immersing himself in characters he was about to play on a stage.

Next day, after a brief game with the builders, James looked down at the window as he passed. The man was staring at the inside of it from two feet away as if he had an intense interest in the anatomy of the fly in its centre.

When James left in the evening - he was to finish the flat himself, Trev beginning another subcontract near his home - he could see basement man walking a few yards in front of him. James decided to follow him. It wasn't difficult, it was a sunny evening and there were enough people around to hide behind if necessary. His quarry got on a Tube train to Stratford, but this time went to an Overground train going westwards and repeated his patter through the length of the train. James buried his head in a newspaper. As intrigued as he was, the man was surely an atypical example; the voice he used when trawling trains was mimicking, perhaps, what he perceived as an accent of the destitute.

James got off, wearying a little of following someone when he could have been in a cosy café somewhere. Maybe it would be easier to talk to the men he'd seen lying around at Charing Cross Station or the one that seemed to be living at the rear of the National Theatre.

James worked hard and fast the next day, but leaving enough space in his psyche to decide to stick to basement man as his pre-study. Maybe he was being lazy, but better the devil you know. He finished what he intended to do and went downstairs and tried the basement door again.

He knocked twice, waiting a full minute between each one. As he turned away the door opened. The occupant was dishevelled, he looked strained and tired. James could see beyond him the rumple of old clothes and sheets of cardboard lying in a corner.

'Hello, I just wanted to see if you were okay.'

'Why?'

'Because you... didn't seem okay when I last saw you, I thought maybe I could - '

'Cheer me up?'

James, forcing himself not to be the therapist, the kind, thoughtful healer, didn't answer.

'Look, I'm having a rather awful day and - '

'Fancy a drink? I could do with a little company, I'm rather hungry, too.'

The man looked at him suspiciously.

'Alright. Hard graft is it, painting those apartments?'

He came out and closed the door. 'I'm Andrew.'

They shook hands. James knew a small café in a side street opposite. They sat; James told him the meal was on him.

'Do you work in the building? I did think you were a caretaker or service engineer or something.'

'But you don't now?'

'No.' James looked at him levelly. 'It's your business; you can tell me or don't tell me, or we can talk about football or maybe the theatre or something.'

Andrew finished his soup, wiped his mouth with a napkin.

'You've guessed then that I don't belong downstairs.' He emphasised the last word. 'You're quite right, of course.' he said, leaning back. 'I'm not your average janitor or your typical tramp, am I.'

They eat their dessert in silence. James watched him eat; it seemed to be the first decent meal he'd had in a while. He asked him how he got by.

'You pick up tips from the others; you wear layers of underwear when you can get it, it's warmer, always wear two pairs of socks, except in the summer, etcetera. You tend to gather, I suppose, where the others do. It's company, you know. I started like that, really.'

'Is it competitive, all seeking a finite resource?'

'No, it isn't really,' he looked a little uneasy, 'though I feel guilty using the basement on my own, but I don't think I could stay there if I bought anyone in with me. The places they, we, stay are pretty institutionalised, been there a while; you can find evidence; little nick-knacks, syringes, dog ends, tins of tobacco, all sorts. Could do a sort of contemporary, urban archaeological study, I suppose.'

He looked at James steadily for a while.

'Going to ask me why?'

'Yes. Or is it too painful? And how long?'

'Too long. You wouldn't know what it's like would you, to wake up so cold it's... the wind, it's so bitter.' He halted. 'You have to give so many damn details to get a job; your life story, NI number, your last job.'

'What was that, then?'

He looked aggressively at his questioner as if he'd never been asked the question before.

'I was stage manager at the Coliseum. As you've guessed, I'm not now.' His fists clenched. 'Do you know, some people don't believe anyone's homeless unless they see them lying in a gutter, you can tell it in their eyes.' He was getting angrier. 'What do they want me to do, then?'

He bent forward and rested the side of his face on the table. He looked up pitifully.

'Please think of the homeless. I've nothing, nobody. I need food, please.' He rolled his eyes imploringly. 'Please.' He sat up. 'I can't do that.'

James quietly asked him where he got his money from to get by.

'Well, it's certainly not from shares in Coca Cola.'

He drunk his coffee, used the napkin again.

'I get it from trains. I sometimes ask people on trains. D'you know, I though about volunteering for the Samaritans at one time?'

James casually enquired if he chose any particular line and what criteria he used, feeling embarrassingly coy as he did so.

'I often toss a coin. Mostly over ground, but the Tube in the late evenings when there's less people, but never in the early morning; nobody wants to give you anything then. You pick up things from the old hands as if it's a trade and you learn the tricks.' He bent his head briefly. 'It's hard.'

James looked around him. There was a girl looking impatiently at them and he realised that there were chairs stacked on the tables behind and that she was waiting to do theirs. He hadn't noticed.

They left and walked back to the flats. Andrew thanked him and asked him to have a drink, he'd saved a little wine from somewhere. James accepted. In a larger room than the one where Andrew slept, the block's boiler filling a third of it, there was a table with an opened bottle of wine in the centre, two doilies, a wilting vase of flower and three chairs. Andrew took a quick look around him.

'The caretaker's quite a nice guy. I look at the boiler from time to time, though I don't really know what I'm looking at, just keep things tidy, put rubbish in the bins, you know.'

As Andrew drank, James, unable to help himself, asked about his childhood. Staring into mid distance, he answered.

'I took it all for granted, of course. The money - dad earned most of it - the talented mum; privilege, I suppose you'd call it.' He was quiet, then, 'I got a third class Physics degree, it should have been a First or a Fail, either would have suited. I was too bright for them. Most of the lecturers didn't understand me; what I was arguing...

their syllogisms with undistributed middles, they'd never heard of Kuhn's paradigm shift, couldn't see that science is a self-contained conceptual system, a belief system that cannot of itself, be wrong, is no different to magic or religion.'

'Why did you do it?'

'Because my father fuckin' did. He and his team won an award from the Royal Society for working on, whatever it was, DNA stuff. He just went along with the research, there was money flung at it, he was conventional, predictable, no shattering insights from him, no breakthroughs, no… you can imagine how we got on, can't you.'

He'd been looking around him while speaking. Now he glanced at James.

'Once, when I was a boy, seeing our cleaner out - I liked her, there was something warm about her - and he probably thought I'd left the house, I heard him shout at my mother, 'Damn bloody boy!' and then a crash. I'd never heard him swear, or shout before. I was so scared. He'd smashed a teapot.'

He was silent for a while.

'I found some old coins the other day, they're mnemonics aren't they. It was their clinks, their whisky malts, the cigars, tips for the tradesmen. He tried to be a well met fellow, the firm handshake, fake laugh; a kind of honorary member of an imaginary club. I was in bed when he shouted, I was curled up, foetal. I ran out across the Heath, flung myself into the grass trying to push through the earth.' There were no tears, but James guessed he was crying internally.

'You're a good listener,' he smiled, 'you should've been a therapist.'

He took a deep breath. 'I used to paint, draw, I wanted to act, I don't know; but not a scientist. Positivism, rigidity, classification, that's what they do; quantify the qualitative to create an illusion of control, and it's engendered an academic and cultural ethos in which creative, intuitive intellectualism is penalised by grey people who think in straight lines and who can't comprehend any other form of mental activity.'

He went into the small kitchen and made coffee. James watched him; hurried, efficient, agile. He brought their coffee to the table, took a gulp, placed the cup back on a doily. He turned to James.

'Look, okay to call you 'Jimmy'? '

James had been called that by only one person; a favourite aunt who'd insisted on using that name till the day she died. Even Trev didn't use it. He nodded acceptance.

Andrew took a deep breath. 'Well, Jimmy. I've got a conviction. It was a child. You may have heard the theories; neuro-science says that where the wiring in the brain is that creates feelings of protection and caring when looking at a child, for people like me there's desire. This wiring analogy's such baloney. But it means, of course that it's not my fault, doesn't it, it absolves me. But, it *was* my fault'

He was suddenly restless, put his hands to the sides of his head, then on top of his knees, then to his head again. James thought he would cry.

'The word paedophile comes from the Greek meaning friendly love for or friendship with a child. I loved my brother's girl, my niece. I stroked her hair, it wasn't really sexual, it was... I kissed her gently, always gently. I touched her a little bit, she was... I *loved* her.'

He'd begun to shout. He looked around him almost wildly, then calmed.

'You're shocked. Yes?'

James wasn't; his professional understanding was invariably at the ready, primed for the attempted objective response, but knew that if he voiced it, it would be met with suspicion - the manual worker stereotype again; 'what's a bloke like you doing talking about psychology?'

'You must have seen a psychiatrist or somebody, surely.'

'No. My family didn't want me to see one. They didn't want to think' - he mimicked again - 'Oh, poor Andrew, it was some sort of abnormal condition, it wasn't his fault.' They wanted me put away, they wanted to blame me. Somehow they made sure I wasn't diagnosed, treated; I don't know how. I think if anybody attempted to help me, they'd stop them somehow. My father's cruel. They're nasty people.'

'Is there nobody in your family who's willing to help you?'

'What do you think, after what I did? I'd just got married. Can you imagine what happened *then*?' It was the rhetoric of anger. 'I have nothing. I haven't a home, I don't even know whether my wife - ex wife - knows I'm out. My parents do, they must know. They don't want to see me, they have no son. I have no - '

He put his head in his hands again. He was crying now. And even then, James couldn't help but take a second's absence from what he felt to wonder if this gesture of anguish was the only symbolic absolute, the universal symbol of pity. He reached across the table and squeezed the man's arm. Andrew nodded silently. James pulled away.

Andrew suddenly stood. 'I think you should leave me alone now. I'm sorry. Thanks for listening, though I'm not sure why I told you.'

As he opened the basement door he bent to pick up an envelope he'd stepped on. He frowned. 'Probably from Bill the caretaker, he's the only one who knows my address.'

James thought he saw the name on the envelope, 'Cummings.' He stepped out.

'Thanks again,' said Andrew, and closed the door.

As James walked up the stairs and out through the thirties swing door the name on the letter seemed branded on the inside of his forehead. He couldn't remember where he'd seen it, heard it. Going down the escalator into Green Park Station, he did.

A recent client who his old mentor Thomas had referred to him, because he was busy and James wasn't, was the father of a girl who had been molested some years before. He'd been increasingly worried about her silences, mood swings, nightmares. He'd brought her to him just the once. Despite the occasional gentle promptings from her father she'd said nothing for the whole session. He didn't bring her again. Her name was Edna, Edna Cummings It was possible it was coincidence, though knowing the probability of two individuals sharing a birthday exceeds fifty percent with a group of only twenty one, it possibly wasn't.

It seemed, then, he knew both victim and perpetrator. He didn't want to face that; the conflict, the strain of trying to detach from this man's actions and the consequences of them, and attempting a thoughtful and even empathetic understanding of them. He wasn't a patient; James had talked with him to find out about a too common social situation he'd been asked to investigate. He'd just happened to be the one he came across.

He thought about Andrew's relationship with his father, it seemed something of a classic: the pressure to pursue the career he himself had chosen, to be like him, but he'd said little of his 'talented' mother, she was in the background. He'd probably got his artistic characteristics from her, though it was, perhaps, an ideologically fractious household with a science-art split and... James couldn't stop himself, didn't know how else to think. He couldn't remember a time when he didn't think like this; analysing, attempting to understand, to grasp meanings, origins. How could he do anything else? Using his craftsmanship, his hand knowledge, had been a welcome change, but it was familiar, easy, there was nothing... worthwhile.

He leant against his office window; he didn't want to sit. He looked at his couch. Someone like Andrew should be occupying it, but it was all too close to his last case. He couldn't see this man anymore, and, of course, didn't have to; he'd finish the flat in two days and be gone. He could help him indirectly by giving him the number of a colleague, a tougher man than James, one who dealt almost exclusively in cases like this, in destructive, familial horror. He would, of course, be warned of Andrew's potentially hostile family, though without money available for any fee it was hypothetical.

And James wasn't sure whether he really wanted to rummage around in the psycho-social reasons for the non-scheduled status passage of homelessness. He felt he could give himself to neither the academic part nor trying, somehow, to marginally ease the situation of the people he may meet. What he was sure of was that the decision on his career was pressing heavily, its priority smothering him.

He questioned himself on whether he was only in it for the satisfying thrill of getting it right or confirming his doubt about an established psychological theory - albeit in a vulgarised inductive way - or even the feeling of a kind of creative fulfilment when patients improved. He questioned whether he *really* cared about his patients' pain - acknowledging he cared more about some than others: the woman whose husband had been missing for fifteen years and was in emotional limbo, but too frail to face the fact that he wouldn't return, and the young boy with the stammer and his own frustration at not getting to its cause.

His thinking left him vacuous; meeting Andrew had done nothing to make any inroads into James' feelings about returning to his job, perhaps even the reverse. He thought longer and harder, trying for something definite and perhaps for all time.

Should he advertise once more, get the friend who'd designed his website to put it up again, maybe create a fresh one, a sparkling new automagic'd, wash-your-hands-of-the-past-and-start-again bit of marketing luminescence or should he, perhaps, make a final decision and contact the British Psychotherapy Association and ask them to delete his name from their Register? He reached for his phone.

FRACTURE

'You look like Daniel Craig,' she said, dropping potatoes onto her plate. She glittered a frank look at him and grinned. 'Well, maybe his older brother.'

Walking into the refectory, he'd seen at the counter a tall, pale, dark haired woman with large black eyes, full lips and, though only afterwards did he articulate it, a vulnerable exoticism.

'Hi, you don't know me, but I'm Mister Right,' he said casually, with what he hoped was a trifling amusement playing around his mouth. As ever, the internal split between the 'I' and the 'me' was active, knowing instantly the impression he was, or thought he was, creating. He asked her what she was doing here. She told him she'd just begun a counselling course.

Putting a coffee on her tray she looked at him candidly and said,

'You're forty five.'

He paused - silence is assent. 'And you are thirty one.' he said.

'How d'you *know* that?' she asked with a delight that was almost childlike; an expression, an attitude he came to know well and was constantly affected by and nearly always with an undertow of sadness. He let her think, as he supposed she still did, that this ageing Bond was fourteen years older than her instead of the twenty four he actually was.

She asked him where he was sitting and he nodded towards the table just inside the door where a student was waiting for him. He wanted to finish his rant against the pernicious *weltenshaung* of political correctness he'd begun as they left the classroom. One of the bonuses of lecturing to mature students was that they tended to listen to lecturers both inside and outside of class. He was up to '...is the most fascistic and repressive form of ideological, social, linguistic and economic control since Stalin. It engenders fear, distorts reality, forfeits fact.'

They left the counter, she asked him his name. 'Tim,' he said; hers was Mercia. The canteen was filling. She sat down with her meal and occasionally glanced across to him. His companion didn't seem to notice. He'd taken her that morning to a local social care office

127

where she was prescribed methadone to help her come off heroin. She lived on her own in a banjo shaped cul-de-sac in the mean maze of an East London council estate and was getting through his political science course with more help from him than he should have given.

He talked to her half-heartedly. Usually, in spite of twelve years of teaching, he tended to proselytize as much outside of timetabled hours as within them, but he was distracted.

He kept looking at Mercia's table, some admin. staff were sitting there, a man grinned at her, she smiled back. He felt jealousy; it was quite strong, thus blanketing his ability to instantly analyse it.

Having a class, he left before her. She glanced up at him, He shrugged, smiled, noticed his student frowning at her as he closed the door.

It had been many years since he'd had a relationship with someone he wasn't teaching, though there always seemed to be some kind of offers from female students to lecturers. He'd been a virgin till he was twenty six. If he hadn't had a need for what he felt he'd missed, or had been more cleverly disingenuous, perhaps he'd have still been married.

When young, he'd wondered what on earth, or in bed, it was really like and sated himself on mind flicks of skinny Iris at number twelve or the silken, misty space inside the thighs of principal boys his dad took him to see at Lyceum pantos, and since then a host of encounters; like ginger Evelyn with the twin sister he'd wanted more, and his mistake of getting drunk and telling them both how he felt.

And Tina from Ghana, who'd made it to the local university, with her two a.m. calls about clinical psychology, dragging him from pumping gyms to thumping night clubs and, when drunk, screeching that he should go back to his 'own colour,' her ex-lover once following him to work and hanging about the foyer for an hour. And there was Charity, a Gambian who had been sexually abused by the ubiquitous uncle.

Next day in the canteen he saw her again. They sat down together where she told him about her course with wide, enthusiastic eyes. The place was almost empty, yet this particular table was psychologically owned by the Humanities Department, the staff of which sat down noisily around them. He could really only play the supportive teacher role, encouraging, informing, smiling, but scrawled a note on a napkin as she got up to leave, asking her if she'd like a drink one evening.

She rang the college the same afternoon to tell him that she had a ten-year old son with hydrocephalus who she lived for and didn't want to worry about or hurt someone else, and was nervous about a teacher-student relationship. He liked her for saying the last. Some mature female students, if they fancied a lecturer, often overtly showed it, sometimes bragging to classmates if they'd been successful. He had never made an approach to one of his own students.

'I think we should start off as friends,' she said, in a rather prim, sensible way.

He took a call from her the day after in the small lecturers union office in the corner of the staff room that he soon came to monopolise - playing the 'who's going to put the phone down first' game with her that, in retrospect, always seemed pleasantly juvenile. She gave him a potted history of herself.

Born and raised in St. Lucia with two sisters and two brothers she'd spent a lot of time as a child sitting outside her father's bar acquainting herself with masculine cursing. She and her siblings were part Norwegian, French, and Carob Indian, whose maternal great grandfather had owned slaves on his sugar plantation, a portion of which was occupied by a large house built by the married eldest sister. When Mercia had visited her siblings recently she had been spat at. The Sanliquot name was not popular amongst indigenous Islanders.

At nineteen she'd married a St Lucian who she met in England and who had returned to the Caribbean shortly after their son had been born. Tim asked what her first memories of England were. She told him how excited she'd been on a school trip as a newly-arrived twelve year old when informed they were going to the sea, and then seeing that flat grey line for the first time and crying with disappointment.

He asked her why she hadn't returned home with her husband.

'He would have treated me as a Caribbean wife.' she said. She was quiet for a while, then, 'I used to lie next to him for months knowing he was seeing other women, but couldn't break free. It was like a chick wanting to get out of an egg and then when it has can only lay beside the broken shell, for comfort, reassurance.'

She was in her bath eating an ice cream when he rang her that evening. Laughing, she asked if he'd like her to eat it or do other things with it. He began to suggest something, then, as if remembering her mother's behavioural instructions to her as she reached puberty regarding relationships with males, said, 'Oh, I'm propositioning you, aren't I.' He could see a long leg raised, ice cream balanced on the knee, widened eyes, slightly pouting lips.

She told him about her course; the Rogerian approach to clients, its emphasis on 'the now' and, so far, no Freud, and about Dan, who ran it, calling her 'My dear lady' as if he was about to kiss her hand, and who would tell the students they shared that political science wasn't a 'proper subject' but not to tell 'the tall guy,' meaning Tim, who imagined Dan's eternal bow tie spinning as he said it, like a music hall comedian.

It was Easter; he was decorating his flat, Mercia was at the hospital where her boy was having his annual tests for his medical condition, and they spoke only briefly. He then rang to ask her to come out with him. She insisted they mustn't be back late, her younger sister would baby sit.

As he arrived outside a Victorian terraced house she was leaning against a large Citroen talking with a slight, Afro Caribbean girl. He could hear their animated patois as he parked and which continued as he got out and stood quietly next to them, feeling excluded.

In a local bar she told him that she didn't feel she was attractive. He told her how ludicrous her statement was.

He wanted her advice on some curtain material. She went back with him, disagreed with his choice of cloth, admired the Egyptian mural he'd painted on a living room wall and said she had to go. As he braked outside her home she said rather archly 'I don't think the evening finished as you'd have preferred it.' Again the slight arrogance, and the vulnerability.

She said things that evening which she would occasionally repeat; that she didn't know much about him, that he intrigued her, that he touched people with his eyes, that he was passionate, and how two people in a relationship should become part of each other. She wanted someone to understand her needs without stating them - she was like a demanding child, she would have loved him to tell her that her command was his wish - and that people saw her as 'a prize vase that was unobtainable.'

In the coming months she would enjoy smugly quoting her favourite brother's opinion that she was an 'ice maiden.'

Phoning him the following day she told him she'd been thinking of him most of the night. But, there was a caveat.

'I'm warning you. You'll fall in love with me. I don't want you to for your sake.' He believed her, didn't recognise it as projection, a defence. This was, of course, precisely when he fell in love with her. He felt the fear, familiar, yet new. We tend not to remember past pain clearly.

'I've always been a sex object to men since I've been on my own,' she said. He could almost see the smiling satisfaction.

Calling him next day she announced firmly that she was 'self sufficient' and repeatedly asked if he'd been thinking of her. 'I just know you have,' she preened. He pictured her with chin raised, lashes lowered, could feel the adolescent narcissism.

A week and many phone conversations later she asked him to her home. He met her son, Julius, was naively surprised at how dark-skinned he was. He was well built, tall, handsome, and with a shy smile. He had just finished a lesson with his tutor who, complete with tweed jacket, elbow patches and old world courtesy, was saying goodbye to his mother. It was obvious he fancied her, most men appeared to. She would say to Tim with a big grin,

'I was shopping today and two men looked round at me and stared, then looked at each other and said, 'Fucking *Hell!*''

She was familiar with using men to get what she wanted, once demonstrating in Tim's garden how she'd got a mechanic to top up her car radiator. Crossing her hands above her breasts, heels raised together, legs looking even longer, eyes wide, she simpered,

'Me? Oh, I don't know how to do things like *that*. Couldn't you do it for me?' Then a plaintiff, 'Please?'

She'd come to him that day for help with her college work. He'd gritted his teeth at the statistics-based research she had to comment on, but was happy to help with her mild dyslexia. She left, telling him she'd been fantasising about them in an art gallery, hands in the back pockets of each other's jeans, laughing, sharing, oblivious to people and paintings, then almost instantly turning around and saying, before getting into her car, 'I don't want to see you for a while. I can't do my work with you in the same building.' Next day she rang and said she'd started waiting by the phone, missing his voice.

She went on work placement for a week and he didn't see her, but she rang constantly. 'It would be fantastic to make love,' she'd say, 'but you'd want more, want commitment, and I couldn't give it.' And, without it feeling at all hackneyed, 'You are my soul.' Next time it was, 'I don't want to share you with anyone, wherever I am I want you to be there,' and, 'This is too intense, I'm so scared, I keep wanting to tell you I won't see you again,' and, 'I'm unhappy when I'm not with you, I can't breathe.'

Calling him in the early hours, she said, 'I don't want to put you on the list of people I've hurt.' Then, with exaggerated huskiness, 'Make love to me gently tonight, tell me what to do.' He did, as if she was in his bed or he in hers. These calls went on. She appeared to be playing at it all, wishing it was real.

Wanting some photos of her he arranged a session with the college photography lecturer. He watched from an unobtrusive distance, not wanting to distract her. She posed easily, sexily, There was something in her posing; her clothes, the slightly dated glamour that reminded him of the front covers of Picture Post he'd read as a teenager. The photographer asked her if she would pose for the students. She refused.

She told him she would come into his class one day and kiss him. She did. As she left the room he said flippantly to sixteen surprised students that although she'd said she'd do it, he never believed her. A moment later one of the admin. staff pushed the classroom door further open and with a concerned voice told him that a young woman was just down the corridor looking distressed. Mercia had heard him. He left the class, apologised to her, and told her to wait in her car for him. He'd never seen her look so hurt.

One evening she came unarranged, insisting she undress in the spare room. He lay on his bed. Half prancing, half mincing, she Marks and Spencered into the bedroom, pale skin, pink lacy underwear, hands on waist, wetting her lips, as if saying,

'Look at me, what a prize, and it's for you!'

He told her to relax, take her time.

'But, I want to *please* you, tell me what I have to *do.*'

But, he couldn't do it, couldn't penetrate her. Her shiny-eyed, demanding eagerness to please elicited merely a tense exhaustion. Briskly dressing, she said, 'I'm disappointed,' and after a pause, 'It doesn't matter, it won't affect our relationship.'

Then, when he'd failed to make love to her again, it was, 'I feel cheated. Why can't I arouse you? You'd do it with a one-night stand, why not me? Am I too prudish, too young for you? I don't want to lose you. I'm so jealous.' She cried, stopped, then, her voice rising, 'If you don't break your brick walls I'll run away and hide behind mine.'

They had sex, of course, but not the final giving, the resolution of love, of lust. Then, after some weeks, he suggested they go away for a weekend. He rented a cottage in Norfolk, her sister looked after Julius. It was small, thatched, with a rose covered porch.

She didn't think it would ever happen, but it did. He'd told her with half-joking bravado before they came that she wouldn't be able to keep up with him and as the East Anglia dawn lightened the curtains after their first night together, she'd whispered,

'Okay, you win, you win.'

They went to a nearby pub, she announcing that she would love to walk into a place where every man's eyes would be on her. As they entered, every woman's eyes were, too.

One afternoon during the following week, and smoothing her love-tumbled hair as she got dressed in the front room of the flat, she said,

'It's too much, it's all too soon. I haven't been with anyone for seven years. When I sit with you while you correct my work, it's like sitting on a volcano. I can never give a man love. I have to protect myself, wrap my child around me.' .

He felt at times as if he was struggling with her to keep any rationality, any semblance of emotional intelligence. As when he'd taken her to Brighton to meet his son who was playing trumpet in a band that played Brazilian street music. She saw his son step out of the group to put an arm around a girl walking alongside and then shortly afterward, marking time till a fellow band member came level with him, and kissing her affectionately. 'I don't like the way he treats women,' she'd said, and wouldn't speak to Tim on the train back to London as if his son's behaviour, whatever it signified to her, was either a genetic trait or learnt and was his father's fault anyway.

And when she said, rather angrily, 'I've been looking for someone to understand me since a child and now I've found you, and you live in a cocoon,' He hadn't the strength to answer. Nor had he when, a few days after first meeting her, she'd said matter-of-factly, 'You live in your head, you surprise me.'

She moved house a week after this, not giving him the address, and a few days later rang to say that she would always be grateful to him for helping her.

'Forget you ever met me,' she said, in that imperious tone she faked so unconvincingly. And then told him that she was thinking of fostering a child and that a care visitor may wish to see him for a reference.

'Don't tell her that I'm the bitch that broke your heart.' she said.

A month ago, and four years after first meeting her, he was leaning back against a pavement barrier outside the local train station waiting for friends to see a football match, when she appeared suddenly in front of him, seeming taller than ever.

She had a low cut top, her skin the colour of honey. She'd been to St. Lucia. He asked her casually if she was shopping in the nearby market and whether she was a counsellor yet. She was a drug abuse team leader now, she told him, barely concealing her pride. She seemed restless, said she had to go.

For the briefest moment as she turned to leave there was hurt and resigned sadness in her eyes. Then her younger sister, who he hadn't noticed was with her, said impatiently and in parody,

'Come on, let's see 'im indoors, Dan, Dan, the teacher man.' Her voice trailed away.

Who was 'Dan,' her psychology lecturer? Wasn't it a Daniel who used to teach Julius? Was she living with one of them? Then her sister was standing directly in front of him, small, thin, looking up with baleful eyes.

'Julius is dead.' she said quietly. 'He died.'

She scampered away. He looked at her back, above her head, could just see Mercia further on, peering closely into a shop window with a characteristic frown.

What had happened? Had Julius's shunt failed? Had...

His friends came laughing out of the station. He walked with them down the slight hill. Pictures, images, that had been lying still, whirled around, released: her trying on tailor-made dresses in her bedroom, the small waist he could almost get his hands around, the full hips, posing in the solipsistic mirror, back arched, looking at every inch of herself; she, in a department store, disappearing, and him, unguarded, panicking, intellectually knowing that it was the child in him being left by mummy - no emotions are new; her phoning him from a shoe shop, tears in her voice, saying that they wouldn't give back her money for a pair of shoes that had broken after a week and, in frustration, tipping a rack over, cascading footwear over the floor; during the college fire drill, wearing a black cape in the quadrangle slightly apart from her new classmates, looking for him, head high, as if uncaring, and him not walking the few yards to her, not knowing why.

And the whole litany of contradictions: the need, the almost fierce independence, arrogance, possessiveness, wanting to give herself, then vanishing into her keep, peering at him through its tiny window; telling him that when they first met me she saw so much sadness behind his eyes she had to turn away. And saying almost disinterestedly as she passed him in a corridor outside the art room,

'Pull me back if I walk away.' He never did.

And he didn't move towards her now, couldn't see her, so many shops, doors, market stalls, people.

He walked along, his pals hopping into the kerb and back again to give themselves room in the crowds, smelt the sharp sweetness of chips and vinegar and the musky cloud of cheap corn oil. He felt for a nanosecond the prick of a tear, then the detachment, the intellectualising, chopping into him like the rigid hands of a masseur on the back of a client.

He silently named the type faces on the shop fascias, observed, as ever, the unnecessary apostrophes, the pvc windows aesthetically corrupting Edwardian houses in a side street, wondered why the mock castles at the sides of the main entrance to the stadium were painted cream, as if Mickey Mouse was going to skip out of this tiny Disneyland and give every fan a hug.

A last image got through; Mercia in St Lucia after being spat upon, head held back at a slight, proud angle, looking defiantly down at the perpetrator, not bothering to wipe the spittle off.

Then he was looking at his match ticket, reading every little word and number on it, noticing the police and behind them a yellow tape, thinking - and wanting to laugh hysterically - that it said *polite notice* and *do not be cross*.

CAFES

James Alan Kent was sitting amongst the white loom chairs and tiffany lamps of the Island Café watching a waitress outside carrying rubbish, appearing and disappearing like a Morse code as she passed the side windows. He was childishly hoping she was Polish because he knew a few words of the language learnt from other waitresses in other cafes. Sometimes he tried to imagine their previous lives. Perhaps the one who had his attention used to twirl *en point* around tables in *Cafe Bleu* placing a cup, a croissant mid step, maybe the girl, plate-stacked in *Paulo's* and curtsying the kitchen door, had once dropped fries and sunnyside eggs in front of a cop on 2nd and Main, and the one he'd seen yesterday had ate a horse hoof in Chechnya to stay alive or fled a looted Kabul window and bloodied apron. Sometimes he saw them as legions of mothers offering surrogate suckling and, continuing to dramatise them as a shaft of sun came through the windows, sensed them surrounding him, smiling as he crossed the road to Fellicci's and more mothers, lovers... He watched the boss at the entrance twisting his shoe on a fag end and then concentrated on his clients' notes which, rather unprofessionally, he occasionally brought with him.

James liked this place, partly because of the variety of baguettes, but mostly for its Art Deco feel. The period represented his first glimpse of a world outside the huddled Victorian terraces of his childhood where he'd read detective picture books showing cocktail cabinets and Lalique glass while their real life counterparts lived in his aunt's suntrap windowed house near Hornchurch aerodrome. He could see her sunray gate, rockery, the front door's leaded glass yacht and, inside, the zigzag wallpaper and feeling a 'don't ask, don't get' nudge from his mother as he swallowed dry cake from a Clarice Cliff plate.

He decided he was allowing himself to think like this because he was in a kind of emotional convalescence. Recently he'd felt forced to make a decision on whether to continue his psychotherapy practice or try something else; knowing deep down that there *was* nothing else. There hadn't, in effect, been a choice.

He had just finished a teaching observation in an ancient office block near London Bridge for a friend and colleague who had set up a counselling school and wanted help from an experienced practitioner he could trust.

'It doesn't really matter about your relative lack of teaching, James, you can tell very soon if someone has a rapport with pupils; it's knowledge and experience that interest me.'

After returning and observing two more classes, the first ineptly taught by a behavioural cognitive therapist, he sat for a while in a room that his friend grandly called a refectory. A woman carrying a tray passed his table, stopped and turned towards him.

'You sat in on a class earlier didn't you? I was in it. I used to do observations.'

He asked if she was going to join the students at the other table and if not perhaps she'd sit with him. She did. She had grey-blue eyes, wide cheekbones, dark brown hair and told him she taught maths in a nearby college and was now doing the counselling course. At first he didn't recognize the accent then noted the slight stress on penultimate syllables and the often hard, trilling 'r'. He took a chance and said with mock seriousness,

'Falsetto: Italian dentures.'

She frowned for a second then gave a toothy, attractive grin and said, 'Polynesia: parrot with memory loss.'

He enjoyed playing around with definitions and it was instantly pleasing to find someone to share with. He asked her when she'd first come to the UK.

'When I was twelve. My father was a clinician in Rome.

'Your eye colour suggests Northern Italy.'

'He's from Turin. It's not all drudgery is it; I've had fun listening to teachers. I've watched pedagogic plumbers, beauticians - 'I teach nails.' I imagined rows of tacks sitting upright on their chairs - optometrists prattling on about pupils' pupils and a Sidcup scientist foretelling a microbial apocalypse.'

'What's the most bizarre thing you've observed?'

'A life-sized Barbie with a worn left breast getting the kiss-of-life from trainee paramedics in a flat-tyred ambulance behind a swimming baths'

She gave him that grin again. 'I know I've only just sat down, but...'

138

She shrugged and, standing up, said, 'Nice to meet you,' and went across to sit with the others. One of them had a leg across a seat. It belonged to the waitress from the café.

Instead of going to the tiny staff room he began writing a report on the lecturers he'd just seen while his impressions were still fresh. He looked over to the table. The dozen or so students were getting up, their chatter bright and fast as they picked up bags and books and turned towards the door, reminding him of the excitement and camaraderie of his own university experience.

After another observation next day and sitting in the café looking at his patients notes - one of whom James felt could benefit from hypnosis, jotting down a colleague's name to contact as he didn't perform this process himself - he saw the girl from the college clearing a table. She recognised him. He told her why he was at the school and asked how long she'd been waitressing.

'A few months, I'm trying to get by without a grant'

There was, for James, something about the way she worked, the brisk and curvy competence, the slightly plump upper arms, the full face with tied-back hair that interested him. She had a slightly working class accent reminiscent of his homely, attractive aunts that used to visit his mother.

He asked about her job. She shrugged, 'It's a source of income; you meet people.' She wiped a table. 'Although some of the people I meet are not worth meeting; the language, the way they eat. And they try to hit on me sometimes. I get tired of it. I dunno why they do.'

'Because you're attractive?'

'I don't think I am.'

The encouraging therapist kicked in. 'But you are.'

She shrugged. 'If you say so.' and with a pleasant, but fake smile, greeted another customer. He was about to leave when she gestured for him to stay. She went into the kitchen and returned wearing her non-work clothes.

'I assume you're a counsellor.'

'I guess my title subsumes that, yes.'

'I've just started. I did psychology and was hooked, though I'm sure the practice is different.'

James had one more class to observe and suggested that if she was going that way she walk with him.

She was. As they walked she asked him about his practice, genuinely interested in his variety of patients and was reasonably cognisant of current theory, but not of Freud, Fechner and others who'd created the foundations of what he did. He turned towards the steps of the college. She didn't.

'I'm going on. Bye.'

He briefly watched her walk away; the purposeful stride, plump rear. For James, female meant tall and slim - he was vaguely aware that it was, maybe, because he was frightened of 'buxom,' a woman that was... real. It hadn't really occurred to him before. He thought of what he might say to a client who felt similarly; it was a frail ego's fear of giving itself, of trusting it to someone who was tangible, solid - but then, that could be translated into 'mother,' what the baby in every man wanted. The contradictions, James knew, would mount.

He didn't see the woman from the refectory until he stood at the back of a full classroom. She was standing by the inside of the door and frowning at the lecturer who was looking around at her students and smiling as if projecting a healing beam onto them. She delivered her lesson quietly, its content as thin as her voice. He was tempted to wait until the students had left and tell her what he thought, but his brief was merely to note it for the colleague who was paying him.

He was the last to leave. The refectory woman was leaning against the corridor wall waiting for him. She shook her head.

'As you may guess, I learnt little in there; we could compare notes about her somnambulistic performance, but... ' She shrugged, 'I'm merely a student here.'

She and the situation suddenly attracted him; her mature playfulness, the walking away from a classroom with a woman carrying books under her arm as if he was an undergraduate again.

'Look, forget this. Let's have a coffee or something,' He smiled at himself. 'I can't resist saying this, but like countless other men at this moment I'm playing a kind of 'hide the id' game. Almost unconsciously, my ego needs to satisfy the demands of the id, but, aware of the constraints imposed by the super-ego, suggests the compromise of meeting in the socially approved environment of a bar or coffee shop.'

She smiled. 'Unconsciously?'

'Come out with me. I don't even know your name.'

She considered the offer for a while.

'It'll have to be tomorrow. And it's Annarita.'

She moved quickly down the stairs and out of sight. He went to the staffroom and looked out the window; down below he could see her and the waitress crossing the road, laughing, animated.

The next day he was wanted neither by the college nor any of his clients. He went to Goldhawk Road, wandered around Brackenbury village and went into its Victorian bakery and coffee shop. He sat there watching an old man with headphones sitting outside concaving his yellowed cheeks dragging on a cigarette. He was reminded of his late brother who he had got to stop smoking, but too late. He thought again of their London walks. The next one, chosen by Stan, would have followed the Overground from Stratford to Richmond along the roads that were nearest to the line. James had moaned about having to virtually zigzag all the way. 'Hold on to the idea,' Stan would say dramatically when an area looked particularly awkward or dismal, 'that there'll be a café somewhere.' It was the laughs, the surreal hyperbole and his brother's detailed memories of their childhood that were the paramount reasons for James being with him.

He looked out at the terraced houses, pavement trees, a distant crane, a glimpse of water - a stream or canal perhaps - and instantly the place seemed an amalgam, a condensed version of their walks symbolising all of them He felt tears moisten his cheeks. Again; images, loss, associations reprising themselves. For a childlike moment he wished the waitress from the Island Café worked there.

When he entered the incongruously named Café Paris Annarita was already there, leaning back on her chair with a slightly mocking smile.

'Have I smashed a stereotype? I even worked out where the south side of the High Street was.'

'A slight crack. And there are reasons why females are no good at spatial concepts,' said James casually, joining her. 'That's why I rarely ask women for directions'

'I know where this is going and you'll lose; but I'm hungry.'

They ordered and ate. He asked her why she'd done maths.

'Because I was good at it.'

'All maths is tautology.'

'I still like it.'

'What about what you're doing now?'

'Okay so far, but - '

'Not precise enough? Not two plus two equals four? That's as it should be, even more so when you get to Freud.'

Their food was brought. They ate, studied the menu for dessert

'Avocado: cry of the Italian croupier'

'I don't think I'll better that,' said James and asked about her parents, genuinely motivated and not seeking childhood tribulations. They'd met in Italy where she was born. It was just her father now. When the waiter brought their drinks she said,

'Prego.'

'Non ho capito, no parla Italiano, mi dispiace.' said James. 'Sorry, that's all I know, I just mimic.'

As they drank he listened to her without really listening; just looked at her, the way she tossed her hair, with its shallow waves spreading out, and that grin stretching her lips. As they left he held the door for her and, glancing back, was aware that he hadn't really noticed their evening's surroundings, his usually precise visual recall pleasantly impaired by her presence. He walked with her to a bus stop; the ubiquitous and often empty, 'Thanks for a lovely evening,' transformed by her smile.

He saw her again two days later. This time it was in her local pub. As they sat in its oak panelled restaurant he noticed, as she turned to attract the waiter, the angle of her neck, the nape, her dark, tight-fitting shirt and was attracted to her again, strongly. He felt he didn't have to try to impress; once more it felt easy, as if they were riding a gentle swell. There was no probing from either of them, just a few more enjoyable bits of humour; her 'Overdue: rabbi' to his 'Ruislip: amusingly Freudian,' till they agreed to stop before they started giggling like a couple of clever school kids.

She asked him if he liked football, her local team was playing the next day and her steward friend had a spare ticket. James hadn't watched a match for a while. He said yes, expressing a mild, but pleasant surprise that she was a fan.

'I have strong memories of the old *Stadio Delle Alpi* when I was a girl.'

They met outside the ground. It was stimulating to see her in a new environment with bustling crowds around them. She was caught in the feel of the game, knew the names of the players, even some of those on the opposing side, and joined in the orchestrated riposte when the home team levelled the score, 'You're not fuckin' larfin' now.' She asked him if he minded her swearing. 'It's the only time I do, I suppose.'

Somehow, he didn't. She even ate the obligatory half time pie.

She wasn't free the following day, but was the one after. He hadn't intended going to the college, but after seeing his only Monday patient he did anyway. They saw each other for a few minutes before her class and then afterwards went to a local bar. It was late when they left. Together they walked back to her flat.

As she let him in and closed the door she turned and leant provocatively against it. He took her gently by her shoulders and pulled her towards him. He looked at her for a second - a filmic hiatus filled by seeing Bogart grab a film noir blonde - and, gripping her harder, kissed her, feeling her teeth thinning her lip. He slowly let go, easing her away from him. She leant against the door again, smiled and said,

'Where did *that* come from?'

'It's what I feel.'

'At this moment?'

'Not just. It's been building for a while.'

She squeezed by him. 'Let's have coffee.'

He followed her through a small dining room to a kitchen, sat at a table and watched her drop spoonfuls of coffee into their cups. He felt as if he'd spent a large part of the last week watching two women making beverages. He wondered idly what one he would rather be sitting near to, but when she gave that large grin again he realised just how idle the thought was. She held her mug up to her mouth and, looking over it at him, said,

'Let's slow down, it's a bit too quick for me. I've got a test in the morning, only a little one, but I want to do well; I've work to get in, too.'

He took an exaggeratedly resigned breath and asked if she needed any help. She didn't, but thanked him for the offer. She gulped her drink and moved towards the front door, saying brightly, 'Sorry,' as she opened it. He stepped out and turned, but the door had closed. He went home feeling in abeyance, in an empty no man's land of emotions unwillingly constrained.

In the café the following afternoon he was immersed in writing notes of one of his patients recent conversations with him when his table shook slightly. He looked up at Annarita's laughing mouth saying,

'I got an A for the test *and* my essay.'

'You've woken me up. What was the question?'

'How far can human motivation be said to be social?'

'What, this early? You did well.'

'Want to celebrate with me?'

'Of course. When? Where?'

'Tomorrow, the Old Drill Hall. You'll find it.'

She got up, gave him a quick kiss on his cheek and left; James, as always, suspecting that when a woman did this to him it was implying something platonic because she wanted nothing else. He pushed the thought away. It was replaced by mild surprise at her being there.

James didn't go to the venue. Neither did Annarita. She rang him as he was crossing the road towards it. She sounded more Italian on the phone, partly because she was anxious and speaking rapidly. Her father, back in Italy to give a series of talks at his old hospital, had been taken ill; it was a family friend who had contacted her. She needed to go; she was on the way now. It was all she said. He was disappointed.

He was busy for the next few days: a referral from a county court, two long-term patients, an emergency call from a woman who frequently cried wolf, but who he would always see, and more observations at the college. While there he found himself surreptitiously glancing around for her. She rang him again. There was some desperation in her voice, her father wasn't any better. Despite her situation he was glad she'd called him.

He thought of her sporadically then more consistently over the following days; thought of her in Italy, in Rome; and of his last visit there; of the sting of sun at Ciampino and the cab drivers shouting and pushing each other as they waited for fares that never seemed to come, and in the city an old aeroplane droning around with a *Vota Forza Da Liberta* banner fishtailing above the *Teatro Dell 'Opera* where the bourgeoisie clapped themselves for being there. Perhaps, one day, they could be there together. The thought excited him.

She rang him late one evening, frenetically using words from her first language. He caught *papa,* thought he understood *buone notizi* and *momento belo.* She was so thrilled; *Grande! Grande!* It seemed that her father was out of danger.

'I will tell you more when I am back, James. It will be good. I miss you. *Ciao.'*

He loved the way she said his name and, even more, the idea that she missed him.

He fretted for days. He wanted to call her, but hadn't saved her number and, knowing he couldn't get it from the college, had decided to ask one of the students. Then she called him. .

'James, he is well and coming home soon. I really have something to celebrate now, haven't I. *Vita e bella!'*

'When are you coming - '

'I am back Do you want to come to the place I mentioned before? Do you remember?'

Of course he did, and of course he remembered. He only then realised just how much he wanted to see her again. It seemed such a long while since he had.

It was a club off Goodge Street. He was early. He'd been to a club only once before, it was called a disco then and he didn't want to be inside that lung-shaking sound again. But this was quieter, with low, melodic music, a horse shoe bar and a dance space at the end of the long room. Getting himself a drink he leant against the counter and looked around him.

There was something a little… odd. He wasn't sure what. A few couples danced quietly under a glitter ball, but they weren't the expected sort of couples. They were, with the exception of two men moving slowly with each other, all women. They reminded him of his teenage dances at the local palais where, under their flashy bravado, lads would look nervously at the girls dancing with each other, bored with waiting for pimpled youth to clumsily invite them.

He'd recently found a black and white photo of two young girls in an East End street, one being bent acutely backwards by the other, her arm around the small of the girl's back, kissing her chin, pretending to be grown up. This, for James, was what these women should be doing; just chatting, playing about. But they weren't; two of the couples were holding each other tightly - 'romantically' was the word that came to his mind before realising how inappropriate it was. One of the twosomes consisted of a woman kissing her younger partner ardently on her mouth. It was Annarita and the waitress.

They moved away from each other, laughing. Annarita gripped her friend's hand and, still laughing, pulled her towards the bar. She looked up and saw him. She grinned broadly.

'Welcome.'

He didn't move.

'You look lost. I believe you know Jade?'

She pushed her forward.

'Hello, Mister Kent.' Her plump, blue-eyed face was flushed. James nodded; he wasn't sure what else to do.

'Come back to our table,' urged Annarita, pulling the younger girl after her. 'Get some more vodkas for us, would you, Jimmy?' she shouted.

He did, standing at the bar still not quite feeling anything. He took their drinks to the table, heard Jade saying, 'Yeh, he's got this psychiatric hotline: you know, 'If you're schizophrenic listen carefully and a little voice inside will tell you what number to press. If you're... ' She stopped, laughing almost hysterically.

He stood there, still holding the glasses.

'Come on, sit down Mister Kent.' said Jade.

'Yes, Mister Kent.' mimicked Annarita, 'but not on *my* lap.' Again the giggling.

'Sorry, we're like a couple of kids, aren't we. I expect you thought it would be just you and me celebrating.'

'Annarita, can you let go of my hand?' Jade said with mock seriousness.

James broke his inertia. He put their drinks down.

'Could we go somewhere else for a while?' He looked down at the girl.

'She won't be long... Jade.'

He walked firmly towards the exit, Annarita following. Outside it was raining. She went to step back inside. He grabbed her arm.

'What's going on?

She frowned, 'Well it's pretty obvious isn't it. Yes, I should have told you. You're a nice man, James, but you're - '

'The wrong sex?'

She didn't answer.

'You don't seem sure. And why meet here, should I have known about this place? Were you trying to tell me something?'

'I thought you were more liberal than this.'

'Liberalism; self-congratulation disguised as humanitarianism. Are you showing her off?'

'I'm sorry. I met her on the course and - '

'And?' He suddenly felt numb.

She pulled away from him. 'You'll be giving me the usual male response next;' she said, voice rising. ''Why? What do you *do*?' and 'Can I watch?' Okay, I should have told you. But I didn't.'

She was silent for a few moments. 'I enjoy being with you, you know that, but - '

'I was falling for you. I thought, I was hoping... does that mean anything? Is the phrasing un-cool?'

She turned quickly and went inside. As he stared at the door, it opened again. He couldn't tell whether she was angry or disappointed.

'Every time you're with me, it seems as if... it's psychiatry, analysing - '

'But, that's what you're doing there, to learn.'

'I know, but there must be more to you than that, there's nothing separate, different. I have no idea what you're really like. I feel that underneath the humour, the intelligence, you're acting; there's... a detachment. The very thing that attracts women to you, pushes them away.'

'What women?'

'The students here. They see you sitting in classes, you talk to them sometimes, they see you and I talking.'

'I'm not interested in other - '

'But, I am James. I want something else. '

She grabbed the door and slammed it behind her. He stared at it again and reverting to a familiar defensive cynicism, said quietly, 'No chance of a shag, then.' and walked away.

He went towards St. Pauls, then along Bishopsgate thinking of her, of them; anima, animus... He automatically went to enter Paulo's, but decided he didn't feel like going to another café, ever. He caught a packed train home.

Next day was a clear, warm, autumnal one, one of those where, if having no clients, he would go to a favourite London spot and walk. He had none; he chose Highgate. From there he walked to Crouch End, trying unsuccessfully to march her out of him. He was hungry and went into a café. He sat there thinking of her; of causes, reasons, and decided that she needed a surrogate mother, but then, what about Jade? He pushed the simplistic equations away.

He had an urge to understand what had occurred during the last few weeks. It had happened quickly. It was a new experience; he'd known very few clients who were overtly homosexual, though many, of course, that were latently so. He realised then how few female clients had been to his practice and felt a growing awareness that here was a whole field of - he hated saying it - ignorance, of unknowing in his professional lexicon. It frightened him.

He'd not long returned from a short holiday in Greece, an area of the Mediterranean he was fond of: Aegean islands silhouetted at dusk, white ferry boats, the light, the landscape and, seeing it through the illustrations in an old Sunday school bible, expecting Jesus to appear any moment on the dirt road in front of him. Perhaps, around Christmas, if he could afford it, he'd go to Sappho's island of Lesbos, see its contradictions; the emerald isle with its eleven million olive trees next to a petrified forest, the *salziknum,* 'daughter-men,' and perhaps he'd get some historical... 'Fuck lesbians,' he said under his breath, laughing at another contradiction. And at his own: an analyst needing an analyst, a man who'd been rejected for another woman and who felt at this moment, though recognising it was all an accident of time, of place, irrelevant.

As he was leaving he heard the East European accent of a girl behind the counter. With his usual reflexive curiosity he asked her where she was from. She looked at him and shook her head, replying that she wasn't going to tell him. A second woman behind the counter said pointedly,

'If she doesn't want to tell you where she is from, then she doesn't want to tell you where she is from.'

Two women again; he felt ganged up on.

'Why? This is *your* prejudice, not mine; don't project it onto me.'

He pushed through the door, barging into someone entering, and knew he had to take hold of himself; he couldn't be like this with clients. But perhaps he should be, let them know he wasn't just a robotic sounding board, a distant entity that just listened. He wished to be in a world where human beings would be just intellects, no wanting, no prejudices, just ... detached, detached.

EDUCATING RITA

It was supper time. I was looking out of the back room window at the aluminium bath hanging on the high fence that separated us from Mrs.Barrett's. My mother was sitting on my left opposite my father, bending his knife to harvest the steak and kidney pie gravy and which he would slide in and out of his mouth with a sucking 'pop.'

'*Must* you do that, Len?'

He took no notice. He never did. She went to the kitchen and returned with the salt. Wiping her hands down the front of her apron she seated herself again, fussily patted her black, greying hair and resumed her meal. I forced my food down as quickly as I could without offending her and left the house. It was all so familiar, like watching an endless loop of the same episode of a kitchen sink drama.

I walked north towards Wanstead Flats, my childhood sanctuary where I'd lay in the tall grass, jump the stream between the houses, return and play 'odds and ends' on the pavement or 'tin can Tommy' in the street till mum called me in for tea. It was nineteen fifty five, I was twenty one, had finished a decorating apprenticeship and wanted to get out, get my own place, not wanting to rent as my father did, with his forelock-touching every week to Mister Surrey when he came round for his money, and who owned half the street.

After several hours of wondering around I found I was walking uphill towards Plaistow Station, homing this way on automatic pilot. I used the station every weekday, sometimes on a Saturday, to get to work, having returned to my old firm and working in the City.

That's when I saw her; a tall, auburn-haired woman, older than me, in a long green coat and bright scarf around her throat, a few yards down from the station entrance. It was dark and had begun to rain. People were scurrying along behind her down the hill. She didn't have an umbrella, she looked bemused. I stood and watched her. She seemed very lost. I walked across to her in front of a bus slowing down for the bus stop, its front wheels turning at an angle, pushing the water away from the headscarved women standing there.

I stood a yard from her, feeling the rain splattering my face.

'Er, excuse me,' I mumbled, not having the energy to adopt a confident, urbane persona, 'D'you need some help? I think you should get out of the rain, stand in the entrance here.'

'Oh, thanks,' she said with a smile that sent startled neurons crashing around insanely inside me. It was Rita Hayworth.

I just looked at her. I didn't and couldn't move. The cynical, intellectualizing little man, perennially on my shoulder, kicked in defensively and told me she was merely another human amongst the six billion on earth, no different from any other stimulus-response mechanism, and yet another media construct. I saw her green eyes. The little man fell to the ground and died.

She frowned, looked even more puzzled. I then, somehow, actually touched her elbow, guided her the few yards to the entrance. We were out of the wet. I managed to say something.

'What, what are you doing here? er, are you okay?'

It was hard to believe that I could say something so rational, so…articulate. I didn't know whether or not she knew that I'd recognised her.

'Well, I was supposed to go to Pinewood Studios and - oh, it doesn't matter, I shouldn't have said I'd come. Do you know the subway well? I left my hotel, got on a train, but I think I've come the wrong way. I was looking at all the station names. I recognised a few at first and then…got off. I don't know where I am'. She raised her eyebrows and laughed at herself. 'I've never been to London before. I've been to Britain once.'

'Didn't you ask anyone on the train? I mean, there must have been people in your carriage.'

'I was tired. I just kept looking at the names, and they sort of …run into each other.' She looked down. 'I'm not sure, really.'

She had a voice I hardly recognised; not the modulated, lilting accent I remembered from her films; this was an obvious American one.

I told her, trying to keep my voice steady, that she was in East London and she'd gone the opposite way to where she should have been heading. She frowned again, then, 'Thank you. I guess I'd better be going back to my hotel if I can find…'

She stopped and leant against the wall inside the double wooden entrance doors. She looked pale…that lovely skin. Her hair was wet and a little flattened on top. I felt I needed to breathe again, I'd been holding my breath for minutes.

'You're not okay, are you' I said.

'No. No I'm not.'

'Look, keep here, I'll get a taxi. You'll be okay if I leave you a minute. Yes?'

She nodded weakly.

I went quickly across to the phone booth near the deserted ticket office and looked for a taxi firm in the phone book. I'd only been in a taxi once, when my father's dog was running in an early race at Hackney Wick and we'd got there just in time to watch it lose. I knew I could pay for this one; my weekly wage packet was in an inside pocket, unopened - I'd wanted the crisp thrill of opening it later, to go out somewhere, the mirage of afterwork; to a café with a friend, arguing about method acting, art, to see a film, perhaps one that she was in. I went back to her, her head was bowed. I was shaking.

'It won't be long.' I said comfortingly. She remained looking down.

'Where are we going?' she asked quietly in a voice that belied any real interest in an answer. She was looking increasingly unwell.

A thud of reason nudged me. A hospital. There was one just behind the station, another a mile away in Stratford. Then a hidden part of childhood treacled over me: not being well meant mum's healing fussiness, the background of which I subliminally saw as my own room where I'd recently painted a night sky and stars on the ceiling, an ancient Egyptian mural on the frieze and pasted a large photo of the Chrysler Building across a wall. I'd managed to buy a black and chrome Art Deco headboard for the bed and found an old Valmier rug and a Diomode light that triple-reflected from a mirror on the figured walnut dressing table I'd got cheap. In an insane way she would complete an adolescent fantasy. The room was behind the parlour. I could sleep upstairs in one of the rooms which had, until recently, been occupied by my father's sister and her husband. We'd taken over the whole unprepossessing, stone-dashed, Victorian terrace house when they left.

I deflected her question, 'You're not really *ill,* are you?'

A pale smile, 'No, well, I hope not, but I need to rest.'

152

I leant on the matchboarded wall next to her. People were coming up the stairs from a train. It was probably the last one of the day. Nobody looked across at us. She had shoulder pads in her coat; I kept looking at her green and pink scarf. She looked vulnerable. The taxi came. Pushing the guilt away I gave my address. The driver didn't say a word. Didn't look, didn't recognise her.

She spent the journey gazing out of a window. She seemed to trust me. I wondered if she was looking through an imaginary lens, having seen countless cameramen squinting at her through their thumbs and fingers rectangles. This time it wasn't a lush setting: the natural frame of the window was filled with a wasteland of rubble and bricks where tower blocks were going to be built, empty beer bottles, a remnant of a bonfire, a frame of a bicycle sticking up like an isosceles triangle, then shabby Victorian terraces, rows of them, shut pubs, cafes, a row of grey shops, all lit, still, by turn-of-the century pavement lamps - a couple of youths, at this late hour, playing floodlit footie under one of them with a bald tennis ball.

I just looked at her, trying not to split open, to explode inside this taxi, to seem relaxed, attempting not to think of hidden cameras filming us for a documentary or something, and not to wonder whether she was just a remarkable look-alike.

I got out, paid quickly, opened the nearside door for her and, again supporting her elbow but more firmly, walked her across the pavement. I pushed the black scrolled gate, unlocked the front door - which I'd recently grained - and ushered her in. I closed it gently.

'Do you live alone here?' she asked.

'No, no, it's my parents place, I thought I'd said, they'll be upstairs, asleep, it's late.'

I looked at my watch, surprised at how late it was. 'It's almost one.' I whispered, 'You can have my room.'

We walked softly towards it. 'The bathroom's upstairs through the first door if -'

'It's okay, I'll go straight to bed.'

She turned, looking weak. She looked smaller.

'Thank you.'

I opened the door, she slid in, closing it quickly. I went upstairs. I'd spent the last two months after work decorating the whole house. The room I entered was the last one to be finished. It was a sort of workshop: dust sheets, tools, brushes, tins of paint on the floor. I made some space, unfolded the sheets, laid them down, fell on top of them without undressing and tried to sleep. I didn't have to go to work tomorrow.

I slept little, thinking of coal mines, tractors, washing whitewash off a ceiling with a double knot distemper brush, anything but thinking of her lying in my bed directly beneath me, perhaps sleeping naked.

Waiting till it was firmly daylight I went to the bathroom, shaved, made myself look respectable. It was still raining. I went downstairs quietly, knocked on the door of my room. She opened it immediately as if she'd been standing there, waiting.

'Good morning.' she said with a bright smile. She had no make up, her hair was pinned back. Her dress was dark blue, loose-fitting, her high heeled shoes were indigo.

'How'd you sleep,' I asked, 'you look better.'

'I am. I slept okay. Your *room!* it's wonderful. And that mirror. I love the thirties period too, I've got a lot of Lalique glass back home. I guess I'm a collector. I assume it was you who painted the ceiling, how did you do it? You could get a job as a scene painter. What do you do, anyway?'

'I'm a painter and decorator.' I said quickly, 'Feeling hungry?'

'Yes. Your parents *are* here, I assume?'

'Oh, yeh, they're having breakfast, let's go in.'

'I don't know your name,' she said.

'It's Chris, Chris Bowes. And yours,' I heard myself saying, 'was Margarita Carmen Cansino before Hollywood changed it.'

She seemed surprised. 'How d'you know that?'

'A friend told me, Tony, he's film mad, I'll cook you something if you want.'

We went past the cellar door to the back room at the end of the narrow hall, but before I could touch it, it was opened by my mother who had obviously heard our voices. She looked alarmed.

'Mum,' I forced myself to say, 'this is a friend of mine. She slept in my room last night, I was upstairs in the spare room, she wasn't feeling well.' I had, obviously, rehearsed this over and over during the night. I could see my father's head turning from his newspaper, looking up.

'Hello,' said mum, eyes looking unusually bright, 'pleased to meet you I'm sure.' She held her hand out. It was taken lightly, with a slight squeeze. My father was standing now.

'Dad, this is -'

'Yeh, I heard. 'ello ducks,' he said in his best cockney, halfway to his seat again, wanting to get back to his paper. He didn't know who she was.

'Come in and sit down,' said mum, 'have my chair, I'll get you something. What would you like?'

'It's alright, I'll do it,' I said. I wanted to do something for her, something she wanted, needed, anything. I was ignored.

'Well, thank you.'

She looked at the half finished food on their plates.

'Oh, I love bacon, eggs and tomatoes,' she said, the latter pronounced with a slight Brooklyn 'tamaytas.' Again, the strong accent, not that husky, almost English one she'd used in 'Gilda.' And when I thought of this, thought of that first shot of her, tossing her head back, the hair, the smile, the mischief, I still couldn't believe that the eponymous star of that film was here, now, with *me,* in Leddington Road.

We sat, she on the nearest chair, me squeezing around the table to my usual place with my back to the small bay window.

'Well, you look all right this mornin', I must say,' said dad gruffly

'Can you help me a minute, Chris?' asked mum from the kitchen eight feet away.

I got up, wriggled by, 'It's alright, don't move,' I said, looking down at the top of her head, her hair, the parting. I wanting to stand there and keep looking. In the kitchen mum slowly closed the door behind me.

'Is that who I think it is?' she whispered. 'It can't really be, can it? She looks so like her.'

I didn't know what to say. I didn't want to say it actually *was* her, as if by not confirming it to anyone I could, somehow, keep her to myself.

'Yes, she does, mum. I won't have a lot, I'm not hungry.'

'But... suit yourself,' she said, moving the bleached broom handle out of her way that she still used for 'stirring the copper,' in which she washed bed sheets and clothes and which I used to help her with as a child, hardly being strong enough to push the stick around.

I stepped back into the room. Dad was saying, 'Where you from, then? You sound a bit like a Yank.' I winced.

'Yes, I am American,' she smiled, 'I live in California.'

'Sunny there, I s'ppose.'

'Yes, it is.'

Mum came through with two plates of fried food and put them down in front of us. She tucked into it healthily. I fidgeted with mine, surreptitiously watching her.

Mum was silent, looking sideways at me and occasionally at her as she ate.

'Wot d'yer do then, luv? asked my father.

She looked across, stopped chewing, 'I'm in movies.'

'Yeh? I don't go to the pictures much meself. I was a crowd extra once in 'Beau Geste' when I was in the army. Took Edie to see it, but they'd cut it out and I wasn't in it.' He guffawed, looking briefly at my mother.

'I know that feeling,' she grinned.

I didn't believe her. He bent his head, scraping his knife around his plate, capturing the grease, but this time not putting it into his mouth. We sat in silence. I felt that I'd brought home a wax facsimile from Madame Tussaud's, she wasn't real, couldn't be Reminding myself again that she was, I watched her eating food five feet away from me, drinking tea, wiping her firm, beautiful lips with one of the napkins hastily brought out for special occasions. She looked over the top of her teacup, commenting that she really liked the way my mother made tea.

She glanced at her watch, began standing up, 'I hope you don't mind, but I really have to get back.' She turned to my mother. 'May I use the bathroom?'

'Certainly dear, you know where it is, don't you.'

She left the room. I could hear her footsteps on the stairs.

'Why didn't you tell me?' mum asked in a hissing whisper,

'I only met her last night, she wasn't well, I thought - '

'Is she going back to America or what?'

'I don't know, I just don't know.'

'Seems a nice gel, very friendly.' said dad, handing his plate to his wife. 'You're a big boy now son, you know wot yer doin'.'

She stood at the door pulling her coat on.

'It's raining,' I said, 'I'll get an umbrella.'

I ran upstairs, put my jacket on, came down again. My mother was listening to her saying how much she loved London, the little alleyways in the city, the Dickensian feel of them, the parks. I don't think my mother quite understood all of what was being said to her.

'Guess I'd better go.' Rita said, smiling quickly at everyone.

'I'll come with you to the station.'

We walked to the front door, to the gate. She turned, raised her handbag - I hadn't noticed it before, it was the same colour as her shoes.

''bye then, and thanks for your hospitality Mrs. Bowes, and you too, Mr. Bowes.'

'Call me Len, luv. It's a pity you can't be here a bit longer, I'm goin' to the British Legion tonight, go every Saturday, there's some good singers there, you'd like it.'

If only she could, would, stay. The four of us at the British Legion, Canning Town Branch - though I'd been only twice - walking up the front steps under the Victorian arch, through the scuffed double doors, along the corridor, past the Ladies and into the hall, the bar on the right, Charlie and Tom propping it up, Gwen with her pill-box tilt hat, Flo with pinned up hair and high heels, all the regulars, the chairs against the lincrusta'd dado, the ribbons of gold tinsel either end of the stage, the inevitable half drunk pint of beer placed on the edge of the apron, everyone staring at her through the sudden silence, except those shouting and laughing inside the door who, after a few seconds, would quieten too. The first person recognising her would be the girl pulling pints, her fist rigid on the pump then slowly sliding down as she whispered her name.

I'd step in front of my parents, dad with double breasted suit, collar and tie, mum, shoulder-padded jacket and too tight shoes just behind him, lead her to the centre of the floor just as George introduces the octogenarian band and the first quickstep, the 'Twelfth Street Rag,' knowing that the English teacher who taught us ballroom at the Tech. would smile proudly as, with a gentle pressure on the small of her back, I would smooth us along, reverse twist here, a spin there, and she would throw her head back, laughing, glitter ball glints sparkling in her eyes...

'Still, ne'er mind, another time, eh?' dad was saying.

'Okay, Len .' she said sweetly, 'And I wish you luck, Edie.'

My mother's eyes were shining, I'd never seen her quite like this.

'Cheerio Miss Hayward, don't get wet, mind.'

I nodded to them, and off we went, my umbrella covering us both.

'I thought you'd ring for a taxi.' she said with a mock frown.

'We don't have a phone, but there's a phone box round the corner.'

We ran, reached it, neither saying anything. I found the number, I was trembling a little. She was outside holding the umbrella, looking around her. I came out.

'Anything interesting?'

'The brick houses. There's so many. You rarely see them in America, they're wood and plastic. Sure, there's the brownstones in New York, redbricks in Chicago, but both sides of the streets around here look like two long houses with lots of doors, it seems so cramped, and there's so many chimneys.'

She looked suddenly contrite. 'I'm sorry, I'm being rude.'

'No, it's okay. The bricks are called London bricks, yellow stocks. They have names. See the kinda burnt ones? They're grey gaults, and the whiteish ones are white suffolks and, Oh, Christ, I'm boring you to death.' I lightly touched the back of her waist while I was saying this. My fingers burned.

'No, no, it's interesting, it's all so different.'

The taxi came. We hurried in and went back to the station where I'd met her eight hours previously. Again, she looked silently out of the window. We scrambled into the station entrance. I shook the umbrella, tried to sound casual.

'What's the next film, then?'

''Fire Down Below.' I think we're starting next week, on location. I forget where. I can be very vague sometimes.'

'Are you going back to your hotel.' She nodded.

'Where is it?'

'Just off Sloane Square. Where's the westbound platform?'

'I'll come down with you.'

We descended the stairs, 'Don't you mind travelling by train? People looking at you, pointing, whispering'

'No, I don't mind. I love subways, the Paris Metro, Rome's Metropolitana, New York, they're great.'

I loved the way her lips moved when she said 'Metropolitana,' her husky voice.

'I don't want you to come with me. Really, it's okay, honestly.'

I felt limp with disappointment. It was visible.

'I'm sorry,' she said.

I wanted to say something that would suggest to her - and myself - that seeing her, talking to her, wasn't anything special, just an ordinary, friendly social encounter. I couldn't, of course, think of anything.

'I hope you... I dunno, learnt something, other than the names of bricks of course.'

'Yes, I did. I learnt that there are some good people about, accommodating. Oh, it sounds corny, I'm not expressing myself very well. I'm better with a script.'

'Do people, the public, know you're over here? I haven't read anything.'

'No. I use dark glasses and a Cansino passport. I've learnt'. She was bending forward, looking back up the rails. A train was coming in. It was a District line. Its clattering seemed so loud.

'This'll take you straight there.' I forced a grin.

'Thanks for your help, you've been kind.'

She took a few steps away from me. I felt suddenly empty.

'Have a doctor look at you.' I said earnestly, 'Does the hotel have one? You can keep the umbrella.' I didn't remember her taking it from me. She looked at it with mild surprise, then came back to me, gave me a quick kiss on my cheek, an inch from the corner of my mouth.

'Thanks again.' She smiled right into me. 'I'll be alright. Brown eyes.' and got into a carriage as the doors closed.

I stood there watching the back of the train vanish in the rain and went up the stairs, out of the station. I missed her, I wanted that feeling again when we'd run to the telephone box together. I'd never felt anything like that before. I wanted to be lying awake again, thinking of her asleep just ten feet below me, looking at my stars on the ceiling, wanted to… just look at her. I incongruously wondered what my mother would be saying to my father at this moment.

'D'you know 'oo she is Len, she's – '

'Alright, keep yer 'air on, you've told me, but it don't matter who –'

'I dunno what this is about, but I'm gonna get to the bottom of this when he gets home.'

And also who I could tell about it. Tony, of course, but not the blokes at work.

'You takin' the piss?' ''avin' a larf ain't yuh?' 'You'll be tellin' us next yer dad's dog won.' 'Pull the uvver one, it's got bells on.'

I walked down the hill; the toy factory at the bottom where my mother still worked, wearing her wedge shoes and turban, the Railway Arms opposite, Desmond's the chemists, Dollond's the grocers, still using his wire to cut cheese, and Doctor Murphy with his huge red hands and his, ''tis only indigestion, mother.' for the amoebic dysentery I had when I was twelve.

But, I *was* going. I would put in for a charge hand's job and if turned down, go to another firm. I'd saved a fair bit for a deposit and there were plenty of building societies around.

I walked quicker, took longer strides, looked up, punched the air and silently mouthed,

'I met Rita fuckin' Hayworth!' It had stopped raining

HATS

Leonard East was sitting at the back of a row of pews looking at an oak table supporting a flower-strewn coffin and listening to Roz's son reading a clumsily written but, rather moving poem. Roz had been an art book publisher who he'd got friendly with somewhere or other despite her dislike of his chunky, banal attempts at figurative painting. In Africa seventeen years previously she'd found she had cancer. During one of her several remissions she bought them both tickets for an Albert Hall concert. She'd asked him a few days later to share a meal with her at her flat in Belsize Park. He hadn't gone. He wished he had. She'd died a week ago in a hospice.

Her daughter had briefly introduced herself to him on the steps leading into the chapel but, having failed to recognise her in the pub afterwards and asking a stout blonde woman sitting opposite why she seemed so miserable, heard,

'Because I've just buried my mother.'

It was his second faux pas within the hour. An elderly couple had given him a lift to the post-funeral get-together and as the husband slowed outside the pub the woman had turned her head and said, seemingly pointing at him, 'Look at that awful hat.' 'All he needs,' said Leonard, 'is a dead deer slung on the roof.' She had, instead, been pointing out of the side window at a vividly coloured piece of headwear belonging to a female friend of the deceased.

There was buffet food laid on, but he didn't eat; the smell of garlic and the appearance of the cold quiche seemed to represent death. It was his third funeral of the week. Unusually, at two of them, he'd known the deceased; at the other he'd known no one; not friends, relatives, nor the coffin's inhabitant.

The first had been an aunt who'd died at 103. He could still see the copy of *Saga* on a sill in the chapel, the plate glass views of pylons, his greying cousins, her Benfleet bungalow and the pampas grass she would pick to spray with lacquer for the vase. And the surprises; Ernie suddenly seeming likeable, a shop steward uncle's reluctant Marxism, a granddaughter's mini skirt and high heels, and the 'Nice spread, Vera,' 'She 'ad a good innin's,' 'Lovely service,' and his own screaming imperative to intellectualize, and still hearing her calling him 'Lenny.'

The second, causing him to get off at Turkey Street station and its adjacent beer can strewn puddle of a canal and deteriorating, sauerkraut smelling pub, was one he'd noted from a local paper. Again he sat at the back and once more listened to a vicar creating an empty, meaningless gospel of faction for a weeping widow and friends. Leaving a fading 'Let's Make Memories' and 'I'm Forever Blowing Bubbles' he walked out and crossed the path to the graveyard.

He looked at the winged angel monuments, a testimony to Victorian piousness and order, at the names on the mossy headstones, Braithwaite, Dobson, Samuels - junior school images settling in his mind - the long grass, the wilting flowers, some still in their cellophane wrappings, and wondered again why he liked graveyards so much. He wondered also, as he often did, what exactly mourners felt at the moment the coffin moved from a decorated facade to the inner workings of heat or earth.

Over a drink in a bowling pavilion afterwards he quietly joined the others and listened to their fake jocularity and superficial memories, ''e liked a good laugh, did Alf,' 'Yeh, 'e once said that if 'e couldn't take it wiv 'im, 'e wouldn't go.' or earnest sadness, asking himself whether any of it hid the reality of their pain; how many there actually felt it, how many a quiet relief?

Usually he would go to a random church or crematorium, not necessarily near his home, and look at the burial and cremation times as a guide for his visits. But this time, a week after his last funeral, spotting a horse-drawn hearse with several black limousines following on a busy City road, he decided to tag along. He was driving the opposite way. He turned and joined the queue of cars behind and, as they gradually overtook, settled behind the last limousine. He wondered who and for what reasons its passengers had been allotted their seats; ''ere, you sit wiv Glad, she's yer aunt,' 'You better go in the back wiv yer baby, Joan,' or, remembering that there hadn't been a floral name laid around the coffin, perhaps it was, 'Do sit with me, Charles, we need to talk arrangements and wills,' or 'Hello George, mind if I plonk next to your good self? I say, are you still in the club? I'm a town member now.' 'I'm a country member.' 'Yes, I remember.' He realised with a smile that he was talking to himself again.

It was a Hawksmoor church in Spitalfields. He was rather surprised that a cortege was allowed this far in; perhaps it was someone perceived as important, one of the 'great and the good.' He nudged up to a parked limo and got out. Everyone seemed to be in traditional black, most wearing hats, some men carrying them in their hands as they walked up the wide steps towards the tall, heavy doors. He followed in his dark clothes - often wearing them, just in case - and entered as the doors were closing, their clanging feeling like a prohibition, of something banned.

Sitting at the back, the nearest mourners a dozen rows in front, he looked around him. It wasn't precious, no Catholic gold and glitz, just white columns, acanthus leaf, rams horns, dulled oak. He imagined a sparrow looking down on the grey heads, black coats, wheelchairs, a corner painting and tomb, hearing a violin dirge in a square nave that had housed hatreds, saccharin cant, and that had never seen a flowered 'Grandad' nor crossed hammers in claret and blue roses; and this before the spirit's weakening to the body, the fidgets, coughs, desire for the wine and smoked eels, toilets...

It was a service - the body apparently being buried somewhere else later in the day - for a Lord Tagellan. There were several speakers eulogising him, most, it seemed, from the House of Lords. He looked around him again, wanting it all to be over so he could follow them to a local tavern or somewhere in Mayfair or, maybe, someone's home, though that one would be difficult. He knew he wanted to argue with one or more of them, wanted to intellectually critique their privileged world views, knowing there was no need to posit conspiracy theories about a ruling class - they ruled because they knew their position in the world and shared the same values. Wherever he landed up with them he wouldn't drink, he wanted to keep sharp. When he saw privilege he was ready for battle.

He noticed a woman, whose dark eyes and fair hair were almost hidden under a veil, standing very still and a little apart from the others. After the growling, oppressive organ music ceased, an elderly woman moved towards her and put an arm around her shoulder and led her out of the chapel. The rest of the congregation slowly followed.

He was about to leave last, as he often did, but on a whim went out just a few yards behind the two women. He stood at the top of the steps and watched them walk along the pavement, the older one occasionally touching the arm of the other. They got into a car, but not one of the limousines. Trying not to hurry he went to his own car. As he reversed he saw them pulling away and, driving around the other vehicles, followed. He wasn't sure why; though he was aware of the seductive mystery of a woman's veil.

They drove to Hampstead and stopped in a pub car park. He waited until they were inside the building and then parked near them. He had no idea where the limousines were.

He got himself a drink and sat at a table behind them. He heard the older woman say, 'It's better here, away from those oleaginous, artificial buggers. Sorry.'

'It's okay,' said the other flippantly, 'it doesn't matter.'

They sat there silently sipping their drinks. He felt himself slipping into his post-funeral conversational mode.

'Excuse me,' he said, leaning towards them, 'I've just been to the service, I thought I noticed you there.' and, pre-empting them, 'I only met him once, but he made an impression. I can't remember where or when, but... I thought I'd pay my respects; that's all.'

The older woman looked at him quizzically. 'He always did make a good first impression, but you have to - '

'It's okay, Aunt May.' said the younger, 'he's gone now, and I need to get rid of this veil.'

She removed her hat and looked at him. She had sad eyes that couldn't quite hide an entrenched glimmer of humour.

'We'll continue to see him differently, Petra, I'm sure, but I must go now, I need a walk.' the older woman said, standing up and patting her companion's arm. She walked away, brushing her hand backwards.

'Goodbye my dear, and you too, young man.'

The younger woman watched her leave. 'I suppose I'd better go, too,' she said, reaching for her hat.

'Don't go.'

'Why?'

'I don't want you to.'

'Do you think I need comforting? It's kind of you, but Uncle Ronald had been ill for some time, so it was - '

'I just want to talk to you.'

She shrugged, laid her hat down and looked at him..

'Did you really meet him? He hadn't gone out in public for years.'

He walked around her table and sat opposite her.

'Or perhaps you just like funerals.' She laughed, the whiteness of her teeth not quite distracting him from his surprise as he attempted an answer.

'Yeh, just love 'em.' He forced a grin.

'Why *are* you here?' If you want to mix with these sort of people you could have gone to the official - '

'I would have, I usually do, but... ' He felt embarrassed. She laughed again, delightfully.

'You really *do* like them don't you.'

'I saw a tombstone the other day, it said, 'Here lies an atheist, all dressed up and nowhere to go.''

She laughed again and said, quietly but pointedly, 'Why?'

He took a deep breath. 'I do go to them, yes. Let's have a drink; I'll tell you why.'

She hesitated. 'Alright then, a G and T, please.'

He got their drinks and sat again.

'What I dislike is that the people who knew the person in the coffin - okay, so she or he is merely a cadaver, shaped by tissue and bone, bodily fluids, etcetera - are now laughing with each other, telling or listening to jokes, saying things like - '

'Tell me some jokes.'

'What's the difference between a lawyer and a trampoline? You should take your shoes off before jumping on a trampoline. It's just the lack of feeling, the false - '

'Like Aunt May says. But, what do you *like* about funerals?'

'I don't want to reduce your uncle with all this, what matters for you, of course, is what you felt for him.' For a brief, strange moment he didn't want her to have loved him. He felt jealous.

166

'It's alright, I knew him mostly as a child and he wasn't really my uncle, more a friend of the family, but those memories came back today.'

'I like churches, especially walking on my own. When I need some quiet, some peace - yes, that's why - I look around the graveyards; somehow, even the trees seem more at rest than elsewhere, they're just... there, as if they could be nowhere else in the world.' And on another whim, he said, 'Come with me. Come for a walk with me. They've usually got decent cafes; we can just walk around and... '

She lowered her head for a second then looked up at him.

'Yes, okay, I'll come with you. I hope you have some more jokes, I like the accents you do.'

Three days later he met her at Nunhead Cemetery, the largest in London. She'd never been there before. It was a late spring day; bright green leaves, daffodils, grass recently mown.

'Let's have tea first.' They said it together.

They found a tea room and, drinking their tea, she asked him what he did. He told her that he was an accountant, but had just finished a law degree, though still didn't really know what he wanted.

'Perhaps you need an all-consuming project, something you can give yourself to.'

'Maybe. Do you think that's why I go to these services?'

She smiled, finished her tea and stood. 'Lets go, then.'

He loved her smile. He asked her more about herself. Her Putney home, she said, was a tiny flat full of hats she'd designed to help out her younger brother's fashion business.

'He was a little ostracised by the family when he went into *that*.' She was wearing a small, dark green one. 'Yes, this is one of mine. Going to tell me a joke, then?

'How d'you know when an accountant's an extrovert? He looks at *your* shoes when he's talking to you, not his own.'

'You're not like that.'

'That's why I don't really want to be one any more. I'd like to go to a New Orleans funeral. The processions are sad going there and happy coming back; the music, swing, the banners.'

'I thought you wanted peace.'

'But, some can be fun. You know, I've always gone out on my own really, like when a child I used to walk for miles along the top of the northern outfall sewer, there's a lot of green there, and you can look down on the back gardens of the Victorian houses.'

'Yes, I like Victorian houses. The flat I've got is Edwardian, but I like most period homes.'

'My favourite period; Georgian's the second. They built the first terrace, known as row houses and - I'm going to stop. I sound like an accountant.'

She grinned. 'I love the sun on trees, maybe a privet hedge, even chocolate box roses around a front door.'

'Yes, and the sun playing on leaves, soft bricks, glistening on window panes... '

They walked on, he excitedly talking of Italianate towers, scrolled balconies, black and white tiled paths, she looking up at him, half smiling as they walked past stone cherubs and leaning gravestones.

'Sometimes I want to become a roof and look down on porticoes and clicking gates, on gardens, and trees higher than me and, say, an unexpected park, a watercolour lake.'

'Now you don't sound like an accountant.' she said, and then laughed again, her head back. He put his arm around her shoulder. She stopped for the briefest moment then put her arm around his waist. They walked on in silence, both feeling the import of their actions.

After minutes she asked him the furthest he'd been for a funeral.

'Lincoln. An accident really, I just wanted to see the cathedral, but there was a service going on and... I suppose that was the first time I went to one without an invite.'

He wanted to stop and look at her, but as they continued walking he said, 'I don't want to walk on my own any more. I want you with me. All the time, really.'

He hadn't yet realised that he had never once thought of her, despite all the signs, as privileged.

He then stopped and looked at her. 'Would you put your veil on for me next time? Please?'

James Kent was digging his nails into his palms as deeply as he could. He could think of nothing else to do. His client had such a monotonous, trivia-espousing estuary drawl that he wished to be either deeply asleep or on his way out of his office through the window, open or closed. She was actually lying on his couch - few patients did - as if to confirm to herself, and her friends in the telling, that she was a bona fide patient, was in fact, mentally ill.

While listening to her onerous droning he thought of his dream the previous night of being with an actor whose accent and brutal East End personae - a profile close-up of him saying, 'You c**t,' epitomising English film realism - he despised. James was listening to his gruff, but jocular and surprisingly caring voice in the parlour of his childhood home. Then they were on a street with privet hedges and their arms lightly around each other's waist. They were both laughing. When James pointed out that it wasn't the usual thing blokes did, his companion, touching his hand, told him that when they got there, there would be sex. Though not knowing where or with whom, he felt a pleasing anticipation.

Even before he was fully awake he knew the actor symbolised his father. The previous evening James had thought of him, trying again to understand, to forgive, and had an image of him not as the alien figure he'd had to live with, but as a weak, unhappy victim of his own father's physical abuse, and someone who, frightened of James' early brightness, had blotted out any wish to understand his offspring. James had almost said aloud, 'I forgive you,' before the obscuration came clouding in again. The actor had become a generic parent, one he'd wanted to laugh with, to be touched by. Perhaps, for a lost child, the wish for a different father was a beginning of homo eroticism, of, perhaps, homosexuality. James had woken from his drowsy analysis and thought, 'I don't *want* to be fucked by Ray Winstone.'

He smiled intermittently to himself for the rest of the way through the woman's moaning, stopping himself several times from telling her that she was so much more fortunate than most of his patients; the previous one was trying to adjust to losing a leg.

When she left, he laid on the couch himself, wondering what his new patient, due in an hour, would be like.

His new client was tall, well-dressed, rather good looking, but looking troubled. A fatuous part of James was hoping that, unlike the woman he'd just tortuously listened to, he really did have problems, something he could get his teeth into and maybe help alleviate. His client sat.

'Why are you here?

'Because. It's difficult.'

'Take your time.'

'I met a woman and… I seem to be falling in love with her.'

He looked at James without expression.

'And?'

'Well, I like funerals.' He gave an 'I'm sorry, but there it is' grin. 'I go to them even if I don't know the deceased or the people there. I just go. I'm driven to, I suppose.'

'Do you know why?'

'I've realised why I like graveyards. I've known her for six weeks and most of the time we're with each other we've been strolling around them. Lately, she's been to a couple of funerals with me. I think I'm here because it's not right. It's a relationship built on… funerals, really.' He laughed and shook his head.'

'What are you seeking? Some sort of solace, maybe? What do funerals mean to you?'

'I don't know; but I love the feeling of quiet, of the peace in graveyards.'

'You can go, as I suspect you do, at any time and walk around them, you don't need to go to the funerals. Is it not that when you listen or talk to the mourners afterwards they're talking about someone who *was* whilst they, and you, *are*? It's a confirmation, Mister East, a reiteration of your own existence. Funerals are rituals and, like many rituals, are comforting, are part of order and order is reassuring; they are a reminder that society continues, *we* continue. And do you dye your hair and, I think, your stubble because the equation is: not going grey, therefore not old, therefore won't die? And yes, you could say what you do is morbid, and certainly it's unusual, but, what does your girl friend think about it?'

His listener looked embarrassed for a moment and touched his stubble.

'She comes with me because she wants to be with me and she's rather gentle and she likes what we do; the calmness, the light, the feelings.'

'Do you want me to help you to stop wanting to go to them or give you permission to continue? Is your disquiet because you feel driven or is it because of the girl?'

His client thought a moment. 'Both. I actually suggested to her that we could visit cemeteries abroad, like the Pere Lachaise in Paris or even God's Acre in Pennsylvania, and the St. Louis Cemetery. I know it sounds mad, but - '

'What did she say?'

'She said, yes. It was hard to believe.'

'Why? Too good to be true?'

His new client looked down and nodded.

'But, I like walking around other places, too. I love buildings, houses; little things, you know, a chimney pot, painted eaves, a shine on an old front door that's had coat upon coat of paint, there's something about the shine, it's deep, it's - '

'Intense?'

'Yes.'

'Buildings interest you, Leonard, partly because they're emotionally easier to deal with than people; there's no hurt, pain, envy, frustration there. Also you're looking for a womb, the womb you'd have liked to have had, an idealised one. And yes, it goes back that far, and perhaps we all, in our primal selves, hunger for the perfect one. A house, for you as a child, would be perhaps... leaves against a window symbolising a mother's hair touching an infant's face, perhaps a cupola would represent an offered breast, and maybe, I don't know, the folds of a caryatid's long skirt would be a place for a child to hide. For *you* to hide. Though it'd be a rather posh house, I suppose. And when you see trees, maybe something small, say a buddleia which often grows from between bricks in a wall, is the experience almost lyrical? Does *she* feel something like this about houses?'

'Yes, in her quiet way, she picks out little things, the minutiae, and tells me what she feels. It's about the light isn't it, it illuminates... softens.'

'I'll say this to you, Leonard, and I hope I'm not committing the sin of projecting parts of myself onto you. I don't know whether you saw the film of 'Billy Liar' - I saw it first as a teenager - and there was Tom Courtenay living in his fantasised world when he meets Julie Christie who actually wants to share this world with him, yet, eventually, he walks away from her. I remember at the end of the film standing up and shouting, 'Don't, don't.' I really did. It's for you to decide, of course, and professionally, maybe, I shouldn't be saying this, but you've found someone who not only wants to be with you - in a context which you think is morally wrong - but also shares the same aesthetic as you, *wants* to share it. It may not be consensual behaviour, but it's *your* consensus, the two of you. Don't walk away from it, from her. You have my secular blessing, carry on. with it; the walks, the peace, trees, the sun on a length of gutter, a window. Go on, however brief it may or may not be. Share it *all.'*

His client frowned at his analyst for a brief while, smiled and handed him a cheque. He shook his hand and went towards the door. James let him out and watched him leave.

He stood in the hall and briefly wondered why his client hadn't mentioned his father. He knew that early trauma could create a partial withdrawal from reality, the inevitable interruption of ego development allowing images and perceptions of all sorts of things; music, flowers, buildings becoming, perhaps, unhealthily significant and... No. He was right to say what he did. It wasn't all a projection of himself. He walked quickly into his study and chose a book. He tried to read.

It was an irony, a piece of graveyard humour that, had he been able to, he'd have appreciated. He'd have told Petra. She would have laughed. It was evening, he was about to finish a walk around a graveyard in East London when he saw a golf ball lying next to a new headstone. He knew there was a golf course at the side of the grounds and was trying to think of a variation of a 'hole in one' joke as he bent to pick it up. He slipped on a mulch of leaves and his head slammed against the stone.

When he was found next morning by a man carrying flowers for an adjacent plaque, the latter thought he was a drunk. He tried to wake him, as did two paramedics thirty minutes afterwards and two doctors in the local A & E Department fifteen minutes after them. But, it's difficult to wake someone whose brain haemorrhage had stopped their breath many hours before.

James Kent had another new patient. Things were going well, though he'd been vaguely wondering why he hadn't heard from Leonard East. He had a new bell also; he opened the door in answer to it. She was quite tall, fair haired and wore an attractive, rather oddly shaped hat. She smiled at him. She had unusually white teeth. He stepped aside so she could enter then closed the door.

LAY PREACHER

Srange day for an atheistic psychoanalyst. James Kent was on his way to church. He'd recently met, by accident, a cousin of an ex-patient who used to bring him to James weekly and, after talking interestingly to him about philosophy and film, had spoken of religion. Each time Jehovah Witnesses descended on James' street like a plague of locusts and knocked on his door with hotlines to God and a proselytizing routine that, with another I.Q. point, could have been a plant, he promised himself that in the face of another ecclesiastical onslaught he would smile patiently and either shut the door or run away. This time, because he liked the man, he raced through well-versed responses merely to get them over with so they could return to their previous subjects.

'Come to an Alpha Course,' the cousin said, 'we need people like you.'

James liked churches, but not what went on inside them; still partly the opiate of the masses - only in recent years had that validation of fatalistic acceptance, 'The rich man in his castle, the poor man at his gate, all creatures high and lowly, God ordered their estate' been scrapped. It was the aesthetics of spires, Norman battlements, leaded glass windows, flying buttresses, the church smell of peaceful calm - though secretly thinking that municipal cleaners used aerosols labelled 'church odour,' 'museum odour,' etcetera - that were the spiritual attractions, but he said no. He rang James every day for the next three till the latter relented.

The church was in Holborn - he'd often passed it - the course being held in a large ground floor room. There were a dozen people there comprising three or four different ethnicities, mostly women.

'Before we begin, let us pray.' said a large, bearded man with a Dutch accent named Dirk who sat at the head of the table and who, James assumed, was a pastor. They did, while James sat there unmoving.

They were asked to introduce themselves. James told them nothing except that he was interested to see what went on. The pastor pulled in his chair, rubbed his hands and said, 'God is good.'

He couldn't resist. 'God is not necessarily good. Your statement's either a tautology or it implies that goodness is independent of God's credence.'

The pastor smiled indulgently at him then looked around at the others who began asking questions directed at their leader and each other about specific parts of the bible. The bible was, as James expected, their bible.

There was a white Zimbabwean woman there, Christina, who talked of The Garden, apples and snakes, of original sin, while her eyes shone preternaturally, her skin holding a slight yellowness, both, perhaps, a testament to pathology. Her belief in borrowed myth was manifest in her eager mouth. The others, looking towards her, nodded emphatically. There were several 'Amen's' - evolution for them, thought James, was probably something to do with Che Guevara. He exaggeratedly shook his head, disbelievingly. They matronised him with subtle smirks. He told them that they could only infer God's existence. A teenager who'd been quiet till then cut in, neatly turning around James' positivism with a mature, 'Believing is seeing.'

Ignoring James, they talked amongst themselves about their 'evidence' for God; personal incidents, biblical happenings. He was about to give them both barrels of his secular shot gun when the pastor announced that as this was only an initial meeting, they would finish. He invited them to pray again.

James lowered his head, trying not to listen, feeling as uncomfortable with prayer as he had as a child, and thinking of Christina and that his garden had neither fruit nor reptiles, nor had it sin for there was no-one to sin with. He wanted, rather sulkily, to be disliked by them, wished them to react to his iconoclasm with suspicion, anger, even perhaps ostracising him, but during and after soup, tea and buns, they were open and friendly, even interested; asking him where he'd found out about the course, what he did, where he lived. He mumbled a few answers and moved away. The person who'd asked him to come had just arrived and was talking seriously with some of the others, briefly acknowledging him.

Attack Christians, he thought, and they become more Christian; turning the metaphorical cheek, courteous, smiling warmly as they gently surrounded him He felt himself reluctantly responding, relaxing, making mildly amusing pleasantries. Christina, looking

175

earnest and tall, was talking to the pastor. She wore high heels, her legs were long and shapely and, he. told himself, was unwell. A few people asked if he was coming again and maybe finish the ten week term. He wondered if he'd had any effect at all, if they had even considered anything he'd said: his entrenched views versus theirs. The pastor was still talking to Christina as he left.

Initially, he had no intention of going again, but had a week with relatively few clients. He saw a friend for a drink, went to two badly chosen films, and feeling a need for a little intellectual stimulus, he went.

Once they'd begun he went through most of the basic arguments against there being a God - some of the people around him seemingly not having heard them before - offered proof that there can be no proof and, after a silence, bore the brunt of a fervent battering by their beliefs, dogma and the occasional use of biblical quotes like back-up sniper fire. The pastor, who'd been quiet for a while, then joined in, enthusiastically explaining chunks of the good book to his delighted flock.

He watched Christina again; she wasn't saying much, she hadn't the week before. He knew little about her. She was younger than him, but could have been married, had children, he didn't know what she did for a living nor where she lived.

After the soup he walked to the staircase and looked through a window, out over Holborn Viaduct towards Farringdon.

'You're frightened to feel God, aren't you. Release it; let it go.'

He turned. It was Christina. He felt almost startled; this didn't seem like doorstep preaching, it felt as if it had been said to *him.*

'What drives your intellectualised disbelief in faith, then?'

'look… there's a need to create a God, we search for order, comfort, a supra-human deity gives us that. If God *did* exist we'd still have to invent him'

'There you go again.'

'I don't know where you live, but if I come a little way with you we can talk more.'

'Here. I live here.'

'What d'you mean?'

'There are rooms here,' she said, as if explaining to a child, 'I've lived here for two years, since I came. The pastor knew my parents, the rent's cheap.'

'And you're nearer to God?'

'I'm tired now. Come next time, try to shake us up again.' She grinned for a moment. He walked with her to the lift.

She turned to look at him. 'Do you want to do some good?'

Before he could answer she told him she was helping out at a South London Christian Centre assisting people coming off drugs. In his naïve, secular way he asked if she was supporting the medical staff in some capacity.

She frowned and said, 'We pray. They're helped through prayer.'

She was going the next day. He didn't have a client until the evening. He said he'd go. She gave him the address.

Another warm welcome, this time by three Jamaican women who appeared to know who he was. There was a young African pastor in a corner office he was introduced to. Christina hadn't arrived yet. He went into the hall.

Long tables were laid with food, mostly cold. There was a pile of sandwiches provided by a large chain of coffee shops with a 'Donated to the Homeless' promotion wrapper. He moved some chairs around, blew up a few balloons, pinned them to a wall then went to the kitchen and washed and dried with some of the other helpers. He went out to the hall again where Afro-Caribbean, East European and other nationalities took their places at the tables and a young, possibly born again Christian told him how he had been cured of his drug addiction through prayer.

The pastor said some blessings. When he'd finished and people began to sing hymns, with the Polish group smoothly word perfect but in a hurry to finish and eat, he came over to James and told him that Christina wouldn't be coming, she didn't feel well enough. He talked to him about her; she'd been coming there three or four times a week for a year. James told him that she'd asked him to come. He was given her number. He left; the yellow street lights against the black sky seemed cold and hard.

He hadn't time next day to call her before his nine o'clock patient came and, when with him, kept thinking of her; the pallor, the quiet

177

mystique, spirituality, the belief and faith she carried with her. He was jealous: envious of the constant drip-feed of assurance, of... certainty. He wanted that belief in him - his baby again, wishing mummy to be interested in nothing but him.

His client was unusually loquacious, but James wasn't really listening. As he left he promised himself that the following week he would give him his full attention and energy. He rang her as soon as he'd gone.

'Oh, hello, you've surprised me. Did you go? What did you think of it?' Did you help out?'

He told her he'd blown up a few balloons. He was going to ask how many of the needy had been religious before they'd arrived at the Centre or was it a sudden conversion when they saw the free food, but felt it wasn't fair to unload more cynicism onto her. He asked how she was feeling.

'Thanks for going,' she said.

'I'd have done more if you'd been there.'

'Such as?'

'Whatever you'd wanted me to.'

She laughed. 'Are you always this compliant with women?'

'Are you going to have a coffee with me?'

There was a silence. She quietly said yes. They arranged a time, a place.

He met her at St Paul's tube, she suggested a nearby cafe. As they walked he watched her. She was casually dressed: flat shoes, jeans, small ear rings, and the spirituality again, which had a depth, a core. He was aware that he had a proneness to be attracted a little too easily by the physicality of a woman, especially if she was tall and slim - his mother was, thus that physique was the norm, short was unthinkingly 'inferior'.

It was a fixed chairs broken yolk kind of place, but it didn't matter; she was there. They sat. She asked him what he thought of the church meeting.

'Well...'

'They seemed to like you.'

'Why?'

'Because they're Christian,' she grinned.

'Precisely. I should save this up for next time, I know, but the only way we can know anything - and no rationalist has yet come up with an *a priori* synthetic truth: something that tells us about the world independent of experience - is through sense data, and God isn't amenable to that.

'You're just a positivist; science, science - '

'No. Science, like magic and religion, is a self-contained belief system that cannot of itself be wrong, plus what a scientific truth is today will be heresy tomorrow, their paradigms shift, 'truth' shifts.'

'Maths doesn't.'

'God created the world in seven days? Maths can only tell us something about the world when it's applied to the world, there's no numbers in nature, it's all tautology: everything behind the equals sign is another way of saying that which is before it. They're also analytic truths; that two chairs plus two chairs make four chairs is true regardless of whether the chairs exist or not.'

'Everything's a construct?'

'Yes, language is the ultimate one. We can't get outside of it and -.'

'You know that I'm not well, don't you.'

Maybe this was a way of shutting him up, to make him feel guilty, knock him off another hobby horse which, with its bit between its teeth, he was about to let ride on and on. He told her that he knew. She looked down then smiled again: such even teeth, such full lips.

'But, you're getting better. Yes?'

She gave an awkward grin. 'Hope so. Look I've got to get home, welcome a new boarder, I think he's from Canada, I should have done my homework. But you'll come next time?'

He asked her what she was doing the weekend

'More church work, I'm afraid.'

She got up to go. He offered to accompany her on the short walk back. He asked whether they could have a chat if he came early next time.

'Okay, I'll see you half an hour earlier. There'll be a service afterwards of course.' She looked worn out, tired.

The afternoon before he saw her, a friend who he'd known for a few years and who had moved back to the north east after living in London rang to say he would be around locally and would like to have a drink with him. When James saw him he realised he'd missed his jocular, but bright crassness and enjoyed the short time they spent together. He then drove back to his local station to get the Tube to the church meeting.

He'd been driving for a few minutes when, as he stopped at traffic lights, was startled by an aggressive fist hammering on his side window. He wound it down. He saw a large face, eyes bulging.

'You hit my car, you know you bastardwell did.'

He remembered that about a mile back there'd been a car parked partly on a corner pavement opposite a traffic island. He'd slowed down to pass.

'Did I? I didn't feel -'

He hadn't noticed the jack handle the man was holding. He pushed the sharp end into the side of James' Adam's apple. He decided instantly to treat him as if he was an angry, potentially violent patient. Looking into his eyes he calmly told him to take the tool away from his throat. He did, slowly. James pointed out that the lights were now green and that he was going to turn left into the main road and stop. He suggested he follow him and they'd talk. He did. James got out of his car, stepped onto the edge of the pavement and leant against the guard rail. His attacker climbed out of his vehicle with another, shorter man.

They came towards him. He repeated that he hadn't known he'd hit the car. The smaller one said, 'Look, mate, 'e's my bruvver, his wife's taken his kid and gone. 'e's in pain.'

'Yeh, I'm sorry mate,' said the one still holding the lever, 'he's right, I'm 'urtin', I really am, but you'll have to pay for the damage.'

James walked round to the side of the car. There was a long scratch on the driver's door. Acting as rationally as he could he asked its owner how much he thought it would cost. He told him; it sounded reasonable. He knew he had a cheque with him, a rare occurrence, wrote it and handed it over. Then they heard a siren. A police car pulled in front of them. They were like a stationary mini convoy now. Two constables stepped out, one with a tube with a lump on the end which James guessed was a breathalyzer.

'Anything wrong, sir?' the officer asked, looking at James.

Surprisingly, jack man said, 'No, it's okay, we're just having a chat, haven't seen each other for a while,'

'Sure you haven't been drinking, sir?'

James told him he'd had a glass of wine. That it was a breathalyzer was confirmed by its use.

'It's right on the line sir, I can charge you or not.'

'Oh, come on, it's Christmas, you're not gonna nab him for one drink are yer?' asked James' previous assailant, putting an arm around his shoulder.

The officer looked at the three of them, nodded and got back in the car with his colleague and drove off. James had forgotten it was two days before Christmas. Bizarrely they wished each other a merry one and he drove away.

Forty minutes later, leaning against the inside of one of the large double doors of the church, he breathed a deep sigh of relief. Then she was standing in front of him asking if he was alright. He told her what had happened.

She squeezed his arm. 'Perhaps God protected you.'

He moved his arm away. 'What's this then, a Lutheran position that the Lord has rewarded my, or rather your, faith, a Calvinist view that his favours are pre-destined' - he'd stepped away from the door, arms out, hands offering the mordant choices - 'or was it written in the stars?'

Realising his irritation was partly due to delayed shock, he took a deep breath and let it out slowly, in little pieces.

'I'm sorry.'

'You get fed up with me keeping on about God?'

'It just happened. Doesn't matter now. God; it's all so dead... meaningless. What are we talking about tonight, then?'

'Do you think you should say anything? If it's so pointless should you even be listening?

'I'd like to see your room.'

'Why?'

'Because… you're in it, you live there. Here.'

She looked at him doubtfully. He sensed a little hurt, expected her to say it wasn't worth it and go off to meet the others and leave him there.

'Come on then,' she said, like a young Girl Guide leader.

They went up the stairs to the top floor, along a corridor and into a room at the end. There was a sofa bed, table, chairs, religious books and the inevitable collection of halo'd Jesus's on the walls. There ware also some photos of red earth, large trees, a house with a veranda which he guessed was the parental home. It was, she said, near Harare, which her parents had insisted on calling Salisbury, still referring to themselves as Rhodesians. They were dead; she had no siblings. She'd begun training as a lawyer, and then … God.

She made him tea. He asked her if she wanted to tell him what was wrong with her.

'It's malaria.' She said it as if the subject bored her. 'It develops within three months of leaving a malaria region, ironically there's little in my country. It affects the red blood corpuscles and my type is plasmodium falciparum.' She said it almost by rote as if she'd heard it a hundred times; the reciting of it objectifying, detaching it from her for a few seconds.

'There won't be much discussion this evening. Dirk will want us to eat and then go to the service. I'd better help get the food ready. Do you want to come?'

He found himself washing up and laying plates again. This was the prosaic, pragmatic side of belief; no searing orange light, no illuminating epiphany, just mundanity, getting things ready, preparing, cleaning. He spoke a little to a few of the others, they were friendly as always. He felt dispirited, wondered how long she'd had the disease, what its prognosis was.

They went into the service; there were a lot of people. After a loud, booming African pastor had finished his spiel, a small band with a soprano played gospel music. People began singing, dancing, Christina stepped into an aisle and he watched her throwing her arms heavenwards. He, too, began moving with the rhythm. As he looked at her again she turned her body towards the people behind her. Then she crumpled and fell on her side. He hesitated, went to go over to her, but others in the congregation already had; a couple of people on the course lifted her, another shouted into a mobile.

The teenager came across to him and said that it had happened before, but was occurring more frequently. The music stopped, the singing petered out, the drummer continued for a few seconds, then quiet. Dirk excused himself and went out behind the two people half carrying her to, James suspected, her room.

He went to the back of the hall and sat on a pew. He heard the siren of an ambulance getting louder, then stopping. The congregation looked lost; some left, others sat, including the singer. He should have gone to the ambulance, but felt he had no right to, felt cut off from her, didn't share her conceptual system, these people, this place, this faith. And what *did* drive this intellectualised disbelief? 'Let it go,' she'd said. But he knew he wouldn't, couldn't.

He went home, half-heatedly willing his intellect to crumble, make himself believe something. She was ill. He wanted to want to pray, but knew who his God was: God the father. Not a bearded man in the sky, benevolent, wise and seemingly righteous, but his late, indifferent, rigid, unaware, weak parent He rang the church. A caretaker answered. He knew nothing. He went online. The malaria variant she had was mostly fatal. Before he deleted he saw 'coma,' 'major organ failure.'

He shouted, 'Dad, fuck you. Fuck you.' But he couldn't feel it; it wasn't even a genuine attempt, just a gesture.

He realised he knew so little about her, wondered why he hadn't asked her more, discovered more. Was there a little bit of him that was wary of getting close to her, to *feel* something for her because he knew she was ill? Perhaps he wanted her as some sort of proxy God; an intermediary between that great psychiatrist in the sky - was he a Freudian? - and himself.

He didn't ring again, was scared to; didn't want to know that she was getting worse, didn't want to emotionally face the concept of death. He was frightened. He knew he wouldn't go to the church again.

Next day was a patient-free one with an overcast sky. He decided to go to a sun bed parlour, not really for a tan he told himself, but to cover up, detract from the lines around the mouth, the pale face. He'd never been to one before. He went in.

'Waddya want, lie-down or stand-up, babe?' asked a walnut coloured peroxide blonde.

Through a partially open door he could see a horizontal, glass-walled sarcophagus and felt a pre-claustrophobic apprehension. He went for the alternative.

Ten minutes was too long. He left, feeling like a baked piece of meat and, arriving home and looking in a mirror and realising he looked like one, decided it was all the remnants of an adolescent narcissism. It was narcissism in the face of mortality: the equation being that if he looked fit and tanned then he wouldn't age, ergo, wouldn't die. It was a subject he'd never studied: the psychology of death. He needed to. And it wasn't the first time 'Physician heal thyself' had mockingly juddered around his head.

SEMIOLOGY

Resting against the whiteboard he looked across to the empty chair on his left where Marci had always sat, until a year ago when her estranged husband's jealousy had finally won and she'd left the course. He knew nothing of her and David, her lecturer; he was jealous of every man.

It was a common story amongst mature female students. Men, feeling inadequate and frightened that their partners or wives were stretching towards new horizons - and wondering who was helping them get there - would occasionally come to the college and demand to know where their women were. When he asked for ideas for research projects a third of the females would opt for something to do with domestic violence, which he would turn into a working hypothesis that they could test.

Hope was such a one. She would sit next to him when discussing her work with heavy bruising under her eye. She was twenty, the youngest in a class of thirty.

'I don't deserve this, do I.' she'd say.

Marci used to sit there wearing a tracksuit, her braided extensions rising above a headband, gazing at him with Bambi eyes and a knowing mouth and occasionally sipping brandy from a plastic bottle. He thought it was mineral water.

It had been a frenetic time. He'd been to a gym with her, seen the frown under the dark, tight nest of hair to ward off posing machos, the burnt umber skin, ear-to-ear grin, watched her puffing out her pain in press-ups, drowning her sadness in saunas, lifted weights with her, and attempted ungainly to keep time with her aerobics group. He'd held her up in a nightclub, rushed to her bedside in a local hospital because she'd collapsed, gazed at the zigzagging, merging colours on the screen whilst her liver was being scanned, and after being dragged for a sunset ride on the *Barracuda* at Southend, lying next to her on his bed like a contortionist dying in his own arms.

The tables and chairs he'd arranged in a three-sided rectangle, for many mature students had had bad educative experiences when young and, especially at the beginning of an academic year, desks set out in well remembered rows would trigger the same fears. Most of the people on this course were from ethnic minorities, mainly African females, and nearly all went on to university.

He played devil's advocate. When he first met them he would explain that under the guise of an evangelical mission Europeans had introduced Christianity to Africa for the purposes of social and economic control of half a continent - the more politically aware would nod wisely - and that God hadn't created us, but we, him; the real question being, why?

The classroom would glow with outrage and anger and, often, pity. He wanted to shock their mindset, to create a sliver of a chance that he just could be right, thus helping them to detach, to step back. They were then halfway to a sociological view of the world, and that's what he was teaching. There were always some female students who would say to him on their way out after the first lecture, lightly touching his shoulder as he sat at his desk, 'We'll pray for you, Mark.' He was sure that they did.

He'd begun the sociology of deviance the previous year at the beginning of term two and started on the semiotics part the day before Marci had left. He'd suggested that the police worked within the class structure, had pre-existing concepts, 'pictures in their heads' of what criminality was and 'criminals' were like. He'd asked them for the signs the Bill pounced on.

The two Dagenham lads, who'd always sat together, immediately and in concert had said, 'Workin' class, innit.'

'They're protecting the bourgeoisie from the proles.' Abosede had shouted, her Catholicism weakening after a month of Marx.

He'd asked for the signals that would suggest 'working classness.' Pam, the Afro-Caribbean had suggested it was the walk; another that it was the 'Sun' stuck in back pockets of jeans. He'd then turned his back to them, bouncing on his heels, squaring his shoulders and asking for, 'Two lagers, John.'

He did this every year, 'the calf muscle move.' He'd then ask if they thought he was mimicking the son of an Emeritus Professor of Literature at Kings College, Cambridge - a cheap laugh, but it made the point. One of several Nigerians had said a car was an obvious clue, another, leisure activities and musical tastes, a usually silent Somalian suggested that accent and appearance were the obvious signals and, rather late, someone had suggested race. And so they'd gone on, most of them saying something and in the end creating a comprehensive coverage of perceived clues.

Marci, as ever, had said nothing, merely looking at him steadily. He'd hinted strongly that there would be questions on this at the end of term and suggested a mnemonic to help them. Their answers came back like drumbeats, and they'd made up a little chant:

dreadlocks, hip-hop, beemer, mean,

tattoos, skins, hard, obscene

Some of them had left the classroom happily singing it - possibly because they were going home to change for a birthday party for the twin girls in the class. He'd reminded them, tongue in cheek, they were to turn up in English time, not African.

Now, he let this evening class go early. His car had been stored in the nearby motor vehicle buildings - and probably used for teaching - for the length of his drink and driving ban, and he was wondering how it would feel when he drove it for the first time in a year. Marci, a lot noisier then than when she'd occasionally slipped into the staff room, unheard and unseen, and put a sandwich - and even an apple - on his desk, had been involved in that, too.

It had been decided that they'd go to a local East End pub for the party. He rarely drank, often being mocked by fellow chippies on the sites he'd worked on as an apprentice years before. The class had settled in well in the three months they had been together and most wanted to go. Marci he'd known outside the classroom since she had tearfully pleaded that her essay had been worth more than the grade he had given it because she had worked so hard; perhaps he should have realised then that she had emotional problems. He mumbled about professional integrity and encouraged her to work harder. He didn't give in. He hadn't the year before when a student who had done a lot of research on prostitution and, accompanied by her tough-looking CID husband and pitiful lame child - a three-pronged attack - had harangued him in front of other staff to give her the Distinction she thought her work was worth. But, he rarely failed any one.

The next day Marci had rung him in the staff room and asked if he wanted to go to a bar that evening with her and some friends. He'd thanked her and declined. Later that night, with tears in her voice, she'd called and asked for his address. A little afterwards he'd seen her walking up a garden path some houses away peering short-sightedly at the number on the front door, a manoeuvre she repeated on the next one. Taking her hand he'd gently guided her to his flat.

They drove to the pub late and on the way he'd made the mistake of mentioning the class flirt whom, apparently, he spent more time talking to in class than the others. The car stiffened; he was scared. She had this effect on him and however he analysed it couldn't prevent. She was out of the car before he'd stopped, towing his fear to the pub. Ignoring wondering classmates she pushed straight through to the bar and ordered a double brandy.

There was a small stage to the side and on it was the girl who had organised this get-together and who was groining her mini-skirted thighs around and pushing them out at everybody standing around. The swot whose name he could never remember was next to her wearing a blonde wig and rhythmically lifting up a kilt, showing his briefs. The two Ugandans, looking like bouncers, were chuckling deeply and the Nigerian women, gold bangles and ear rings glittering, were quietly smiling, their Victorian values not far away; not for them the two inch band of flesh at their waists, tops of knickers showing. He noticed the Ghanaian women were wearing traditional dress, which seemed to glow, as did their smooth skins, and saw the Romford Marxist leaning against the flock-papered wall frowning disapprovingly. Most of them looked very different from the way they did in class and seemed genuinely glad to see him.

He circulated, drank some wine - someone seemed to keep filling his glass - learnt more about Robert Gabriel Mugabe from an extrovert Zimbabwean student, and one of the older women came over to talk to him about social work. Then Marci was by his side, eyes narrowed. She turned and minced to the stage, jumped up and started dancing about in a clumsy, clattering way in front of a track-suited skinhead, repeatedly pressing herself against him. As she briefly pulled away there was a noticeable bulge in his crotch. She looked round at Mark and grinned. He strode across and pulled her off the stage. He could hardly see through the noise.

'Get off, get off, get off!' she shouted. 'Let me go!'

She tried to pull her hand away; he gripped harder, dragged her across to the door and, in a tiny chip of cold detachment, saw them performing some exotic dance where the man strides smoothly across the dance floor dragging his sylph-like partner horizontally behind him. He was angry, and as he pulled the door open glimpsed one of the Dagenham students hiding under a table. She continued to shout at him to let her go as he hurried her to his car parked across the road. He held her against the passenger door for a few seconds then ran around to open the driving-side door. She kicked the side of the car and continued doing so as he got in. He leant across to open the door for her and saw two women run from the pub towards her. He didn't know them.

'He's her tutor, he's abusing her.' one shrilled. 'He's using his authority.'

Again, the distancing irrelevance as he thought that this could be a cue for a lecture on perceptions of power. In the wing mirror he saw some men hastily cross towards him. He'd left the window down; the other woman pushed her arm in and grabbed his hand as it turned the ignition.

'She's with me.' he said, as calmly as he could,' I brought her here, she's - '

'I'm not!' Marci screamed.' I'm not with him, I'm not, I'm not!' and then she began crying. He pushed the hand away and drove off.

He stopped after a hundred yards or so and then went around the block to go back to see if she was okay. Slowly he passed the pub; a group of women were comforting her. He could hear her sobbing. He drove homewards.

A few minutes later he was driving the wrong way down a one-way street and realised he was drunk. He stopped the car; it just happened to be outside of a small police station. A constable told him to get out. He did so and irrelevantly emptied his pockets, placing their contents on the roof of the car. He heard himself giggling as they slid slowly down.

She was leaning against the porch when he got back. He opened the door and closed it behind them. She followed him to the bedroom. He let out a tortuous explosion of the evening's emotions.

'You could have got me lynched.' he yelled. 'Why did you lie?

Why?'

She suddenly slid down the wall and knelt on the floor. He picked her up and gently laid her on the bed. She slept instantly in his arms. He hadn't mentioned the breathalysing. He held her tightly throughout the night.

The last of them left the classroom - Hope remarking facetiously that she'd seen a squirrel in the college earlier and wanted to know if it was deviant - and just to make sure that the motor vehicle lecturer had got his message he glanced out the window to see if the car was outside the workshops. It was. He hurried down the stairs, wondering why he felt such anticipation at driving again, something quite ordinary, mundane even. He'd got used to buses.

It felt immediately familiar. Driving slowly out the gate he turned westward, overtook two lorries and accelerated towards a main junction a mile away. As he neared it he became gradually aware that what was irritatingly taking his attention were flashing blue lights hitting the driving mirror. Their significance escaped him - he even flicked the mirror up to dull the flashes - until he heard the siren and saw the panda car suddenly behind him. The traffic lights in front were red. He slowed and stopped. Turning in his seat he saw two policemen step out from either side of their car, their movements synchronised.

He'd taught for nine hours in a twelve-hour day and was tired; he assumed he'd been speeding. He remembered the last time police had approached his car; the unbelieving shake of the head from the older one, the embarrassed grin from the other as he'd picked up his wallet, small change and comb from the roadside, and thought of Marci with her bloodshot, beautiful eyes telling him the following morning that her husband was coming back and she wouldn't be able to see him again. He thought also of the last lesson she'd had with him, what they'd all been discussing, and the little chant.

Quickly he pulled two paperbacks from the glove compartment, *Sociology* and *Philosophical Theory*, and dropped them face upwards on the passenger seat. And as the two uniformed figures looked in at him from both sides of the car he lowered the window and raised the volume on *Classic FM.*

STACKS

It was the Flying Fortress that brought back the instant prejudice - not, for some reason, the 'Memphis Belle' parked on the edge of the apron outside the hangar - and of course it came from dad. It was his father's teenage 'bleedin' Yanks' response to the 'They're over 'ere, overfed and over sexed - and you're underfed, under sexed and under Eisenhower' wartime joke. It had passed onto James; another bit of familial internalization lasting for ever.

He was at Duxford, a museum now but once a Second World War operational aerodrome. On a nearby wall was a large black and white photo showing, from the foreground to the background of a high, wide, stylized columned façade, a sea of helmeted soldiers sitting backs to camera. In front of them, mounted centre top, was a huge concrete swastika - all reeking of the Moderne, of fascism, of a deep, controlled mass hysteria. He felt a childlike awe. He felt also a momentary guilt as if his aesthetic sense and the appreciation of the shot had pushed out the emotional meaning. It was a willing seduction, burying the repugnance of death.

James Kent was here partly because he'd overheard an enthusiastic train conversation about the place and because he had time on his hands. There was a paucity of new clients. There'd been no referrals for some time and two of his long-standing patients were now coming once every two weeks instead of one. It could be, of course, that they were finding his therapist fees difficult, though he hadn't increased them for five years. There may have been other variables, but he couldn't be bothered to think what they were.

He went out of the hangar to the parked civilian airplanes on the edge of the runway: the Ambassador, Britannia, the VC 10 and, wandering into a second hangar - the sight making him feel less sombre - the elegant lines of the Comet. He needed a coffee. It was a choice between 'Wingco Joe's' - a strained alliance of transatlantic nomenclature - and 'The Mess,' a tidy, characterless space serving little but tea and buns. He chose neither. On the train home he recalled another photo in one of the hangars of a Lady Bountiful frowning down at a bedridden airman and amused himself by hearing, 'Rectum?' 'Well, it didn't do 'em much good, ma'am.'

It was still light and warm and although walking around the lake in

Wanstead Park would have been a more appropriate summer evening experience he wanted a little urban stimulus, so broke his journey and wandered around Dalston and Hoxton, the latter - known by workmates when he was an apprentice as 'oxton' - he'd never liked. When a child it was seen as an inner city slum even by people living where he did in Plaistow, and the image overrode whatever he saw as he looked briefly around him.

Turning a corner he saw a shop tucked between a warehouse and a storage unit with second-hand books, prints and photos displayed outside and similar bric-a-brac, plus furniture, mirrors, lighting and clothes inside. A large African man sprawled on a thirties sofa asked him, with a big grin and a cockney accent, if he was interested in anything. James told him he was just looking. The man explained that he and a mate had just pooled their scant resources to see whether a growing local professional demography would enable them to make a living.

'Hey,' he said to a broad, long-haired man putting up a wall picture, 'let's take pictures of people as they come in.' He waved a smart phone.

James suggested, a little disinterestedly, they stick them on the inside of the window below an 'our customers' sticker to make the place feel more communal.

'Nice idea,' said the long-haired one, turning to him and smiling.

James recognised him; but wasn't sure from where, then as he came towards him, hand outstretched, he did. He was an ex-patient.

'How are you?' James asked lightly.

He just smiled some more. He rarely smiled when James knew him.

'Fine, fine.'

James wished them luck with their venture and left. He was thinking how incongruous it was for someone as bright as this man to have a shop - too much time doing nothing, waiting, restless. Then he was at James' side.

'Mister Kent, I'd like to see you again; as a patient, of course.' He seemed nervous. 'It's the same, really. Could I? I still like the jokes you used to tell me; you know, the hotline with the automated messages: 'If you're obsessive-compulsive, please press 1 repeatedly. If you have multiple personalities, please press 3, 4, 5 and 6. If you -' '

'If you need to see me again you have my number'

His ex-client seemed hurt for a second, as if he expected a consultation in the street, then thanked him and went back to the shop.

On his way home James thought about Roy Brookland who he'd last seen four years ago. He remembered something the latter had written for him. When clients did this he'd ask them to tell him what they'd written and to look at his eyes while doing so. Writing what they felt, thought, could be an escape from actually feeling it

When Brookland had done so James knew he wasn't emotionally experiencing his words; he'd turned them into images of the words, could see them in his mind. He was very visual, partly because he'd been escaping himself, not facing what was there, denying, in effect, that he lived in his own skin, *had* to live there. Thus, a sometimes intense preoccupation with the design, the architecture, the feel of houses, buildings, streets was a facile, part compensation for not facing his fear of real relationships. James knew how utterly lonely he had to be.

He'd left treatment suddenly. James had called him, written to him; there'd been no reply. He'd assumed rather lazily that he was feeling better, stronger, and felt he didn't need help any more. James once asked him what he did for a living. He'd just shrugged. 'This and that.' he'd said dismissively.

James lay on the couch in his study, as he occasionally did when attempting to understand better the patients who had sat and tried to relax on it, and remembered more of his ex-client: the intense annoyance .when James would say or do something he felt was 'unintellectual,' such as watching football on TV when he came to him - as James turned it off he'd sneer - or forgetting who wrote 'Catch 22,' what *chateau forte* meant and many random opinions, bits of behaviour and an arbitrary lack of knowledge he selectively hated.

James was of course - to the man's child - his father; the man that had never been aware of or understood his needs since his birth. He came, detachedly, to recognise this. Sometimes his cognisance would be immediate, but to transfer this into an emotional awareness was too difficult for him. Perhaps, James thought, he'd left him because he knew he wouldn't, couldn't get better.

He looked in his filing cabinet - preferring the texture of paper to the bright flatness of a monitor screen - and found a short play Brookland had written. centred on the '68 student revolution in Paris. James occasionally went to fringe theatres and would seek out someone involved in the show, tell them of his client's work and whether they knew anyone it could be sent to. He managed to find someone who read plays for a small theatre company based under a South London railway arch. Brookland sent it and was asked for a writing CV. James remembered what he'd said to him.

'The written word is all; surely, no matter who writes something it's *what's* written. I refuse to be a supplicant.'

He though it was about power and writers meant to 'feel like Twist with his bowl.' It was, for him, a case of who you knew and being young.

'I feel like sending them a forgotten Strindberg or Chekov play and telling them I'm 75, live in Scunthorpe and have never written anything in my life.'

Whatever James had said to him: how talented, creative, perceptive he was, he wouldn't, couldn't accept praise. He could win the Nobel Prize for literature, James thought, but his emotional impoverishment would swallow it up like a cloud, it would vanish; yet recognition was something he seemed to crave more than anything else.

James found what he was looking for with the play:

'The 'me' is a tiny creature living inside the 'I', the body, watching the 'I' - the constructed 'I' - all the time, watching the face, limbs, the flesh age. (Sometimes I feel that when the body's too old, I'll find another vehicle for myself - or rather, for 'me,' as there is no self - and carry on.)'

This was an interestingly warped account of the internal 'known' and the 'knower,' and was, James knew, him escaping, forever escaping from whatever he was so frightened of.

He rang James the next morning. There were no patients the following day and he agreed to come. He was on time, sat down and, attempting a wry smile, looked across at James.

'Well, here you are again,' said James lightly, 'Anything new?'

When James had last seen him in this room his hair had been short, cropped and he'd worn his usual tie.

'It's the same really, like I said, just … the same. I wonder if serial killers feel like me: everybody composed of just moronic molecules, just mechanisms that get in the way.'

'You mean, your way. And you're not going to kill anyone, however you feel. Who do you hate most, men or women?'

'They're just… bodies.'

'You reduce every person to that because you're not facing very early feelings toward both your parents, especially your father. I told you this some time ago. I know you remember.'

He shifted uncomfortably, was quiet for a while.

'I like windows, not just when they're lit at night and you imagine warmth and love there, but on a bright day and the glass and glazing bars glinting…'

He looked far away for a moment, almost smiling.

'I remember you telling me this.'

'Mostly, I love chimneys, there's something about them.'

'You've never mentioned this before.'

He didn't respond, his face returning to the same vacantly musing expression.

'I was on a flat roof recently in Soho, plants and stuff, a friend lives in a top flat, and I could see the chimneys of the terraces stretching out into perspective. I stood by the chimney stack; it was bigger than I thought. I wanted to hug one of the chimneys. It seemed huge. I reached up, but felt frightened, horrible, I couldn't.'

He narrowed his eyes and grimaced. as he said it. Then he relaxed, was quiet for a while.

'I was thinking about the big one near the slag heaps at Becton power station. When I was a teenager I climbed to the top of one of the heaps. They're not there any more. Perhaps, like my life, they've turned into a hill of beans.'

He paused, looking sad.

'You know, it's as if I saw you yesterday, nothing has changed, nothing has happened, time doesn't move. I carry you about in my head, anyway.'

'That's because you won't, can't, separate.'

'I know,' he said quietly.

He got up suddenly, took out his wallet and held out a cheque. James shook his head.

'Thanks.' He turned to leave.

'I wish you wouldn't go again.'

'I have to.' .

'You've been here ten minutes. I don't really know what your reasons are for going, nor why you're starting a shop, but - '

'Because I can't do what I used to do.' he said over his shoulder.

He opened the front door and walked quickly up the path. In answer to James' unspoken question, he said, without turning his head,

'I was a civil aviation pilot,'

James caught a glimpse of angry, bitter eyes as he looked back for a moment while opening the gate. He didn't close it.

There was a dull, slowly building shock: the realisation that this man who lived inside himself in a tundra of a place where nothing grew, had controlled a faked ego and a body that pulled levers, reacted to instruments, spoke to Air Traffic Controllers, joked with his co-pilots and stewards, looked casually out of toughened glass windows at mountains, seas, clouds - James wondered if, like his passengers, he'd seen shapes in them - had made instant decisions: on whether to switch to computerised control in a tropical storm over Malaysia, if and when to abort a trip if there'd been a violent passenger aboard, and whether to actually climb a gangway and get into his aircraft

James wondered what his old friend and colleague Thomas would have said about some of this. He thought he knew what it would be.

'Chimneys are the father's penis, James. As a young boy he was terrified of loving his father, he looked into his eyes and couldn't, just couldn't love him, it was wrong. The intriguing, fascinating thing about chimneys for him is that from a sunlit, tree-framed distance they are, if you like, perhaps soft penises, things that won't

196

hurt him, but, close up, they are hostile, brutal, nightmarish. And yes, before you say it, this is before culture gets in with its taboos of incest and homosexuality. This is primal, James, and I'm surprised there's not more people messed up, more queues outside places where people like us work.'

Then he'd probably say, as he'd once suggested,

'I'm coming to the conclusion that the id - that ineradicable bundle of animal instincts, just to remind you quasi-Freudians - within the child wants to be taken over by the father, at an unconscious level, wants to be fucked by him.'

James had grimaced. This last was too Freudian, even for him - he probably didn't want it to be true - though it could have been pure Thomas. He could hear him saying,

'That's the look I get from fellow analysts. I can now understand how Sigmund felt about the reaction to his theories by the Viennese middle classes.'

James felt disappointed, weary, it seemed so pointless. He'd done nothing for Brookland. He'd carry on as he was now for ever. Maybe he should have tried harder to persuade him to stay; the year or so he'd seen him for was no time at all, a mere beginning. James guessed that he hadn't been told what he'd done for a living - and perhaps had still been doing when he was coming to him regularly - because he thought he'd be shocked, certainly surprised. He was. He was curious about how he'd got through his assessments, psychiatric checks - he assumed he'd had them - but, as he'd been like he was virtually all of his life, he'd have acted it; it wouldn't, perhaps, have been too difficult.

Brookland didn't stay in his mind for long, but a month or so after he'd walked out James met a friend at the old Reeves Paints factory off Kingsland Road. They talked mostly poetry, his friend wanting James to have a final proof-read of his erstwhile collection before sending it to publishers. James took it with him and went towards a nearby café he'd enjoyed some time before.

He was vaguely aware that he was near Brookland's shop, in fact, virtually had to pass it. From the corner he could see scaffolding along the front of it. As he got nearer he could see a man sliding tiles down from the pitched roof. The cheerful African from the shop was standing on the edge of the pavement looking up, listening to the clacking, swishing rhythm of the spinning tiles. James went across to him, received the big grin.

'Hello, I know you. I've got a picture.'

He pointed to his shop window, at the rows of small photos. stuck on a large sheet of paper.

'We did what you said'.

James commented that his business seemed to be doing okay and asked how his partner was.

'Well, a little strange. I'm a bit bothered. He went up the scaffold the other day, in fact he's been up there more than once. The roofers were away for lunch, though he does it sometimes after they've knocked off. He climbs up, looks at the chimneys, sometimes as if he's waiting for white smoke to come out to show the pope's been elected. I've watched him. He goes up the roof close to 'em, never touches. He's crazy. I love him, though. But he didn't like it this morning. This plane flew over, unusually low, really, and he pushed his fists in his ears. I thought he was gonna flatten his head. He looked shocked.' He laughed.

'That's a bit danger - '

'No, you can see it's boarded above the gutter, he'll be alright But yesterday I heard this crash and there were bits of broken chimney like pottery on the pavement. I don't know how it could have got there unless it'd been thrown down, really. But he said nothing when he come in again.'

'Perhaps you shouldn't mention I... it's okay, doesn't matter.'

James again wished his business well, and left.

As he walked he was thinking that if Thomas was right then Brookland must have been so frightened: the old, soot-grimed chimneys getting larger as he moved towards them, seeming, perhaps, to symbolise his father as an awful nemesis. It must have taken nerve to climb the scaffold each time. He briefly wondered if the phallus was circumcised - it certainly would have been for Freud - for the chimneys, going in slightly towards the top and the thick-lipped head, could have represented an uncut one. Maybe he'd seen his father's, erect or otherwise. The fear would then, perhaps, have been engendered by the reality, not just the symbolism - if, of course, Thomas was right. Perhaps, just perhaps, he'd smashed or broken off one of them and threw it down in an attempt to destroy his father

Trying to push these images away James realised he needed fresh air. He remembered there was a roof garden café on top of the Reeves building. He turned back to it, climbed the stairs, opened the door at the top and immediately saw a newly pointed chimney stack against the side of the café. He sat with his back to it, sipped his drink and took deep, refreshing breaths. He looked around him. On the slate roofs were chimneys. Everywhere.

He was at Hendon RAF museum; it was like the previous museum, but with fewer hangars, the planes crammed in, not so many hanging from the ceiling, more military aircraft, information, stories.

When he came out he looked up and saw a large Boeing climbing higher in the sky. He imagined the cabin crew, practised and efficient, a smart, smooth-faced American-looking pilot like an advert for Lucky Strike smiling at a curvy stewardess, she grinning back. He froze it there, turned him into a Tussauds waxwork, into the man who was once his patient, and looked closely into his face to see what he was thinking, hiding.

He remembered then the immaculate navy blue, brass-buttoned Captain's jacket hanging in the centre of one of the walls of the shop. There was a rack of quite singular garments below it, but he doubted if the coat was for sale. It could, he thought, have been for effect, though for Roy Brookland it was, perhaps, a defiant, gleaming badge of courage.

PSYCHES

He began therapy six months after leaving his wife and child and moving in with Con and her two children. Guilt is a corrosive suffering and for most of the time Adam lived in her home it felt like having a terrible injury and being stuck inside a wall. - other than the exhausting joyousness of the sexual scenarios they played out when they had the house to themselves. He was the wartime American pilot over here picking up a debutante, an East End spiv seducing a waitress, a monsignor claiming his rights; occasionally, the quick aside from the impromptu scripts where he'd tell her how convincing the accent was, that glance; the quick scribbling of *rape!* on a torn sheet of paper and throwing it out the bedroom window and her coming back to herself worrying that somebody just might find it. Their room became an everywhere.

Never having been in love and compensating for an inimical childhood by creating a movies-inspired fantasy and a desire and an expectation that he would find it - being unable to create it with his wife, a triumph of substance over imagery - he had invaded Con. She'd been a child minder and had looked after his son for a while whilst he and his wife worked. It was always Adam who'd picked him up, staying far later than needed.

His son, Sam, who was eight, stayed three evenings a week and every other weekend and, when possible, Con's daughter, Tara, a bossy, precocious child who argued with him constantly, stayed weekends with her father. Using energy he didn't have, Adam cleaned out a large coalbunker in the garden and wrote, 'Tara and Sam's Club House' in bright blue across the door. They never used it.

Con had an older brother, Ray, and it seemed obvious to Adam, though knowing little of psychology then, that Sam, in fact, represented her father's favourite offspring. Her father, an army captain, had shot himself; his unfortunate daughter was now stuck in that role forever.

Adam would take his son over the park and, between a traffic cone and his jacket, teach him to keep goal, and on their return Con and her kids would be sitting with their backs to them watching TV as they passed down the hall. There was no greeting. They'd play for hours, not wanting to get back

She'd cook the evening meals for the children and afterwards, while he read to Sam and tucked him in, Sam would want to know why they couldn't eat together like other families. He couldn't tell him that Con wanted only her and himself sharing meals. She also resented the time his father spent putting him to bed.

Whenever Adam was lying in bed with her on a Sunday morning, Sam came rushing in from the adjoining bedroom - she insisted Adam didn't call it 'his' - crying, 'Daddy! Daddy!' and threw himself over the bed. The room would tense and she would walk grimly out, wrapping a dressing gown around her in that deliberate, beautiful way she had.

She became introverted and began writing long notes to him begging him to talk to her, to communicate, to leave her a note when he went to work. Writing what she felt for him always ended with, 'Your turn now.' He could feel her silent desperation, but didn't have the energy to respond.

Some days after Tara casually told her mother that she had purposely swallowed a generous amount of paracetemol - not saying why - Con, handling the incident practically and efficiently, quietly suggested that he should seek help for himself.

It could have been one of many names from the directory, but this belonged to an address that was reasonably near, and so he had his first appointment with Malcolm Jule, psychotherapist.

Jewish, tall, grey haired and some years older than Adam, he lived in a large thirties pastiche house with a long through-lounge and a white hand-painted grand piano in the window bay. He was also a lyricist and had written *Nectar Kiss* and a Eurovision song contest winner *Ring a Ling* some years before and was still receiving occasional royalty cheques for these and other songs. Later in their relationship he would play some pieces by Gershwin and Porter while Adam was standing by the piano.

Adam used to think how attractive to women Malcolm must be: the patriarchal nose, stern, but sensitive profile, the lilting sounds from under his hands. He was divorced and had a daughter, Michele, who Adam once saw before she began studying psychoanalysis in Paris under a student of Lacan. Her father had never encouraged her to pursue his own profession.

He saw his clients in a small upstairs room. After some time he changed the setting of these sessions to his through-lounge, which was almost as upsetting to Adam as watching, in the beginning, another patient enter the house as he was being seen out. Immediately he recognised that they would all feel this, each wanting to be the only one. As Malcolm pointed out in the early years, when he listened more than he talked, no emotions are new. It was obvious where this one had come from, as Adam learnt over time where others had, though initially these were intellectual recognitions, without emotional understanding.

One of the characteristics of his condition was that for a long while he couldn't rid himself of an analytic detachment that was ever present; couldn't do or feel anything without intellectualising it, 'knowing' it, couldn't yawn without seeing himself yawning, couldn't speak without hearing himself speaking. There was a separation of thought from feeling, of being locked into an alien world by his blocking off of early trauma.

After a while, having helped Adam realise how trapped in his childhood terrors he was, Michael talked of sex. Though a fan of Freud, he was aware of his flaws: for him, it wasn't culture that denied an impossible infantile attempt to consummate the desire for the mother, it was innate.

Adam would tell Con of some of these conversations.

'He's competing with you sexually.' she'd say, with the nonchalant assurance of someone who would remark that it was raining when hearing it on a window pane.

Malcolm saw her once when she was waiting in a car for Adam, commenting on her attractiveness.

'It took me a year to read Freud,' he once declared, 'but he didn't go back as far as me, or into the areas that I have; schizophrenia, psychosis… and people like you.'

When he said something like this, there was a quietly expressed authority, a casually stated, but unarguable truth.

He told Adam of a patient nobody would treat who, after seventeen years of just sitting silently with him, spoke for the first time two weeks previously, and another who, after half a lifetime, was now remembering his birth.

'It's horrible watching him.' He'd say.

He allowed Adam to say what he wanted, to cry - he rarely did - and there were no 'shoulds.' Also he never broke the fundamental rule of not judging. Sometimes Adam would lie to him and then tell him he had. He would just shrug, and, when suggesting free association and Adam telling him he'd play games with him, intuitively knowing what paths he would travel in response to his responses, he'd be countered by a weary,

'What would you gain from that?'

He had been brought up in an East London borough adjacent to where Adam had been raised, and sometimes called him 'son' - though as Adam's father had always used this term instead of his name, it took some time to accept that Malcolm wasn't goading him by using it. Out of his royalties he'd bought a flat in Miami where he stayed each winter and would always say to Adam,

'It's okay, I'm coming back.'

Inevitably they became friends, but not outside Malcolm's home, another cardinal rule. They talked psychology, initiated mostly by Adam, gradually depersonalising it. He knew it would stimulate Malcolm; knew also that he wouldn't have to think about nor try to get back to early experiences in their fifty minutes together, and suspected that Malcolm knew what his patient was doing and willingly joined in, knowing that Adam wasn't yet ready to do other than deflect and escape.

He'd been in therapy himself for five years, starting when he was twenty, and believing it essential if he was to minimise the projections of his own attitudes onto his patients. A year was spent observing babies.

'Where else does it start?' he'd say.

Though initially scorning his ideas, his fellow professionals would describe them as 'innovative,' especially after they became absorbed into mainstream psychoanalytic theory.

He was adamant that Melanie Klein should have gone further back into the early genesis of behaviour, and that all religions, in some way or other, are to do with faeces and the physical and psychological cleansing of it. For him, people's initial sensations other than from the breast came with the wiping away of faeces, and their first internalisation of guilt came when they messed themselves, thus indicating they'd done something 'wrong.' Baptism, the pilgrimage of Hindus to the Ganges, the word 'salvation' arising from the Roman word for salt used for cleansing. were some of his obvious examples. *'In the beginning was the body'* was a foundation stone for Malcolm Jule.

There was no smugness when he spoke of these things, merely a slight questioning raise of the eyebrows and a smile in his eyes. Rarely would he disagree with a theory derisively, but when he did, there was no doubting he was alluding to propositions created by intellectual pygmies.

Adam moved away from Con's soon after Sam told him tearfully that he couldn't come to stay with him any more because of the way she and Tara still treated him. To his delight his father rented a flat.

He began to see Malcolm less as the years went by, from once a week to once a month - though Malcolm wanted to see him more often - and, eventually, much less.

He received a letter from Malcolm's daughter telling him her father had died a week before of a heart attack the day after returning from Florida, and inviting him to his funeral. He assumed she'd found her father's appointments book, always on top of the piano, and written to his clients.

A few days afterwards Adam drove through the cemetery gates and parked. There wasn't the sense of peace here that was to be found in spreading, unkempt cemeteries with their large trees and wild bushes hanging over blackened, eroded tombs and headstones and long grass growing over inscribed slabs of granite. This place was built in the thirties: low, cream-painted buildings, Palladian style roofs, discreet chimney above the crematorium, neat symmetry of rose bushes measured along red-bricked walls, sculpted hedges bordering curved paths, small numbered plaques telling whose ashes were uniformly spaced in the earth with its cropped, tended grass and patterned plastic wrapped flowers, like a strange new Victorianism protecting naked plants from the lascivious eyes of men.

Walking towards the burial ground he noticed how small it was, the oven obviously doing more business than the gravediggers. His timing was right, he hadn't wanted to be part of the service, be trapped in that melancholy, and fifty yards in front of him thirty or so darkly dressed figures were turning away from a rectangle of newly turned earth.

He saw Michele first, the only person he'd expected to recognise, her dark eyes looking down in her plump, sallow face. Then he realised, it was Con's arm she was holding with such casual familiarity. She turned her head and smiled wistfully at her companion who continued looking down. A young man behind Con moved to her side and squeezed her arm. She looked around quickly and gave him a grin of recognition. He said something to her and she laughed, showing those perfect teeth, lips pulled back slightly more at one side of her mouth; the kind of laugh he'd heard at parties with her as if she was responding to a lover. She carried on walking towards him, tall, upright, looking straight ahead. Her spitting eyes were now quieter, and he'd never seen her so untroubled. There was sadness, but something else; a stillness, a sort of completion.

Her hair, still auburn, spread out from the centre of her hairline, a partly opened curtain covering her high cheekbones. He wanted to rush to her, place his hands gently on the sides of her face, stroke her hair back as it used to be, long and flowing, wanted her to tell him why she was here, what she had to do with Malcolm. The world was incomprehensible. He was frightened. He didn't move.

He looked at her as if his eyes were a camera, she in the centre of the lens. He moved his head slowly to one side, keeping her central, the background - mourners, gravestones, trees, a low hill - moved across behind her. She filled the lens. She was gone.

Silently, the rest of the group passed him, some making brisk, untidy goodbyes, others getting into cars to go to Malcolm's or perhaps his daughter's house. Adam stood where he was, watching them, until there was no one. He walked outside to the pavement where he felt he could hear a faint tinkling of *My Heart Belongs to Daddy,* stood on the kerb's edge, looked through the asphalt of the road, saw endless dark canyons. He is standing there still.

PERIOD

'Yeh, I got me boy back, but she told the social worker she 'ad parental responsibility, but the court 'ad given it ter me. Wot a liar! But they believed 'er. Is this the right way?'

James Kent was in a plumber's van scurrying around East London looking for a place to get a valve for his bathroom tap.

'Er, yes, there's one on the next right, I think.'

'And this geezer she was livin' wiv then, Bert, my boy said 'e was always sniffin', well, 'e would be wouldn't 'e, 'e was on cocaine, like she was. She slept wiv me bruvver as well. I went round, kicked 's door in and beat 'im up. Anyway, this Bert - 'e was a known paedophile an' all - turns out bits of 'im was found in a lake. It was in the papers, 'Guardian' an' that. They arrested a bloke next day. 'e'd chopped 'is arms off and put 'em in a garage in a Tesco's bag. They ain't found the rest of 'im yet. 'e said it weren't 'im, but they found a receipt for reward points in the bag. So it must 'ave been.'im.'

James felt a vague sense of the surreal in the combination of severed limbs and supermarket points.

'This it, then?'

It was. They bought the valve, drove back and the tap was fixed. He'd never asked the man anything - except about the tap - but as soon as they were in the van he, along with his restricted code, had begun. He was unaware that James was a therapist, so maybe James had 'that sort of face,' and if so, then all to the good; it was that little bit more of an encouragement for his clients to want to talk to him, to share their burdens.

He felt hungry. He rarely cooked; like gardening it's been hyped for centuries as an art form; take hunger away and the aesthetic of food, especially cold, tends to dim. Waitress Agnieszka was back from Poland so he went to Paulo's. Her little boy was with her now, though she had to use a baby minder as her chef hubby worked a fourteen hour day and slept large chunks of her life away. James let her complain to him for a few minutes while she served him and got ready to finish her shift,

'I must go.' she said, 'Pick up the survey card from the counter and say something good about Agnieszka, and come every day, now.'

As she went out a woman with high hair and wearing a bonnet came in. He stood to leave and looked at the face under the hat. It was a delicate face, small nose, petal lips. She quickly glanced at him. He noticed the colour of the eyes, a colour that was difficult to describe; they also barely hid a tiredness, a frailty. She had a wan smile; like a cliché, but real. Gently, but deliberately, she leant against the counter. He asked her if she was alright.

'A little poorly I'm afraid,' she said, putting a slim, pale hand over her eyes.

He moved towards her.

'Can I... ? '

She shook her head, pulled her shoulders up. He hesitated then walked out. He turned to look at her again through the glass entrance door. He didn't see her, but saw the cook come from his kitchen at the back looking down, concerned. James could see the back of her hatless head as, with the cook's help, she pulled herself up from the floor and leant against the counter again. James went in, prompted by nothing more than the long-learned response to help a woman, maybe climbing up a station's stairs with a baby buggy or carrying shopping from the boot of a car.

'Anything I can - '

'I dunno; she's not well, I think.' The cook slowly released her.

She turned her head towards James, her half-smiling mouth ready to apologise for any inconvenience caused. The cook went back to his workplace while James stood near her in case she fell again. She stared at the floor for a while, then sharply up at him. She frowned.

'Thanks. I don't know why I did that.'

'Or, rather, what happened,' he suggested to her in his sometimes pedantic manner.

'Yes, I suppose so, but I'm okay now, so... thanks.'

She smiled. Such an attractive mouth. She went towards the door. He picked up her hat and handed it to her.

'It's a nice hat.'

She took it from him quickly, nodded and went out. He did also and began going the opposite way but couldn't resist turning his head to watch her. She clipped away on her high heels and bumped into a big man, almost spinning off him.

'Sorry luv,' he said and jumped on a bus as its doors were closing. She walked unsteadily across the pavement and leant against a shop window. She was pale, colourless. James went across to her.

'That wasn't my fault was it?'

'Probably not, he was in a hurry.'

'I don't come to London often; think I'll get back to the flat.'

'Not a stunning apartment, is it? I imagine new home buyers all over the city staggering about, looking bewildered, holding their heads.'

'There must be more comfortable places to talk than you holding me up against a shop window in the middle of a rush hour.'

He'd forgotten that his hands were still gently cupping her elbows. He felt lost for a second; they'd just met - not even met.

She smiled again, blinking her eyes. 'It's alright. It hasn't happened before, and thank you.'

'Well, if that's so… glad you're okay.'

He turned away, thinking of the glut of 'okays' and 'alrights' there'd been in the last few minutes.

'Excuse me.' She was grinning now, mocking them both. 'You have my scarf.'

He had. Somehow this green, silky thing was hooked on the shoulder of his jacket. He handed it to her. There was colour in her cheeks now.

'Well, bye-bye Mrs. Scarf Lady.' he said, returning to a boyhood where he and his friends habitually called people, 'Mr. Off Licence' or 'Mrs. Fish Shop Lady.'

'It's Jude. And again, thanks.'

He told her his name and turned away as it started to rain. He looked back at her; the long coat, hair piled up at the back, bonnet now back at an angle. He heard himself asking if she fancied a drink one evening. She didn't turn. He had a choice: catch up to her or shout. She stopped, turned towards him and waited. He walked towards her, thinking he could see a David Lean tracking camera closing in on them. He asked her where and when. She suggested Saturday, he volunteered Camden Lock. He asked why she was in London.

'I've been looking around some antique fairs, Victorian, mostly. There's one at Alexander Palace, .Sunday.'

He told her it was 'Ally Pally' to the native, and asked why she collected it.

'Well, in my twenties, you know, you just collect Victoriana.'

'You make it sound like a rite of passage.'

He noticed the rain again, she was getting as wet as him.

They parted, neither of them saying goodbye; though he gave her a wave, she walking across to the station, him to a bus, where he could look out at brollies in a swirl of impressionism and Magritte to Barons Court and a French café where he would sit and look at an overgrown, sparsely tombstone'd graveyard backing it and write a letter to a patient he hadn't seen for a while and so far couldn't contact.

Other than graveyards he'd felt an animosity towards everything Victorian since a child: the narrow, lincrusta'd ugliness of the house he was born and raised in with its Nike bronze on the mantle piece over a zebo-blacked range stove, dark spindle struts of the banister rail, brass stair rods, and his parents bedroom with the mahogany wardrobe and chest where he'd seen a packet of 'Ona' contraceptives inside a partly open drawer, and which still evoked a heavy, claustrophobic grimness - the smell of lavender furniture polish filling him even now with an olfactory repugnance - and the Roman pediments and heavy lintel windows of the local library with its oppressive Gothic scrolls and heavy doors draping over his spirit like a tarpaulin.

He was habitually early, she was late. Her hair wasn't so piled, a wider hat, pulled forward, a long skirt, brown leather boots buttoned to her knees.

'You look like an up-market Bisto kid' he said, assuming she'd know the reference. She raised a leg, kicked out a little.

'What am I now, a chorus girl?'

Her action surprised him, it didn't go with the urban respectability of her clothes and made her more… carnal. He immediately knew why he felt this: it was the excitement of watching the high-kicking chorus lines and the misty, silken space inside the thighs of the principal boys at the Lyceum pantos his father had taken him to as a boy.

They were outside the canal-side café where the narrow boats were. He asked if she wished to go in. She wanted the market. They went across to it. She was like a gentle throwback in the centre of a circle of the young, with their pierced noses and striped stockings. She bought a filigree brooch and suggested they eat.

They went back to the café. Just before they sat at a table she saw something which made her laugh. It was a sound that seemed to light the room like the sun that suddenly illuminated the bridge and crossing train over the canal.

As he ordered he noticed the music, alien at first, then he was back at the Palais - ballroom taught them by a teacher at tech - leaning on a wall wearing a draped jacket, Tony Curtis hair, a glitter ball glinting on lacquered waves and flared skirts, and his mates' 'ere, she might let yer put yer and up 'er skirt.' He watched the 'Jenny Wren' tying up and thought back to the market: Goths gear, rockers, punks, the past…

'Are you still with me?'

He apologised. He was doing this increasingly: wandering back to early and teenage years - he wished some of his clients could do it as easily. It seemed obvious that her comparable times were an emotional and cultural remove from the experiences that had formed him. As his mother analogously used to say, 'Chalk and cheese, son, chalk and cheese.'

He let her do the talking. She had no children, was divorced, and was now filling her time 'collecting,' selling a little, keeping a lot. The flat she was staying in for a few days belonged to a friend.

They enjoyably used the few hours before she caught her train with a boat trip to Little Venice then walking back to the café on the bridge over the canal tunnel. She was talkative, animated. He detected a hint of South Downs quasi-establishment from far back and of a rather insular - though not parochial - sense of security which informed the world she saw. He was envious. It was an envy he hadn't outgrown.

210

But he was intrigued by her, not least by the hats, the ruffle shoulder pads of her blouse, the way she walked; a slight, attractively awkward shuffle, as if steel tips on her heels would have made no sound. And her laugh, coming from a bright, loved, honest place that he wanted to know, childishly wanted to share.

Looking down on the canal, he mentioned that this little piece of London reminded him of Norwich, where he'd been a student and whose river valley had now been turned into a lake for the richer students to sail on. She asked him when he was last there. He told her it was a year previously when he'd read some of his poetry in the English Faculty.

'I read poetry. Don't write it.'

'You can be my groupie next time.'

'You're on,' she said, raising her glass of tea as if it was wine.

He walked to the Tube with her. As if expecting his question, she said,

'No .Tomorrow will be more boring for you than today, and I don't want to get back late. But, if you want to come to Hastings...'

She expressed the invitation a little archly. They agreed he would see her in her home town the following weekend.

It was a busy week: He had two female clients who were stealing; one quite regularly, the other erratically, one more calculating than the other, both because they wanted to take, grab something they felt they'd never had; namely, he assumed, love.

Her house was in a Crescent, one side of it curving steeply upwards. Standing on the steps outside her three storey Victorian terrace, his eyes were level with the top of the chimneys on the flat roofs of two Georgian houses diagonally opposite. Before he knocked on the original door which, by self conscious design he assumed, hadn't been painted for many years, he noticed in the bay window a large, hanging Cupid draped with Chinese lanterns dangling above a candelabra. It was the sort of window he wanted to press his nose against.

She opened the door, wearing a kind of cheongsam with red and white flowers, hair loose on her shoulders. She looked at him steadily, silently, then walked down the rose-pattern papered hall and into a room. She seemed provocative, almost teasing. He followed her. She looked briefly around.

'Voila.' she said quietly.

There was a high ceiling, cornice, frieze, a picture rail from which hung pictures of deer and hills, sunsets and dawns, a painting of a young girl lying on her back in a bed of white roses, another girl lying by her side about to kiss her watched by a curly haired boy peeking from a bush, full of sensual, sentimentalised Victorian sexuality.

There were framed pieces of fabric, one with 'Looking Unto Jesus' stitched on, reminding him of a childhood tabernacle with a painting of a tall, blonde, haloed Christ resting his hand on the head of a black boy holding hands with a Chinese girl, the stiff formality of it oozing a contrived, caring liberalism. There was a linen tablecloth with delicately sewn patterns, two huge baroque mirrors and chests of drawers with stencilled trees. The large kitchen area had a butler's sink, ornate copper taps, stacks of flowered, crinkly-edged plates, baskets with pairs of black scissors, pot-pouri and painted egg shells. He noticed a game bird lying on a chopping board.

Every square metre of wall: the bird strewn French paper, tapestries, framed butterflies, a papier mache deer's head, the painted chairs, cabinets and clocks held a symbolic fascination.

Through the tall box sash on the end wall he could see a spiral staircase leading up to a garden - he glimpsed a life-size Romanesque statue - and a terraced row of high gabled houses slanting away into perspective. He must have been looking around him shaking his head. She laughed. The sound increasingly attracted him.

'Come with me.'

He followed her down the hall past music hall posters and a host of supine nudes, one three dimensional, another languorously holding a feather duster in front of her crotch, through to the end of the passage and a frosted glass door panel with 'The Green Room' etched on it. She opened it. Filling almost the entire end wall was a stained glass ecclesiastical window pattering coloured light around the walls and floor.

'Let's have tea.'

They sat at the table. He asked about various trinkets and objects until she became restless and decided they should eat somewhere. To satisfy his art deco curiosity they went to the Pavilion, looking in on an art installation of three potted plants with a wire leading from them to speakers making an unpleasant whirring sound above a notice that said the artist was '… ignoring a narrative of chronology to allow the viewer to explore multiple avenues of meaning.' A uniformed attendant sat in a corner wearing large earplugs and a look of utter ennui.

They walked across the beach, then up a hill, seeing the town unevenly, attractively lying in its little valley, the music from the fairground on the front just audible; then back to the house. All the while, try as he may, he couldn't help the urge to attempt to second guess her, analyse her, and wondered, as he'd done before, if he'd occupied his professional role to the exclusion of an ability to relate to a woman other than intellectually, sexually - and not even that, yet. Her occasional mock grimace and the smile afterwards was a gesture of wanting to know him. She was perceptive. She was waiting for something. Him, perhaps.

Returning to the house, she went to the kitchen. He leant against the inside of its door watching her wipe some cups, fill a kettle. He decided he wanted her to try to get to know him. He asked why she hadn't bothered to find out what he did for a living.

'I know what you do. You weren't at that place just to read poems were you; you were at the Association of Psychotherapists conference.'

'How did… ?' he was too surprised to say more.

'Can you remember what you did there?'

'Of course. I was lucky there was time to fit me in. I critiqued Glazer's 'Some Temporal Aspects of a Non-scheduled Status Passage.' It was about relatives gathered around someone's deathbed. The author was drunk on syntax, blind to semantics. Though, to be fair, he… sorry, I shouldn't expect you to - '

'You gave your opinion on other things, too, didn't you' She said it in a flat, dead voice.

Then he recognised her. She'd been on her own and spoken to him rather hesitantly, almost timidly. She'd looked very different to what she did now. She realised that he knew who she was.

'I'd just started as a therapist then. I knew nobody in the profession. I wanted advice. Mistakenly, I chose you.'

He remembered more clearly. She'd been on the edge of a group of practitioners he was talking to about why he still thought that drugs used to lessen the fear and quieten the internal voice of paranoid conditions - which he still tended to refer to as a persecution complex - were, in essence, counter-productive, a cop out in helping patients face their own devils, struggle through them and develop a more solid identity. More came back: one of her clients was, she'd said, calling her, often in the small hours, to either gush out frenzied, hollow descriptions of his day or just cling on to her voice to keep him sane.

'As I recall, you were - '

'Convinced by your argument? Yes I was.' Her voice was rising. 'So convinced that I convinced him too, and he told his doctor he wouldn't take his drugs anymore. So I talked to him, James, talked and talked and listened and listened for hours thinking I was helping him, but in the end he was sectioned. I've seen him. He's *really* desperate now despite the resumption of his drugs.' Her anger swirled around the room.

'I... I never suggested that it was for all paranoics at all times. They need to be carefully chosen.'

'This is *your* fault. Its okay, I didn't fall down purposely just to lure you here for some sort of evil revenge, I barely looked at you, didn't see you, didn't recognise you until that man bumped into me.'

'Why did you ask me here?'

'Because... '

'Why didn't you tell me this before? Why didn't you just let it out?'

'I didn't feel strong enough.'

'Yes you did.' He was shouting now. 'You wanted me here on home ground, you feel secure here, it's your own fantasy world, isn't it; an imagined perfect past of peace, colour, knick knacks, and the paintings, soft, easy, lazy; there's nothing harsh for you here, nothing alive, no physical, sexual reality is there.' He was shouting at her as if she was a patient he was trying to shock into facing her needs, her appetites, break her emotional mould of feeling they were morally wrong

'Interesting that you've chosen this most repressed of eras isn't it; a validation of your not letting go. It's all around you, a confirmation of emotional safety, this decorative, escapist haze of comforting compensation. You've...' He stopped. She'd backed away from him, looking hurt, distressed.

Why was he so angry? Was it just because she'd blamed him for her patient's troubles or - and as he looked at her pained eyes, tears on the verge of sliding down her cheeks, realised it was so - because he wanted to shake her, wanted to take her to the bedroom, actually carry her, drop her onto the four poster bed - she must have one - surrounded by statuettes of fawns, Greek Gods, young negroes holding out gifts on trays?

He felt confused, heavy... jammed, unable to express himself to himself. He strode to the front door, yanked it open, marched out, directionless, down the front steps and the grassy bank at the edge of the road, downhill to the end of her street, up steps by the side of a church, a curving Regency road, tall, bow-windowed houses, and then more steps and a small Greek restaurant looking like someone's front room. He had to stop somewhere.

He sat. He could feel his clenched teeth, hands rigidly curled. There were no other customers. There was a picture on the wall, like a Lempicka without the humour, of: two women leaning a little apart against a bar counter, one holding a wine glass, looking at each other with a hint of sensuousness, or was it his projection? He was analysing again; the painter, himself, everyone, including the patriarchal, grey moustache'd patron with a menu in one hand and worry beads crunching in the other. Was it a habit learned from his culture or was he playing with them for a specific reason? He willed his retsina to drown the anger, not knowing whether it was turned against her or himself.

He shouldn't have shouted at her. An instant image he was pushing away was of her wide, wet eyes - he still couldn't define their colour - perturbed, alarmed. Perhaps it was her criticism - mum 'jawing' his infant self, telling him not to do something, stopping him expressing himself innocently, freely; and blaming him. 'I didn't. It wasn't me. I didn't.'

Perhaps Jude had a point. Maybe he'd sensed a convert, been a little too enthusiastic, not caring that - as he now knew - she'd been new to the game, unseasoned, had been, perhaps, looking for some certainty, something black or white, not wanting the more realistic shades of grey. It could have been she'd wanted to create an image of herself as the therapist who went against the strengthening norm of drug solutions. He doubted it. He should have talked to her, have listened.

He walked back to the station, vaguely aware that at another time he could have enjoyed this town: a genteel Brighton, with its small, urban hills, churches, passages, ancient steps. He felt as if he'd come to the end of a relationship that had never begun.

Moving homeward on a bus through the East End streets he passed the builders merchants where he'd bought the tap valve a few days before. He seemed to have moved from Bert's body, or parts of it, in an Essex lake to Millais' 'Ophelia' floating on bindweed in a front room in Hastings.

The old hatreds returned: the ugly, ornamental trusses under bay windows, heavy colonial pediments, acanthus leaf capitals, pointless swags. It was as if it was all inside of him, his bones made of it.

He thought of Jude again, and then, intuitively, the concept of transference. He remembered the clear, cold textbook definition from enthusiastic undergraduate days: 'The unconscious tendency to redirect feelings, attitudes, desires and repressed experiences retained from childhood to a new object; this could be an erotic attraction to. the therapist.' He also remembered answering a question using the definition in his seminar group, eliciting 'Ooh, hark at him,' from some of the other students, and being annoyed that they weren't taking it seriously: the course, their future profession, *him*.

The transference was supposed to be hers, not his. This, for some psychiatrists, was a cardinal sin. He had committed it.

He thought of the old saying that psychoanalysts don't suffer from insanity - they love every minute of it. Not quite. And perhaps he'd see Jude again. It was a pity; he'd almost started to like the brass stair rods.

BETE NOIRE

'I told the wife I'd come into some money. I said she could buy anything, do anything, the world was hers. She said she wanted to go somewhere she'd never been before. I said, 'Try the kitchen.''

He continued. 'What did the inflatable teacher in the inflatable school say to the inflatable schoolboy the day after he'd given him a pin? 'You've let me down, you've let the school down, and above all... ''

He'd been doing this for as long as he'd been in treatment: the jokes, the one-liners, the quick corner-of-the-mouth ripostes.

'This bloke goes into a psychiatrist and says, 'I feel I don't exist.' The quack says, 'Next, please.''

As ancient as it was, James Kent had to smile at this one. It interested him how the ideas, terminology, the bits and pieces of psychiatry, the theories of its founding fathers, had become known, had entered into common parlance and been generally accepted, except for the occasional, defensive squeals of 'psycho babble.'

He grudgingly agreed with Kit, a Marxist acquaintance of long ago, that the reason why apprentice plumbers, Mexican peons, rhubarb growers and sagger makers bottom knockers had all heard of Freud was that, assisted by the media and its control of the dissemination of ideas, 'those who own the means of material production control the means of mental production,' the ruling class had thrown its weight behind his theories to further its own interests. In short, if the world perceives its troubles, its violence, its pathology as a result of the unconscious, attention is then taken away from a critique of its major capitalist institutions.

It was obvious whose side Kit was on in the two theorists contrasting models of human nature: Freud's being that man was lazy, hedonistic, self seeking and competitive, and Marx's that he was naturally co-operative, born 'good,' but made 'bad' by a contemporary society. One, arguably, used by all authority to justify itself, the other like Rousseau's 'noble savage' with his unlimited potential for altruism and virtue. Kit had demonstrated his bias by causing as much legal and, sometimes, illegal disruption to the political status quo as he could. Perhaps he still was.

But these musings weren't helping James' patient, weren't aiding him in breaking the defences that manifested themselves in his relentless repertoire of gags and wisecracks. He left James, as ever, on a high - though not as a result of anything his therapist had contributed - chortling his way down the path, though the gate, past the hedge and off home. By the time he'd reached the station the part of him that he wasn't facing had grown more virulent for its neglect. Next time, the intensity of the humour would be ratcheted up that little bit more, the gags delivered that little bit faster. James needed to think harder, try a different way to get to him.

He went upstairs to his study thinking of his ex-colleague again. When they'd first met, Kit had been lecturing for several years in social science at the same London college where James had arrived to do an abortive one term teaching placement After his evening class of plastering apprentices had decided that this was, as their self-appointed leader told him, 'the unacceptable face of education,' and had walked out early and straight into the long arms of the patrolling Principal, who'd told James sternly that he wanted his domain to be 'ship-shape and Bristol fashion,' he'd bumped into Kit. Noting his dispirited expression he asked James what was troubling him. He told him. Kit laughed.

'Yer gotta be 'ard sometimes. They're victims. Yer gotta 'elp them get though their course. Exploited labour though they are, they need to mek a livin', they cannna live outside o' society.'

James hadn't noticed before how strong his Durham accent was. He came to know it, be aware of how he exaggerated it and used it to his advantage. In union meetings if he criticised the college's management or the political and economic system in general, it would strengthen, become harsher, as if confirming his working class credentials.

He once asked James about his own occupational background. James told him some of the things he'd done. He mentioned time spent as a decorator, then a commercial artist. Kit frowned as if James had betrayed his class.

'Yer canna be wearkin' cluss and an uttist, mun, yer canna.'

The first words he ever said to James were,

'You coomin' to the office, then?'

This was a reference to the college bar, a log cabin type building in the middle of the grassy quad where he'd take students in warm weather to form a circle round him while he sat there talking politics then saunter in with some of them to have a drink.

He was, initially, a distant figure to James, one who had a little mystery about him. He'd gone to Ruskin College, courtesy of trade union membership, became a teacher, and went on innumerable demos against the state, the 'system.'

One Monday he came into the staff room with plasters on head and cheeks and bruised arms he'd suffered from the 'filth's' batons in an alley off Trafalgar Square. For him, the primary function of the police was to protect the property class's interests from attacks by the property-less masses. The other lecturers seemed to defer to him, mainly because of the forceful expression of his political narratives.

'Where do unions coom from?' he'd ask rhetorically, not just at union meetings, but occasionally in the classroom or the refectory, 'from t' guilds who were more concerned wi' maintainin' differential incomes an' status between skilled artisans an' labourers than any unified opposition to the status quo. They're essentially conservative; strikes are just institutionalised agreements between owners an' wearkers.'

In answer to James' question of why he was so active in the unions then, he shrugged and said that they were just an accepted step to his hoped-for anarchism.

'I grew oop in t' north, you in t' south; yer very name, James, is respectable wearkin' class, mun. I'm from rough, an' as a kid I saw inequality all aroun' me, people 'ardly getting' by, mun. I've stolen, 'ad to at times. I used to think, even as a kid, why? Why do some 'ave so little and others so much? Does it 'ave to be? I were so angry abou' it.'

'James understood this, but felt that there was a more personalised anger within Kit. There was. Its source, it seemed, was Reginald Thomas-Heading.

Reg was a Sierra Leonean teacher on the staff who Kit didn't speak to and obviously disliked intensely, partly because his own teaching timetable of many years had been decimated by him. Reg had a lot of teaching in a faculty where he wasn't wanted by its lecturers because of complaints about him by their students. Though too scared of his anticipated cries of 'racist' to do anything about it, they let it be known covertly. This was quietly acted upon and he suddenly got more work in his own faculty teaching Kit's subject, the latter, less, having to take over Reg's previous classes.

Reg's teaching style, whatever the subject, was to get his pupils to read and then copy from a text book, though this didn't stop him striding into the staff room after a class, metal tipped heels clacking as if to confirm a delusory sense of importance and, rubbing his hands together as if to celebrate a job well done, say, in a smug, self-congratulatory tone,

'Well, that was a good old discussion there, got the old debates going.'

Reg didn't have a degree in the social sciences and it was doubted whether he was a graduate at all. He was short, broad, inarticulate, and a club bouncer in his spare time. Students, as well as some of the more predominantly middle class lecturers felt a latent physical intimidation in his presence, compounded by the liberalist ethos of the college creating a fear of showing any hint of bias against an ethnic staff member. Reg was aware of this situation and would use it blatantly, once getting a representative from union HQ to visit the college to inquire into his perceived discrimination, though no-one seemed to know what it actually meant or what would have counted as evidence.

There was another episode where he was accused of hitting a student in the library. Kit had hung around outside the Hearing in case he was asked to speak a few words on behalf of Reg, which, because of his political principles, he was willing to do, but wasn't called.

'Ter think ah were sut there ready to say soomit good abou' 'im,. Ah di'nt know 'im then. Ah were an idiot.'

Nothing had been proven - a pupil's word against his, the library virtually empty at the time - but he'd been suspended on full pay for six months.

'It were in local paper wi' a picture of his smug, round-eyed innocence. It said summat like, I dunno, 'Lecturer Claims Suspension Racist.' Aye, and 'e got money for doin' nowt.'

Kit enjoyed teaching, especially mature students, particularly Africans. He would tell them in his introductory lesson that God was either a well-intentioned deity who was obviously not omnipotent, or *was* all powerful and therefore a bastard or, a third alternative, was both weak *and* a bastard, and anyway, he didn't create us, we created him. This was met with either open hostility, shock or a disbelieving shaking of heads - though at the end of the ninety minutes, half the women passing his desk on the way out would squeeze his shoulder and tell him they would pray for him.

He did, apparently, have extra-curricular relationships with several of his students, though it was difficult to pinpoint his attraction. He was average height, thick set, with cropped sandy hair, wide pugilistic nose and made very little concession to matters sartorial. James once overheard one of his students say of him that he looked like 'a lorry driver with brains.'

He once mentioned to James that he was attracted to a Ghanaian girl in one of his classes. Sitting in the refectory with James one lunch time, wanting to know some things about her course, she asked him if he knew much about Reg. Before he could answer she said,

'Who does he think he is? 'He asked me to go to that YMCA place in the high street with him and get a room. I've hardly spoken to him. It's because I'm black. What an insult.'

He asked her if she'd told Kit. She had. He thought of Kit's remark when he first began to talk to him of Reg.

'I canna imagine 'im, yer know, smoothin' a woman's 'air... runnin' 'is 'ands gently through it, spreadin' it out wi' 'is fingers, like.' his own splayed digits mirroring his words.

James wondered if Reg, maybe, represented the infant Kit's father. If this was so, and the latter hadn't got through his oedipal phase, it would, partly, explain his need to have relationships with students: they were the mothers he was *allowed* to have, free of dad, of Reg. He tried to imagine what the child in him had felt when hearing of Reg's propositioning of his Ghanaian student; dad coming after mum again, not letting him have his own love object, his possession. It seemed obvious that his dislike had, or would, become hatred.

Aware that he was playing around with what he'd learnt from his psychology degree completed a few months before - when he'd half-heartedly decided to see if he was capable of teaching for a living - James could see that he was, with intellectual naivety, perhaps using Kit as someone who 'fitted' a theory, or theories.

Between classes James had been spending time with Kit indulging in coffee, specious bits of intellectualism, quasi-humorous hyperbole and discussing James' decision not to carry on teaching, though intending to finish his placement. On the last afternoon of the Spring term, Kit came into the refectory late. He sat slowly down opposite James.

'Fookin' 'ell, me wife's just rung. She wants me to clear out, wants me ter leave. 'er friend's movin' in.'

He stared down at James' empty coffee cup. He looked up.

'It's not a mun, it's 'er friend, Vera. I 'ad me suspicions, but she's gonna move in, or she 'as moved in, and I've gotta get out. Viv and Vera; like an old Workers Playtime double act '

He looked down again, wringing his hands.

'I reckon they'll laugh at me won't they, 'avin' a lesbian wife. I'm glad I've no kids, aye.'

He looked around him and back at James again.

'We 'aven't been gettin' on wi' each other fer a while, but I wasn't... She should have told me at 'ome, not rung me. I'll 'ave to get a flat. I don't wanna live 'round 'ere. Fook it.'

Standing up, he said, 'I'm off. I'll cancel the class, canna be 'elped. I'm goin' 'ome.'. He stopped moving for a second. 'back,' he corrected himself. 'Get me stuff together.' He loped quickly out the door.

The first day back after the short break, Kit told him that he'd moved out and found himself a couple of rooms locally.

'It'll do for now. If I'm not wanted there's no point in stayin'.'

James didn't ask him how he was feeling, though there were certainly the foundations to build a sustainable wall of anger and bitterness on that would take a long time to crumble. But he did ask him what would happen to his ex-council house in Bloomsbury which he'd bought cheaply as a sitting tenant some years before.

'Dunno, mun. She can 'ave it, anyway. I canna be bothered,' he said, flicking his hand away from him.

He stopped coming down for their little chats then and, when James saw him in the staffroom or a corridor, he looked grimly busy. No more did he walk into James' classroom, stand in front of the students and say, with almost total conviction and ignoring James' initial annoyance,

''e dunno what 'e's talkin' abou', take no notice, he's a right wing fascist,' and shaking his head with mock sadness would wheel around towards the door, punch the air and shout, 'oop the revolution.'

James had to return to his training college before the end of term, but didn't say goodbye to Kit because the latter was involved in teaching observations at various places around the borough, rarely returning to the main site. Rather lazily, James hadn't bothered to find out his contact number.

A month or so after leaving the college James was on his way home at the end of the first week of a psychotherapy course in East London, when he saw a lecturer who he'd spoken to a few times when with Kit. He was at a bus stop. James crossed the road to him. Almost immediately he was asked if he'd heard about Kit, what had happened to him or rather, what he'd done. James had neither seen nor spoken to him since they'd stood by the staffroom's photocopier two weeks before he'd left, Kit tensely silent, not answering questions. Assuming ignorance from James' expression, he began the story. It seemed obvious he'd been told it in detail.

Kit was finishing moving to his newly rented flat, a matter mostly of taking his books, clothes and bric-a-brac on buses, trains and the occasional taxi, for he didn't drive, and was carrying a backpack and case along the high street one evening when he stopped for a few drinks at a pub. Soon after leaving he passed a night club, its beating noise hammering the air around him.

He saw Reg standing outside wearing a dark suit and tie. He was looking around him, legs wide apart, with a patently contrived look of menace, closing and unclosing his fists hanging at his sides. He looked at Kit from ten feet away, the latter unsure what his expression meant, but went across to him anyway. He pushed his face into this ridiculous bouncer and began yelling at him, apparently not remembering what it was that he'd shouted. Reg tried to push him away.

Kit bent down, grabbed his case and swung it against Reg's head, knocking him against the smoked glass window of the club and cracking it. The case had come open; sock, vests, exercise books and framed photos scattering over the pavement. He began picking them up, turning his head and shouting staccato obscenities at Reg, then kneeling down and repeatedly and relentlessly beating his fists on a kerbstone, until a club employee had helped him up and led him inside.

It seemed he remembered little of what had happened immediately after that, though he did recall, apparently with some pride, that he'd stood over a horizontal Reg, head limply resting against the damaged window, and said to him,

'You're every thin' I'm not, and nuthin' I am,' and walked away.

So far he hadn't returned to work. James asked about Reg. He'd been paid off by the college with no public reason given, though the purveyor of this information thought its origins lay in the library incident and its denouement; complaints from students.

James' ex-colleague got onto his bus, turned towards him, gave a noncommittal shrug and went on his way.

Walking home, James tried to think of Kit and this event with an ice-chip of detachment - something he knew he would have to acquire if he was going to pursue a career in psychotherapy which, he realised, had been a desire long forming. He had to try to see it all as clearly and as analytically as he could. If Reg represented an infantile Kit's father - though he'd told James that, as an adult, he'd liked him - what did his wife and her lover symbolise?

He remembered as a child the reaction he had to household visits from female neighbours or one of his aunts, and his mother's animation and laughter. He disliked their talking, their cackling, their 'oohs' and 'ahs,' their 'so she said'…'so I said,' and the continual nodding in sympathetic circularity to each other, and realised, though not then, that it was jealousy. He wanted mum to himself, not sharing her with these lipstick'd, henna'd hair women. If Kit's ego was frailer than it appeared, both to others and himself, then maybe the figure of Reg *was* an intensified complication to an oedipal situation.

And there was another cause for his frustration. James had noticed it when taking him to a poetry venue in Islington. He'd looked uncomfortable and left before it had finished. The following day he'd explained that he didn't like 'those sort of people.' He meant that they were 'posh' and that he was from 'oop north.'

James was becoming aware that, from soon after he had met Kit, he'd been using him as a sort of crude case study and that perhaps he'd been overanalysing it all. But this was retrospection, and as such, teleological; the effect preceding the cause. There were, though, some intuitive elements, some flashes of a kind of pleasing warmth and, as insignificant an addition to the symbolic universe of psychiatry as they were, these moments seemed to have been part of the slowly evolving impetus that had led him to his present work.

His neurotic, gag-telling patient, now coming twice a week, was with him again, sitting on the couch. There was the tense restlessness and rictus smile as precursors to stand, hunch his shoulders and, offering his palms to him, begin yet another joke. He was effectively paying James as an audience of one for a fifty minute comedy gig.

James asked him to talk about his favourite game as a child, about his home, his mother. He stood.

'Two guys in a bar. One says to the other, 'I made a terrible Freudian slip last night. I was having a meal at my mother's and meant to say, 'Would you pass the butter, please,' but it came out as, 'You fuckin' bitch, you fuckin' ruined my fuckin' life.''

Perhaps they were getting somewhere now, thought James.

POETRY WARS

'You can tell me to fuck off if you like, but our guest poet's from Northumberland and it's a long way to come to read in this noise. I've no right to ask you to move, you've come for a drink and you want to enjoy it, but could you move a little further down?'

Bad choice of days: a monthly Friday night in a pub under London Bridge. Generally, they'd smile and reluctantly move.

Mike was tired of doing this; the poets, the non-reading audience looking at him with weary déjà vu as more customers came in, more drinks, more noise. It was his third venue in five years. He needed a new one. The first had been in Borough Market, a second floor room in a Georgian house above a shop - you could look through a twelve-paned box sash at a railway bridge less than ten yards away, the building vibrating as trains crossed - with the smell of grilling sausages filling the room from 'Posh Bangers' below. Although the room had, as an American visitor put it, 'the classiest lectern in town,' the fumes were getting thicker than the camaraderie and the congregation sparser.

After three years or so they went across the road to the 'King's Head' and a large, badly lit lincrusta'd room with a pool table at one end - though made good use of by a performer reading poems often involving snooker tournaments which, as a professional actor, he'd demonstrate entertainingly - and a disused bar at the other with a relentlessly whining air conditioner above it.

It had begun almost accidentally; Mike wandering into a Charing Cross Road bookshop where there was a reading going on with open mic spots run by a Ghanaian poet. One evening, a few weeks later, he didn't show up. There were a dozen or so people waiting so Mike offered to take over. This he did for two months till the bookshop changed hands and there was no more poetry - at least, spoken. Being congenitally unable to self-propagandise and push himself around the poetry circuit, he looked for a place he could run and in which he would occasionally read his own work; realising very soon how naff it was to read at his own venue.

He believed, somewhat hypocritically, that, like Victorian children, poets should be seen and not heard, reading aloud being merely an audio version of the real thing: that singular, elemental contact between reader, writer and the written word. He was aware of his double standards for he listened to poets and would-be ones - wondering what the collective noun for poets was, someone once suggesting a 'malice' - at least once every four weeks; listening to the posturing indulgence of rap poets ruining rhythm, murdering melody, the rhyming, still clung to by those who held on to their nursery experience, the post-modern poets with their pseudo-original stream of disconnected, inanimate objects going nowhere and saying nothing; and neo-surrealist poetry dwelling in its own arse and whose only frame of reference was itself. Aware that it's not known what we have to presuppose to settle an aesthetic matter, Mike opted for craftsmanship, clarity, and a hoped-for originality. He wanted this place to be for genuine poets, both established and those at the beginning of a love affair with poetry and, to satisfy the kernel of the teacher in him, to learn from others.

So here he was at his fourth place; a coffee shop off Brick Lane. He'd found it while walking around the city as he was wont to do: the Dickensian alleyways, Georgian terraces in Spitalfields, the churches, guilds, markets, and half-heartedly looking for the buildings he'd worked in as a young tradesman years before (still hearing Jock the foreman telling him that if the plaster was too wet to prime, then, 'blow on it till it's fockin' dry').

It was a Victorian shop painted Buckingham green with no name on the fascia and inside, lining a match-boarded wall, sacks of coffee from around the world: Ecuador, Ethiopia, Columbia, Chad. The small counter was made of sanded pine, the same as the floor boards, with a piece of corrugated iron from an old Anderson shelter partly supporting one end. The tables and chairs were as eclectically fashionable as the art exhibits on its jade green walls.

'This'd make a nice poetry venue.' Mike said to the girl behind the counter with attractively unkempt hair, black hot pants and tights, and wide smile.

'My uncle is a poet.' she said with an Italian accent, handing him a cup of Venezuelan coffee Mike explained what he did and that Mere Poetry needed another home. She was Sophia, and her co-worker, the likeable Carlo, was her cousin. Mike asked her if she wrote poetry, she was young enough for this to have been a recent teenage trait. She did, but Giovanni was the real poet. He asked her what sort of poetry he wrote. A specious question. 'Italian,' she said. He wasn't there, but would be later. Mike had a sandwich. They talked. Giovanni was really her stepfather. They, 'Rivenda UK,' as the cards on the counter stated, had been open two months. Business was slow, they didn't advertise, Giovanni believed in word of mouth for his trade.

A man came in; tall, stubbled, with a slow smile and an arm lightly touching his companion's shoulder, sharing a joke. He wore a tan corduroy jacket, faded jeans, casual brown shoes, hinting, Mike thought, at cultural interests he'd worked at and not an easy part of his familial tradition. He was introduced to Giovanni and Martin, an 'Italian translator.' They liked Mike's suggestion.

'We are open every day except Christmas, whatever day you say.'

The accent was there, but he'd obviously lived in this country for some time. Sophia said something to him. He replied in Italian, went across to her, came back.

'Ah, my ex. Women, women, uh?' His accent had got more pronounced, as if he felt he should, for Mike's sake, appear a little nearer to a stereotype, to his roots.

'You look annoyed,' Mike said.

'No, I am angry.'

He went down to the basement, beckoning Mike to follow. It was a square, commodious space with white emulsion'd walls, Victorian sofa, tattered Regency chair and two large, very ordinary paintings on the wall. Mike suggested they could hold the poetry there.

'No. Upstairs, you can have upstairs.'

They agreed he could use the place on the first Monday of each month and Giovanni would supply home-made cakes and any kind of coffee chosen.

A few days later Mike sent emails to people he'd added to his contacts: those he'd inherited from his publisher and those collected from places where he'd been guest poet: a pub in Greenwich, a library in Lincoln, an Art House in Brighton, Cabaret Voltaire, Kerouac's, trying to flog copies of his collection, and from people who had wandered into the pub, the bar, the café, seeing someone standing and reading and people seated, listening, sometimes laughing, occasionally clapping, and wondering what was going on.

A week afterwards, Carlo and Mike were rearranging the tables and chairs, Sophia putting cakes, coffee cups and glasses on the counter next to the wine Mike had brought, and Giovanni, having an evening free from the Soho restaurant he managed for a friend, standing around smiling quietly, waiting for Martin to arrive and read some of his own and Giovanni's poems in English. Mike asked the latter if he would read in Italian. He enjoyed the sound of the language, himself knowing only, *mangiare beni, grazie* and *tu sei una bella donna.*

Looking around them at the new place a few regular Mere Poetry fans came in. Some who hadn't been to the last venue for months arrived making jokes about the passports and tetanus jabs needed to cross to this side of the Thames, the exhibiting artist, some students studying nearby and two Afro-Caribbean gays; one, lean and frowning, wearing brief shorts and black and white hooped leggings, sat with a small dog on his lap and limply stroked it for the next hour and a half.

Mike's guest poet, Josh, walked in. He'd seen him read once and chose him out of laziness, not having the motivation to look around for anyone else at the time. They half-heartedly chatted about poetry, Mike mentioning that he wasn't fond of rhymes - too easy, cheap - nor music if that was the main event, telling him that he'd recently read at The Den, a Soho club where a pop group topped the bill and that to read poetry immediately afterwards was like walking through porridge and that he wouldn't do it again, though he had been generously paid.. Just then, Pete 'trumpet' Barlow, who ran the club, came in and settled next to the star turn. And then Colin with his guitar. Mike was glad he'd come. Colin smiled shyly and sat in a corner on his own. He used to be a regular, writing and singing songs with Melissa, a middle aged, blonde East End Jewess who'd moved away. Mike hadn't seen him for some time, and had known little about him till a recent email from him:

'Hello Mike,

I'm sabotaging myself. I live virtually isolated amongst an uneducated enclave of jaw-gapingly narrow-minded, ignorant, arrogant, emotionally retarded, fucked up, white-vanned fascists, where I am known as 'the poof,' 'the queer,' and other denigratory terms. They have been making up my life as they go along on a daily basis for at least twenty five years. I've never slept with men, but according to them I do little else. Melissa was my only friend; her and my music are my psychic antidote in this unstoppable nightmare. You might imagine how all this erodes my creative enthusiasm. And this is sheltered accommodation! I was offered it because, in my last residence, I was harassed to the point of fleeing the place in fear of my life. The story is endless. The creative potential enormous. I want to write a hilarious play about it all. Stacks of material. No play comes. It will. Poetry first, perhaps.

I've risked a revelation. But it's just the plain facts of my existence. I've always enjoyed coming to Mere Poetry. I'll come when I can.

Colin.'

There were twenty five people by eight o' clock, and they started. Mike gave his usual welcome, a little longer this time as it was a new place. His resident singer songwriter - a Welsh Dylan Thomas fan who was almost pitch perfect - hadn't showed, but she always came just after the interval where she sat and sang, either with her own backing CD or guitarist. He had taken the names of the readers as they came in, most people wanted to read, and called on a couple of poetry gig veterans to open so two anxious twenty year olds who had never read in public before wouldn't have to begin.. After half an hour there were twenty eight people, including Sophia and Carlo, the café only just able to accommodate them. Tony then strode in.

'Hi Mike, I've just been hostesssing at a club in Stepney that finished early, so here I am.'

A big, friendly smile, .red gash of a mouth, black wig, earrings, stilettos and a red cheongsam split to the thigh covered with gold dragons. He ran a place in Wapping, with an octogenarian band struggling through salsas and rumbas, for cross-dressing friends and other people including families with children, who were looking for something different, and where Mike hadn't been for years. He was from New Zealand, and was always planning to go back there.

'Whatever will my grandchildren say when they see me? He'd jokingly ask.

Using his usual slightly cynical banter Mike introduced the poets: Jimmy 'jazzman' Curtis, self-appointed bard of south London, with his tambourine-like velvet hat, t-shirt with *does my society look big in this?* across it, sixties beads, baggy trousers, all calculatingly flung together, his huge glasses, long, wispy grey hair all part of his 'look.' Barry, nervous and showy, with his poems, rather arbitrarily, about

Ealing and New Cross, young Betty Beth Smith shyly reading two pieces about cats and old ladies, a cockney journalist who had never read in public before and who kept looking across to James appealingly each time he finished a poem for him to raise a finger, indicaing he could read another, and Tony, who read some work from a well known New Zealand poet, complete with convincing kookaburra sounds.

After the interval, during which most people had pointed at the coffee beans of their choice, and Giovanni, drinking large glasses of red wine, smilingly watched Carlo make it, it was Martin the translator, with his perfect English enunciating every consonant, reading Giovanni's work with a quiet pride. Mark noticed 'shard,' 'juxtaposition,' but thankfully no 'soul,' in his verses, and reminded Giovanni that he was going to read in Italian. He did so. Mike could have listened to him all evening.

Idris, just arrived, then sang, *A cappella,* her recently written ballad about the Welsh valleys, low and lilting.

Then Colin, who had a parody 'Russian' song to sing, 'It sounds like a Russian song, but it's not a Russian song, it has no Putin nor a Tsar, and it hasn't got a samovar, but, it sounds…' and another about his best friend who'd recently died and who he thought wouldn't have minded him trying to emulate his Kingston Town accent. Strumming his guitar he began, his lopsided smile convincing himself that his attempt had succeeded. It hadn't.

Josh suddenly stood up, as did Pete Barlow a second later. They turned and walked out the door. Trying not to show concern as most of the audience looked at him questioningly, Mike began clapping as Colin strained his last notes. They joined in. Mike guessed, perhaps too hurriedly, that his guest poet was another disciple of the stifling, middle class guilt trip of liberalism and that what had upset him was not the mediocrity of the song nor, perhaps the singing, but the attempted accent, which, maybe, he'd thought was 'racist.' (He found out some time afterwards that James not only rhymed all of his poetry, but, knowing that he was going to put him on immediately after the music, thought that Mike had done so purposely. Mike had no idea why).

He clapped some more. Sophia was looking amazed at all the people in her café, unaware of what was going on. Carlo spoke to Giovanni, coming quietly back from a few moments in the basement. He looked suddenly angry, not the anger of a cultured Roman, but a rougher, more savage emotion on his dark-skinned face. He looked across to Mike, his grey eyes like metal.

'I won't be long, Mister Mike.' he said, and strode through the front door. Mike didn't know where he was going. People were looking uncomfortable, bemused.

Then two hooded white faces were looking through the large, low window of the shop.

'There 'e is. Nonce. Pissiin' nonce.'

One of them pointed at Colin, sitting, guitar leaning between his legs. He looked unbelievingly at them, horrified.

'Yeh, you, we followed yuh. Nonce. Nonce.'

It was obvious they'd been drinking. Nobody moved. Mike felt Colin's fear. He went towards the door just as Giovanni appeared. The latter grabbed them both, one in each fist. He lifted the shorter of them who, six inches off the ground, started to pedal the air as if he'd forgotten his bike, and flung them onto their backs, the taller one briefly sliding along the pavement like a tobogganist going the wrong way. Giovanni's face was set in an expression Mike felt he was comfortable with, as if what he'd done was nothing new. The two lads got up and ran. Giovanni then turned and said to someone the other side of the doorway, his Italian accent thicker, stronger,

'You apologise to Mister Mike and the other people. You must not walk out like that, it is discourteous.'

Pete Barlow and Josh apprehensively pushed their heads into the café. Josh reluctantly nodded towards Mike. They disappeared.

'You must -'

'It's okay Giovanni, it's okay, come back in.' Mike said. He did so, easing by him.

'I am sorry. These things happen.' Giovanni smiled. 'Excuse me.'

He went down the stairs to the basement again. Mike looked around. People were quiet, concerned.' He .leant over the banister rail and looked down. Giovanni sat in the chair, chin resting in a cupped hand like Rodin's 'Thinker.' Mike took a deep breath, turned to the others.

'Right, er, let's continue. I think Idris should give us another song.'

She did, as if nothing had happened. It was one of her early songs, 'Times of Conflict.' Mike caught Colin's eye, silently appealed for him to accompany her, knowing that he knew this one. To his credit he did. There was one more reader, one of the public-reading virgins, looking strained. Then they'd finished.

Mike thanked everyone who had come, wondering whether they would again, those who had read, and Idris and Colin, the latter getting an enthusiastic clap. People chatted to each other, but not for long, most wanting to get home. Mike helped Carlo quickly put the tables and chairs back and started to go down to Giovanni.

'Don't.' said Carlo, 'He won't talk. Not while he's like this. He musn't do this stuff. If he gets reported to Parole...' he shrugged. 'Sophia's with him.' Mike didn't remember her going down. 'Best you go. *Ciao.*'

Mike asked him to thank his boss for him; investigating Carlo's cryptic remarks could wait till next time, or maybe when he brought some fliers to put on the tables before the next event. He wanted to speak to Colin, but he'd gone; though Mike knew he'd have company back to his home, anyway, Idris lived nearby. He picked up his collection and a few poetry pamphlets he'd scattered around as he always did whatever the venue: on a mantle shelf, leaning against a jar of plastic flowers, on beer bottles, and here, on a sack of coffee beans, and left.

Three weeks afterwards, carrying a few fliers, Mike turned the corner into Leyland Street and wondered why there were no tables and chairs outside the cafe; they'd been put out before on a day as warm as this. As he got nearer the reason became obvious; the place was closed, a grafitti'd shutter covering the front. He was unsure whether Giovanni had decided to close for the day, maybe to give Sophia and Carlo a rest, or...had closed. The Alpha Deli was next door. Mike went in. The girl sweeping the floor didn't know why they weren't open. Her boss did. Standing up from behind the counter, he said,

'They've. gone. No business. Not enough customers.'

Mike turned away thinking of when he'd told Giovanni of the trestle board advert the Deli had put on the street corner fifty yards away and asked him why he didn't do the same.

'We are poets,' he'd said with a smile, putting his arm around Mike's shoulders, 'not traders.'

He dumped the fliers in a waste bin and walked back to the station. As he reached the bottom of the entrance steps he heard, 'Mister Mike.' He knew of course who it was. Giovanni was right behind him.

'Hey, I was going to tell you, Sophia gave me you email address and-'

'You've finished then. No more Rivenda UK?'

They stood there, people jostling by.

'I'm managing a restaurant in Piccadilly now'

'And Sophia and Carlo?'

'They're working there part-time. Pity. No more poetry, uh?'

'Well, I'll find somewhere else if I can. If not… I'll let you know. Ok?'

'Sure, Mister Mike. I enjoyed it you know'.

He gave a big, bristly grin, got to the top of the stairs and had gone.

'You can tell me to fuck off if you like, but our guest poet's from Manchester and it's a long way to come to read if nobody can hear you. We've been away for a couple of months and I know I've no right to ask you to move, but d'you think you could, please? Just around the corner there?'

They were three men. One seemed a little hostile. He looked behind Mike, got up, quickly gestured to the others, and they moved quietly to the end of the L shaped bar. Mike turned and nearly walked into Giovanni who was looking grimly at the backs of the three suited customers. He wondered quickly why he hadn't asked Carlo more about Giovanni's story when he last saw him. It didn't matter. Giovanni smiled at him and they returned to the small scattering of people sitting in a half circle in front of a large, scruffily dressed man with an open book in his hands.

'Right, before I introduce Tom again, I'd like to say that we're all pleased that Colin's here and, of course, Giovanni, who'll read a poem or two in Italian accompanied by Colin on guitar. Tom Barrett

won the National Poetry Competition a few years ago, all five grand
of it, and I'm hoping that this evening...'

GUNS AND ROSES

From the bus, sitting with, seemingly, a representative speaker of each of London's 400 languages and dialects, he could see through the damp twilight the wet chairs outside Charlie's Café like a dispirited, doomed attempt to create a Boulevard San Michelle bar in Canning Town - a black and white photo of the Eiffel Tower just visible on its wall - the tatty but stylish thirties bus garage currently a supermarket, a few grey-leafed trees and a stretch of the Northern Outfall sewer now desperately called 'Greenway.' Somebody looked up from the pavement, she in her bubble, he in his, pondering the futile relativism of everything, and as this statement cannot claim privileged exemption from itself is thus self-stultifying and therefore there is no absolute and if there was, for whom or what would it be an absolute? So, warts and all, it's relativism. There is no meaning. Guided by the imbalance of instincts and society's non-codified laws, people make their own and, in this nihilistic mood, James Kent was incapable of making his.

He was thinking of his patients, wanting to put his hands inside their heads and grab neutrons, electrons, change placements and strengths, bend neural pathways, alter structures to make them feel better without them having to go through the pain, the work, the struggle to get there. Perhaps all the answers lay in a neurophysiological future. Meanwhile, there is a cornucopia of drugs and the fatuously labelled 'talking cure.'

This was the ontological space in which James worked; patiently listening, the occasional question, the infrequent satisfactions of clients improvements and genuine adjustments to themselves and their lives and, of late, wondering what else there was for him if he stopped what he'd been doing for six years, assuming he could afford to.

He was on his way to meet Mia where they often met, at a café near London Bridge. He'd first seen her four years ago at the launch of his poetry collection at an art gallery in South London, and where he casually asked her to have a drink with him the next evening.

They'd met near the Cutty Sark, her fair hair and rich blue-eyes confirming the Agnetha Faltskog likeness, and begun walking alongside the Thames She told him she was from Cape Town, had been here for two years and that it was all rather grey, the colours absorbed by the streets.

'There is no distance, no sky.'

The colours she loved were gold and red, russet and green, he realising later that they were the colours of apples. She then, in one of her many impromptu actions that still surprised and pleased him, reached over a graveyard railing of the Thames-side church and picked a large petal from a rose, saying with a smile, 'Eat it, it's nice.' He did, and it was. After a silence she enthused about the ultramarine dusk, the pink reflections on the water, and asked where he would take her if he wanted a romantic evening. He told her, only half jokingly, that it would be a pie and mash shop. There was one nearby. She enjoyed it. They talked poetry and England, she telling him bashfully that she wrote bits of Victorian whimsy about the Queen having tea with Dickens and Dick Whittington, and he telling her about its capital city and of his late brother and himself walking over a thousand miles in the last few years around its streets. When the pink reflections turned to the grey-cream splashes of embankment lamps, they caught a bus towards St. Paul's, near where she was living.

They passed her stop accidentally, him realising it sooner than her and with a rather out-of-character deviousness said nothing until they were a couple of miles eastwards of their destination where she realised she didn't recognise the area around her. It was October, dark and getting late, hence his suggestion that she may as well stay at his place. She did. Lying next to him - having just moved in there was neither couch nor spare bed, which he hadn't mentioned - she gently kissed his shoulder before saying goodnight and turning her back. In the morning, his frustration still clinging, she said to him,

'It's better to be friends than lovers.'

He felt this to be a mature woman's gambit, the earth mother offering a comforting, 'There, there,' to a little boy. Since that time, they'd become good friends, having a genuine affection for each other.

After they'd met for the third time, she told him her story. Born near Cape Town to a teacher mother and German naturopath father who left them both a month after her birth, she finished a theosophy degree at twenty one and married. Her and her husband bought a farm and an orchard on the outskirts of Cape Town and had a son, Daniel. A few years afterwards her husband met another woman, divorced Mia and sold the farm, leaving her nothing. He never saw his son again, but not for want of trying.

Daniel, on his way home from junior school on the back of a teacher's motor bike, was thrown off as the machine broadsided, skidding on a bend of the cinder road. His leg was broken. As his mother began nursing him to health his father appeared, demanding to see his offspring. After being refused he threatened to take the child. Mother and son then spent the next three years staying in several places in South Africa, she having evidence that her ex had traced them to the first two.

She earned a living for both of them by waiting on tables and sketching people's portraits while Daniel attended various schools. Feeling, after a while, relatively safe, she met a musician who had recently left the army, and married again.

For two years she stopped telling James about her past. He didn't insist, merely suggesting that she tell him if and when she wanted to. When she did so she told him that, as she sang well and played piano competently in those days and her husband's song writing career was blossoming, he had decided they should team up professionally and tour the USA.

During this time he wrote the hit, *Sophie Marie,* soon after which he invited Mia to meet the song's eponymous heroine. She refused. Just after this she discovered that a song he'd written, for and about her, had been sold to a well known rock musician who had, through recordings and tours, made a lot of money from it. This started a long series of jealousies and recriminations, eventually leading to divorce.

Before their split and after returning home to South Africa, her husband - she'd adamantly refused to tell James his name - became a mercenary for the government of a European country, later leading a band of other mercenaries on a successful raid on their rebel-held embassy in a West African country.

Two days before the assault a member of the mercenary group, who Mia knew, came and informed her that her husband had ordered him to 'Get rid of her.' She told James this, as she had other stories about her life, with the preamble of a weary and resigned, 'You won't believe this.' But he always did. He could see no reason why she'd lie. Keeping as calm as she could she'd asked the man why.

'Because you've been in the house when we've had meetings and you've heard things, you know things.'

She protested that she'd never listened, and always closed the door of whatever room she was in; the little sound bites of conversation she had heard she'd rarely understood anyway, especially when they were in French.

'I don't want to do it. And I'm not. But you've got to get out of the house tonight, the latest by the morning. Go, Mia.'

Thus Daniel and his mother began wandering again; the jobs, hardships, different schools, and the fear again. When offering this information she would nonchalantly shrug, as if she'd decided to accept some sort of generalised nemesis to explain it all, a de-personalisation; a 'wrong place at the wrong time' randomness.

But there *was* something vulnerable, an almost ethereal vagueness about her, as when she was immersed in an activity like painting or drawing. She was teaching at her local school and would, perhaps, work all night in her Rotherhithe studio before realising she'd be late for work if she continued. And there was a sporadic forgetfulness, especially in the context of time. She insisted he always carried his mobile phone so that she could ring him when she was late in meeting him. There was also her proneness to 'accidents.' They were in an almost empty Islington bar one evening when, as they turned to leave, she discovered she no longer had her bag with her.

'It was that couple near us at the counter,' she'd shouted. He had never heard her raise her voice before. They ran out. Of course, the pair had gone.

Another time, as she left him in a crowded tube train, him playfully pushing his face against the door glass, she looked suddenly shocked and shook her head at him as the train took him away from her. She rang him later to say she'd had her bag cut away and taken. He remembered they'd been pushed up tightly against two men. He imagined her standing on the platform staring at the back of the departing train, a strap hanging uselessly from her shoulder.

He once asked her if she ever felt frightened of her second husband finding her.

'You're assuming he wants to find me,' she snapped. Then, 'I'm sorry, it's just that I try not to think of him.'

Her run of misfortunes continued: having two of her paintings stolen from a Cape Town gallery when she went back for a few weeks to see her son and her passport taken as she was going through Customs on her return; leaving her bag in a cinema, knocking into someone when she and James were walking along the South Bank and the man hurrying off with her purse which she discovered was missing only later when remembering that it was James' birthday and she'd run off to a Covent Garden shop to buy a present.

And so they continued: sharing interests, ideas, humour; their friendship. Then, a new client came to him.

He walked into James' study; fair hair, early thirties, tall and skinny with lips pressed together in a tight, shy smile. He stood there expectantly. James beckoned him to sit. He did, frowning down at the length of the sofa.

'It's okay, you don't have to lie on it.' said James.

'Didn't Freud stand behind his couch, hide away somewhere so his patients would find it easier to talk?' He had an accent that sounded familiar.

'Apparently, yes, but I think he realised the folly of it. Patients, in order to face themselves, face what they're struggling with, must eventually have eye contact with their therapist; there's more chance of feeling what they're saying, less chance to escape, which a large part of them wants to do. And what are you struggling with?'

'I don't know where to begin.'

James didn't use the easy response of, 'Try the beginning,' the real beginning may not have been remembered.

'Why do you ask?'

'Because you've come to see me.'

'I didn't want to, but…'

'But what?'

He looked at the door, got up.

'Where are you going?'

'I don't know,' he said to the door, 'I don't *know*. I don't want to be here.'

'Have you thought, Robert, it is Robert, isn't it? that when someone listens to you it's as if they're giving you love, of a kind. I need that, too, but not as much as you. I'll listen to you for the next fifty minutes and for the next fifty and the next, and so on. Will you talk to me?'

He turned, walked slowly back to the couch and sat again, this time seeming a little more comfortable.

Taking a deep breath he said, 'My friends tell me I'm paranoid.' He bent his head and looked at the floor for a few minutes.

'A characteristic of paranoia is hearing voices. I suspect that you don't. Am I right?'

'Yes, but it's when people look at me, anyone really, it's just that expression in their eyes, I don't know.' He dropped his head again.

'What *is* the expression?'

'They're against me, they want to… attack me, I suppose.'

As gently as he could, James said, 'Maybe you feel that they, somehow, *should* attack you, a sort of redemption; that you deserve to be punished. Do you, Robert?'

His client didn't answer; continued looking down.

James let him stay in this position until his time was up. As he went he asked if he could come the next week. James suggested he see him weekly. He agreed.

During that week he saw Mia just the once; at an open night at her studio. There weren't many people, mostly the other artists, little of whose work he liked; contemporary art had, for him, such diffuse criteria, not just for what 'good' art was, but art itself, that, without an obvious craftsmanship, he felt dismayed in its presence.

The next time his client came he sat on the arm of the couch where he'd sat before. He looked down again.

'This 'attacking,'' James began quietly, encouragingly, 'where do you think it comes from? I'm not really expecting you to have emotional knowledge of this,' he added quickly, 'but, use your intelligence. I feel that this began when you were a boy. Picture him, this little boy, with his parents, without his parents, with a family member, with whoever.'

His client said nothing for precisely forty minutes. During this time James merely said twice, 'You can talk to me, you know.'

Then he looked up, narrowed his eyes the tiniest bit; there was an internal stiffening. 'There was this... this uncle; he was hard, a tough man, he frightened people I think.' He looked down again. 'He scared me. He sort of dominated my parents. He was my mum's brother. He didn't say very much. Dad was timid, especially when Uncle Peter was there.'

When he said 'Peter,' James belatedly recognised the South African accent and rather clipped, almost formal English,

'And when he looked at me it was as if he... knew something, just knew something, maybe wanted revenge, I don't know.'

He looked at James, tears coming into his eyes. He was asked if he had any idea what this man represented to him. He shook his head emphatically.

'God, Robert? Society? Somebody who knew you did something you shouldn't have? Something awful?'

'Don't know. Don't know.' He was almost shouting. James let him calm down. He was about to tell him that he had only a few minutes left with him when he looked up and said, with a slight smile,

'They said he was a soldier, he was in a raid somewhere, but he wasn't allowed to get a medal. He had this... mystery. Apparently he was a singer or something, though I couldn't imagine him doing that, he was too tough. He had a wife or girl friend, it was all hush-hush.' Pronounced in his accent, the dated colloquialism seemed odd. He stopped smiling and frowned.

'When I was growing up I remember him saying to my father, I forget where we were and I don't really know why I remember it, but he said, 'She has to be silent.' I don't know who they were talking about, but I felt frightened for her, whoever she was. I try to convince myself now that it was a bit melodramatic, I was only a boy. Perhaps it was, who knows?'

He then kept repeating in a tense, but level voice, 'He frightened me.' until James gently told him it was time to go and that he wanted him to try to think about this man and what he, himself, might be feeling guilty about. He quietly left.

Coincidences, synchronicity, often happened to James, but mostly in a minor vein. He would be half listening to the radio and reading or thinking of a particular word when he would hear that word in that exact second. It may have been a word as ubiquitous as 'hello' or, as happened recently, 'avuncular' and, an hour before that, 'recusant.' Mostly he'd smile to himself, just accepted it; a common phenomenon.

This coincidence, however, wasn't amusing. His response was a slowly building disbelief. This one was too real.

Should he tell Mia what he was dreading to think? He imagined her with her young son in a South African mining town searching for a room, a job, and when managing to find them, needing someone to look after him. And then maybe overhearing a conversation between a teacher and caretaker or a chance remark from a child when picking Daniel up from school that a man had been seen standing outside the building and, obtaining a description that could have fitted her farmer husband, rushing to wherever her offspring was being looked after, grabbing him, getting him home, gathering what belongings she could and fleeing again. And a few years later, after the soldier's warning to leave, taking a teenage Daniel to some other town, city or village and hiding again.

He'd look at her in his car or while she was watching a film or leaning against the parapet on a bridge looking at the Thames go by, look at that sensitive profile, neatly cut highlighted hair, almost fussily colour co-ordinated clothes, and felt he understood why she'd stopped telling him about her life and its ordeals; in her home country, in America and, now, potentially, here.

He went on-line, found that *Sophie Marie's* lyrics and music was credited to a Bobby Bins. Then he searched for every name that was linked to him, however tenuously, until, as he was about to end the search, a 'Peter Brand' came up, a guitarist who'd been in a group managed by someone who'd been associated with Bobby Bins. There was nothing else except the link.

Mia and he met two days afterwards at the Festival Hall cafe and, while they listened superficially to the muffled sound of a symphony, as casually as he could and working hard not to convey his angst, asked her if her ex had sold his songs to anyone else or written any other well known pieces that even James would be familiar with. She gave him what his mother would have called an 'old-fashioned look' and didn't answer. He'd seen it before when he'd asked her something that had gone over an invisible boundary she'd set. And then, while drinking tea and chatting, the obvious came to him. He could, when he felt his patient's mood was conducive, ask him what his uncle's surname was, though a part of him didn't want to know, didn't want to hear it spoken.

This almost surreal situation, this worrying topography was ever present. He had to shake himself when with his other patients, force himself to listen, to understand and not do them a disservice.

Robert didn't come the next week. James rang him in the evening. There was no answer. The next morning was the same. He could feel his quest becoming an obsession: He had to know whether this man had been Mia's partner and could still represent a danger to her. He assumed he was alive, but needed to know; surely Robert could help.

James rang him repeatedly over the next few days and then went to his address. He lived four miles away, or rather had. He wasn't there and, according to his subletting landlord, after staying in the second floor flat for a year he'd left six days previously to return to South Africa.

James was just turning to leave when he was asked, not challengingly, but out of polite curiosity, who he was. He said that he was a friend and that he may know his ex-tenant's aunt.

'He left some things in his room, I shouldn't think he wanted them, you may as well have them. Come in.'

He followed the landlord up the stairs to a living room. It was very tidy. The man took a plastic bag from a table.

'He left a couple of t-shirts, a few books, there's a pair of trainers here, too, and a few photos. I've only just found them, I was going to chuck 'em, I have no forwarding address. Do what you will.'

James sat outside in his car. He was supposed to have been helping a man with paranoid tendencies to get to their origins, to try to help him illuminate them, not in a flash of incandescent recognition, a healing light suffusing his universe for ever, but to help him feel…innocent again, to cope with this knowledge, alone. Now he couldn't.

He looked in the bag. There were two colour photos: one of tropical trees in front of a white painted timber clad house and, torn diagonally, but not completely in two, a black and white picture of an angelic looking boy of about six or so looking up dotingly at a handsome, rather gaunt man in army uniform. Behind them, to the side, was what could have been a case for a musical instrument or, perhaps, a rifle. It seemed as if his client had made a decision to leave this piece of his life behind.

And then he wondered if he was not about to use this object to create an exaggerated image of this man's dichotomous talents because he, fancifully, wanted to add even more mystique to Mia's past, give it an aura of some sort of glamour, of what he'd felt as a child for film goddesses and for far away lands and, of course, to soften the hard, hollow starkness that was filling him.

His decision whether or not to tell Mia of Robert and to show her the photograph was hastened by her deciding to return home to Cape Town for a month to see her son and the house she and Daniel were buying on Magina Bay. Her timing was arbitrary but, as he travelled to Heathrow with her on the Tube, glancing at her expression, her quiet anticipation of home and seeing Daniel, he felt that telling her that his now ex-patient was, possibly, related to the second man in her life that she'd been forced to flee, would bring it all back to her, and maybe she wouldn't be tough enough to cope. He could see her panicking and roaming the British Isles or Europe or somewhere, hiding, working, frightened.

But then, other questions: was it just a series of non-serendipitous coincidences after all? Was it him not only putting pieces of the jigsaw together, but *creating* the jigsaw, constructing it out of a piece of conversation overheard by a small boy, from a song, a photograph? Again, the therapist's eternal problem: the projection of his own self, his feelings, attitudes, ideologies onto his patient and, now, in a scattered, fragmented way, onto his client's situation, his past. Either way, so much of Mia was scar tissue, and he didn't wish it opened up.

He wasn't surprised when, as they got off the train, she thought for a panicky moment that she'd left her passport behind. He comforted her and carried her bags up the escalator. Again it seemed the norm when she discovered she'd read her flight's ETD wrongly and that there was an hour or so before check-in. He sat her down in a near deserted airport café and brought them coffee.

He wasn't sure how to begin. Would she see him as interfering too much in her life, the part of her life she'd stopped telling him about some time ago? He could hear his mother telling him it wasn't any of his business, just as she would have said of his chosen career that, 'All this meddlin's not right.'

He told Mia while she was eating a croissant. She looked surprised at the beginning of his narrative and was, at the end, frowning and nodding her head, but a little distractedly, as if she was feigning interest. He hadn't mentioned the photograph. He began reaching into his pocket for it, intending to place it on the table in front of her so that he could see her reaction. She suddenly stood up.

'Do you realise the time? I'm late,'

He hurried after her to check the bags in. He stood next to her in the small queue, watched her, full of her tickets, boarding pass, her son, her house. He wondered if he'd told it, explained it all accurately enough, strongly enough. Had she really listened, heard it all through the echoing flight announcements?

A uniformed female looked briefly at her bits of paper. Mia hastily put them in her bag. She went through the low gate and turned.

'It's okay,' she smiled. 'It's alright, really.'

She took a few steps towards him, gave him an affectionate kiss.

'You have one angel, I have two. I need them.'

Then she was gone.

On the journey back he was asking himself what she meant by saying it was 'okay.' That she'd caught her flight and would be seeing Daniel tomorrow? That she'd picked up the allusions, inferences and the possible meaning of the story and that it didn't matter? Or was she protecting him? He imagined her sitting in a window seat looking out unseeingly at sky and sea, and feeling a fist of anxiety turning in her stomach. But he knew that this was as far as it would go. If he raised it all again her eyes would convey an obdurate refusal to respond, a wish to hear no more.

Arriving home, he put the unrepaired photo inside a never used childhood bible he wondered why he'd kept. He was hoping that its memory would lose its jagged resonance and become a dull, lessening weight or even an embarrassing irrelevance.

He would send her the occasional text or email while she was away, but she wouldn't reply; it would be summer there and she'd be busy painting, drawing and sitting under her favourite waterfall near Table Mountain - though she'd probably send him a picture of her, laughing and wet in a bikini.

He went out to see a film, passing Charlie's Café again, its owner piling up his metal chairs to carry in out of the rain. The lit windows seemed to have a bit of Impressionism about them, Van Gogh, maybe, or Monet, until he decided that they didn't and, in a rare slip into anthropomorphism, that the dark East End night didn't deserve colour, had done nothing to justify it, wasn't good enough for it. Somehow, the rain suited the night.

TREES

'You've got a great face,' Ben heard from somewhere to his right. A young man came around in front of him and handed him a sketch: the lean, lined, fifty year old profile, the dark eyes, long nose like his mother's, designer stubble, greying hair. His gut response was one of rejection; no, he didn't look like this, but having attended a recent life drawing class he knew he did. He was sitting in Café Rouge at Heathrow; as a Francophile he enjoyed the Lautrec posters and scrolled gestures to *Art Nouveau*.

'Hope you don't mind. I love drawing people.'

Ben told him it was okay by him, heard his flight called and went towards Departures. He was going to see his son who he'd last seen in Memphis, Missouri, where, just after he'd left a commune shared by others indulging in a well intentioned bourgeois fantasy, had gone to live near Seattle to work for an IT start-up company and was now freelance.

Spending much of the long flight seeing in the clouds fluffy dogs, countless chicks and an elephant stamping on a mouse, he arrived at Minneapolis for a short stop-over between flights. Going through the covered walkway after landing he mentioned to a flight attendant how surprised he was that an aircraft that large had only two engines. She pointed to her braided, peak capped companion, 'Ask him, he knows about planes, he's the captain.' 'I *know,*' he said, with wide eyes and drooped wrist, 'they make them so *big* these days.'

It reminded him of when he and Paula had flown to New York some years before and, like a scene from a fifties musical, the captain had sung a chorus of 'New York, New York' as they came in to Kennedy.

Having failed to conceptually validate *curry and mushroom croissant* and *marinated pecans and balsamic reduction* at the French Meadows Café he went to the gate where a fourteen stone female Customs Officer told him to remove his footwear and belt, 'No shoes, no go,' followed by a security guard, hands cocked at his hips, who ordered him to, 'Step back sir, take yer hands outta your pockets.' Ben wanted to tell him he'd seen the movies. All of them.

After an overnight stay at a bland, beige airport hotel, Tom

248

welcomed him with a hug and they resumed their bantering, pseudo-combative interaction as if they'd last seen each other the week before: He was without his partner, Marion, who was visiting her mother on nearby Bainbridge Island.

Ben felt lifted. It was good to see his son again. They got the light rail to Downtown Seattle, wandered around Central market and through the small square under the rooftop *Cantina* with its samba band, hip-swaying Mexican Seattleites and the creaking arses of the English tourists just missing the beat.

The ferry trip to Bainbridge Island was like a mini-cruise, with the distant Olympic Mountains ahead of them and the city dwindling away at the stern. They caught the bus to Poulsbo and the house Tom had found for Ben to rent.

It was a large one with plastic clapboard cladding and rocking chairs on the wraparound porch. Ben had to smile, something he'd realised recently he rarely did; it was so American. The estate could have been used for The Truman Show: the automatically sprinkled, bright green front lawns, range rovers and pick-up trucks in front of double garages, the pale blues and greys of the houses backed by pine trees and maples.

The owner told them his wife, Ann, would be back shortly and led them to his guest's room past another which, with its over-styled mahogany desk and a card leaning back on it saying 'CEO,' Ben guessed was his office. Downstairs was a large carpeted area with kitchen bar and more beige ceilings and walls.

The plan was that he'd be here for a week then they'd pick up Marion and the three of them would go to Paris for eight days. She had never been, and Tom only as a child a few months before his mother died of leukaemia. It was the last time Ben had been, also. When he thought of the city it was always behind Paula's face, at a distance, its perspective exaggerated, her smile shining out as if from a tourist poster.

Leaving his bags in the room he and Tom walked into Poulsbo, its Nordic origins seen in the flags and shop names - the deeply cut fjord-like bays surrounding the town would have held a comforting familiarity for its early immigrants. They ate in the Mexican *Casa Luna* overlooking the Bay with the waiters' constant, 'D'yer wan' it boxed? as they scraped the remains of meals into polystyrene boxes, and then wandered into the Poulsbo Marine Science Center, locally known as the aquarium. Ben had little interest in things piscatorial, but a fluffy, sponge-like creature in a large glass tank caught his eye.

'We call it Ginger, it's an octopus. It's kinda small and pink, but there yer go.'

She was tall, slim, dark frizzy hair, deep set brown eyes, olive skin, and perhaps in her late twenties. He asked her if she knew a lot about fish.

'A little. I'm part-time, I help out back with the kids sometimes, it's mostly voluntary.' She bent down. 'Joey, go back in the room with Ellie, good boy.' He did.

'You're not working your way through college, then?'

'Well, yeh, but not here. I'm majoring in Developmental Psychology and I have a job.'

He asked her what she did.

'I'm a lumberjack.' She laughed; the white teeth, one slightly crooked, the flesh puffed a little under her eyes.

Tom, who'd been looking for somewhere to use his laptop, walked by humming Monty Python's, 'I'm A Lumberjack and I'm Okay' out the corner of his mouth and pointed at a window in the side wall behind which Joey was being read to by a helper, indicating he was going to sit in there. Ben asked her how she became a lumberjack.

'My father was one.'

'The son he never had?'

'Maybe.'

He asked her where she worked. It was near the rain forest north of the State.

'It's full of virgin lumber.'

'You've just commoditised nature.'

'Maybe we're all commodities.'

He asked her if she knew Piaget's work and that, as a sociologist, he felt he had to point out his ignoring of cultural variables.

'Perhaps he does. We read Freud, too.'

'Do you think that a backpack is, symbolically, a placenta?'

'Maybe. And would you accept that a child with a good birth experience will tend to draw circles rather than angular shapes?'

He suggested that it could be a compensation for a bad one, and then asked if she was going to attack sociology.

'No, no need to. Science has settled the nature-nurture debate in favour of nature.' She grinned, 'We're at war.'

He felt suddenly stimulated; that familiar feeling when he'd been teaching - now being a new and reluctant Head of Department at his local college in London.

'You've got to ask who benefits from the power accorded to science to 'settle' this debate, and the answer, other than the ideologically vested interests of science, are the drug companies.'

'Are you always this cynical? Do you always intellectualise the world like this?'

Ben didn't answer. She narrowed her eyes a little. There was a smile in them.

'What are you running away from?'

He'd been asked neither of these questions before. He felt, for a second, a confusion, a kind of emotional interruption, Then she said,

'Look, I've gotta get something out the car. Be back. Incidentally, I'm half Jewish.'

She walked towards the entrance and into the small car park. He watched her through a window go to a red, fifties Eldorado convertible with a bonnet as long as the rest of the car and a MIZZROZE license plate. She returned with a piece of paper.

'It's a logging itinerary. Sorry about the number plate, my dad bought me the car and the plate came with it.'

'I assume your name's Rose.'

'Yep, and I'm at a private university and feel very privileged.'

'I could count on the fingers of one hand the female, undergraduate, Jewish lumberjacks I've met this week.'

'And I never expected to meet an English sociologist in an aquarium in Washington State. I need to go.' He didn't want her to.

'I lunch with the guys sometimes at the Junction Diner down the 101 aways if you're ever there.' She gave a take-it-or-leave-it shrug. 'See yer.'

And out she went again, all flower patterned blouse, black tights and hair. He went back to the window of the arts and crafts room and saw Tom snuggled in a corner tapping away while Joey quietly ran around in circles watched by Ellie.

They left the aquarium to get some groceries and then to Tom's rented, run-down bungalow off a dirt road behind *Silver City Tattoos* which would have had a view over hill-ringed Freedom Bay had it not been for the chalet-like condominiums obscuring it. They shared a few beers and a hyperbolic sense of the ridiculous and then, along with a flashlight, Ben went up the hill to his room. After living on his own for so long he couldn't get used to sharing a house, despite Ann's plea, delivered from the fake leather sofa she seemed to constantly lie in, to 'Treat the place as yours, our home's your home.'

Tom had arranged a bus trip for him next day to Crescent Lake because it was blue and tranquil and thought he needed it. He was picked up outside a McDonalds, the occupants all elderly women except for a baseball-capped male. A few miles along the highway, with its occasional yellow smudges where paint trucks had veered off the lines, they passed the steeple-less First Church of Christ The Scientist and then more dark green hills as they neared the peninsula. They were held in a queue while trucks with long trailers full of logs passed them. He thought of Rose. He thought of her again while on the lake jetty listening to Larry from the bus telling him he owned twenty acres and a cow.

As they tracked casually through the forest surrounding the lake Larry told him what he knew about logging and about the resinous cedar wood he built his stock fences with while Ben stopped under the biggest tree he'd ever seen. He looked up and imagined Rose at the top balancing in a harness, seeing just her boots and hair through the branches. The sun came through. He saw it light up the skin on her arm. He couldn't see what she was doing. He felt protective towards her, ridiculously proprietary, then excited; her thighs, knees, boots, pressing against the trunk, her upper body swinging out. He caught up with Larry and went across the log bridge to the falls.

Tom had to work again next day. Ben felt restless on his own, he needed to walk. He wandered into the local windowless Wal-Mart,

As he left he asked the check-out girl why she'd wished him a great day and told her if she knew him she'd probably wish him a bad one. She frowned, put her grin back and said' 'Have a...' and turned to the next customer. He wasn't quite sure why he was in this mood.

After leaving his groceries at the house he went to the Junction Café a mile away at the side of the highway: melamine walls, gingham tablecloths, ketchup or gravy on every square inch of steak, omelettes and biscuits applied by large men sitting on high-backed bar stools. One of them, looking out at a lumber truck in the parking lot next to a *Honey Bucket* mobile toilet, was wearing an *old guys rule* t-shirt. There were a few pony tails and backwoodsmen beards, but no Rose.

He still wasn't certain why he kept thinking of her. Even amongst the large number of mature women students he'd taught he could think of no-one he'd met just once who had caused him to think about them till the next time, the next lecture. He'd had relationships with women during the last fifteen years, but each had gone back to something, or someone.

He went to Bainbridge and walked along the jetty where seniors who'd been with Microsoft since the early days had bought techno-rich, high-bridged boats with names like *Ratpack, Poodie Gal* and *As Time Goes By*. Wanting something more restful than conspicuous nautical consumption he went around the back of a nearby Unitarian church, part of which was a pre-school with a cosy allotment of sweet peas and rhubarb with the Stars & Stripes planted firmly in a corner.

Out of curiosity he thought he'd have a quick look inside the building. He went in. Someone was awkwardly spinning a ball off a bat over a table tennis table. It was Rose. He went towards her,

'Hey, what are you doing here?' she asked, glancing up briefly. He told her.

'I'm not stalking you, honestly.' he said lightly,

'I do voluntary work here too, out of semester. Coincidence, uh? The kids have gone now. D'you play?'

He remembered when he'd first learnt the game at thirteen in an East End school, using partly open books triangling across a desk for the net.

'I'll beat you.' he said. 'You serve.'

He hadn't held a bat since playing for a youth team. She was good; a little gauche, but effective. He childishly felt he had to beat her, to impress, he couldn't let her win.

It all came back: smashes, devious serves, defensive chops, back hands. When she served he watched her breasts move beneath a white t-shirt, her enthusiasm in hitting the ball made them seem, somehow, innocent, unknowing. He won two games, the next he didn't, possibly because he was watching her, intrigued by the way she smashed down, the irregular tooth showing as she grimaced, her crouch as she chopped back, the firm slap of her flip flops.

'Wh-hey, I beatcha. There's coffee through here.'

She put her bat down and went into a small room with a coffee machine and a table. He followed and sat down.

'How you gonna sociologise that, then?'

'I could say that, like all games, it's rule-bound behaviour, thus its competitive nature affirming the capitalist ethos. But I won't. Tell me about logging.'

'Well, there's forty three saw mills in Washington State, though some are stopping production 'cos of the recession, and some are exporting to China and India and - '

'You're telling it by rote, why?'

'Well, I don't really relate to that side of it, I just... like getting out there, working.'

He asked her to tell him about the different kinds of trees she worked on.

'Western red cedar, Alaskan yellow, and don't forget it's not tie hacks and axes any more, it's chain saws, Douglas firs - '

'What about the sequoias that are so big the trunks are carved out and cars drive through.'

'That's for tourists, and I know that word's got all the vowels in, and I don't want to talk about this stuff anymore.'

He felt hurt. He asked her if she was finished here and perhaps wanted to eat.

'I need to be going, but we could go to Campana's on Thursday, if you want. About eight?'

'That's another three days.'

'It's in Poulsbo.'

He'd seen the place. He said goodbye to her as she hurried out. A few seconds later he saw the red car drove away up Madison past the fifties blue and silver diner he'd had a coffee in earlier.

Other than going to Tom's friend's house the next evening, and the one after to a cinema, the next two days, because his son was working, he spent in Bainbridge and Poulsbo, preferring the latter. It was cosy, the former more affluent, more self-consciously fashionable. The aquarium was shut.

After making his stubble a little more designed he got to Campana's early. It was an old schoolhouse converted into an Italian restaurant with a spacious bar at the back and favouring Dean Martin and Sinatra numbers. He sat there appreciating the post-modern irony of menu items like *Dago Deli* and *Wop 'n Wahoo,* and started thinking of the differences, the little ones, between here and home: the light switches going down for off, the high water in toilet bowls submerging the testicles of the unsuspecting, the lack of people walking.

She came in with her usual black tights and no make up, but with a red band around her hair. Waiting for the waitress he started telling her how filmic he found America, how, for instance, nearly everyone in Memphis had made him silently ask, 'Weren't you in...?' and, 'Surely, you played the sheriff with...' and the courthouse clock stuck forever at four, with Roy Bang's gun store on the corner of the square and his wares on trestle tables on the sidewalk, so alien to the English eye

They ordered Nina Campana's secret recipe lasagne and talked about films. He liked sharing them: those he'd loved in his teens such as Bonnie and Clyde and asked her if she remembered the garage scene with Michael J. Pollard who he thought Tom looked like as a baby. She didn't because she hadn't seen the film. It was a projection again; he assumed she had and, he realised, adolescently needed her to have, the same interest in films as him, the same enthusiasm, a similar knowledge. He felt disappointed.

'What sort of music d'you like?' They asked it in unison, her in her confident, pleasant drawl, him in his flat, posh cockney. The music he mentioned she either hadn't heard or wasn't interested in. Again, his disappointed child. He told her he didn't analyse music, He liked it or he didn't.

'It's like Joe Blogs being asked about a piece of art - and 'art' is that which is an art gallery of course - and saying, 'I don't know much about art, but I know what I like.' which is just as valid as the art critic of the New York Times calling it 'a turbulent arabesque of significant complexity.''

He knew this was a populist thing to say to her, to help her see him as unpretentious, 'cool,' even. She didn't answer. He subtly suggested she change her mind and tell him more about her work.

The meal came. It was good. They hardly spoke except to comment on the food. They were both hungry. When they'd finished she said,

'Okay, there's a European tradition that we're sworn enemies of werewolves, vampires and Mormons and also immortal. We're still sometimes called professional assassins by the way, and I didn't get into it because of my father. There was a high school competition for axing and sawing logs. I won it. I got my proficiency certificate in one year instead of two and I've been doing the job for three years.'

He asked her what happened at the tops of trees, partly because he'd pictured her there.

'We tie lines sometimes to help the direction of the fall, but not often. There's not many camps now either, though there may be one where we're going, it's pretty wild, we usually use a motel if its too far to get home.'

Feeling a kind of pre-jealousy in anticipating her reply he said, 'Do you have trouble with - '

'No. I put 'em down, they don't make passes any more.'

She said it with a quick flint of hardness in her eyes. He felt a ridiculously adolescent relief.

'So, what about you?'

Through long practice he told her there was little to tell. She asked if he lived on his own. There was a slight mocking in her eyes.

'D'you wanna talk?' she asked matter-of-factly.

He had his hand flat on the table and suddenly felt the slightest touch. She'd put the top of her middle finger on his. He'd been looking down. He looked up at her. She seemed very still.

'Tell me about Tom's mother.' she asked quietly.

He paused. That was how he wanted to think of her; as his boy's mother, someone who'd produced a child for him, performed a function, helped him bring him up, looked after the house, and not as someone who'd loved, who'd shared so much with him that...

And then Paula flooded all over him, into him. He could feel the tears shivering across his face, down the side of his nostrils, into the corner of his mouth. He raised an arm a little, like a wounded animal. It was like being trapped in a freezeframe that went on for minutes, the inside of his body shook.

He didn't know what to do. He had no behavioural guidelines for this. It was an internal anomie. He felt she'd cut through an emotional impoverishment, ripped it till it was hanging open like bloodied entrails, felt he had to grab it, pull it shut, hold it till it was closed again. He wanted to bind it tightly with his years of escapes, journeys, his compensations; films, Mahler, galleries, and the cafes; sketching, writing, staring.

He looked up. She was watching his eyes, her head slightly to one side, her whole hand now on top of his. He tried to pull it back. She pressed down, gave him a slow, serious smile, and said gently,

'If you don't talk to your pain, it will talk to *you,* shout and scream at you.' Then, just as gently, she suggested they sit at the bar. 'There's no one there,'

They did. He forced himself to point out that the large, baroque mirror at the back was for cowboys to shoot at while the barman ducked behind the counter just in time.

'You really have seen too many films, haven't you.'

And then her cell phone rang. She said several 'okays,' nodding in between them. She put it back in her jacket pocket, looked at him earnestly.

'Look, I know it's not right, but I have to be going More big man sawing tomorrow. I'm sorry. That was Rick, he's got my stuff and he'll pick me up on the highway. We'll share the bill.'

He told her he'd pay. She thanked him.

'You don't want to listen to more Perry Como then?'

'Never heard of him,' she said, smiling. He went to get up.

'No, it's okay.'

He asked her when she'd be hack, if he'd see her again. She moved around the table. He felt her near him. She bent over and quickly kissed his forehead. He felt her hair brush an eyebrow. She walked away quickly.

He stood. 'How did you know...?'

His voice sounded weak, inarticulate. She always seemed to be leaving She half turned her head, lightly touched her puckered lips and bent her hand away, then just before she pushed through the exit door she became a silhouette; exaggeratedly upright, in profile; the high frizzy hair, retrousse nose, full lips.

He stared at the door, heard Sinatra's, 'One For My Baby' and sat down again. He heard her car pull away. He didn't want to leave, wanted to keep where he was, where she'd been. He wiped his face

The waitress came over, asked if he wanted a refill. He absently nodded.

'No problem.' she said.

He felt an instant anger. 'Should there be? It's a restaurant, it's Italian, you've got bags full of coffee beans from five continents. You have cream, milk, sugar, the loudest *Gaggia* machine in the world. *Should* there be a problem?'

He was shouting. He stopped, took a breath, apologised.

'Bad day, uh?' she said, defensively deadpan, not looking at him. He paid the bill. He usually forgot that waitresses here depended largely on tips for a living. He left a large one.

He went back to the house, its beigeness drooping over him like a spiritual blanket. He suddenly felt tired; tired of people walking dogs on beaches that howled most of the night in gardens, of having to ask for 'war-der' in cafes to save minutes of baffled frowns and complex negotiation, of obese women living in solipsistic bubbles loading dipped fries into their mouths and licking their fingers surrounded by chrome boxes of napkins, the ubiquitous verbal tic of 'like,' the dead racoons he'd seen on sidewalks and, what he saw as another example of America's technological obsession with the unnecessary, a crank-operated *for emergencies* TV set in a shop window.

Laying on his bed he tried to let the good things sift though: the courtesy of drivers unnecessarily reversing to let people cross, the politeness, the occasional 'sir,' the friendliness of the local bus drivers, the non-stop joking of the two female ones both named Daphne, and the interest when people discovered where he was from, telling him that their family had once come from Edinburgh or Merthyr Tydfil to emphasise that they, too, had an ancient lineage.

He thought of the hills, the green-blue, clear water lakes, the seventy foot cliffs leading down to them, the mountains that looked from a distance like pink-grey cloud banks. And he wondered if Rose had experienced the smaller beauties, like the glint of sun on a London canal, forsythia hanging over a Victorian window in Hampstead, the curved Art Deco windows of a Chelsea apartment block, a steeple rising above chestnut trees, a teenage Sloane guiding her horse gently over Kensington cobbles or whether, even, she had ever been outside of her country. He hadn't asked. There hadn't seemed to be time.

On the way to an internet café the next day he passed a man on a freeway bridge waving a twelve foot American flag to commemorate an anniversary of 9/11; below, and by the side of him, cars honked loudly. He went to the aquarium. She wasn't, of course, there. Nor was she on the Seattle ferry the day after as he listened to floating bits of conversation from passengers looking out across the water, 'Two hundred Starbucks have opened in China, two in Vietnam.' 'Yeh, he's the seventh best hand surgeon in Seattle...' He missed her.

The following afternoon he was at Tom's watering the vegetable patch and parched lawn with a hose. He went inside to help him cook their meal. Tom was leaning against the sink with a copy of the Kitsap County Herald in his hands - his relaxed, nonchalant stance would remain in Ben's mind for ever.

'There's a little piece here about a fatal accident; logs and cables and a ravine and stuff - what's 'highlining?' - down in North Oregon, some sort of tornado. Looks like it was a freak one or something, there wasn't a warning. There's a Miss R. Kratz mentioned. Wonder if it could be that girl in the Marine place, she was a lumberjack wasn't she?' He looked at Ben. 'Maybe it's her. That'd be a shame.'

He'd told his son nothing about her. As far as Tom knew they'd merely spent a few minutes talking together.

He couldn't quite equate 'accident' with 'Miss R. Kratz'. Then he did. He didn't know her surname, but knew it was her. He felt paralyzed, not knowing what to say, to feel. Larry had told him about 'highlining:' slinging a cable across a ravine to carry a cab with logs from the side with no roads to the one that did. He wondered if it was this, wondered if she had ever done it before.

'Anyway, its Paris tomorrow, dad. Eighteen hours in a chair in the sky, hope the Wi-Fi's working. Marion's really looking forward to it. We're meeting her at the ferry.'

It was soon after the aircraft took off that he felt the longing. He saw the grin, the red hair band, then a still, white face partly covered in leaves. He pushed the images away. He was going to spend time in his favourite city, a place which had meant so much to Paula, a city where kerb grills gushed water all day cleaning the cobbles, yet still surprising him, trickling around a corner, where the Left Bank and the smell of *Gitanes* still excited him.

And it was as if he hadn't done anything else for the last week than go to an aquarium, play table tennis and have a meal with Rose, as if he hadn't seen deep, cloudless skies, nor sat on a beach looking at the silhouettes of Seattle's towers through the swaying, tick-tocking yacht masts, nor tasted the freshly caught salmon under the fairy lights at Tom's friend's barbecue watching a deer in the garden and, almost, as if he hadn't spent precious time with his son.

As they fastened their seat belts for the descent into Charles De Gaulle, Tom leaned forward from three seats away and grinned at him. He smiled back and looked out the window. There'd been no fanciful shapes this trip, just the merging lines of grey land, sea and sky. He thought of the house he'd stayed in and trying not to wait for the sigh of the lid closing on the kitchen's automatic bin and Ann's fat, white, squiggling feet in all that sofa. He thought of Paris once more, of boulevard trees almost touching verandas and eaves, but not quite close nor tall enough, and not high enough to see from the *Sacre-Couer.*

And he thought he knew how Rose had died; falling silently, just the shattered air screaming through the leaf-stripped branches above her. A line from Galsworthy's The Forsyte Saga came back to him: 'Beauty is a rose that a fair wind blows… '

CINEPHILIA

It was six thirty on a Friday evening and James Kent had no more clients till Monday. He walked to his favourite café in Wanstead and watched Alice the waitress sitting under its awning with a cigarette. Parked behind her in retro art deco glory was the owner's jade green and ivory Nissan Figaro with its cream leather seats, stylized dashboard, white-walled tyres and boasting a price tag out of the reach of a mortgage-laden psychotherapist. The sweet froth gulp of James' cappuccino took him back emotionally to early maternal feeding; a reminder that such places represent our first silent succour in a tender universe.

On the way he'd passed a mosque with its open double doors and a speaker with a twenty decibel call to prayer - wondering what would happen if he stood outside with a megaphone preaching atheism - and went into a shop to have a photo of one of his paintings enlarged. It was a poster he'd done when younger for London Transport; a stylized representation of the metropolis with the Thames curving through bits of cityscape and a swan gliding into the suburbs. It wasn't wanted.

A distraught little boy with his parents were there preparing to have their photos taken. An elderly Chinese man came in wishing everyone loud, good-natured good mornings with repeated 'Herro darlin's' like an oriental Benny Hill and offered the boy a lollipop. His father frowned and told him that if he wanted his child to have confectionery he would buy it himself. James was about to point out to him that the man merely wanted to make his son feel better, when he guessed that his 'would' really meant 'could' and that he'd probably known, somewhere, a level of poverty which ensured that when he was capable of paying for something he wanted the world to know.

James knew he was doing it again: habitually analysing, using energy he should be saving for those who came to him for help with their varying degrees of pain and fear. And, perhaps, one in particular.

He came to him first a month ago. James tried not to be affected by the physical appearance of someone unless an obvious abnormality was part of the problem, but Hayden Chivers was rather different:

tall, slim, late middle aged, dark eyes, greying hair, a balance in the way he moved, sat, held his head upright and a slight, but modulated London accent; an attractive man, though James pushed the latter characteristic away; it could influence diagnosis, its charm could cloud, skew any objectivity he may succeed in holding.

He looked briefly at James then the room, still a restful shade of green with some of the latter's watercolours on the wall, then back to him before gazing again at the walls. James usually said something benignly facetious to interrupt the silence at these first meetings with clients, and did so.

'Seen any good films lately?'

His eyes widened.

'Yes. Yes, I have, 'Gilda', at the weekend. I've got the poster at home with a shot of her that's a reversal; initially her cigarette was in her right hand and the smoke, drifting slowly upwards like a kind of helix, is really a symbol of Noir, like *contra jour* shots, as in 'Build My Gallows High' with Mitchum in Acapulco heat, slatted light across his jacket and Greer walking in against the sun, and Dietrich's films; strolling a highway, headlights stroking her back before she becomes the night, the palms, fedoras, wise guys, bars…'

James was immediately tempted to join in this cinematic monologue, but resisted the indulgence. He was about to hold up his hand to signal his client to stop and explain that his question hadn't really been literal, but, remembering the number of patients who had sat across from him and said nothing for minutes, hours days and, one, for years, asked him if he'd always been interested in movies. His client's eyes narrowed a little.

'Yes, but not when my father took me. I loved going with my mate, though.' He paused for a second, 'Bill, a friend when I was a teenager.'

When people get excited, pleasured, sad, angry, they revert to those feelings experienced in their early years, especially in the language and accent they were expressed in; his had been cockney. Theoretically, maybe, James should have let him continue as he wanted, but he wished to know how much knowledge, in this context, his patient had of himself.

'Why do you think film is so important to you?'

'They're an escape, just as they are for everybody.'

The second part of his sentence, James felt, was a deflection from his awareness that his 'escape' was, perhaps, unhealthy and wanted to present his intense interest as a mildly eccentric foible. He wondered if he was aware also, as James suddenly was, that they were part of a larger running away, a much bigger avoidance. As if he knew what James was thinking, he said,

'I rarely get carried along completely with a film, there's always a part of me, I think it's located above my left ear,' he smiled, 'that's continually aware of the camera angles, the framing, the script, the... it's always there, though I went recently to an afternoon movie, knowing it had already started, and there was a close-up of a girl's profile staring across a stretch of water. There was a tear on her cheek, though this time I didn't look for the camera's reflection. Then there was the static shot, full face looking sad as she drove along a road, not even the upward arcing camera angle could lessen the intensity, and I wondered what had happened to her; a crushed child, a father dying maybe. But you knew that soon the scene would end, she'd get out the car, technicians would take the camera off the bonnet, a unit director or someone would pinch her arse and the chief grip drive the car away, then she'd probably light a cigarette and tell the stunt man jokingly to piss off. And all the time that first shot of her was flooding my mind and I wanted to be with her, just with her, looking across the water.'

He was living this little moment again, eyes concentrating inwardly, head nodding very slightly. James was a little surprised that he'd allowed himself to imagine her actions off-screen, to picture her outside the set, the script. But then, the reality, the behaviour of the girl was still 'within' a film milieu, he wasn't really going outside of it. He was silent for a few minutes then began talking of childhood things.

'I do get stuff from films, I know. I mean, when I kissed Pauline from over the road, I wasn't aping my parents, I'd never seen them do it, nor even my mate Terry from the corner house where we used to play odds and ends, the street game; you know, flinging the ball at the pennies, tanners if you were flush, on the paving slab against the wall, and you catch it, but no one ever seemed to knock the money out the square, and then mum would shout down the street for your tea. Perhaps you don't know the game, I'm older than you. When I kissed her though, it was really the boy kissing the girl in the porch in the background of a foreground Danny Green in 'The lady Killers.' And I like fair haired women, not a Monroe blonde, but, say, Cate Blanchett...'

His voice became background. James immediately went back to his own first piercing sensation of some sort of infantile love, of standing outside 'The Anchor' on the corner of his street in Plaistow looking in at the yellowed silhouettes of drinkers in the public bar with his father coming out occasionally to bribe him with penny arrowroot biscuits, and hearing, amongst the 'gi's a kiss darlin'' and 'like to give 'er one up the jaxi' and the sentimentalising of pint-raised celebrations of 'if you was the only gel in the world,' the song that, he realised now, came from 'Casablanca' and which his mother had taken him to see. He hadn't understood it, but the tune came back: a soft focus Bergman lah-lah-lahing it next to Sam's piano and then the full orchestra and the timeless 'Its still the same old story, a fight for love and glory...' Although too young to comprehend 'glory,' he felt, standing there in chafing grey serge shorts and socks wrinkled around his ankles, a kind of gloriousness filling him.

He looked at his new client, felt at that moment they were experiencing the same nostalgic frisson, the same pre-pubescent meaning, and he knew instantly that he should stop this implicit sharing, this beginning of an unprofessionalism that wouldn't do this man any good. He was a client. He wasn't a friend. James could relax later; the interactive process had hardly begun.

His client continued talking of films, sounding like a 'Guardian' reviewer, but was genuinely excited, as animated as he was articulate. James looked at his watch, he'd let him run over by ten minutes. He couldn't remember doing this with a patient before unless it was some sort of emergency. His client was surprised at how long he'd been talking. They agreed he'd come weekly. He left, looking flat, a little dispirited.

James thought about him a little through a busy spell with clients for the next six days. He then, without feeling surprise, saw him in a local cinema. James was sitting at the back, his client coming in after him, looking even taller than he remembered, and went straight to the middle of the front row; it was a matinee, few people were there. James looked occasionally at the back of his head, it didn't move. He wondered whether he always, when able, sat front centre whatever

265

the cinema or film, and if so, why. It could be merely for room to stretch his long legs, but the nearer he was to the screen the bigger it was and there was less peripheral area to distract his vision. He imagined his expression: still, intense, eyes wandering, occasionally widening, trying to let the film occupy his head, not so much identifying with this or that character, but empathising, almost becoming them.

When James left he was still sitting there, just as motionless, perhaps wanting to hear the theme music again or to see who the Second Assistant Director was before the shock of an empty black screen and someone in casual uniform picking up an empty drinks can from under the next seat; and reluctantly having to accept the need to leave this warm, dark space and face the harsh light and the traffic outside.

He came next day exactly on time and almost having to stoop to miss the top of the door frame as James let him in. He sat, his knees together, and tried a smile.

'Yes, I have seen some good films lately.' He laughed. 'Well, not really. I saw a recently made silent film, but wasn't impressed. But those pencil moustaches did bring back a magical world, magical I suppose because it was so unlike my world, my rather grimy life.'

'Where was this world, this life?'

'He waved a loose hand as if flicking a fly.away.

'Doesn't matter.'

Then off he went, describing, at times vividly, scene upon scene from film after film, remembering whole chunks of dialogue, from the last words of, 'Towering Inferno,' 'So long Fire Chief. 'So long, architect,' to 'Play it Sam. You played it for her, you can play it for me.' 'I can see the back of the head of an actor who I haven't seen for years and recognise him instantly, as I do from the first syllable uttered by a minor off-screen actor I haven't heard for ages.

'The 'bit above the left ear?''

'Yes.' He was quiet for a while, then almost shouted, 'Yes it is.'

Again a silence.

'Do you think you're obsessed with film?'

He laughed easily, swinging one leg over the other restlessly.

'No-o. Some people drink, others take drugs, this is my addiction.'

He laughed again, took a deep breath and carried on with his 'addiction.'

James went through the motions of listening to him, nodding when he thought appropriate, and wondering whether the speaker was imagining himself as an observer on the film sets or dwelling in the scripted fantasies.

He stopped him when his time was up. Again the surprise that he'd been with James as long as he had.

During the time before his next appointment, James wondered, in between seeing other patients, how real the world was to him. He'd never said in quiet desperation to him that it wasn't, but James felt that underneath the relentlessly detailed memories of movies the world outside of them wasn't quite real. How unreal he didn't know, nor how long it had been so.

When James saw him next he enquired about his relationships with women. There was no answer.

'What did, do, you feel? Love? A nebulous word I know, but... what?'

He took a long, deep breath, looking alternately around the room then down, then at James.

'Look, I left my wife for... a woman who looked like Paulette Goddard. Remember her?' He half smiled. 'I know it seems superficial, but there it is. She....' His voice rose. 'I act, act all the fuckin' *time.*' He brought a fist down on the sofa arm.

'Everything's an act, I'm acting with you now. I don't *want* to anymore.'

He stopped. The silence was like something hard and heavy hitting the room. He stood, went towards the window, looked out. He was completely still for a while, then raised his shoulders, turned quickly, took some money from his jacket pocket and pushed it into James' hand.

'I'm going. Have to. See you next time.'

He strode quickly to the front door, opened it and left, closing it loudly.

James went to his study and thought about him. He didn't like using the words 'classic case' for it depended on what period of psychoanalytic history a quintessential example of a condition came from, but it was tempting. His patient, when dealing with people generally or in significant relationships, would have used characters he'd seen, mostly in movies, and squashed into an amalgam of different pieces of a constructed personality. This would have been a finely honed process; a fluid, shifting plasma of protection.

He was pretty sure that this was the first time he'd hinted to anyone that his behaviour had been, was, influenced by filmic images, how much of his actions had been internalized from the picture palaces of his childhood onwards; fused into multilayered bits of behaviour in which he could artificially respond to social situations, not just everyday ones, but intimate ones. James was suddenly convinced that his real self wasn't bearable, had become fragmented, impoverished, unreal. Hayden Chivers had created a false self.

He examined his diagnosis, contradicted it, attempted to put other conclusions in its place. He'd seen the man only three times and had been told very little until his last emotional speech. But, assuming he was right, he tried to think of what this experience would have meant to his client. Sitting there, James dredged up his knowledge of the patients he'd treated over the years, trying to find symptoms, characteristics, actions that he could validly relate to this man. He didn't look at past notes, the experiences were virtually all in his head; but a correct analysis depended on whether he was right about his patient's lack of reality.

There had been, he guessed, a perceived destruction of himself, an annihilation of self as baby, at birth perhaps or, a contentious view, in the womb. Whatever the source, he had pushed it away from himself all of his life. Every perceived incident of neglect, however trivial, every raised voice as a child, would have left him unutterably estranged and lonely, carrying a pain unbearably harsh. He would have filled his emptiness not only with the monochromic and technicolored conjuring of childlike emotions, but with an intellectualisation of the world; perhaps constantly, relentlessly looking at his every thought, every action, wondering why and where they came from and analysing them in discrete, staccato bits of introspection; a prohibition on *feeling* a self.

He tried to imagine what it would have been like for him in a relationship with a woman. If she told him she loved him he'd have forgotten it the next day as if it had never been said, there would have been no emotional memory of it. He could see him, hours afterwards, writing down the exact words she'd used in a notebook he'd secreted in a bedside chest of drawers to look at repeatedly to convince him that they had been said. The pain of the bad things that had been magnified throughout his life would have been remembered, but rarely the few good things. But, he wouldn't have loved, he couldn't, except for the fantasising of it, the fantasised emotions.

He made a few notes and then prepared for his next clients, two that had been with him for some time, another new, and decided that when he saw him next he'd probe deeper, shake him a little, interrupt his flow of excited, beguiled escapism, and to elaborate on those revealing last words.

Over the preceding few years there had been some upsetting phone calls from patients, some calling to see if he'd give them free time listening to their talk of small, often mundane things, yet crying inside for help, others literally crying for some sort of salvation, from him, from God, from anything, but none so alarming and confusing as Hayden Chivers' call on the afternoon of the day he was due to see him. He rang at exactly the time he should have been lifting the knocker on James' front door.

'Hello. Mister Kent?'

He didn't recognise the voice immediately.

'I won't be coming today unfortunately, because…'

He could hear a momentary squeaking sound, slightly muffled, like someone trying not to laugh in case it tipped into hysteria.

'I've killed someone.'

James' mind went into inertia for a few seconds. The voice asked if he was still listening. James asked him to explain what he meant.

'You see, when I was a kid someone hit me once and I hit him back hard and I could see I'd really hurt him and I felt so sorry and then he kept hitting me, but I just felt so sorry, though I don't now.' He said it quickly, in one long sentence.

James steadied himself. 'Can you tell me exactly what happened? Do you want to come to me now?'

'No. No. I hit him. I hit him.'

The line went dead.

Who had he hit? Was he talking of the childhood incident or the person he'd said he'd killed?

James rang back. There was no answer. He was tempted to get into his car and drive to his address, but this was a mobile number, he could have been anywhere. He thought of ringing a local police station, but, what? What would, could they do? He did nothing for an hour, except mostly try not to believe what he'd just heard. He shook himself. This indecision was a weakness that he knew could tell him things about himself he wouldn't like. Then the phone rang again.

It was the police. His patient had seen one of their cars slowing down at traffic lights, had knocked on its window and told the driver what he'd told James and then asked them to ring him. Apparently, he hadn't told them who or where the victim was. They asked James about himself, then to hold for a minute. It became five. Then a different voice was telling him that they'd found something and that they would contact him.

After a fretful night for James, they did. At their request he went to see them. He waited for an hour in a small room till two plainclothes policemen came in and spoke to him. They told him briefly what had happened. It was related in a matter-of-fact, almost casual manner, ritually not wanting to show what they felt, or perhaps partly inured to the aftermath of violence

His patient had smashed a hole above a man's left ear. It seemed, from an early pathologist's report, it was the result of repeated blows from a house brick. James wasn't told who the victim was or the context. They then had to leave, telling him that they may need him and, if so, would let him know 'in due course.' One of them shook his hand.

As soon as James heard where the wound was a thought had flashed. Had Hayden Chivers, in an ultimate act of projection, been attempting to smash his *own* intellect; that detached, obsessive game which prevented the films he watched from completely taking him over, both the undeveloped self and the fake; prevented him from giving himself up to complete, bewitching, comforting fantasy, or was it merely a meaningless coincidence? He wasn't sure, and he realised that he hadn't been fully aware of the man's anger. Depression is often anger frustrated, perceived as having nowhere to go. This time, for him, it had found somewhere.

He ordered another coffee. It had been ten days since he'd been told he may be officially needed. As yet, it seemed he wasn't. He'd given his professional opinion to authorities before, but had always felt a little fraudulent. Based upon what a client told him, his experience with other patients, theories and some intuition, he'd told them what he knew, or thought he knew. He tried to find truths and to communicate them as precisely and articulately as he could. What was done with them afterwards he couldn't influence.

He looked around him: the photo of the lunching riveters astride a New York girder tilted on the wall, a Cartier-Bresson of the Sacre-Couer next to it; bright leaves on the graveyard trees of the church opposite seen from under the awning where Alice sat with yet another cigarette, her smoke blowing across the open door.

James liked to learn a few words from foreign languages, now rapidly becoming local dialects; 'Hello,' 'Please,' and 'Thanks,' which, after a struggle, he'd remembered in Turkish, Polish and Lithuanian, but not in Romanian. He held up his scrawled phonetic of a Romany 'Hello.' Alice frowned, shook her head and mouthed *Bunaziua*. Theirs were the only movements inside or outside the shop. Its owner, legs apart, looked at nothing, a customer stared at his cappuccino froth, the local butcher, grey hair thick at the back, rested his chin on a hand, a woman sat in a corner reading. James wanted to harvest it all, bind it, carry it home, place it on a sill in the sun, sit and look at it, every piece of it, slowly, considerately, thinking of nothing else; certainly not of a violent death.

Alice put on her coat and passed him as he rose from the table.

'*La revedere*' she said.

'*Lahreveedaree,* he replied. She shook her head again. He was still struggling.

271

RABBIT REDUX

He sat opposite him on the train, ginger hair cropped closely at the sides, wide, thin-lipped mouth, stubby fingers operating a smart phone with casual precision and rather effeminate movements - though James Kent may have perceived the latter through an evaluative screen created by the man's buddy, a lost looking 20 year old with a large earring who was snuggled up to him. They were sitting cuddling travel bags with their wide-apart legs. As Harry would have said, they were a couple of old Marys.

Harry he'd known since university a dozen years ago and although gay himself intensely disliked the younger ones who he saw as aggressively flaunting their sexuality; one which, cynically, he felt was enshrined by the media in its treatment of celebs deaths through AIDS in a sort of triumphal martyrdom. When someone hates an individual or a collective it's almost always as a result of fear and, or, jealousy of the hate object.

It was Harry who had tried it on with James at his flat in Bow. They were both a little drunk, but the latter was sober enough to grab his friend's hand as it wandered up the inside of his leg and firmly tell him no. He was the laziest man James knew. He'd never decorated his home, rarely walked anywhere and his dislike of exertion, except with his punters, many of whom were married men 'just wanting a cuddle,' was made obvious when in James car as it suffered a flat tyre. Standing there with a look of mock astonishment when asked to help jack up the wheel, hands cupping his cheeks he'd shrilled, 'My Dear, I couldn't possibly.'

Driving home, a police car flashed its lights and pulled up in front of him. Getting out and slowly walking towards James' car as if he'd seen too many road movies, the driver asked James why he was driving so slowly. He told him it was because he was tired. He was wished a good evening and slowly drove away. As the officer passed him he pointed out of his window and mouthed, 'Lights.' They were put on with a grateful smile.

There's something about a police car's flashing lights that screams, *You!* and elicits in James an immediate childhood apprehension

272

which, he thought, possibly represented God, and a reminder of his dad's sharp elbows and his 'Stop bleedin' fidgetin' in a cold Victorian church. But, this was his little problem and as long as it, and others, didn't get in the way of helping his clients, it was okay.

Hatred was a common theme in his working life; his patients' relentless grinding out of detestation, its genesis, as usual, in their childhoods, hating for many different reasons one or both parents and, as adults and locked into their childhood as large parts of their psyches often were, forever projecting it onto people and objects.

He'd been treating a man in his early seventies, though looking much younger, for the last six months. Tall, thin, intelligent, and a teacher of political culture, there was an immense sadness behind his eyes, except for rare flashes of humour and when exuding abhorrence for so many things, particularly the shouting into mobiles and tinnitus of music on buses and trains, the smell of hot food being eaten and sitting next to or in the proximity of women recreating their faces. He told James that he half expected one day to see a woman on the tube unbutton her bra, pencil a dotted line under her breast, cut it with a Stanley knife and push a jelly-like mould into it before stitching it up and resuming her reading of 'Hello.'

Before getting onto a train he would move quickly along a platform looking into carriage windows hoping to find one without food, phones or make-up in order not to have to ask with muted anger, 'Does the concept of 'other people' have any meaning for you?' and then going through to another carriage. When in a cinema, the crisp rustling of confectionery wrappings lacerated him and there was the inevitable turning on someone with a hissing, 'Have you finished your breakfast yet?' Sometimes, for him, people just living appeared to be an indulgence.

It was obvious to James that at an early age his needs hadn't been met. He was equally certain that he had been left to cry on his own and that when his mother did eventually come to him he had emotionally switched off, disassociated himself from her and, possibly, his father. He had little doubt, also, that it went back to him needing the breast yet having his nappy changed, being given the tit when he'd shit himself. That was the beginning, and his psyche would never fully compensate.

He would tell James of his Blitz experience: being lifted from a warm bed and carried to the bunks in the garden shelter, of a stray German fighter strafing the houses while he looked up, frightened and fascinated; the doodlebugs, a nearby V2 explosion and other vivid, almost autistically detailed descriptions of his experiences of that time. In his bedroom he'd read 'The Blackout Book,' words and illustrations in fluorescent ink to enable them to be seen in a darkened room with, as well as crosswords and puzzles, diagrams of tactics pilots would use to shoot down the Luftwaffe. One was of a spitfire looping back over an enemy fighter to come behind him and fire. He wondered whether the Germans had access to this book and decided to hide it in case, somehow, they discovered it.

He related a spasmodically recurring nightmare where an aircraft spiralled down from a bright red sky in slow motion over the terraced houses, the screaming pilot hanging from its wheels.

'He was so… lost.' he said. It was himself, of course, who was lost.

An alienating, frightening episode which almost certainly confirmed his fear of a hateful God, *his* God, was his evacuation to an Essex farm on the day after war was officially declared.

He showed James a photo of himself at five taken with his dad's Kodak an hour before he was put on the train. It showed a small, thin, pale faced child with a puffed peak cap, coat neatly buttoned to the neck, socks ending midway on his calves, shiny shoes - a tortoise by his right one - some sort of bedding on his back and a neatly ribbon-tied box hanging from his shoulder holding a gas mask, as if it was a present he was about to take to someone.

The farmer, a large, rough man, caught rabbits, and one morning the child he was temporarily responsible for tripped over one of his many hidden snares. He was sworn at and cursed in a rural blasphemy he didn't understand, but which terrified him.

He remembered little of the man's wife who, looking like a stout-armed advert for country goodness, cooked huge slices of fried bread and taught him, ironically, to say 'White rabbits' as his first words on the first day of every month to bring him luck. There were only three of these, for after crying himself to sleep every night he was brought home.

His first night back, standing on his bed, head resting on the wall, he heard through it his father shouting at his mother, 'That soddin' boy.' He was in effect, though never consciously knowing it because it had

274

been so for ever, an emotional orphan. He would always be one.

The dictum that every man you meet is your father, every woman your mother, at an unconscious level still holds. His attitude towards women was ambivalent: the need for a mother figure of course and, equally obviously, the slightest sign of any form of rejection, however trivial and in whatever stage of the relationship he was in, was interpreted fearfully as a desertion, an abandonment. And then the hatred, the anger.

He had occasionally mentioned political correctness or, as he called it, 'liberalism's para-military wing' which he seemed to loathe as much as or more than preening cosmetic aestheticism and the satisfying of appetites in inappropriate public spaces. At their last meeting he held out a letter to James.

'I wrote this. Read it, please.'

It was dated a year previously. He began pacing around the room, rhythmically pushing a fist into a palm then wheeling round and pacing again.

'Can you imagine how I felt? Can you? *Can* you do that? I -'

'You know I can, Edward.'

'Call me Ted, why do you treat me so formally?' He was becoming increasingly agitated.

'You've been coming here for a while now. I can understand your feelings, can absorb them. Intellectually you know this to be true. Try to feel it.'

He took a deep breath, nodded, rested.

'From what I've told you about my relationship with students, do you not see how unfair this is?' He looked across at his therapist appealingly, the palms of his hands turned out towards him. James thought of Shylock's, 'If you prick us, do we not bleed?'

He started explaining the background to the letter. After retirement from a permanent position at an institute in west London, he'd been teaching three classes composed almost entirely of mature ethnic students at a north London college. The money was relatively little, but, as he'd said, he needed the stimulus of debate, controversy, the banter with the class and that he would, if necessary, have done it for free.

After three weeks he'd been asked by a female Admin. staff member what he thought of his pupils. He'd replied, apparently in a jocular tone, that it was sometimes rather difficult teaching them as they were 'full of religion,' and then forgot about it as he went to his class.

The following day his agency rang to say that his contract had been cancelled. No explanation was offered, it hadn't been given one. He'd rung the college. The co-ordinator, who he hadn't met, told him briefly that he'd made a racist remark against African students and didn't want to discuss it any further. It was the 'racist' and 'against' that had enraged him, hence his letter to her.

While narrating all this and being obviously frustrated and angry, he was relatively still, but then began pacing again as James began reading the letter.

It started with his reaction to the call.

'I was both embarrassed and annoyed by your behaviour which seemed inarticulate and accusatory. You sounded a little desperate and put the phone down. Is this really the rational behaviour of a manager? You said that I had made a 'comment about Africans' to a member of HR. (I assume this title is to distinguish it from 'Animal' Resources). *And*? What then? You refused to tell me what I'd said or what you'd been told I'd said which may have been very different to what I did say. You made a decision upon the hearsay of another person. Was this not irresponsible? Should you not have asked *me* what was said? What were you frightened of?'

It stated that the writer had nothing to defend and went on to explain that his subject dealt not with value judgements, but with social facts and that the relevant social fact here was that Africans, along with many other nationalities, were often very religious and that religion was a cultural product and part of his job was to get students to question where their beliefs came from, and who benefitted from them.

'You do not need to be a historian or a Marxist' it continued, 'to know that, under the guise of an evangelical mission, Europeans exploited most of Africa. The way they did this was to spread a religion, in this case, Christianity, to gain economic and social control. Indeed, the more politically aware students know this long before they meet me, as they also know that little politics is taught in their continent below H.E. level; meaning that they often come from an anti-intellectual culture, one in which they are not encouraged to analyse nor criticise the social institutions in which they live; certainly suiting the likes of Mugabe, Kabila et al.'

The letter pointed out that just as there isn't a value judgement in the statement 'I see a dog,' the statement that 'Africans are generally religious' is, likewise, value free, value neutral, a social fact. 'Nowhere do I imply that the dog was either 'good' or 'bad' or that I 'liked' it or did not, and neither, therefore, was the students religiosity 'good' or 'bad' or 'right' or 'wrong.''

There were lines attempting to demonstrate the absurdity of it all.

'If I was to say that Jack and Jill were, respectively, male and female, am I a sexist? That 2 plus 2 is 4 means I'm a numberist? That the sky is blue, a colourist?'

When James mentioned the effectiveness of these little pieces of hyperbole to him his pacing quickened, as James imagined it would at a particularly intense part of a lecture he was giving, pausing for emphasis, hands moving as if preparing for a karate chop, legs bent as if he was going to kneel, then straightening and moving again.

'Suppose I refer to you as a 'white Englishman.' What do I get for *that* then,' he sneered, 'two life sentences running concurrently?' He tried to calm himself, sat again, restlessly. James wondered why he hadn't used something like, 'black Ghanaian' as an example.

The letter continued. 'I have taught approximately 400 students of 40 different nationalities in the last two years, *mostly Africans.* I love teaching mature students, especially the latter group with their Victorian values and infectious humour - ask my Zulu partner - and have discussed religion frequently and the part it plays in legitimating both a ruling class and social inequality. Part of my brief is to get students to *question.* Surely this is the aim of education?'

James asked him about his partner.

'They want to control emotions. They tell you, you *shouldn't* feel something. That's a normative statement. How can a feeling be *wrong?* It's an ontological reality. How can an emotion be put into an evaluative sphere?

'Your partner?'

He took deep breaths for several seconds. 'It was a long time ago.

We'd sit in a pub: the inquisitive looks, the faces turned away.... I was in a relationship with someone else at the time, a nurse. 'What are you trying to prove?' she asked when she found out, 'that you're as liberal as the next man?' He gave a brief chuckle at the irony. 'No crisp-uniformed compassion from her; gentle Nightingale turned scalpelled surgeon. 'What is it about black pussy?' she'd say, 'Where does it all come from? Teenage documentaries of bouncing tits in tribal dances, I bet, and do you realise there's an AIDS epidemic in Africa? How will you feel,' she asked, 'when two old ladies in a café serve her burnt toast and a dirty mug because they know she's with you? Bitch.''

He gave an unconvincing man-of-the-world smile, as if these encounters were merely some sort of enforced, relatively unimportant rites of passage.

At the end of the letter he quoted a recent Home Secretary's definition of racism as, 'any incident which is perceived as such.' If we go along this road and I was to perceive you as a giraffe then, ergo, you are.' It accuses his accuser of a knee-jerk reflex based on the internalisation of PC, which he states is 'a pernicious, stifling, all-permeating form of public control.' It ended with, 'Here endeth the lesson.'

The whole tone of what James had read was angry, sarcastic and patronising. He'd used his intellect, as he suspected he always had, as a weapon, a defence

'Why is truth so important to you?'

'Because...' he was briefly made inarticulate by his fist-clenching anger, 'iI we have an evaluative context like the one I've talked about, then it... distorts, it's... I should have gone to the college governors.' He was snarling and grinding his teeth.

'Why didn't you?'

He ignored the question.

'We are asked to assimilate all cultures,' he said, with exaggerated calm, 'respect their differences, their mores.' He stood up. 'Oh look,' he yelled, pointing past James, eyes wide in mock horror, 'There's an adulterous Somalia woman being stoned to death on the pavement. Let's give it up for Sharia law!' He punched the air.

'You've made your point. Why didn't you go to the governors?'

'Because...' He sat, slouched, slowly shaking his head.

'I'll have my say now,' James said. 'Without a value system to internalise - a distorting system for you - we are psychotic. Arguably, everything is distorted, everything's a construct. It's a particular *form* of distortion you hate: political correctness, and as minor and laughable as it's made out to be, it represents for you a denial of what is, a disbelief. You hate it because it's saying truth *isn't,* therefore *you* are *not.* '

'The reason you didn't report it to the governors is because you felt that they'd be as liberal and misguided as your co-ordinator was, They would be on her side. What are they, Ted? They're your father, aren't they, she's your mother. He's taking her side. You did nothing because you thought that, yet again, you would be taken no notice of, be ignored, unrecognised. You were the frail child again, lonely, in despair. Yes? This liberalism stuff is just a presenting case for you, isn't it.'

James could hear himself shouting. Perhaps his professional experience calculated that this was the time; the time for his client to pour it all out, or at least begin to, loudly, traumatically

He didn't say anything for a while, then, quietly, 'Yes.' Then louder, 'Yes, yes, yes.' He repeatedly beat his knees with his fists as if hammering a table. He began to cry. 'They won't believe me, they won't believe me, they won't...'

Between sobs he tried telling James, as if he wasn't sure even he would believe him, about the students who, at the end of the academic year and passing him in the corridor, would tell him that he was 'the best,' and of the student group who, though never having met him, merely hearing stories from their pals, had gone to the Vice Principal to demand that they be taught by him; and the ex-students who would, years after he'd taught them, come up to him in the street, in a shop, and thank him for his support and encouragement. It was difficult for James to understand all he was saying.

Suddenly he stopped and stood up, rigidly, bent slightly backwards, his face wet. He looked at his watch.

'I think my time's up. Thank you.' He said it formally as if it was the end of a meeting, as if he and James had never met before this brief fifty minutes. He offered his hand. James shook it, the automatic reaction filling the sudden emotional vacuum.

He floated around the back of James' mind continuously for the next fortnight. He was hoping that his client was struggling through his outpouring, his frustrated rage, maybe even feeling some of the original pain, and that he would come to him at his next appointment feeling vulnerable and apprehensive, but open and ready to start some sort of healing. He didn't come. James didn't ring him. He expected him to call with an explanation and an apology as he'd done once before when he couldn't keep an appointment. He didn't.

Three days after James was supposed to see him he was idly wondering, as he picked up a local paper, why such publications still used the stereotypical headlines that they did. They were like a time warp, like a Captain Marvèl comic. This one was, 'Man Runs Amok In Butcher's Shop.' Turning the page, not intending to read it, his peripheral vision noticed his client's name.

Apparently, he'd been standing outside a local butchers looking through its window for some time before he went in and grabbed two skinned rabbits and smashed them repeatedly against a white-tiled wall. James imagined his tall, thin body leaning over the pig trotters, steaks and sirloins to reach them. He also saw him slouched in a corner, slowly sliding to the floor, head in hands, blood, bone and flesh smearing the tiles above him.

He wondered what to do. Whether he should find out where his patient was being held and go to him, offer support, ask him whether he wanted him to speak for him at a future Hearing or... he didn't know. He knew he should have.

There were other questions about whether his own outburst had been the right thing to do. And why had he? It hadn't been because of the subject of his client's attack - an all-pervasive ideology that he also disliked for its implicit patronising, fake righteousness, and its contradictory haze of conjecture and opinion. His client had developed intellectually, but parts of him, James had initially guessed, were still about five years old. He'd suffered his rural distress at that age, so he seemed to have got that right, but wasn't quite sure about the rest of it.

It wasn't just his timing, it was a loss of control, an indulgence, a problem, and this one it seemed had got in the way of him helping a patient. He liked this man, felt that outside the confines of his study they could have been friends. He felt he needed more long talks with his early mentor, perhaps a refresher course. He tried to convince himself that, maybe, it was a good thing this had happened, he'd be better at his job because of it; though he hadn't been of much use in the end to Edward Reeves.

Harry rang him the next day, but not being in the mood for seeing him and, potentially, more hatred, he decided to take a train to Kingston or, maybe, Bray and walk along the Thames for a few miles. There was a twenty minute wait at Paddington before the train left. He found himself ambling along the platform looking in its windows. There was a girl solipsistically putting on make up; the widening gaze to brush the lashes, the narrowing for the rouge; her eyes, twin miracles of mascara, like crows flying into a white chalk cliff.

WINDOWS

He was sitting in *Halal Kebab* looking out at hip hop teens loping along in jeans with knee length crotches and shoulders yawing as if they were auditioning for Richard the Third. Around the church opposite, Sunday best Africans coiled like a technicolor snake while over the road in *Bindira Sarees* were silks that spoke of duty, wife and mosque, where a girl lifted gauzy cottons the colours of her moods, had perhaps ridden bikes in one and played peek-a-boo in others.

Going out to the East End heat he saw acronym fruit, *guava, eddos, saag,* on pavement stalls, look-alike heroes on Bolywood posters and girls in *salwar kameez* playing hopscotch as a posse of 'Wha cha' 'bout mun, innit' young Asians slouched by.

James Kent, psychoanalyst, was going to a football match. As he neared the ground fans jostled past him singing, in an orchestrated piece of tribalism created to elicit fear in the opposition's fans, ''oo are yer? 'oo are yer? 'oo the fuckin' 'ell are you?'

He decided it was too hot to watch the game. Something he'd never done before. As a child he'd braved snow and ice on the uncovered terracing in the north end to watch reserve matches against the likes of Lincoln City and Scunthorpe, but this was sapping, sweating heat, as if it had solidified around him. He walked against the crowd back to the station and caught the tube to the City and sat in Paulo's, the station café.

Trying not to listen to the Cityspeak of margins, equities and the esoteric language of profit, he watched two young waitresses laughing across the room to each other then gazed up at the sun glowing through the station's roof struts onto the elaborate symmetry of Victorian Roman columns, and down to the trains and the Lowry-like figures on the nearest platform. One of them was Arthur Clifford.

He looked appreciably older that when James had last seen him about ten years previously, a few months after James had aborted the PGCE course they were both doing at an institute in Putney; though there had been the occasional greetings card along with a batch of newspaper cuttings and indecipherable comments down the column sides. He'd been keen to teach. James hadn't.

As usual he was moving quickly with firm, long strides as if he was going somewhere specific and had to be there at a certain time to get something done, never just wandering about to look at this, at that. His lank, wavy hair was even longer than James remembered and he was wearing a tweed jacket which could have been the same one he always seemed to wear.

He wasn't a handsome man, but women seemed to respond to his outgoing persona instantly; perhaps unconsciously females are drawn to this characteristic because it suggests an emotional health, an essential attribute for a father. James' hand was halfway to the window to knock on it when he realised that, as his friend was forty yards away, it would be a pointless way of trying to attract his attention.

When they'd first met, few of their fellow students seemed to like Arthur. He was outspoken, opinionated and occasionally uninformed, though there was always intellectual credibility. If he disagreed with anyone, as he often did, his response was accompanied by a sneer and, sometimes, a silent snarl. When listening to someone he'd exaggeratedly angle his head and frown as if the speaker was either slurring his speech or was linguistically challenged. He was pedantic, often dogmatic and possibly the least spendthrift of anyone James had known. In the cinematic haven of the Scala, which offered cakes and coffee in the foyer, he'd bring a thermos flask of tea, and while in the National Theatre cafe he'd order a tea and for the next few hours, holding court to a small, captive audience, would make swift journeys to the counter to have his cup filled with hot water into which he'd drop one of a large supply of tea bags he always carried with him.

For a brief period he'd taught English, but couldn't seem to find any work teaching film studies, his main pedagogic passion; he was completing a thesis on Tarkovsky at the time.

In his twenties he'd taken up photography, his work well-known enough for an exhibition of local landscapes in D.H. Lawrence's house at Eastwood in Nottinghamshire, the same county he himself was from. There was a London exhibition of his East European work, too. He'd sent James a shot of the barley sugar onions and lighthouse spires of Moscow's St. Basil's Cathedral against a pre-digital ultramarine sky and a photo taken at the back of Krakow's Glowny station where the prostitutes chalked their fees on the soles of their shoes, raising a foot to catch trade from passers-by, their commerce scratched away on a pavement should the police come clumsily grabbing. It showed an out of focus leather sole with part of a number inches from the camera, in the background was a white face, red gash of a mouth, black-lined eyes and breasts like white eggs.

James decided to ring him, if just for his entertainment value, though he was mildly interested in whether he'd managed to get a full time lecturing job. They arranged to meet in Holborn a week hence, and it was here that Arthur took his most memorable shot.

They were in a café, Arthur telling him that he'd found neither the job nor the woman he wanted, but had enough interests to keep him almost content. He asked James nothing about himself. They decided to have a look around the nearby Freemasons Headquarters, certainly not for any ideological interest, but to satisfy James' own in Art Deco.

As they were leaving, approaching a side exit, they heard a swishing, humming sound which got louder and more intense as they went through the swing doors and onto the pavement. To their left was a crowd of people at a street junction, some holding up flashing phones as if they were at a festival, others stretching upwards to see the source of the sound.

They went towards it, getting as near as they could, catching glimpses through a rush of paramedics of a stretcher, oxygen mask, ambulance, and a broken shoe in a gutter. The people not taking pictures were quietly looking on, perhaps part of them wanting to watch death.

Inside the circle of onlookers was an overturned car with a red helicopter by its side hanging its blades over it like a huge, broken sycamore seed; it looked, for an insane instant, as if a visiting funfair had arrived. Then, from the huddle of medics, a thumbs-up, the signal for blades to stretch, rotate and rise, the sound alien in the narrow streets, an infinite regress of noise trapped in echoes.

Hanging onto the outside of the rising cockpit, feet on the ski, a uniformed figure looked down at a body in a red blanket being winched up from the road, then across as he saw an open casement and screamed. 'Shut it. Shut it.' A hand slammed the window in, slivers of glass glistening as they fell. James saw Arthur taking his camera from the bag he always carried, raising it towards the window and taking a shot in one seamless movement. The machine hovered for a few seconds, rotors flailing and then rose, the swinging stretcher being pulled nearer the red belly. As it cleared the buildings and flew westward, people slowly moved away, some still looking up as it vanished ever higher across the rooftop.

Glancing up at the window, James thought he saw a face, and wondered if the man's thoughts had been smashed from his brain by twelve foot blades a fork's length from his dining table, food jumping from his plate. He turned to Arthur. He looked pale and shaken and said that he'd had to battle to be able to even move through the sound. James guessed that taking the photo was a reflex action for him however he felt.

They walked to a bus stop where Arthur told him that he was going to Venice on holiday in a week's time and suggested they meet again when he returned.

It was almost three months before he contacted James again and when he did so suggested they meet in a restaurant on the South Bank. He lived in a block of fifties flats a mile or so south, an area that James, because of his rather parochial territorial attitudes, found alien.

After a meal, and in answer to James' question, Arthur, with a pleased grin, showed him the photograph. The face behind the window was hazy, the open mouth a reminder of Munch's 'The Scream,' but the foreground fist gripping the window handle showed clearly the white of the tightened skin and the stretched veins.

Taking it from him he said, 'I should have told you this before. I actually met this bloke a couple of weeks ago. I was going to a shop to pick up a tripod and walking on the opposite side of the road when he came out of his building. I was sure it was him. I asked him, jokingly, if he'd seen any good choppers lately. I made a spiral sign. He looked alarmed. I told him I'd taken a snap of him closing the window. He stood there, trembling. I asked him if he was okay, I felt sorry for him. Anyway, I chatted to him and we went to this café and he told me what had happened, though I don't think he really wanted to talk. It was hard work, really.'

It was neither a surprising nor unfamiliar tale to James, though contexts and details obviously differed. Soon after the helicopter incident the man had experienced increasingly inimical dreams of long steel blades smashing through glass and tearing his throat - James instantly saw the opening scenes of 'Apocalypse Now' with its silhouetted helicopters rising from behind a hill and filling the screen, their cracking staccato vibrating the cinema. Arthur hadn't asked his name and referred to him as 'the window man,' yet while telling James about him he seemed genuinely sorry, almost as if he was a friend he was concerned for, a trait James hadn't really associated with him and certainly not visible to the students and pedagogues they'd known at college.

The man had stopped working almost immediately after the incident and confined himself to his flat for a month, rarely leaving it, and then becoming a voluntary patient at a psychiatric unit.

James knew something of these environments; he'd spent several months in two of them gaining experience. He imagined the man leaving a local surgery after being told to pull himself together and stepping out into a spinning High Street, into a noisy, desolate nothingness, a whirling void filled with fear. He saw him board a bus, hands pressing his ears, managing to pay his fare, get off, struggle through a Gothic gate and somehow reach a room where somebody wearing a white coat with a name like Doctor Schoenberg, thrusts her face at him over a mahogany desk and asks him why he's there as he timidly offers up an exercise book full of his scrawled, screaming hurt because he doesn't want to speak, to tell it all, for he'll have to face it again and he cannot. And the grim martinet of a head male nurse he tries to be nice to because he doesn't want to be with the other patients, one masturbating every night, another terrified of the atomic bomb, another of everything in the trapped obscenity of it all.

Arthur told James how pleased he was with the photo and asked him, belatedly, what he'd been doing since Putney.

'You didn't take up teaching, did you. Am I right?'

James told him that he'd gone back to his original interest in psychology; not to positivistic studies of trying to quantify the qualitative such as why pupils learn better in some situations than others and then ignoring the educative relationship between teacher and student, but to the theoretical, the insightful, the experiential applied intuitively, pragmatically to individuals, to his patients.

He quoted an anti-positivistic verse he'd indulgently written as a student:

Freud discovered the instincts

The fears, the lusts, the hates.

But if only he'd found some data

He could have been one of the greats.

'Are you successful, James?'

'In my job? Yes, sometimes. Not always.'

He didn't tell him that he seemed to be increasingly taking on people who had tried other therapists but, either immediately or after two or three visits, had asked to see someone else. He was apprehensive about accepting such clients for they were often running away from themselves and projecting this onto their therapists. They had to stop somewhere. Many of his patients were long-term. He had three who had been coming to him since he'd started his practice and would be with him much longer.

Arthur returned to his theme. 'I wondered whether he was still being treated. I don't think he was. When he was with me he kept looking about nervously as if he hadn't been out of his flat for weeks.'

He looked at James with a slightly mocking smile, 'Perhaps he needs your help. You know where he lives, it's the front flat on the third floor.'

James told him that he couldn't just knock on his door and ask if he wanted help, though the chances were that he was quietly and desperately wishing for something like this to happen. They talked of other things and then parted, Arthur's last words being, 'Think about it, eh?'

James did, for the next week; thought of his trauma, his pain; his shadowy three quarter profile in the photo wedging itself into his head unwanted, sometimes even while he was with other clients. As he seemed to be fading from him, Arthur rang to say he'd seen him again.

Passing the building on his way to meet a friend he saw the man in the doorway of the block, looking frightened, as if he didn't want to be there or to go back inside. He seemed to have been standing there a while. Arthur had gently talked to him and, with some persuasion, had been invited into his flat. The place was frugal, minimal, the only colour seemed to be a print of Tretchikov's 'Green Girl' taped to a wall.

'He didn't say very much, but he's in a lot of stress, he really is. He did admit, though, that he needed help. Isn't that a good thing in your profession? I've got his address and... Look, I mentioned you. Perhaps it's not ethical or something, but, that poor bloke.'

James told him that though it was a little unconventional, he would see him if he contacted him, though it had to be on his own initiative.

His would-be patient rang two weeks later. It was a quiet voice that lacked energy and direction, as if it hadn't full contact with the world. He made an appointment. James was, unusually, fully booked for a week, but didn't think a few more days would alter the situation.

He saw him when he was within a few yards of his house. Above the privet hedge his head, seemingly disembodied, moved smoothly along till the rest of him appeared as he tentatively opened the gate before stepping back and quietly closing it. James felt a glimmer of admiration for Arthur's ability to recognise him from the photo. He then pushed the gate firmly and took two strides along the path and looked in the open window - it was a warm day - and saw James sitting back in an armchair as he had been for twenty minutes, waiting for him. James smiled at him encouragingly. He looked surprised.

Something told James not to get up, not to move, certainly not to go to the door and ask him in. He suddenly looked frightened, edged back up the path a little, his eyes on the therapist, and stood there, very still. James slowly crooked a finger and silently mouthed, 'Come in.' The man had to make a decision. All he had to do was begin the first step then another would follow, then another. But it was like a wall in front of him. He couldn't move. He turned quickly, opened the gate and scurried past the hedge. James could see only the top of his head again.

That evening Arthur rang him to ask how it went. When told that it hadn't he seemed disappointed, though James suggested that his potential client could, possibly, come again and this time enter his home. His friend suggested he would go to the man's place again and talk to him, persuade him to try once more - in effect, and unconsciously on his part, attempting to set up an ersatz counsellor-client relationship. It was one that never began.

He was opposite the apartment block and about to cross the road to begin his mission when he heard screeching brakes and somebody shout. He saw a woman in front of him point upwards. He looked to where she was indicating and saw him kneeling on his sill, the window open, looking across to the cranes on the building site sixty yards in front of him.

Arthur's first thought, pushing away the significance of the crouch, was that the red tiled sill must be hurting his knees, the bottom of the metal frame, his shins. He fell forward, his arm movements like a quick-motion, butterfly stroke. Arthur never saw anymore. He turned away, hands covering his face.

In Paulo's, where they'd first seen each other again just a few months before, he described it to James, living it, feeling it all. As he talked, James wondered if, when people jump, some of them uselessly whirl their arms because they suddenly change their minds and want to stay airborne or at least slow their descent; but in this case, the man could have been emulating the red helicopter that had smashed the air outside his home and, eventually, the mind inside it.

He asked Arthur how he felt.

'I'll get by.'

He shook James' hand as if it was going to be another long while before they met and strode away from him.

Walking home through Green Street, he realised that he hadn't always been aware of the qualities his friend had. People see others who they think they know superficially, lay down a stereotype or a batch of stereotypes on different characteristics of them. They do this because they want order, a shorthand way of 'understanding,' a quick fix. He hoped that his training and experience had prevented him from doing this with his patients. Sadly, he doubted it.

He thought of the dead man who had told neither of them his name. Arthur had seen some handkerchiefs when in the flat that had 'F P' embroidered on a corner, which told them nothing. James knew it would have been noted in the tabloids, but decided not to bother, there was little point.

He thought about what remnants of actions and images had welled up in the man as he'd jumped; perhaps a flicker of concern for someone who saw him fall, or came across him, legs akimbo, sprawled across the pavement or, maybe, it was the casual ease with which his body would be carried into an ambulance or the sound of a sweeper's brushes pushing his debris away, or the impenetrable dark, the despair, the kneeling on the sill, or an image of the patch of worn floral carpet he'd raised himself from and looking down at a shoe he hadn't tied properly. James also wondered whether he knew when he'd shut the window the night before that it would be the last time he'd do it, and perhaps even a dull awareness that he wouldn't need his door key any more.

And the questions. Could he have made time for him before the aborted attempt to meet? Should he have gone into the garden and made himself benign and welcoming, broke down the man's fear; changed the possibly hostile, perhaps even threatening picture he had of him?

He passed 'The River of Life Pentecostal Church' again; the dark-suited African men standing outside with their Christianising pamphlets and booming evangelising spiel, the women offering single flowers to passers-by, their children solemnly restless by their sides.

Walking by a ladder against an old Burtons building where a window cleaner was leathering a suntrap window, he fancifully thought that, maybe, through the grime, he was seeing reflections of pantile roofs, white render, stylized shells, perhaps imagining foyers of chrome and black, walnut and jade, the glistening spire of the Chrysler... though he was, James suspected, probably just thinking about cleaning a window.

VIC

The most trivial encounter I had with Vic Denby was on the first day at my new school. My father had insisted on accompanying me despite my protests, for not only did he constantly embarrass me when out with him by telling me to pull my shoulders back and to breathe deeply - a leftover from his army days, the only cockney in a Yorkshire regiment serving in Delhi when he was seventeen - but, seeming to wait purposely till we were in earshot of a dozen people. It was 1947, I was thirteen and starting at the local Tech.

Nearing our destination, a twenty minute walk from home, isolated groups of boys in the silence of newness were standing around outside a wide, sloping incline leading to the main doors of the building. Not one of them had their fathers with them.

As I walked towards them, looking down and away from my father, there were the tinkling sounds of giggling and the snarl of barely controlled snigger. Glancing up, I saw a big, dark haired boy with a rough, pitted face looking from side to side at his newly found cronies and then pointedly at my father and me. I looked straight at him His lips twisted in an exaggerated sneer of contempt. I turned away, unable to hold his eyes. I looked up at my father, willing him to return home. He was looking around him with a self-satisfied air, rocking slowly backwards and forwards on his heels with his hands held loosely behind him and repeatedly pushing his shoulders back and vigorously sniffing and nodding his head in approval as if in the middle of the countryside admiring the scenic beauty spread before him.

'Yes, it looks a nice school, son. They seem to be decent boys. I think you'll be okay here.'

He probably said it quietly, but it seemed to bellow out, echoing around the forecourt. The sound of a bell came from somewhere and we all moved towards the entrance.

'You'll be alright then, son?'

I gritted my teeth and momentarily closed my eyes, *'Yes,* dad*'*

He looked uncomfortable and said hesitantly, 'Well, cheerio son.' and walked away. I saw Vic for a second turning for a final sneer then went into the building.

That morning we were told that for the first of the three years there we would be taught the usual academic subjects; after that, one day a week would be spent getting acquainted with the basic principles of the building trades and at the end of that period would be expected to choose the one we intended to specialise in, the remaining trade teaching time singularly devoted to it. There were, after a while, a few extra-curricular activities not mentioned then that were to lighten the class and workshop rituals; one such created by an English teacher who decided that if we were at the School of Building then, by definition, we must be louts and in an attempt to civilise us he taught, in the main hall and after hurriedly scoffed meals in the lunch hour, ballroom dancing.

It was, in retrospect, quite bizarre to watch boys, some with cement or paint-spattered overalls, dancing with each other; the ones who had to play the woman's role gritting their teeth inside a howl of sarcastic comments. One particularly small lad was, as a teaching aid, made to stand on the teacher's shoes and be whirled around like a puppet at a seaside fairground.

I realised after very few weeks that I had little interest or ability in any of the trades except the more artistic elements of decorating and it was in this workshop a year or so later that Vic's contempt for me came into the open.

He had quickly established himself as one of the dominant personalities of the class and gathered around him the majority of the rougher lads. He attempted to prove his physical superiority on every possible occasion. If there was any furniture moving or desk arranging to be done he would be the first to get up and push and carry, his expression meant to convey that he was only toying with small pieces of wood, mere child's play, and after sliding a desk recklessly across the room would spread out his hands and curve his arms up over his head in an exaggerated follow-through. If there was cement to be made up in a brickwork lesson his hands were the first to grab a shovel. He'd pick up sloppy wads of 'muck' for the mortar boards then stack a large number of bricks in a hod and carry it unnecessarily around before depositing the bricks in piles in front of the walls the students were building.

Vic had a native shrewdness and an aptitude for quickly grasping a practical subject and, considering the finer points of communication superfluous, was basic and direct.

In one decorating lesson we were all, either in pairs or singly, painting murals on the workshop walls. My associate for this was a normally quiet boy whose father, it was rumoured, had his own decorating business. The particular creation we had evolved was a six feet square relief map of the Bay of Biscay and part of Spain, the land mass being formed by a stippler made of short lengths of rubber strips placed at right angles to each other we repeatedly pressed onto a thick layer of alabaster. This, when hardened, rubbed down and shaded in various tones of brown and green was a reasonable topographical representation of hilly, wooded land. The trade teacher, seeing that his class was absorbed in its work, was indulging in one of his periodic absences from the room.

We'd been working silently for a while and I mentioned to my colleague something about Dali's moustache dropping off if he could see the misshapen mess we were making of his country and, in a slow, scholarly manner, he surprisingly began to relate what he knew of the artist's life. He rolled out a string of interesting facts and observations and as I aired my meagre knowledge of the subject, I became more absorbed in our conversation; was stimulated and loquacious.

'What you on about, Bowes?'

I felt myself flush even before I turned and saw Vic looking down at me from across the room. He was standing on a pair of steps from which he was working on a version of the mailed fist and motto of the Tank Corps. He leisurely swivelled round, leant his back on the steps, drew one leg up a couple of treads higher than the other, rested his elbow on a knee and cupped the side of his face in a hand. He sat smirking and closing his eyes in an affected manner of nonchalant superiority and, thrusting his head forward, said condescendingly,

'What is it this time then, your artistic appreciation?' He carefully emphasised the last two words as if they were foreign to him.

'Why ain't you like Jim and Lofty and the uvvers, Bowes?' he asked, narrowing his eyes. 'We're gonna get motor bikes when we can. Get the gels, too.' he grinned, looking around at the others.

The largest of his sycophants looked up from his work and sniggered. 'You don't wanna know nuffin' about art.' Vic said with infinite conviction, his eyes moving from side to side as if thinking of a significant sequel to his statement. He looked down at his board again, shaking his head and saying almost absently,

'Nah.'

Turning the steps towards us, he used them as a pulpit, leaning his folded arms comfortably on top of them.

'You wanna watch wrestlin', he said, holding his arms up like a weightlifter. 'Strength,' he shouted, 'Strength.'

Somehow he represented the whole world, and I felt that familiar, panicky isolation.

'Muscles,' Vic was saying. 'What yer wanna do, is -'

'The biggest muscle you've got is between your ears.' I blurted out angrily in a sudden flash of bravery. The silence made the words seem even more inadequate and stupid. A few of the boys who had heard them laughed in a preoccupied way for they were, in varying degrees, enjoying what they were doing and there was nothing hostile in their amusement. I sensed that Vic had failed to see this and he glared around challengingly, his lips tightened in anger.

Nobody looked at him and if they had would probably have been surprised to see him so annoyed. His eyes caught mine in the second before he turned away. I stood tensely, trying to concentrate on my mural, wanting Vic to do the same with his. No one was speaking. A few boys were humming or whistling quietly and I relaxed a little.

Then, a slipping, juddering sound, a wooden clatter, a heavy thump. I spun round. Vic was laying spread eagled on his back with the steps across his legs and red paint, like blood, spattered over the floor around him, his paint can describing an arc in the air, its curve decreasing as it slowed. There was a momentary stillness, and then the sound.

They were shrieking, mouths wide open, lips stretched back over teeth, pointing down at him. One boy abruptly sat on the floor, head dropping back loosely and then whipping it up again to stare incredulously, his eyes moist, laughing hugely and soundlessly. I was watching Vic closely as he viciously kicked the steps away and clambered to his feet. His white face was expressionless as he calmly and methodically brushed himself down, hands slapping over his shoulders and the back of his thighs, eyes almost vacant.

The room had quietened a little, then without warning he strode across to me. I pushed my arm up defensively and pressed back against the wall, but Vic's fist chopped it down with such force that I slid to the floor, cradling my arm to my chest. He then knelt in front of me, his back upright and erect, hands tightly clenched. He was quite still. I stared back at him, gaping. Nobody was laughing now. There was no noise at all.

He raised his fists high above his head and swung them down onto my shoulders, one at a time, as one came down the other would go up as if he were ringing imaginary church bells. Strangely, there was no force behind them, they just lightly touched me. I was holding my hands palms upwards in front of my face, turning away in anticipation of heavier blows and catching short glimpses of Vic staring unblinkingly at a point above my head, detached, frowning hard as if he were desperately trying to remember something or grasp the reality of his actions. Slowly and, at first, almost inaudibly, he choked hoarsely,

'I hate you, I hate you,' and then quickening until he was screaming it into a high-pitched rhythm of, 'aitchew, aithchew, aitchew,' over and over.

A few of the bigger boys pulled him away from me and as soon as he was on his feet he shook himself from them and with head hanging walked limply back to the fallen steps, pushed them upright and slowly looked around him for something to clean the paint up, none of which, fortunately, had touched anyone's work. Someone tentatively offered him a piece of rag then wandered back to where he had been working. The others returned to their places, also, some looking over at me and shrugging their shoulders, but shock showing in their eyes. Vic was kneeling on the floor, body stretched forward, rubbing the bunched-up rag in wide ineffectual circles, his shoulders spasmodically jerking. He was crying. The class then helped clear up the mess. I did, too.

Vic was quieter and less aggressive for a while afterwards, but not for long. His strident voice could soon be heard again and he seemed the same old Vic, except that he never spoke to me at all and when he eventually did it was only at moments when he more or less had to.

Eighteen months later and just prior to leaving I had an interview with a large City and West End painting contractors and a month afterwards started work.

A pressure on my shoulder. A rocking motion, gentle, rhythmic, my arm firmly gripped, the rocking more vigorous, my head lolling loosely about. A name was being called, gently, insistently; it was mine. I opened my eyes and stared at my mother who was telling me that there was a cup of tea on the bedside table and not to knock it over and don't be too long getting up. I nodded slowly, feeling sleep clamping my eyelids tighter and was only barely aware of the door closing, and then the slow realisation that it was Monday morning, my first day at work. I hung my head backwards over the side of the bed and stared at the ceiling.

Images of myself travelling to work drifted around my mind and concreted themselves in movie form: a straightforward shot leaving the house wearing a grey, black-flecked sports jacket, neat, wool tie and worsted trousers. The camera pans towards me as I walk quickly along the street showing a back view with head bent forward on stooping shoulders, then a dramatic close-up, the camera on its trolley twelve inches from my bobbing face, minute particles of sleep in the corner of an eye, yellow filling in a front tooth and the pallor of the smooth skin.

The houses in the background are seen as the camera moves away, travelling faster than I'm walking. The corner of the road, a blank wall, a dog trots past then I appear again, turning quickly, flashing from left to right of the screen. A side view this time as I begin running to catch a bus pulling away from the stop, a slowing down and then a casual leap onto the platform with an aerial shot looking almost directly down at me swinging around the pole with one hand and instantly disappearing into the interior. The blue-grey acrid air of the crowded top deck, a low shot showing boots, black shiny casuals, corduroys and a pair of brown suede shoes. Stark close-ups of men with a day's growth of beard and the just shaven ones putting home-rolled or factory made cigarettes between their lips. Faces with closed eyes endeavouring to finish off harshly interrupted sleep, faces with narrowed eyes reading the pages of the Daily Mirror or Reveille, those with mouths open, panting with the effort of the double exertion of having run for the bus and coughing from a too-early fag.

The vehicle slows and just when it has almost stopped starts away again. An early morning office girl climbs the stairs and looks around her with distaste. Nobody stands for her and, leaning against the side at the top of the stairs, she brushes imaginary smuts from her clean, crisp dress with the back of a gloved hand and stares fixedly out of a back window. The bus slackens its bouncing, rolling speed, the camera pans away and points through a side window and in the natural frame lorries and cars, motorbikes and cycles sweep across the lens and, after them, a wasteland of dust and bricks, squashed drink cartons, remnants of bonfires, old newspapers and the frame of a bicycle sticking up like a scalene triangle. The rectangle is then filled with shabby Victorian houses, and a shot from the top of the steep, curved stairs as bodies helter-skelter down and jump off the bus - the majority before it has stopped - into the grimy entrance of the station, makes them look like squat-bodied giants with huge feet.

My gaze strayed from the ceiling to the underneath of a saucer rim protruding from the top of my bedside table and in a moment of full wakefulness I lifted myself from the bed in pleasant anticipation of the hot, sweet tea. Ten rushed minutes later I was on my way to the bus stop. There were no cameras.

I was to report at eight o'clock to the foreman painter, Mister Fox, at a building in Finsbury Circus. I was carrying a small case containing shiny, newly purchased tools and a packet of sandwiches. Walking from the station I swung this about disdainfully in an effort to hide from the world that this little lad, who I was sure it was looking at with comforting smiles and women with inclinations of heads and looks in their eyes which suggested an inwardly exclaimed 'Aaaah' of pity, was not really going off to work for the first time, but had, in fact, started years ago and was now accepted as one of the men. Squaring my shoulders, an old habit, I crossed the road to the entrance.

A staircase with a rail supported by iron balustrades wrought in heavily ornate designs spiralled upwards. I climbed carefully, passing floors with metal partitions, false ceilings, recently plastered walls, new window frames in the process of erection and men just starting work for the day, slow moving and reluctant. One of them told me where the paint shop was and I found the foreman there who, when informed timorously that I was the new apprentice, gave me a look of disapproval, a paint kettle full of pink priming and led me along the large, semi-partitioned floor to the windows at the end and told me he wanted ten completed that day. Half way across were pairs of trestles, scaffold boards stretched between them, and working in pairs on them were six painters, their brushes casually pounding the ceiling with hollow flip flops of sound. I hoped that, in time, I could pick up their effortless expertise.

They were laughing, voices and guffaws echoing around and one of them, with quick glances at an immaculately dressed man sporting dustless brogues, looking irritated and flicking a steel tape measure from hand to hand, was making a gesture towards his workmates by gripping an arm above the elbow and, still holding his brush, swinging it with tightly clenched fist mock-furiously up and down, lips curled back over gritted teeth - a universal gesture unknown to me at the time.

There was a cliquishness in such incidents, an unconscious knowledge of the right things to say and do, the correct responses, the right feelings. These things were seemingly a natural part of them, unthinking, unforced.

I walked over to a window which seemed to soar above me, the others vanishing into a pinpoint of perspective. In my brand new white bib and brace I began searching anxiously for a pair of steps. I explored the floors above and below and the only pair that weren't being used were painted brown and an electrician, before grabbing them back from me, stuck his face through their inverted 'V' into mine and with a patronising, mock severity as if he had just caught his youngest child sticking a finger into a pot of jam, slowly and deliberately shook his head then burst into laughter while I stared with fascination at the small dots of amalgam in his mouth glistening with spittle.

I returned to the floor where I was supposed to be working and heard the foreman sarcastically say to one of the men, 'If you can't finish it till the first coat's dry, stand there and blow on it.'

He turned to me.' Haven't you started yet?'

'I can't find any steps.' I said.

'Well, bloody look for 'em. Anyway, we're off to tea now, they've got a big area down there and they'll have a long run, so we'll have a bit of dinner now.'

I sat in the nearby café, the other boiler-suited or bib-and-braced painters laughing easily, ordering food; 'Two airships on a cloud, darling,' 'Babies on a raft, luv' for sausages and mash and beans on toast. And then, swaggering in, shoulders rolling, long hair slicked down, was Vic Denby.

He sat down in a corner, had a quiet chuckle with a couple of painters, looked at me, gave a slight nod then turned his head away. I had no idea that he had come to this firm, was working on this job.

For the next few days I only saw Vic in the café; it was a big job, painters, mostly in twos, were spread out on various floors, the other tradesmen; electricians, plasterers, carpenters were thinning out now, their work almost done. He never spoke to me, never gestured. At the end of the week Charlie Fox took me to the main entrance and pointed at the ceiling which was scaffold-boarded about eight feet below its surface and where men were brushing cream eggshell onto it, finishing it with large, fine hair stipplers. He pointed up through the gap where the ladder entered through the boards to a large, elaborate Adam ceiling rose.

'You been to Buildin' School ain't yer? Well, pick that out; the swags in red and the egg and arrers in white; do the round rim in blue. Ted's got the colours; get 'em from the paint shop.'

This was more like it. I had a sudden urge to ask for the boards to be raised so I could lie on my back to paint and pretend it was the Sistine Chapel. I carried three paint kettles and brushes up with me in one go then went down for the white spirit and rag. I started enjoying myself immediately; standing on an old stool, cutting in the Roman swags with a large chisel-edged sable, pushing the white into the tongue and dart with an inch tool. Time was irrelevant.

I stepped back. There was nothing there. My chest hit the metal edge of a board as I fell; I seemed to bounce away and then my buttocks and the back of my head were hitting ladder rungs as I fell, strangely upright. I landed vertically also, and then fell forward on my knees. As I pulled myself up I glanced down at a shoe. It was hanging off, almost broken in half. I stood and looked around dizzily, perhaps for the brushes, the kettles… I don't know.

I just stood there, alone. None of the painters on the boards above me seemed to have noticed. One was singing in a casual voice about a country girl he was in love with, I could hear his foot tapping quietly to the rhythm of the song, and his brush. And then I looked to the corner of this big, dust-sheeted area and there was Vic, ten yards away standing in a doorway. In a moment of pointless irrelevance I noticed he had cut his initials into the handle of a filling knife he was holding. He was smiling, almost likeably, a forefinger lightly tapping the side of his nose. He stopped, nodded his head slowly up and down, still smiling. I looked away. On the sheets around my feet was a spattering of red. Like blood.

COIFFURES

'I'll make the tea, ain't got no sugar again, but have a bicky. I'll wet yer 'air, ooh, it has got long, I know you like it full at the back but I like it short, if anyone sees you with yer shirt off they'll think I've got a man in 'ere, see in the mirror? perfick, ooh, look at all that 'air on the floor.'

Perhaps, he thought, she expected it to be on the ceiling.

'Yeh, we 'ad a nice cuppa tea outside Marks, you know, it was lovely, then Sainsbury's, you know, lovely shop, packed with people.' As if it was a welcome change from the usual lions and wildebeests.

Ann had been cutting James' hair in the kitchen of her home at two monthly intervals for fifteen years and was the most vacuous person he'd ever known. Every time he came he'd politely ask her to turn down the sound of her daytime TV soap and if he used a word containing more than three syllables she would ask a deflective, 'What d'you think of the weather, then?' Her son regularly took her on Italian holidays where she hadn't learnt a word of the language. Her raison d'etre was shopping. James wondered why, other than gossip, the working class - that annoying nano-second flick of awareness reminding him that it was a social background he also shared - had so little curiosity At a house agents recently he'd asked a girl at the desk why the estate in which they were in the centre of was so popular. Not a word of the Edwardian villas, late Victorian houses and established trees, only 'Well... it's nice.' dividing the last word into the estuary 'nie-wess.'

He was darkly hating the world because his younger brother had died a month previously. Stan had worked in some sort of security post for much of his life after finishing an engineering apprenticeship and them delivering pies and soft drinks around the East End. They'd spent most Sundays for the last eight years walking around London's terraced streets, past Georgian houses, magnolia gardens and magic mews, gazed at steepled skylines, laughed and occasionally argued around Hampstead and Highbury, Pimlico and Putney, along the Thames to Henley and the Lea Navigation from Limehouse Cut to Ware. And there were the trips to Paris, Rome, Madrid and Prague, and striding the five boroughs of New York.

Stan had lived for a few years just four miles away, though James had hardly seen him. Then their mother died and while doing the necessary chores of doctor's, solicitors and estate agents the old humour began to return - the cynicism along with the cockney hyperbole - and they'd revisited the streets they used to play in and saw more of each other. And when they did so it was as if Stan was old enough then, after decades and different lives, to come with him on his journeys; James not having to force smiles anymore as they sat on a rocking horse in Aunt Gwen's garden, help him cross the sewage pipe over the brook or push him on a swing, his boots smacking James' back as he turned, nor to feel the blows from the big boys he taunted. They walked streets with bits of cemetery and Epping Forest touching back gardens as James told him of childhood escapes following tramways and canals and standing on the bow of the Woolwich ferry for hours going back and forth across the Thames.

He'd married a Barbara Windsor look-a-like who'd moved up from rough to respectable working class by buying a house courtesy of Stan's years of 'working all the hours God sends.' He'd describe the glow he got from the money he'd saved from the years spent at his work place, the drinking of hundreds of gallons of tea, reading a thousand Daily Mails, his saveloy fingers red and dripping sweat as they trudged along, his eyebrows rising in surprise as James explained a joke.

It was near the end of a canal walk when he told James about it: his wife's dislike of his sallow jowls, thinning hair and incessant smoking and that she'd left him the day before, saying in a note propped against the kettle that she'd gone off with the accountant from next door. She'd left a number. Stan had rung her an hour later to ask if she was alright and did she want anything.

Stan remembered things about their early life James had forgotten: dad's roll-up dangling from his lip, the echo of his key in the cheaply grained door, the grim mat stamping, the shaking of a wet raincoat, the grey line of sea from a Canvey Island chalet, mum square-jawed in a deckchair.

It was his nephew who'd rung James. Stan had died in his bathroom the morning after a single dose of chemotherapy that James had taken him to a hospital for, convinced his body wasn't strong enough to cope with even that. James had delayed the shock for a moment by wondering how people learnt to manage death; through other people's anecdotal experiences? films, obituaries, novels?

He'd moved blindly around the house kicking doors and scattering books, while brittle images and mosaics of urban architecture filled the pain: the streetscapes of an endless city, Stan behind, gasping for a caff and becoming dad lying at the bottom of the stairs clutching his kidneys, James staring forever before running next door for mum. When Stan's six year old eyes had looked up at him, not thinking how he'd die, James couldn't know that his father would always hover inside of him, almost strangling the tears, the love.

To escape from the more harrowing aspects of life as a psychotherapist James wrote poetry. He'd been asked to read at a venue in Hackney, yet another up-and-coming East London 'events' café. On one side was a silver graffiti-covered pub, on the other a Victorian biscuit factory being converted to apartments trendily called 'The Biscuit Factory.' They were surrounded by sixties flats and a run down nineteenth century industrial estate.

He felt listless; most of his clients seemed to be in limbo. Satisfaction came from seeing a patient unclenching, loosening, allowing, with James help, deep-rooted defences to uncoil, to slowly release the lead-walled psyche. There'd been few signs of this; it had been an unrewarding week.

He didn't really want to read, he had no new work; most of it was in a collection. He had a few copies with him to sell to anyone interested; if they weren't he wouldn't be bothered to persuade them. A reviewer had written of the 'remarkable clarity' of his work. He knew it thoroughly, had overworked it; felt that 'remarkably dull' was more appropriate.

The café interior was the result of raids made on fifties junk shops and bargain Victoriana, but with wine menus. There were fifty people, a dozen, at most, there for the poetry, a third of the women were in Alice in Wonderland tresses, and a similar proportion of those men who hadn't turned themselves into Jesus look-alikes wore flat caps, tight white jeans and sneakers; the 'young, urban professionals' beloved by developers. The host had told him that the drinkers would have to listen because 'they had no choice.' They did, and they exercised it. He excused himself and left; there were other readers anyway.

It wasn't just his filial loss that was troubling him. He wanted grief to take its natural course - difficult for someone with a long-lasting habit of relentless self-analysis - but there was Martha.

He'd first met her at a poetry workshop he'd run in a local library for the Essex Poetry Festival. She was one of ten people whose work he'd photocopied for them to read to each other and comment upon; the obligatory intro of attempting to define poetry he'd reduced to 'the best words in the best order' and moved on. She sat at the end of the long table. She was almost skinny, with dark auburn hair and an adjectival surfeit of romanticised verses that made him bite his lip so as not to be unkind to her. She was dyslexic, but had a hard worked for articulacy which partly compensated and a way of intensely but flowingly gesticulating that conveyed ideas and meanings convincingly. There was a little strangeness about her: she would drift away for a few seconds as if she didn't know she was being spoken to or, sometimes, speaking herself. As the group left he heard one of them say quietly to another that she seemed a 'bit whacky, bit of a nutter.' It was a term he disliked.

He met her again a few days later when she was driving slowly past his home. He was going out and had just closed the door. She was looking at him, smiling. She stopped. He went across to her. She had to see her ex for something; apparently he lived in the street that ran off his.

'Now I know where you live,' she said, laughing, and drove off.

Soon afterwards he saw her when meeting a friend who was lecturing on a Fine Arts course at a Silvertown college. She was being taught by him and was with him in the pub. She merely said hello to James and left. His friend got a little drunk and told him about her. She was a good student who he found hard to believe was fifty, as did James, it surprised him; she had a skin of a thirty year old. Her ex was, apparently, running a brothel in a flat above some local High Street shops. His friend had once slept with her, literally, she telling him she had a nineteen year old boyfriend who wanted sex all the time and she needed a rest. He'd reluctantly given it to her.

The next evening there was a knock on James' door and she was on the step looking down at a piece of paper she was writing on.

'I've come to give you my mobile number.' she said, not looking up. She wore big sun glasses, a black, lacy shawl and sandals. He asked her where she was going. 'Nowhere.' she answered still looking down, and gave him the number. She went back to her car and drove off. He briefly wondered why he hadn't asked her in.

He saw his teacher friend on a local train a week afterwards. He told James she'd been behaving erratically; working intently for hours in the studio then sitting and staring at her work, unmoving, for long periods. She'd then miss a couple of days and the next be standing outside the college an hour before it opened. He'd tried to get her to tell him what was wrong. She wouldn't. He asked James whether he would see her professionally.

'No. I know her, and you know the rules.'

He told him he knew someone who, perhaps, could help. He rang a colleague, Robin, who he'd met at a British Psychological Association conference a few years before who, although tending to remember such gatherings solely in terms of the food that had been served, 'Ah yes, that was the smoked trout one' or 'the chicken l'orange conference,' was very competent.

A week later James was asked to read again at another new venue: an upstairs room in a converted warehouse with a small fringe theatre underneath not far from his previous short-lived performance. He was the last on; a dubious honour for he had to listen to and clap politely virtually all of the sets. She came in at the end of the short interval and sat familiarly next to him. He hadn't asked her to come and wasn't quite sure how she knew he'd be there, though it could have been a coincidence. She was fiddling around inside her bag. He imagined her not looking up since he'd last seen her. Then she did, along with a wide, red lipstick'd smile and large green eyes.

'I've put my name down to read. I've written two new poems and, before you say it, I've cut the adjectives down.'She showed them to him just before the second half started. She was on first. She stood behind the mike with no intro and re-affirming his theory that females are more likely than males to write of the body, the visceral; 'woman equals nature, man culture,' someone once said. After his ten minutes and the surprisingly appreciative applause and the selling of a few books was over he went to leave. She got up and put her arm in his - the reflex action initially being acceptance, not the pushing away - and they went out as if old friends, or more.

During the short walk to the station he gradually eased from her and said he was going westwards, not the other way. She looked disappointed.

'I'll come with you,' she said brightly.

He told her he was seeing a patient. She frowned. He didn't think she knew what he did. He didn't explain. It was mildly embarrassing to stand six metres from her on the opposite platform watching the disapproving look and the sudden, beaming grin. He was annoyed at himself for lying; most people tell the truth most of the time; as well as the social taboo against not doing so, it's easier. Her train came and left. He crossed to the platform and waited for the next, feeling like an artful little boy. On the train he thought of her poems and the raw but interesting treatment of primitive subjects, and scribbled some stanzas which he thought captured the feel of hers.

Two days later, placing a book mark in Laing's 'The Divided Self,' he glanced disinterestedly out of the window and saw her car outside. As he moved to get a better view around the hedge she turned her head to grin at him and drove away with a squeal of brakes.

He realised he'd pushed away the idea that she was, he wasn't sure how to express it, 'following' was inaccurate as was 'harassing,' stalking him. He knew the concept referred to a spectrum of behaviours and an even wider continuum of motivations. As a practitioner they should have interested him They didn't. He was tired. He was sure there was little more involved than a somewhat skewed curiosity.

The following weekend Robin called him. She'd been to him twice.

'I don't know how much you know about her, but she's obviously very insecure and perhaps this is manifested in her work. She's shown me some of her paintings, they're rather second rate, but I don't think that's important. One moment she's all excitement and energy, seeing them vividly, explaining them; objects of worship if you like, then the next... well, she said she slashed one. There's hatred there, maybe fear. I feel there's obsession, too. Anyway, thought you should know. Pity, she's an attractive woman. So, how's your world James?'

They talked about how their practices were prospering or not and whether they would be going to an imminent psychotherapists conference, but he kept thinking of her: the dark, auburn hair, giving him her number, a slashed painting, wondering what or whom it was of.

Then she rang his home number. He'd given this to the students at the workshop in case they wanted to talk about their work.

'Do you want to come to my birthday party tomorrow? It's just a little one, you'll enjoy it.' He didn't answer.

'Please.'

She gave him her address and, having no clients the next day and thinking that there just may be some interesting people there, he went. She lived nearer than he thought.

It was the ground floor flat of a fifties block. She was dressed for a party.

'Come and sit down, have a drink.'

He went into a music filled room. No one else was there.

'Am I the first? I'm usually last, I like to make an entrance.'

'No, it's just you and me. It is my birthday, though.'

It was the last bit that got to him, he could feel the loneliness; he knew his. She sat opposite him. He didn't notice the décor, contents, colour of the curtains; she and the situation stopped the visual recording. She gave him a glass of wine, changed the music. He asked her about her work. She talked of Hockney, Bellini, a Turner exhibition.

'Let's dance.' she said, pulling him up and pressing into him. He went through the motions, sat down and mentioned Turner again, 'You know more about him than me.'

In phrases which he assumed were straight from her course book she unenthusiastically told him a little more. He was feeling uncomfortable, told her he needed to go.

'Why?'

He hesitated. She came right up to him, her face inches from his.

'Don't go.'

He kissed her forehead as if he was kissing someone who he was fond of, perhaps a sister or a child, and turned to leave.

'I hate it when you do that.'

He was thrown; the implication was that he'd done it to her before.

'Look… I'm going.'

'Really?'

Then she punched him. As he twisted away he was caught on the side of the neck. He could feel her breath. When film noir heroes hit women there was seemingly something deserved and satisfying about it. He couldn't. He opened the door, walked to his car and drove away.

He was shaken, but what was bothering him was whether he should tell Robin. He decided not to and guessed she wouldn't either.

She came around next day. He could see who it was through his art deco glass door panes. He opened the door quickly and asked her firmly what she wanted.

'I'm sorry, so sorry. Please let me come in. I want to apologise.' She was crying.

He let her go before him into the front room. She looked briefly around then stopped, grimacing at a shelf holding a framed sepia shot of two of his aunts, one who'd died recently at 97, it seemed to have been taken during the twenties, both wore peacock feather hats and flapper skirts.

'Who are they? What are they doing here?'

Putting her hand on top of her head she clawed at her hair which he could now see was a full wig. It fell. She stepped over to the bookshelf. He noticed a knife in her hand, held loosely, incidentally, like a piece of scrap paper. She swept the photo off the shelf along with books and an urn holding Stan's ashes which James intended to scatter around somewhere his brother had particularly enjoyed in London. He looked at the floor, the books and the urn - lid still tightly on - rolling slowly to a stop. The image came fast: a flash of his ex sister-in-law at the funeral frowning at him from ten yards away outside the chapel of the crematorium as if she'd seen him a week ago instead of years.

'When's the service start then? You can 'ave the ashes. You 'ave 'im.'

Martha began to stride to another shelf, arm and hand outstretched, but he grabbed her shoulder, pulled her backwards out of the room and along the passage and, opening the front door with his other hand, aware for a second of her grey, cropped hair, turned her towards the path and pushed her along it, the gate stopping her momentum. She opened it frantically and ran across to her car. He slammed the door. He'd never done this to a woman before. He was scared. He sat down and tried to calm himself.

'Obsession.' His colleague seemed to have been right. But why him? James would tell him this time; he knew he had to. She could be, she was, dangerous. And he knew, too, that he'd been kidding himself thinking that his brother's last words to him had been, 'I'm so glad you showed me around London.'

He had said it, but it wasn't the last words he'd said to him. As James had turned from him to go, Stan, sitting on a chair in the middle of his kitchen extension, had said,

'Nothing matters: your job, your problems, nothing.' He'd looked so ill. He should have gone back to him, squeezed his shoulder, kissed him and said, 'It's okay it'll be alright.' But he hadn't.

As he picked up the phone he looked at the wig where it had dropped: the fine, long auburn hair, the thin nylon mesh inside it. He could hear Ann again,

'Ooh, look at all that 'air on the floor.'

GEOGRAPHY

James Kent had just been treated by his osteopath. He saw him annually where he would hear the same tale about his graduation and wearing a 'God made human beings so there would be osteopaths' t-shirt. It was an injury James received when, looking out from his Nordic-Brutalist flat on the campus of his sixties plate-glass university and seeing a first team trial game, he couldn't help joining in. He hadn't played football since youth clubs and when the game had finished he couldn't stand upright. After weeks he could. After years he was told one of his legs was half an inch longer than the other; his left sacroiliac joint having twisted a long time before. It was put back in its natural position in under twenty minutes and when it happened again James returned to the same man.

As he left he passed a girl pasting theatre posters to the font wall of the Young Vic. They were creased, corners peeling. He'd learnt to hang wallpaper during an apprenticeship and went across to her, gently took the cloth from her hands, quietly asking her permission as he did so and explaining while demonstrating that she'd do a better job by beginning in the centre and pressing outwards, suggested a firm brush or straight piece of hard plastic acting as a spatula would be better than the rag. She smiled her thanks as he walked away to the nearby home of a friend who wanted him to paint the outside of the windows of her ground floor flat.

They'd known each other sporadically for years and she'd recently asked whether he still did any decorating for anyone. She'd intimated that a positive reply would probably be a long shot knowing that he'd been a practising psychotherapist for some time and would, perhaps, have forgotten the skills of his old trade anyway. Of course he hadn't, they seemed as natural to him as walking. It would, and should, have been an outside bet, but client numbers as well as finances were at an all-time low so he agreed to do the job for her at a reasonable price.

His friend was working so he borrowed a key from a neighbour. When he started he noticed himself automatically pulling the top sash down, lifting the bottom one up a few inches to get to its top bar, then the glazing bars, frame, reveals, methodically tapping his inch tool inside the kettle - he could hear himself thinking in the

310

language of his ex-trade - and cutting in quickly and easily. He put two coats on in a few hours and decided not to charge her, leaving a note for her with the neighbour he'd borrowed the key from. He could see his friend another time.

The next day, another clientless one, the neighbour rang him. She'd heard from James' friend what he did for a living. 'I have a son,' she said in a rather weak voice. 'He's sixteen and he's very depressed. He is so unhappy. I'm not sure why. Would you see him? Please?'

He told her he would, but that he didn't live locally. She knew this, but it didn't matter; nor did his fee.

A few days afterwards a slim, dark haired young man looking no more than fourteen knocked on James' door. He was pale, tense and appeared very nervous. He was asked to come in. He followed James' through to the room where he saw patients and was offered either the couch or armchair. He chose the chair.

The slight figure sat uncomfortably still, looking across at James' kneecaps, slowly blinking. James said nothing. Looking into the middle distance between the therapist and himself, his patient said,

'I'm sort of... lost.'

'Try to describe what you feel.'

'I can't.'

'Anything to do with your parents?'

He didn't answer.

'Do you hate them?'

He looked bewildered, frightened.

'I... how did you know?'

'I didn't, but you're not alone, Alan. Really, it's okay.'

He looked down and nodded slowly, his lips quivering. It was obvious he wanted to cry. James knew he wouldn't.

'I've got Rick, though.' he said, looking up.

'Friend?'

'I've known him since we were kids, infants really, we played together, you know, we... ' His voice trailed. He looked down again.

'Has anything happened?'

He didn't respond for a while, then, 'He's got a motor bike, he goes out with his, with his, his new friend sometimes.' It was almost a stutter.

'Are you jealous of his friend? It's alright, you can say it.'

Still looking at the floor, he nodded again.

'You don't want a motor bike, too?'

'I'm too young, anyway?'

'Anyway? Do they frighten you? The noise?'

'Yes.'

'So you decided that your fear of motor bikes outweighs your feelings of jealousy about your mate's friend? I don't mean it was a clear cut, logical decision, but in effect?'

There was no answer. After a time James asked him if he was studying or had a job.

'I started as an order clerk for Jameson's, but I can draw, should have gone to Art College.'

He was asked why he hadn't. He said nothing. James pointed out that he could still go and rather pointlessly asked if he enjoyed art.

'Yes, I've always done it, used to copy a lot, fine detailed stuff. I remember the night before an art exam at school. I found a pen and ink sketch of the chantry at Wells; not sure what it was, but I copied it. It took three hours. Next day I remembered every line of it, every scroll, each bit of shading and drew it in the exam. I was top.'

He didn't smile, there was no sign of any satisfaction at all.

'Does it please you, this ability?'

He shrugged.

'Do you really *feel* it, Allen, this expertise, this talent you say you've virtually always had or is it a little fantasy world you go into when you draw. I suspect it's not very real, is it.'

He looked alarmed. There was a long pause. 'No,' he said quietly.

'That's all you've got, isn't it. You and Rick, that is.'

'Yes.' He was barely audible. He put his head deep between his knees.

James could see that if his patient carried on untended, in a year or so

312

he would break down; he wasn't too far from it at that moment.

'Have you always felt this dreadful, this insecure?'

After a while he nodded a reply.

'Your parents. Do - ?'

'Mum. There's just her. Always has been, really. She's so fuckin' distant, so... I'm sorry, I don't really swear. Anyway, I've got Rick,' he said again, clenching his teeth and hand. 'We do things, always together; make up crosswords, he draws too, go everywhere together, go to the movies a lot, we joined a film club, 'Close-up,' see French films, Japanese classics.'

The latter genre seemed to James to be a little alien to this would-be cineaste, as if he and his friend felt that somehow they *should* enjoy them. James let him feel, think, muse for a while then asked about his mother.

'My mum works at Waterloo station, don't know what she does, manual job I think. We haven't always lived around here; we used to live in Bow, the Stratford end.'

James allowed him, because neither of them wanted to go any deeper on a first meeting - an often unsatisfying experience for the analyst and a potentially dangerous one for the patient - to talk effortless banalities, he would ask about his father next time. James guessed the origins of his insecurity went deeper than a missing father and more than the norm for the period stretching from childhood to late teens and beyond, as was a pubescent, potential homosexuality.

As he left, more animated than when he arrived, he asked whether he could see James sooner than the following week. He was told he could. He came three days afterwards.

He immediately waved away questions about his father and talked of art and his crossword compiling. Again he was articulate. Crosswords, thought James, wouldn't mean such an easy escape as drawing, but a visualisation of the words would still provide him with a pleasing aesthetic satisfaction to compensate for his morbid fears of the real world.

James interrupted him and said, 'Motor bikes.'

His patient stopped. He looked apprehensive.

'What about them?

'Have you thought about asking Rick if you could ride pillion? Why not suggest it, you'd be together.' His patient was silent.

'What frightens you the most, the bike or being refused the ride?'

He was obviously distressed. James said nothing. His patient didn't want to talk at all. James let the silence dominate for minutes then said gently,

'Jealousy's okay you know, its part of being what we are. It can be horrible I know, but it means that you - '

'I might, I've been thinking about it for a while now. Perhaps I should. But, I'm sorry Mister Kent, I can't keep here long, honest, I'm going to see a film with Rick tonight.'

James reluctantly encouraged him in his deflection, let him talk about a drawing he'd just finished, a movie he and his friend had recently seen and the one they were going to watch that evening. He then said that although he felt he should come again in less than a week he didn't think it would be fair on his mother. This, James felt, was about principle more than a genuine caring for her purse. James told him he'd waive this one.

'Have it on me.'

Another first. There seemed to have been a quite a few lately: having no patients in his office for four consecutive days, getting tired of Paulo's and sitting instead in local cafes to read newspapers and to jot down retrospective observations on his few current patients, and refusing an invitation to read his competition-winning poem. Newmarket Town Hall seemed too far.

They arranged a time for five days hence. His patient didn't show up. James wasn't unduly concerned and resisted the impulse to ring the mother. He left the call for two days then rang twice during the next week. There was no answer; no way to leave a message.

Clientless days were stretching ahead of him like an endless vacuum. Halfway through the next one he decided to do something he'd been putting off for a long time. He hadn't been back to the street he'd lived in for the first 20 years of his life since he'd left home. He'd had little desire to do so until a year before when his late, younger brother had persuaded him to write to the present occupier asking whether they could, perhaps, have a quick look around the house.

Predictably there'd been no reply.

He went to Stratford and walked through the old recreation ground. After a new appreciation of the thirties Tudorbethan public toilet he and his mates had chalked stumps on and played cricket outside, either before or after playing conkers under the numerous chestnut trees, he noticed a basketball pitch in place of the old sandpit and swings with their see-saw escapes from his church and school's God-fearing Gothic. The bandstand, where the second rate brass bands with their patched red uniforms played on occasional Sundays, had also disappeared. He turned along The Portway. Everything, of course, had changed: the old Kinema, the 'Gaf,' had been obliterated by new-builds, Fox's the greengrocers, the fish shop, the garage, even the Toby Arms had gone, though the original fascia of the tobacconist's with its faded sign-written 'Bye's Lolly Shop' revealed while the shop was being refitted, remained. It was a vivid mnemonic of his childhood and of his early teens, of Trebor fruit salad, sucking Spanish wood, and persuading the woman behind the counter to sell him a cigarette from a packet of five Weights.

He turned into the street, walking slowly. The pavement trees weren't there then, nor the leaded glass in the Simms' cricket-balled fanlight. He passed Mrs. Burn's, the Thornton's, and then 26; now stone-dashed and with PVC windows and door. He didn't stop, just walked on. There was no point, there'd be very little left except the curved wall in the passage, the side door and maybe the outside toilet, now probably used for junk. There were no slatted blinds and matt front doors then either nor, at the end of the road, the Latvian deli as comfortable as a Paris street corner; but opposite, the City Corporation sign at the Park entrance proudly black in the sun was as, barely visible, were the genitals he'd carved on its edge when he was twelve.

It was still bleak and dark as he continued to the local station, the only welcoming thing was the LT bull's eye sticking out from the sooty bricks. He realised it couldn't have been far from where Allen had spent his own childhood.

His back was stiffening, he moved easily but it presaged the joint twisting again. He thought it prudent to call his osteopath. There was a cancellation; he could be seen in an hour. He thanked the part-time receptionist-cum-secretary whose name he'd never known and was about to ring off when she said,

'There's bad news, James, about Bill's son. I'll tell you when I see you.' When he arrived, pressing the bell slowly and gently as if to diminish its demanding buzz, the door was opened with a kind of dignified slowness. He sat down, looking at the receptionist enquiringly.

'He'll see you in a couple of minutes.' She shook her head. 'It was awful. It was a crash. Rick was out on his motor bike with his friend and they crashed. It was a lorry or something, apparently they skidded. The funeral was only two days ago. I told him he shouldn't come in, but you know what he's like, him and his work. The other boy was alright, I think he just fell off. They'd been friends for years. It was awful.'

For a brief moment James felt as if he was part of a bereaved family which had lost one of its members: osteopath Bill, his son, whose name he hadn't known, the receptionist... He was part of an affectual social entity - he could hear the psycho-social phrases he'd learnt to effectively switch subjective reality onto a dispassionate level. He was about to ask her the name of Rick's friend, but already knew the answer. He was aware that Bill had moved from near Bow Church a dozen years previously after his wife had died, thus James' client, this frightened, lonely boy, had possibly lived no more than a few hundred yards from his childhood mate for most of his life. He assumed Bill, along with his son, had moved first to start his practice. Maybe Allen's mother had moved nearby because of her job.

He sat there, thinking of their horror as they saw the vehicle coming at them, an absolute fear diluted minutely by the optic nerve's fascination with a large object coming straight at the eye. He saw the tip of a foot support gouging the road, sparks spattering.

Had Allen been aware of what was going to happen? With his hands on his mate's waist to keep on the bike and head bent he may not have seen anything. James saw his arms clasped completely around the body in front of him, so relieved, happy, wanted.

He wondered how much a part he himself played in this. It had been his suggestion that... The treatment room door opened, an elderly woman came out followed by Bill. The receptionist opened the front door for her. Bill looked at James quickly, hardly catching his eye and turned back into the room. James followed. The osteopath excused himself briefly while his patient stripped.

When James had previously been there was always Bill's chortling laugh pushing into the waiting room, his proud voice speaking of his son's trial for Spurs, hinted at by the school team photo that was, James had noticed, now no longer on the wall, in its place a clout nail and cracked plaster.

His hand was shaken then the usual thumb and finger placed firmly on his hip.

'Leg's long again. Sacroiliac.'

There was no conversation. Neither of them spoke, as if there was an externally created law of silence which neither of them could or wanted to do anything about. His arms in the crux of James' he pulled his patient up and around, up and around, but James imagined that in his head he was lifting a child onto his shoulders, podgy legs around his face, releasing James the boy, helpless with laughter, falls across his bed in the mock fight, and kneading his patient's neck he turns the child's head and sees wide eyes playing hide and seek. As he gripped James' calf perhaps he saw his lad slide into a tackle or flying up the stairs as his fingers climbed James' spine, and maybe ruffling the boy's hair as his hands dug deeper into the back of his patient's skull.

James left. It had been thirty minutes of emotional limbo; Bill hardly knew he was there; he was an object, the leaden stimulus to the automatic response his training and experience dictated. James guessed that it would be months before he began muted, trivial conversations with his patients again.

Perhaps, James thought, he should visit Alan's mother, if not now then at some other time. He should, at least, ring her and perhaps talk to her son. He'd lost his friend; a large part of his frail, vulnerable ego. He may need James. He would certainly need somebody. James had met her only twice; to take and then return a key. He would be a reminder that her son hadn't been well, had been sent to him for help. She could, at this moment, do without that.

He thought again of the connections, the links, and the internal voice asking pointlessly, 'What are the odds... ?' but there were no mystical forces, no fatalistic, pre-ordained meetings, events, consequences. The determinants of this were simple and mundane: arbitrary places, arbitrary times.

On automatic pilot he realised he was walking into Paulo's and waitress Agnieska's smiling 'Haven't seen you for a time. How are things?'

'Like show business, no business.' he said, knowing she wouldn't understand the quip. But then, it wasn't funny; it was about as unfunny and pointless as sending a teenager to be a participant observer in his best friend's obliteration.

He sat down, looked at his miserable grey-brown macchiato, aimlessly stirring it and splashing some on the oak table. Looking at the pattern of the spillage he saw it as just another arbitrary accident of nature. Like death.